Sommerhjem Journeys Series:

*Journey's Middle*: Winner of the Midwest Independent Publishing Association (MIPA) 2012 Midwest Book Award for Young Adult Fiction and finalist in the Fiction: Fantasy and Science Fiction category.

*Journey's Lost and Found*: Finalist of the MIPA 2013 Midwest Book Awards in both the Young Adult Fiction and the Fiction: Fantasy and Science Fiction categories.

*Journey's Seekers*: Winner of the MIPA 2014 Midwest Book Awards in both the Young Adult Fiction and the Fiction: Fantasy and Science Fiction categories.

*Journey's Crossroads*

# Journey's Crossroads

## B. K. PARENT

*B K Parent, 2015*

**⊙iUniverse®**

# JOURNEY'S CROSSROADS

iUniverse books may be ordered through booksellers or by contacting:

iUniverse
1663 Liberty Drive
Bloomington, IN 47403
www.iuniverse.com
1-800-Authors (1-800-288-4677)

ISBN: 978-1-4917-6978-2 (sc)
ISBN: 978-1-4917-6980-5 (hc)
ISBN: 978-1-4917-6979-9 (e)

Library of Congress Control Number: 2015908829

Print information available on the last page.

iUniverse rev. date:   06/23/2015

# ACKNOWLEDGMENTS

Many thanks to the Chapter of the Week Group members who have been my main readers, critics, suppliers of ideas and support, and have kept me on track; to Celeste Klein who encouraged me daily; to my sister Patti Callaway, Flika Gardner, and Joni Amundson who insisted on their chapter every week and let me know if the cliff hanger at the end of the chapter worked; to René Carlberg, Cathy Carlson, Sarah Charleston, Glennis Cohen, Sarah Huelskoetter, Beth and Josh Irish, Vickie Keating, Jenni Meyer, niece Anna Perkins, Connie Stirling, and Robin Villwock for also being members of the Chapter of the Week Group and reading the story.

Once again, many thanks to my niece Katherine M. Parent for her cover art. I can only hope the inside of the book is as good as the cover she has designed.

Special thanks goes to Linne Jensen for surviving editing yet another book with me. I am extremely grateful for her knowledge of grammar and punctuation, and her ability to make sure the stories have consistency. Thanks also to Gale Stone and Mary Sturm for finding errors we missed.

To Patricia Callaway, who laughs at the funny parts of the stories, groans at the cliffhanger endings, and who has always been supportive. Thanks, sister.

To CEK, always.

# INTRODUCTION

*Journey's Crossroads* was written as a serial. The chapters were each approximately four plus pages long and sent via e-mail to friends and relations once a week. A cliffhanger was written into the end of each chapter in order to build anticipation for the next chapter or, in some cases, merely to irritate the reader. You, as a new reader, have choices. You can read a chapter, walk away, and then later pick the book up and read the next chapter to get the serial experience. Another choice is to just read *Journey's Crossroads* as a conventional book and "one more chapter" yourself to three o'clock in the morning on a work or school night. Whichever way you choose, I hope you enjoy the journeys of Piper, Jing, Lom, Taarig, and a few surprise folks.

# Prologue

The rulers of the country of Sommerhjem had traditionally been chosen by the Gylden Sirklene challenge. That tradition and much of the knowledge surrounding the Gylden Sirklene challenge was lost during and after the very long reign of King Griswold. As he crept up in years, his daughter began to take over the day-to-day ruling of Sommerhjem, and when King Griswold finally died, she just assumed the reign. She also lived for a long time, and by then, it seemed natural that her son would rule as the next king. After him, his daughter, Octavia, became the queen.

When the beloved Queen Octavia died, her daughter and heir, Princess Esmeralda, was not of age to rule. Following the death of Queen Octavia, there was a time of turmoil and intrigue as those who sought power vied for position. Eventually, Lord Cedric Klingflug was appointed regent until Princess Esmeralda became old enough to rule as the next queen of Sommerhjem.

As time passed, Regent Klingflug gained more and more power and followers. By his abuse of his power, Lord Klingflug acquired more land and wealth. His edicts and taxes caused a great deal of outrage from both the nobles and the common folk who were loyal to the Crown, but that had not stopped him. He levied higher and higher taxes and created special licenses, resulting in hardship for many in Sommerhjem. Those who aligned themselves with the Regent benefited greatly in coin and property, while many loyal to the Crown lost their lands and livelihoods.

Determined not to give up the rule of Sommerhjem, Regent Klingflug plotted and planned ways to maintain power and discredit Princess

Esmeralda. He set in motion a variety of plans, which would continue to allow him to rule even after the princess came of age, if she managed to survive that long. One plan, which worked well, was to keep Princess Esmeralda isolated so she could not gain any popularity among the folk she would come to rule. Also, by keeping her from getting to know her subjects, she could not learn how upset they were with the Regent's edicts.

Regent Cedric Klingflug was very aware that the one sure way to prevent him from continuing to rule was the calling of the Gylden Sirklene challenge. He knew, while many had forgotten, that the position of king or queen of Sommerhjem had not always been a hereditary position. Only in the last few hundred years, since King Griswold's reign, had the title been passed down from father or mother to daughter or son. Prior to that time, upon the passing of the old ruler, the new ruler of Sommerhjem was chosen by the Gylden Sirklene challenge. Regent Klingflug had ordered scholars loyal to him to find out as much as they could about the Gylden Sirklene challenge. Then he had tried to find and destroy all of the parts and pieces needed for the challenge to be called and carried out.

On the third day of the great summer fair in the capital, when Princess Esmeralda was to have been declared the queen, the Regent discovered he had failed in his quest to maintain power and to prevent the Gylden Sirklene challenge from being called. He was forced to relinquish his position as regent. At the same time, Princess Esmeralda stepped down from becoming queen. An interim ruling council was formed to rule Sommerhjem for a year from the day the challenge was called, as was set out in the Book of Rules governing the challenge.

According to the Book of Rules, an object called the oppgave ringe was required for the challenge. Made up of nine pieces, all needed to be found and returned to the capital of Sommerhjem by a year from the day the challenge was called. Also on the day the challenge was called in the Well of Speaking, seekers, royal librarians, royal historians, and others were charged with finding out more about the Gylden Sirklene challenge and where to find the needed pieces.

By fall, six pieces of the oppgave ringe had been returned to their proper place in the Well of Speaking in the capital. Two were placed in the vessteboks located in the sea wall in the Well of Speaking by the rover Nissa during the great summer fair. Later in the summer, one was placed in the vessteboks by Greer, a former street boy from Høyhauger, a rough and tumble border town in the country of Bortfjell, just across Sommerhjem's northern border. The fourth piece of the oppgave ringe was brought to the capital by Meryl, who came upon it by chance. By fall, Chance, a member of a Høyttaier trading family, and Yara, a rare book restorer in the royal library, had each found and brought one piece of the oppgave ringe to the capital.

Three pieces of the oppgave ringe remain missing. These last three pieces are being sought both by those who would have them returned to their proper place so the challenge can proceed and by those who would prevent that from happening

# PART ONE

# CHAPTER ONE

Piper hoped the fog would continue to stay thick and conceal her as she paddled her small reed boat out of Farlig Brygge's harbor. She had known the time would come when she would have to cut her losses and leave the smugglers' haven. Piper had hoped folks would just think she was moving on when she eventually left town, just another drifter who had come for a while and then left. After this night's bit of work, though, she was not going to have that luxury. She hoped no one had noticed that she knew the man others called Bertok, or that she had not shown up for work just when he had left town. With eyes and ears everywhere in Farlig Brygge watching everyone's every move, she could not be sure who had seen what or had noticed her movements. While her stay in Farlig Brygge had always been fraught with danger and imminent exposure, it had become even more dangerous for her to remain.

Piper was glad to be leaving Farlig Brygge. The seaport on the far southwestern shore of Sommerhjem was certainly not a place most folks would choose to live. While it boasted a fair harbor, the town itself was a squalid, festering place of weather-beaten, cobbled-together buildings, housing the dregs of folks. Farlig Brygge was a haven for smugglers, thieves, and folks of nastier ilk. It was a dangerous place, filled with dangerous folk who would sell their own grandmothers if they thought they could get good coin for them. For the right price, one could probably obtain almost anything in Farlig Brygge, or hire someone who would get it.

Piper had ended up in Farlig Brygge following several rumors that there was information to be had there concerning a piece of the oppgave ringe. After her quick conversation with the man those here knew as Bertok, but who was in reality her foster brother Elek, she knew one of the rumors was true. However, since she had been here, she had heard several more rumors that might be worth either following up or passing on to others. First, however, she needed to get as far away from Farlig Brygge this night as possible, hopefully without being followed. If she could just make it to the foothills of the southern mountains, she would have the advantage.

Piper had always been good at direction. She had an uncanny sense of just where she was, even in the dark or, in this case, the fog. Paddling across the harbor through the fog had its advantages and disadvantages. One advantage was that others would be hard-pressed to either locate her or see her in the enveloping fog. A disadvantage was that she would also have difficulty knowing who else was out on the water at this time of night. As she slipped silently past the town dock, she could hear the creak of rigging on boats tied up there. Occasionally, she caught the faint glow of lantern light through patches of thinning fog. As she passed under the establishments that were built out over the harbor and held up on pilings, she could hear roars of laughter, the sounds of a fight, and the pounding of booted feet overhead. *Just a normal night in the waterfront establishments of Farlig Brygge*, she thought.

When Piper was almost to the beginning of the salt marsh and a channel that would lead her inland away from the harbor, she slowed her boat, stopped paddling, and drifted. She did not know what had alerted her, but something had. She had learned to listen to that inner voice, or whatever it was that was demanding caution. As she sat in her boat drifting, thankful that the tide was coming in rather than going out, she thought she heard folks talking ahead of her. It was often hard to tell what direction sound was coming from in the fog. Her boat came to rest against the marsh grass, and she knew she was not far from the channel she was seeking.

"Can't never sees a blasted thing in this here miserable fog. How's we supposed to spot that gel, Piper?"

"Quiet, you dunderhead. You wants her to hear you? Besides, we donna has to sees her, we jus' has to wait until she runs into our nets."

Slowly backing away from the channel opening and the trap, Piper stayed close to the marsh grass, putting some distance between her and those who were waiting for her. It would seem she would need to go with another plan. She just was not sure how this next plan would work.

There was a grizzled old marsh man who would come into the eating establishment where she worked and brag about how he could get anywhere in a marsh, swamp, or bog, with or without a boat. She was a good listener, and he liked to talk. One night, when business had been particularly slow, and he had been particularly talkative, the old marsh man had let her in on a few of his secrets.

"I has me these marsh shoes," he had told her. "Ya need some good flexible wood to form the frame, and then, some rawhide for the webbing. Course, ya also need to know where to step," he had said, and then sat back holding his stomach while he had a good guffaw.

At the time, Piper had thought he had been pulling her leg, but several days later he had motioned her over to his boat and invited her to come aboard. There on the deck had been a pair of the marsh shoes he had told her about.

"Had me this pair for a long time now, and they's pretty much worn out. Thinkin' I be makin' me some new ones. Ya want ta learn how?" he had asked.

Piper had, and so the old marsh man, whose gruffness turned out to be more bark than bite, had taught her how to make marsh shoes. Unfortunately, she had not had an occasion to try them, and still did not know if they would work. In theory, the marsh shoes should be able to spread her weight out so that she would not sink into the marsh grass up to her eyebrows while trying to walk on it. She had packed light, so her belongings would not add too much more weight, and she would drag her boat behind her. Now all she had to do was find a place where she could get out of her boat and onto a bit of semisolid marsh grass. While the prospect seemed risky, it was less risky than heading out to sea in a reed boat.

Pulling in next to the marsh grass, Piper grabbed her daypack and put it on her back. She then checked to make sure her waterproof pack was securely lashed down in the boat. Standing up in the boat, she put one of the marsh shoes on the marsh grass and slipped her foot into it. *Now comes the real test*, she thought. Placing the second marsh shoe on the marsh grass, using her paddle to help her balance, she put her weight on the first marsh shoe. When she did not immediately sink into the marsh grass, she stepped into the second marsh shoe. Again, she stayed on top of the marsh grass. Piper slowly bent down and fastened the bindings of the marsh shoes to her boots. Using her paddle to test the grass ahead of her, she stepped forward, pulling her boat behind her.

Fortunately, Piper had chosen a place to begin to move across the salt marsh where the channel she had hoped to travel on turned. Unfortunately, she was still too close to where the two she had heard talking waited. She did not want to put her boat in the water for fear that others might be waiting farther down the channel. Walking slowly across the salt marsh grass was tedious and tiring work. Each step had to be carefully placed, and she needed to test the marsh ahead before taking the next step. Pulling the boat behind her was also taking a toll on her. It had been a long day, and the night was proving to be even longer. Piper knew she did not dare stop, nor did she think the hunt for her would end when dawn arrived. When she finally thought she had gone far enough, she found her way back to the channel and slipped her boat into the water.

Piper knew she had left an obvious trail in the marsh grass that anyone with a modicum of intelligence would be able to follow. She hoped that they would expect her to be heading farther into the salt marsh and northeast. She was, however, paddling southeast toward the mountain foothills.

Paddling as quietly as possible, Piper tried to put as much distance between her and Farlig Brygge as she could before she ran out of stamina. She had no doubt that the search for her would center on either the sea coast or the main channel of the salt marsh. It was good that she was going to be in neither place.

Piper was grateful that the old marsh man had taken a shine to her for, along with the helpful instructions on how to build marsh shoes, he had also let her look at the map he had made over the years of the salt marsh around Farlig Brygge.

"Folks around here are too lazy to really know the marsh these days. They only follow the main channels, and most don't even knows about the wee byways and hidden channels."

Piper could only hope that no one had paid attention to her conversations with the old marsh man and might think to question him. He had shown her a narrow channel that flowed all the way to the foothills of the southern mountains. She could also only hope that the old marsh man would keep his own counsel if he heard she was being sought after.

If her sense of direction had not failed her this night, that narrow channel, which flowed all the way to the southern mountains, was where she had turned her boat in just as dawn was beginning to break. Once she got to the mountains, she knew she would have the advantage, for she had been raised in the southern mountains and had served time there on the border patrol. As the morning hours passed and the fog burned off, Piper began to look for a break in the marsh grass that might lead to a place she could pull into and conceal herself and her boat so she could rest. Fortunately, just when she thought her arms could not take even one more stroke with the paddle, she spotted a promising little gap in the salt marsh grass. It proved to be just what she had been looking for. Pulling her way through the gap, Piper found herself in a small pond, just big enough to turn the boat around in. She fell asleep to the sound of frogs croaking.

It was the absence of sound that pulled Piper abruptly out of a light doze. Straining her ears, she listened intently, hoping to catch a sound, any sound, which would tell her why the salt marsh had become so silent. Several minutes passed, but she heard nothing. Several more minutes passed, and she caught the faint whisper of a paddle snicking out of the water. *Someone, or several someones, is out there being very quiet and stealthy,* Piper thought. *If they discover the place where I pulled out of the narrow channel, I will be well and truly trapped.*

"At this point, I'd be willin' to put coin down that that lass who was seen talkin' to Bertok, and disappeared about the same time he did, couldn't have made it this far. She could not be as fast as us, and certainly had to go slow in the fog last night."

"I'm thinkin' you be right. Can't imagine hows she would've got past those guarding the main channel, and even if'n she did, hows woulds she have known about this narrow channel? Let's paddle a bit farther on, and then head back."

Piper lay back down in her boat and kept as still as she could, listening. Soon the normal salt marsh sounds returned. She could hear bird songs start up again. Frogs began their croaking chorus, and the air filled with the deep croaks of the bullfrogs and the higher-pitched piping of the peepers. Long moments passed, and Piper was hard-pressed to keep her eyes open. The sun was warm, and the buzz of insects was mesmerizing.

As gradually as the sounds had returned, they began to cease, and Piper knew the men she had heard were returning. Now, if only her luck would hold a second time, and the men would again not notice the small break in the salt marsh grass. Soon, she once again heard the snick of paddles being drawn out of the water. She sat frozen in place and held her breath. Her boat rocked slightly as the men's boat passed by. Gradually, the marsh sounds once again returned, but she made no move to leave her place of concealment. Several hours passed before she felt comfortable enough to leave the small pond and venture back into the narrow channel.

Piper paddled well into the night before halting again. She was going to need daylight for the next leg of her trip. She needed to find a small stream that flowed into the salt marsh. The old marsh man had told her that the small stream was just wide enough and just deep enough to accommodate a single-folk reed boat. He had also told her its current was not so strong that it would be a struggle to paddle upstream. More importantly, the stream would widen out the closer she got to the foothills of the southern mountains. He had showed her on his map that the salt marsh would change to swamp, and then, after a way, would change to scrub land. Finally, the land would become more solid and forested. He suggested that if she ever went that way, she might have to portage around fallen trees and small stretches of gentle rapids. Eventually, she would need to go by foot where the stream tumbled out of the foothills.

Several days later, Piper reached the foothills, dirty and exhausted. She had never been happier to come to the end of a long paddle than she was this day. The salt marsh had been a pleasant trip compared to the swamp and the stream beyond. It had taken two days of getting out of her boat often to pull it through the swamp before she had even come to the stream. By then her clothes were slick with smelly swamp muck, and she was sure they were crawling with things too fierce to mention. The marsh man had not been joking when he had suggested that she might need to portage around fallen trees and small rapids. There had been several days during which she had spent more time out of the stream than on it.

Finally coming to a place where she could no longer follow the stream, for it cascaded down the hillside in a series of small falls, she removed her gear from the reed boat and began gathering large river rocks from the streambed. After filling the boat up with rocks until it was barely floating, she pushed it out to the deepest part of the pool below the first falls. Piper added more rocks until the boat sank to the bottom of the pool. If anyone managed to track her from Farlig Brygge, a reed boat this far from the salt marsh would certainly be telling. She hoped that by sinking the boat it would not be easy for anyone to know she had come this way.

Tucking her daypack into her waterproof pack and slinging that on her back, Piper began to follow an animal path that ran parallel to the stream. Even though she was back in the foothills of the southern mountains, she knew she was not out of danger, for the trek home would not be an easy one.

# CHAPTER TWO

Despite being back in familiar territory, Piper did not relax. The southern mountains held their own dangers beyond the two-legged kind, who might or might not be on her trail. The southern mountains of Sommerhjem consisted of foothills, taller tree-covered mountains, and then the higher craggy snowcapped mountains that formed a spine running west to east along the whole of the southern border. There was only one good pass that connected Sommerhjem with the country to the south, and it was Piper's family who held the holding that guarded the pass. Because of the varying terrain of the southern mountains, a great variety of wildlife lived there, some in less-than-peaceful coexistence with folk. Most avoided places where folks lived. However, she was in their territory now.

Piper was traveling along trails that ran through the tree-covered section of the southern mountains. She had chosen to travel there because she wanted to avoid the sparsely-settled foothills. The forested mountains were extensive and, although several forester clans held guardianship over them, the foresters were spread pretty thin. Piper knew she might run into a lone forester, or a group of foresters, but she preferred to avoid them for as long as she could. It was not that she felt she was in any danger from any of them. It was just that she hoped to put as much distance as possible between herself and those from Farlig Brygge who might still be looking for her before anyone knew she was in the forest.

The shadows had grown long and the day had begun to cool before Piper grew close to the place she had been working her way toward all afternoon. It was one of the old places, which had been built long before her ancestors had settled in the high mountain pass. It was just one of a few scattered in the mountains, and they had always drawn Piper. Her friends could not understand her fascination for the old places, and many had remarked that they were uncomfortable spending any time near them. Piper, however, always found the ancient places peaceful and safe. She had never been quite able to explain why she felt that way and had given up trying.

The ancient place might give her some protection from both two-footed and four-footed predators. The place was a series of open stone archways with an alcove at the far end. She thought it looked a bit like a giant ribcage and was certain she never wanted to meet any living creature that was that big. Piper felt camping in the alcove would be a little bit safer than camping out in the open, so she picked up her pace, wanting to get there while there was still some light.

Upon arriving, Piper placed her pack in the alcove and set about gathering some dry wood. She chose dead branches from the trees surrounding the archway, for she knew they would be the driest. She did not want plumes of smoke rising from her cook fire for someone farther up the mountain to spot. A warm fire and a warm meal would be welcome this night, since it grew cool in the mountains this time of year once the sun set. Just outside the alcove was a fire ring, for which she offered thanks to the unknown builders. She was not sure if the fire ring had originally been part of the site, or if it had been added later by some other folk needing shelter. She just hoped that she was not offending the original builders by camping in this place.

Piper had just come back to the alcove after filling her water skin at a nearby spring when she felt like she was being watched. Carefully setting the water skin down, she reached for her short bow and quickly nocked an arrow. Her cook fire had burned down to just glowing coals, so she really did not have much light to see by. The woods that surrounded her were filled with dark shifting shadows. Stepping farther into the shadow of the alcove, Piper held herself still and waited. The birds continued to sing, she could hear small rustlings in the trees and underbrush, and the wind gently stirred the leaves.

Finally, Piper set her bow and quiver down close at hand and set her cook pot in the hot coals. Keeping a watchful eye, she prepared dinner and ate. The feeling of being watched continued. While uncomfortable and leery of what might be out in the woods, for some odd reason she did not feel overly threatened. Once dinner was cleaned up, it was full dark. She knew she could not stay up all night and climbed into her sleeping roll.

Dawn arrived in a blaze of brilliant color. Piper spent a short moment standing back from the edge of a rock outcropping, looking over the land bathed in the early morning light that lay below her. She wished she could somehow stop time and capture the moment. *It would be nice to just spend the day without a worry on this rocky ledge taking in the scenery below,* Piper thought, as she adjusted her pack, turned, and began the day's trek.

Following the animal trails through the forest was certainly going to lengthen her walk home, but, by avoiding the more well-traveled paths, Piper would be able to put more distance between herself and Farlig Brygge before her passage might be noticed by the folks who patrolled the forest. The feeling of being watched had subsided somewhat from the night before, but had not entirely gone away.

Storm clouds had been gathering all day, and the sky was getting darker and darker. A heavy rain would be bad enough, but there was always the chance of a snowstorm this time of year. Piper needed to find some substantial shelter, for the wind was picking up and there was a bit of biting cold in the air. Shivering and pulling her thin cloak closely around her, Piper thought she had spent too much time in the damp, but warmer, salt marsh region. She was no longer accustomed to the mountain cold.

Scattered throughout the mountain's forest lands were rocky outcroppings. Piper hoped she could find an overhang that might protect her from the coming storm. Quickening her pace, she was huffing and puffing by the time she reached a wall of rock that held some promise. She worked her way swiftly along, looking for an overhang, a shallow cave, or a very dense pine tree growing right up next to the rock wall. She could hear the thunder begin to boom and rumble, drawing ever closer, and she was being hit by a mixture of rain and small icy pellets. Just when she was beginning to despair because she was going to have to sit out the storm huddled under inadequate shelter, she spotted a small cave opening.

Quickly ducking into the opening, Piper noticed in the dim light that the cave did not extend very far back. It might have once, but there looked to have been a recent cave-in that blocked her from going farther back. Cold and damp, she moved as far into the cave as she could to get out of the cold wind. When her eyes finally adjusted to the light, she began to notice her surroundings. The floor of the cave showed signs of recently being disturbed, but she did not think it was done by animals. *Maybe someone else sought shelter here not too long ago*, she thought.

Piper was not going to go out in the blustery weather to gather firewood, so she resigned herself to a cold supper and a miserable damp night. Taking time to clear away the debris on a section of floor, she spread out her sleeping roll, sat down on part of it, and leaned back against the cave wall. She found that she was having difficulty keeping her eyes open, even though it was early. She realized she had not yet adjusted to being this high in the mountains. Having dwelt for some time in the lowland humid sea air, she was having trouble breathing. She hoped it would not take very much longer for her lungs to get used to the thinner mountain air.

When Piper caught her head nodding once again, she decided she should probably just give in, curl up in her blanket roll, and get some sleep, but something stopped her. Sitting very still, she listened, for she thought she had heard the sound of rock hitting rock. It made her a bit nervous, for she worried that the recent cave-in she had noticed at the back of the cave meant that the cave might be unstable. Piper had weighed that possibility when she had first entered the cave, but had dismissed it. Being just inside a possibly unstable cave was far preferable to being out in the storm that was now raging outside.

*Just an errant rock falling*, she thought. *Just an errant rock*. Moving to settle in, Piper heard the sound of rock on rock once again, and then again. When she really began to concentrate on what she was hearing, she noted that there was a pattern to the sound which was too consistent to be just random rocks falling. It was then that Piper realized she had been hearing the rock-on-rock sound for quite some time, but it had taken a while for her to recognize what she was hearing. It sounded like someone or something was moving rocks on the other side of the cave-in at the back of the cave.

Cautiously moving closer to the cave-in, Piper called out, "Is there someone there?" She thought she heard a muffled shout. "Can you hear me?" Again Piper thought she heard some yelling.

Picking up a rock, Piper tapped it on another rock three times and then listened. Nothing happened. She tried again, tapping the rock three times a bit harder. Piper listened once again. She heard rock hitting rock three times. She slowly hit her rock on another rock five times. She heard rock hit rock five times from the other side of the cave-in. To be sure she was not imagining things, Piper hit her rock four times rapidly against a rock. She heard four rapid hits from the other side of the cave-in. It would seem she was not alone in the cave after all.

At first, Piper began to frantically grab rocks randomly from the pile of rocks blocking the back of the cave and pitch them behind her. She soon found herself leaping away from a small rock slide and decided she needed to be much more methodical and cautious. After that, she began to move the rocks more carefully and slowly. After the first hour, she removed her wool sweater and decided if her hands were to have a chance of having any skin left on them, she should put on her leather gloves. She had also built up a strong thirst, so she took a moment to get some water. As Piper stood surveying whether she had even made a dent in the jumble of rocks in front of her, she listened. Other than the rain falling outside the cave, there was no other sound. Whoever was on the other side of the curtain of rock was no longer moving rocks.

Concerned, Piper again called out to whomever was behind the rocks, but there was no answer. Wiping away the sweat that was trickling into her eyes, she began working on the pile of rocks again, now more determined than ever. Soon she lost all track of time. She had no time for thoughts, caught up in the rhythm of picking a rock out of the pile and tossing it behind her. She began to despair, for it seemed like she was no closer to breaking through to the other side than when she had started. Doubts began to assail her. *Was this a fool's errand? Am I really hearing someone tapping on the other side of the wall of rocks, or is it just my imagination?* A cramp in her hand caused her to stop.

Piper straightened and shook out her hands. Placing her non-cramped hand in the small of her back, she pushed at the tired and sore muscles there. She did not know how much longer she could continue to move rocks. As she stood there, drenched in sweat, covered with dirt and dust, very discouraged, she thought she heard a very faint voice calling.

"Is someone there?" Piper asked.

"Yes," came a very faint reply. "Trapped. Can't help anymore."

"You're trapped?"

"Yes."

"Are you hurt?"

"I don't think so."

"If I move more rocks, will that put you in more danger?"

"Not if you're careful. I'm next to the cave wall to your left. I have cleared as much from this side as I can. Can you reach the rocks on the top?"

"Yes."

"Good, then carefully remove the rocks from the top and work your way down, then repeat."

"Yell if I move something that causes rocks to tumble on your side."

Piper heard only a faint reply, as if talking had worn the folk on the other side out. With renewed effort, Piper began moving rocks again. Finally, she removed a rock and could see no rocks beyond, but she could not be sure if she had broken through. By this time, she was working almost blind and by feel. Since the sun had set, she had been working by the light of just one small candle in her very small travel lantern. Just as she moved back to pick up the lantern and bring it to the opening to see if she actually could see beyond the cave-in, the candle sputtered and died.

# Chapter Three

With the candle light extinguished, Piper was left in total darkness. Very slowly and cautiously, she inched her way back down the cave-in until she felt she was standing on the cave floor. Earlier, she had been tossing or moving rocks off the cave-in to the same pile. Once she had been able to talk to the folk behind the cave-in, her task had become more real and urgent. It was then that she had begun tossing rocks willy-nilly behind her. That could prove to be a problem now since she needed to move away from the cave-in to get to her gear and could not see where she had littered the floor with the rocks. Piper began to slowly shuffle her way toward where she had left her pack. It would not do either of them any good if she were to trip over a rock and sprain or break something.

Several stubbed toes later, Piper located her pack. She had to feel around to find her one remaining candle and then get it lit. With the minimal light from the small candle lantern, she picked her way back to the cave-in. Just a little to the left of where she was working was a ledge at waist height, wide enough to hold her lantern and give her just barely enough light to see by. Piper once again moved up the cave-in and moved a few more rocks to enlarge the opening.

"Are you still with me?" Piper inquired.

"Yes," came a very faint answer.

"Can you see any light?"

"Yes, and I smell rain in the air coming in through the opening you have made. I will always cherish the smell of rain from now on because I don't think I have ever smelled anything so wonderful."

"If I get this opening bigger, can you climb up from your side?"

"Well, there's just one wee problem."

"And that would be?"

"I'm wedged under a rather large rock and can't seem to get myself out."

"Ah, that could complicate things."

"Now that I have fresh air, and if you can lower some water down to me somehow, I should be all right if you want to go and find others to help, as long as you don't take too long."

"Actually, there are a few hitches with your idea. There is a raging storm going on outside the cave, and it is pitch dark except for the occasional flash of lightning. Second, I have been trying to move as far through the forest heading east as I can because I think there might be folks who are looking for me that I don't want to find me. So, going out searching for help could be problematic," suggested Piper.

"Ah, that could complicate things."

"Indeed. I'll be right back with some water for you."

After lowering the water skin down, Piper suggested that she should get back to moving rock while she still had some candle light. Once this candle burned out, she would have to wait until daybreak before she would again be able to see what she was doing. She finally had to quit when the candle flickered several times, dimmed, brightened, dimmed, and finally went out. She apologized to the folk on the other side of the cave-in. Shuffling her way back to her blanket roll, she lay down and fell into an uneasy, exhausted sleep.

The sound of the crash of rock upon rock had Piper sitting up abruptly, only to have her lie back down due to the pain in almost every joint and muscle in her body. Rolling carefully to her side, she noticed a faint light coming from the cave entrance. Easing herself upright, Piper walked over to the opening she had made near the top of the cave-in and called in.

"Are you there?" she asked.

"Unfortunately yes, since there is nowhere else I can be at the moment," came the reply.

"Not a morning folk, eh? A bit grumpy this morning, are we?" called Piper back, attempting to lighten the mood.

"I get this way only when I'm hungry, and, oh, incidentally trapped under a large rock."

"Good to know. Well then, I'll just start removing more rock and see where that might get us. Looks like a few fell on their own. I think that's what woke me."

It took all morning and halfway into the afternoon before Piper had an opening cleared so she could clamber over the remaining rocks and get into the area where the folk was trapped.

Once she reached him, she was surprised to note how young he was and, from what she could see, how short. She now also had a better view of what was holding him in place. It looked like his foot was wedged and a large rock needed to be lifted up in order to get his foot out.

"Perhaps introductions are in order," Piper suggested. "I am Piper of the clan Wynda, guardians of the southern pass." She did not know why she was being formal, but for some reason it seemed appropriate.

"I am Collier of the Günnary," the young man said with equal formality. "I hope that taking the time to try to rescue me has not allowed those who might be searching for you to catch up. I hope my plight has not put you in more danger."

Piper realized with a start that, in all the hours she had been shifting rock, she had not really considered the possible consequences. It never occurred to her that she should just push on and leave this man behind. Swiftly on the heels of that thought came the next one. *Had he just said he was of the Günnary?* Piper wondered. She had heard of the Günnary in stories and legends. The tales suggested that they used to prospect in the southern mountains, but Piper thought they had all disappeared sometime back in time.

"Well, ah, Collier you said, ah, let's see if we can get you out of here," Piper said, feeling somewhat flustered, for she did not know what to think of this Collier who claimed to be a Günnary.

"If I might suggest, you are going to need a good stout tree limb. If you can lift the rock across my foot a little at a time, I can shove a rock underneath it to keep it up. If we keep very carefully raising it a little higher each time, I should be able to free myself. You will need to find a number of flat stones besides finding the sturdy log."

"You think that will work?"

"I'm hoping it will work."

Piper had no difficulty finding a very sturdy tree limb that had cracked off in the storm the night before. It actually took her longer to find the flat stones. Once she had everything together, she asked Collier what he wanted her to do next, since he seemed to have a very clear plan in mind.

"Move the flat stones closer to me. I will try to wedge them under when you lift the big rock. See that larger stone to your right?"

"This one?" Piper asked, pointing to the rock she thought Collier meant.

"No, the one just beyond it."

"This one then?"

"Yes, that should do."

Following Collier's instructions, Piper placed the rock he had indicated on the cave floor close to the rock that needed to be lifted. Putting the sturdy tree limb between the rock on the cave floor and the rock that had Collier's foot trapped took some adjustment, but it was soon in place. Piper pressed down as hard as she could on the limb, and the top rock lifted up just enough for Collier to get a very thin flat rock wedged underneath.

"Are you all right?" Piper questioned.

"Still stuck, but fine. Let's try again."

Again Piper pressed down on the tree limb and the top rock inched upward just enough for Collier to place another flat rock on top of the first one. Inch by inch, the top rock began to rise.

"I think if you press down and can hold it, I might be able to get my foot out. Give it a try," Collier told Piper.

Piper put the tree limb in under the rock and put all of her weight into her downward press. A moment passed, and then two. Her arms were beginning to quiver and her muscles were burning. She was just about to tell Collier that she was not going to be able to hold it much longer when he scooted himself past her. She let the tree limb up slowly and sank to the cave floor.

Collier thanked Piper and sat there rubbing the foot that had been trapped.

Once Piper determined that Collier was indeed all in one piece, she asked the question that had been on her mind through the long night and day. "How did this happen?"

"Well, it wasn't a natural occurrence, I can tell you that much. This is an old mine. Most probably it was made by Günnary in a time before my folk went into hiding, which is a story for another time. Maybe right now we could take a short break from explanations while I take time to clean up and get something to eat and drink."

"Oh, I'm sorry. Normally, I'm not this thoughtless. My curiosity got the better of my good manners."

It surprised Piper that Collier, rather than moving out to the cave entrance, got up, and began moving farther into the cave.

"Collier?"

"Yes."

"The cave entrance is the other way."

"Oh, I know that. It's just that all of my gear is back this way. I'll be back in a little bit."

Piper got up, climbed back over the cave-in, and walked toward the cave mouth. While she had been inside moving rock and then freeing Collier, the rain had stopped and the sun had come out. She walked out and began to gather firewood, for a hot meal sounded like a very appealing idea. When she returned to the cave for the third time, her arms full of firewood, Collier was at the cave mouth to help her.

"I've already moved the wood you brought in before farther back into the cave. There is a natural chimney farther back. From the looks of that sky, I think it is going to rain again, and there is a bite to the air," Collier remarked.

"I had best go grab a few more armloads then," said Piper.

Collier had suggested Piper gather up her gear and move farther back into the tunnel to his campsite. While she was packing up, she again asked Collier what had happened.

"During the time that the former regent Cedric Klingflug was controlling Sommerhjem, the forester clans were moved out of their home forests and scattered over the land. A rover named Shueller, who is of the Günnary, had a conversation with one of the head foresters from this area. She remarked that their clan history mentioned that at one time the Günnary had worked in these mountains. Mind you, that was a very long time ago, before the troubling times that caused the Günnary to withdraw from most areas of Sommerhjem to protect themselves. In the olden times, other folks wanted the gems the Günnary found or mined. They enslaved my folk and made them mine and cut gems for their own wealth. It was a very bad time. Now, most of my folk are afraid to leave the places they have withdrawn to."

"But not you."

"No, not me. I guess I take after Shueller, for he left and became a rover. Must run in the family, since he's my great uncle. I was restless at home. Felt closed in. I was surprised, to say the least, that when I approached the head of our clan and told him I wanted to go exploring, he encouraged me to do so. So I left home and I came here to see if I could find any trace of the Günnary ever being here."

"And did you?"

"Yes. These mountains, which are between the foothills and the higher craggy rocky mountains, are quite old. Older I think than the higher mountains, the spine that separates Sommerhjem from Rullegress, the country south of us. From a distance, they look like higher tree-covered foothills. However, when you get into these middle mountains, you soon discover that there is a rock base not too far under the soil. Oftentimes there are sheer rock walls like the one we are inside. The opening you went through is a natural one in that rock wall, but it was once only a shallow cave."

"Go on," Piper encouraged, for she had become so caught up in what Collier was saying she had forgotten her original question.

"Going back from where the cave-in is, there are clear signs that this cave was once mined. The tunnel was shored up the very same way we do it back home, and I found other reasons to believe that this was once a Günnary mine. But you want to know not what happened here a long time ago, but what happened to me."

21

"Yes."

"I've been in this area for over a month with the blessing of the foresters. These mountains are definitely worth taking a second look at. Here and there I have found some promising areas that might produce a gem vein or two. I have also found a number of really fine gems that I'm anxious to have someone cut and polish. Not my best skill I'm afraid. I actually stumbled on this cave due to a storm much like the one that drew you here to find shelter. I had gone fairly far into the tunnel and was excited with what I was seeing. On the third night, I was too wound up after what I thought I had discovered very late in the day. I had to return to my camping spot within the tunnel, for I was very low on lamp oil, and it is most unwise to let your lamp go out when you are deep within unfamiliar tunnels. Anyway, I knew it was not going to be smart to go back so late in the day, but, as I said, I was too wound up so I started working on what looked like a promising vein near the tunnel entrance."

Piper found herself leaning forward, intrigued.

"My father would be appalled by what I did next. I know better."

"What did you do?"

"A good miner always knows he should check all around the area where he is going to start swinging his pickaxe. And I did for the most part. I checked the wall I was going to swing at and noticed that the tunnel support posts were fairly close to where I wanted to try to chip away at a rock protrusion that looked promising."

"Let me guess. You took a wild swing and knocked out the support post."

Collier, looking acutely embarrassed, went on. "I might not feel so foolish if that were the case, but I swung up in order to bring my pickaxe down hard and hit the ceiling support beam."

When Piper looked at the very short Günnary man and the high ceiling above the cave-in, she cocked an inquisitive eyebrow.

"Trust me, the ceiling was a lot lower before I caused it to come down on me. Right now, regretfully, I once again find it too late in the day to go back to the area I was exploring before I brought the ceiling down on me. Wait until you see what I found there."

# CHAPTER FOUR

Collier lit a lantern that gave off a great deal more light than Piper's candle lantern ever could. He held it aloft to light the way and indicated that Piper should follow him.

"Is it safe to go farther into the tunnel?" Piper asked. There was a great deal of concern and trepidation in her voice.

"This tunnel is very safe, as long as there is not an overly eager Günnary swinging a pickaxe and forgetting all of the rules about mining that he had been taught from birth," Collier answered ruefully. "Be guaranteed that I won't make that mistake ever again."

When the two came to a side tunnel, Collier indicated that they should turn down it. "What I found down the tunnel we turned off from was what might be a vein of a very rare stone, firestar gems. The vein of it at home played out long ago, but I don't think this one is played out. Even if I find no others, I want to show you what I did find. I noticed something back in the tunnels that suggested to me that this tunnel was made by a Günnary. I would tell you more, but that would be giving away clan secrets. I hope you understand."

"That's fair. I certainly would not be sharing with anyone some things my clan knows about the southern mountains and the southern pass."

"Thank you for understanding. Ah, here we are," Collier indicated. He headed straight to a pack and pulled out some dried fruit, apologizing to Piper and explaining he was still very hungry, and did not think he could wait until something was cooked.

Piper looked about and saw that Collier had set up a cozy camp in a side room off the tunnel. He had made himself a fire pit near one wall. There was also a cobbled-together table and several benches near the fire pit. On the opposite side of the room, he had set out his blanket roll on a bed of cedar boughs. What surprised her was she could feel a slight breeze.

"All the comforts of home, I see," Piper remarked.

"Actually, I can't take credit for it. The table, benches, and fire pit were here when I arrived. Since the dust was about an inch thick, I decided that the former tenant was either a really bad housekeeper, or this place had not been anyone's home for quite some time. Once I got it cleaned up, it is quite an adequate place to hang my hat for the time being. One of the nicest parts about this place is it has a natural chimney, and that fissure straight ahead lets in fresh air."

"So this is what you found that you wanted to show me?"

"No. When I was exploring this room, I found a cache left, I think, a very, very long time ago. It is what is in it that I want to show you. I'm trusting you will continue to be the good lass you have so far proved yourself to be. If you would be so kind as to sit at the table facing the fire pit, I'll fetch it."

Piper did as asked. She felt it would be rude if she turned around, for Collier was undoubtedly fetching whatever he had found from where he had hidden it.

A moment later Collier sat down beside Piper, placing the lantern on the table. He also placed a small intricately carved wooden box on the table next to the lantern. Collier opened the box and drew out a pouch that was made of golden pine spider silk. He set it on the table and reached into his back pocket for a fairly clean kerchief. Collier spread the kerchief out on the table, untied the cord holding the pouch closed, and then tipped the contents out on the table.

Piper sat looking down on nine stones that were like none she had ever seen before. There were nine polished stones of extraordinary beauty. At first glance they appeared black, but when Collier held one up to the lantern light, she could see tiny specks of fire within in reds, oranges, and yellows.

"They're beautiful," Piper commented, her eyes fixed on the gems.

"They are indeed, but what is remarkable is that they are cut and polished. I'm not sure that there is anyone now who could do that. It is a skill that was lost back in time. Even if I find some firestar gems here, I'm not sure I'll ever find someone who can cut or polish them. When I get back home, I will need to talk to the head of our clan, Torger. I think there is a rover elder who is also a highly esteemed gem cutter, now what was his name … hum-m-m …. Oh, sorry, got lost in my own thoughts. While these are quite amazing, there is something else I want to show you."

Collier lifted something else out of the small box that was wrapped in golden pine spider silk cloth and unwrapped it, laying the contents on the table. There, nestled in the silk cloth, was a thin bracelet. The band of the bracelet was carved in much the same design as the box that had held it. Set in the top center of the bracelet was a firestar gem. The bracelet was also uniquely designed so that, once it was fastened onto one's wrist, it would not rotate about the wrist. It was like a narrow cuff, and yet not.

"It's like nothing I have ever seen before," Collier stated. "I don't know what material the bracelet is made of, nor am I familiar with the design of either the bracelet or the carvings on it. What I do know is I'm not meant to keep this bracelet. I want you to have it. It's but a small payment for your saving my life for, if you had not come along, I surely would have perished all alone in this cave. My family would never have known what happened to me."

"I can't accept it," Piper protested.

"You can and must. By delaying your journey home, I know you have placed your life in more danger. You have risked your safety to save me. In addition, and please don't ask me how I know, for I would not be able to explain. I think this bracelet is meant to be yours. There is a rightness to your having it."

Piper did not know what to say. Collier seemed so convinced that what he was telling her was true. In addition, there was something about the bracelet that was pulling at her. Finally, Piper reached out and picked up the bracelet and put it on. Surprisingly, it felt warm against her skin and fit as if it had been made for her. When she looked at the firestar gem, she noticed a soft glow within. When she went to show it to Collier, it was gone. Piper wondered if she had imagined it.

"Are you sure you want to give this to me?" Piper asked.

"From the look on your face when you put it on, I think I would not be able to get it back from you," Collier said with good humor. "Now then, let me put this back while you start a cook fire. I don't know about you, but I think I could eat a whole deer by myself. Unfortunately, I don't have one handy."

"Just point me in the direction of your supplies, and between what we both have, we should be able to put together a fairly filling meal."

When the meal was finished, Collier sat back with a sigh. "I'm not sure that I have ever tasted anything so good."

"After being trapped under a rock for several days, shoe leather would have tasted good to you," Piper quipped.

"That may be true, but the meal you put together was very tasty, very tasty indeed, and once again I'm in your debt. I have a little more energy left, so what say we get the chores done so we can settle in? I expect you are just a wee bit tired from your rock moving, and I admit I'm a bit worn out myself."

For the next hour, Piper and Collier gathered wood, hauled water, and cleaned up. Once the chores were done, they pulled the benches closer to the fire and sat in silence for a while, sipping cups of hot tea. Finally, Piper broke the comfortable silence.

"What are your plans now?" Piper asked.

"I had planned to spend about another week here and then head home. I left my horse and pack horse at one of the forester outposts about a two day walk to the east from here. I'm actually less anxious about leaving here than I was before."

"Why is that?"

"Having found something and then having to leave is usually worrisome, for you hope that no one else discovers what you have found while you are away. Before I leave, I'm going to fill in some of the cave-in you removed. I think the looks of that tumble of rocks might discourage most folks from exploring beyond the shallow opening of the cave. I intend to come back during the warm season next year. I suppose you will head out in the morning."

"Yes. I need to get home. I have been gone longer than I like." *If anyone saw me with Bertok, or suspected I helped Bertok, that could be a reason to send folks after me. Plus*, Piper thought, *I have some information that needs to be passed on, along with a few things I acquired while in Farlig Brygge which others might not be too happy to discover are gone.*

The next morning Collier walked Piper along her back trail for about an hour before they parted ways. Collier was going to make sure no one would know she had found his cave, and she was going to take a different trail lower down on the mountain. She bid Collier farewell and wished him luck and a safe journey home. She hoped their ruse worked, and that she had not led anyone to his discovery.

The day was exceptionally clear and crisp. It was just the type of day for an enjoyable hike in the mountains and the trail Piper was following was an easy one. Yet, she felt less comfortable on the trail since it was probably more well-traveled than the animal paths she had been following. It was allowing her, however, to put more distance between Collier and herself.

Piper again began to feel as if she were being watched, but she could not spot anyone or anything. As the day progressed, that feeling grew stronger and stronger. She began to weigh the options of staying on the more well-traveled trail, which allowed her to move faster, or moving off onto a narrower animal path, which would slow her down. Animals did not always head in the direction one wanted to go, nor did they make it always easy to walk upright, due to their being shorter. She finally decided, since she had lost several days rescuing Collier, she would stick to the well-traveled trail and to try to make up some time.

Toward dusk, Piper began to look for a place to settle in for the night. Though the temperature had cooled down as the sun set, it was not overly cold. The sky was clear, and it did not look like rain. Piper needed a place she could safely build a fire, and one that might have a large rock at her back. Most of the animals in the mountains did not bother folks, unless one threatened them or their offspring. It was that one exception to the rule that could severely harm one however. It was better to be cautious.

Piper found a suitable place near a small stream before the light was gone. Others had camped there before, for there was a fire ring and a stack of wood. Piper set about gathering more wood, putting fresh water in her water skin, and cooking a hot meal. She also set out some snares, hoping to capture something edible since her supplies were running low. Being very cautious, Piper repacked her pack. She wanted to be able to grab it containing all her gear, if she had to suddenly flee. It would not do to have to leave quickly without her gear. Having banked the fire for the night, Piper was just about to untie her blanket roll from her pack when she heard voices coming up the trail.

"She can't be more than a half hour ahead. We should catch up with her soon. You're sure it's her we're following?"

"Yes, I'm sure. Those other tracks we saw belonged to someone with a much smaller foot. Almost looked to be wee lad's or lass's size. None of our concern if a youngling is out here in the woods. Probably some forester lad or lass. Wait. I just caught a whiff of smoke."

Sound carries in the woods, so Piper did not know how far away the speakers were. *Too close*, she concluded. Quickly, she spread the dying coals apart and dumped the contents of her water skin on them. It would not do to set the forest ablaze. She knew putting water on the coals would certainly create smoke and a wet burnt-wood smell, but it could not be helped. Hoping she had put the fire out, but not willing to spend any more time, Piper grabbed her pack and headed into the woods.

There was very little light to see by, for it was past dusk and the moon had not risen yet. Piper was trying to move as quickly as she could, but also needed to move as quietly as she could. She looked over her shoulder and saw a flare of light coming from her campsite.

"She was here just moments ago. This fire pit still has some heat to it. There, you can see she entered the woods there."

Piper turned back and began to pick up her pace, heading higher up the mountain. She could hear the two crashing through the woods behind her. Piper raced on, brush snagging her clothes, tree branches hitting her in the face. Several times she stumbled, and twice she tripped over tree roots and fell, only to pick herself up and continue on. Her breath was coming in gasps, and she felt her legs beginning to burn as she moved up and up the mountain. Piper could feel the two behind her gaining. Suddenly her feet hit smooth rock, which allowed her to move faster. After several hundred feet of running across the rock, she burst through the sparse trees into the open, only to find herself on a rocky outcrop. She could hear her pursuers close behind her and knew she could not go back the way she had come.

Cautiously looking over the edge of the ledge she was standing on, Piper could see a wide ledge below her. Knowing that she surely would be caught by those pursuing her if she stood there much longer, she eased herself over the edge and dropped down onto the ledge. It narrowed very shortly beyond where she was standing. Inching her way along the ever narrowing ledge, she came to a place where there had been a rock fall. Debating what to do next was not an option when she heard the sounds of someone dropping onto the ledge behind her. Moving as quickly as she could, she began to scrabble across the loose rocks. Suddenly the rocks beneath her feet shifted, and Piper found herself tumbling down the rock slide, over and over, at an ever-increasing speed, until everything went dark.

# Chapter Five

At the edge of the rock slide, a heated debate was going on between the two men who had been pursuing Piper. One of the men was trying to convince the other to make his way down the rock slide and try to locate the lass they had been following.

"I'm's not steppin' one foot out onto that rock slide in the dark. I canna' hold a lantern to try 'n pick my way down and keep my balance. If'n you think it's such a grand idea, you do it."

"I'm's the one what's in charge here, so I says you do it."

Their argument was cut short when the full moon moved from behind the clouds and lit up the area below the two men as if it were almost daylight. The light of the moon gave them a true idea of what lay below. The rock slide went down several hundred feet. Lying at the bottom, half covered by rocks, was the still form of Piper. They also caught movement of something carefully slinking across the rocks. Before they could get a clear view, the moon was again hidden by the clouds.

"Now I'm's fer sure not goin' down there, not 'tils daylight I'm's not."

"Yer right fer once. If'n she's still there in the mornin', or if'n there is anythin' left of her in the mornin', we can find out then. If'n she somehow lives through the fall 'n whatever it was slinkin' across the rocks, we'll just catch up with her on the morrow."

Piper heard someone moaning softly and finally realized she was the one moaning. The blackness was beginning to fade as she figured out she had been knocked out by the fall. Slowly and cautiously she began to try to find out if she had broken or sprained anything. She was worried that those who had been chasing her would follow her down the rock slide and catch up with her. Lying still, Piper listened, but could hear no movement from above her. With the clouds covering the moon, everything around her lay in deep shadow.

Gingerly moving her left arm, she found that her hand and arm, though sore, did not appear to be broken, just scraped. Reaching up, Piper checked her head and what she could reach of her upper body. Bumps and scrapes, undoubtedly bruised, but, nothing broken as far as she could determine. Her back felt very sore, but since it was arched awkwardly over her pack, that was understandable. Slipping her arms out from the pack's straps allowed her to sit up and check her legs. Though buried under some of the rocks, she could feel them, which Piper thought might be a good sign. As quietly as she could, she began to remove the rocks one by one. She did not want to alert those who had been after her.

After Piper had removed the rocks covering her legs, she tentatively moved first one foot and then the other. Both seemed to be in working order and moved without pain. Next, she flexed both knees, and the results were the same. While her legs and feet were sore, nothing appeared to be broken. Settling her pack on her back, Piper was about to scoot the remaining few feet down the rock slide when she caught movement out of the corner of her eye and froze.

The moon had once again come out while she had been checking out her bumps and bruises, so she could see quite clearly what was now sitting right in front of her not more than five feet away. Though she knew better than to look directly into the eyes of a mountain cat, she found herself doing so and could not look away. As strange as it seemed to her, Piper was sure she was being measured, and for some odd reason did not wish to be found wanting. *My immediate concern,* she thought, *is how to prevent myself from becoming dinner, or more likely breakfast.*

Piper whispered a plea to the mountain cat. "Please, I mean you no harm, and I'm sure I don't taste very good."

The mountain cat just cocked his head, as if listening intently.

Piper would never be able to explain afterward what had prompted her to reach out her hand in supplication to the mountain cat. When she did so, her sleeve slipped back, exposing the bracelet that Collier had given her. An arc of light flashed between her wrist and the mountain cat's neck. When Piper could see again, the mountain cat was gone.

Not taking the time to wonder about what had just happened, heedless of any noises she might be making, Piper slid the last few feet down the rock slide and stood. Her body ached all over. Pushing that aside, Piper began to move as swiftly through the woods as she could, hoping to put distance between herself and the two who had followed her to the edge of the rock slide and the mountain cat, wherever he had slipped off to.

Piper began to question whether she should even be concerned about the mountain cat. She wondered if she had really seen him, as tired as she was. She thought her imagination might have been playing tricks on her. But, on the other hand, he certainly had looked like a mountain cat. Had she seen the mountain cat in the daylight, she would have seen that his back fur was the color of dried pine needles. The fur on the back of his head and back was longer, and his sides and underbelly fur was a lighter rust color with dark spots. His cream-colored face was very furry with a thin black line running from the inner corner of his eye and outlining his muzzle.

The clouds had cleared off and the light of the full moon was bright enough to make walking in the woods less of a hazard. Piper quickly found a deer path and began to follow it. It wove in and around trees, but generally went in the direction she wanted to go. Every once in a while, she would stop, look, and listen, but she could neither see nor hear anyone behind her. What was worrisome was she knew she would not be able to keep up her fast walking pace for long. Sooner rather than later, her aching body was going to refuse to move much farther. Piper knew she was going to need a safe place to hide. She needed food and she needed rest.

It was midmorning before Piper stumbled to a halt and realized she had just run out of what little energy she had left. Wanting to sink to her knees and then just lie down on the deer path, she began to put one foot in front of the other, making herself push on, trying to concentrate on the woods around her, and looking for a place to stop. Seeing nothing that would suit, Piper stumbled on. Soon she lost all awareness of the woods she was in, for it took all of her concentration to remain upright. She did not even know she had entered a mossy green glade until she caught her foot on a moss-covered rock and tripped, landing flat on her face. At that point, she just did not have the wherewithal to get back up.

It was there that Foster and Wileen, accompanied by several mountain cats, found her sprawled face down, head pillowed on her arms, fast asleep.

"You were right to insist we follow you, Jing," Foster said, addressing the young mountain cat. "I have heard rumors that Neebing blessed walked the land again, but I thought they were just that, rumors."

"Ah, I see you noticed the bracelet, too," Wileen remarked. "A very old one of a design long lost in the mists of time. I wonder how it came into her possession."

"I'm sure we will be able to ask her. First things first, however. Let's see if we can wake her up without scaring her. We will then have to convince her we mean her no harm, and then try to get her to stay on a mount long enough to get her back home."

Wileen reached out, very gently touched Piper's shoulder, and then stepped back, not knowing for sure how Piper would react. Piper's eyes snapped open and she tried to spring up, only to moan and flatten herself back down on the moss.

"We mean you no harm, Neebing blessed. Jing led us to you so we could help you. Can you sit up?" Foster asked.

It took Piper a moment to gather her wits about her and look up. At first, she could not take in just what she was seeing. Piper closed her eyes and opened them again. The vision before her had not changed. A couple in their mid-years stood before her, along with three mountain cats. She reached down to pinch herself, thinking she must be dreaming, but the pinch hurt, assuring her she was not.

"Can you sit up, or do you need some help?" Foster asked again.

Piper drew herself up on her knees. When she tried to push herself upright, she almost made it, but, losing her balance, ended up unceremoniously dropping back down, landing on her seat. The smaller of the mountain cats quickly moved her way. Piper stiffened, but the mountain cat just circled behind her and sat down, leaning into her back, supporting her. It was a strange sensation, Piper thought, like leaning against a fur-covered and very warm pillow. It got even stranger feeling when the mountain cat started purring. The rumbling vibration against her back was oddly comforting. Strange, but oddly comforting.

"Do you think you can ride?" Wileen inquired.

"I'm not sure of anything right now. I guess if I can get my body to stand up, I might be able to answer that question."

"Take your time, dear. We're in no rush. Our cottage is about half a day's ride from here, and our guest bed would be a whole lot more comfortable than continuing to sleep here, although the moss does look somewhat soft. Here, let me give you a hand up."

With a groan that Piper could not hold in, she rose, swayed a little, and then steadied. Though stiff, sore, and tender in some places, once she was standing and had stretched a bit, she felt she might, just might, be able to walk. As she followed the couple, it occurred to her that maybe she should refuse their help. After all, she did not know who they were or their intentions. The fact that she was surrounded by three mountain cats at the moment, and the fact that Foster was carrying her pack, kept her from saying anything.

As if reading Piper's thoughts, Wileen said, "We really do mean you no harm. I am Wileen and my companion is Foster. We are caretakers, you might say, in this area of the forest."

Piper thought about what Wileen had just said and suspected she probably looked as confused as she felt. These two were not dressed like any foresters she had ever met, but then she had to admit to herself that she was much more familiar with the forester clans who took care of the forests closer to where she grew up. She was not as familiar with the clans who took care of the southwestern edge of the southern mountains.

"Ah, I see that Wileen has confused you," stated Foster. "I will try to explain. We are caretakers, for want of a better word, not of the forest, at least not directly. We are not foresters. We are caretakers of the animals who live here. We work with the foresters to make sure the animals who live in this section of the southern mountains remain healthy. For some reason, the animals do not fear us."

*Nor do you seem to fear them*, Piper thought, *since you seem quite comfortable surrounded as you are by mountain cats.*

One was always very cautious when in the vicinity of a mountain cat. While not as large as the hunting cats that roamed the eastern mountains, mountain cats could be as fierce and were not to be tangled with.

In a short while they had reached the place where Wileen and Foster had tied their mounts. She did not know why she felt somewhat comfortable following these folks, despite being practically surrounded by mountain cats. At the very least, they seemed to be heading in the direction Piper wanted to go.

When Piper glanced up, for she had been watching the path so she would not trip and fall, her mouth opened in surprise. She had been expecting to see two or more sturdy mountain horses. Instead, standing untethered were three storm deer. Larger than the mountain horses, the storm deer were a type of deer so named because their call sounded like thunder. They were dark fawn colored and sported huge racks of antlers. What was even more amazing to Piper was that each of the three was saddled for riding. She had never heard of storm deer being tame enough to be ridden. Just who were these folks who had seemingly come to her rescue?

# Chapter Six

Piper discovered that a storm deer was surprisingly comfortable to ride. It had a smooth gait and was very surefooted on the narrow mountain paths. She had been riding for about half a day when the group came out of the forest into a wide meadow. In the center of the meadow was a stone cottage with a thatched roof. In addition to the cottage, there was a long stone building, a stillhouse, a fenced area, and the remains of a huge garden. The homestead looked well cared for. Piper could see that paths led into the meadow out of the surrounding woods from several directions. As Piper grew closer, she noticed the flowers. Near the cottage was the kitchen herb garden and late fall flowers bloomed in the window boxes. She also noticed there was a wisp of smoke coming from the cottage chimney and wondered if some others lived here.

Piper's mount followed the other storm deer to the long low building which Foster explained was part stable, part tack room, part kennel, and part storage for hay and grain among other things. In addition, he told her, there were several rooms where they could treat injured animals. Piper expected that they would ride into the stable part and remove the blanket saddles and tack from the storm deer. It was not to be the case. They stopped short of the low building and dismounted. There they removed the riding gear, and with some ceremony, Foster and Wileen thanked their mounts. Since that seemed expected, Piper thanked her mount, but felt rather foolish doing so. Upon being dismounted, divested of their riding gear, and properly thanked, the three storm deer turned and with great dignity walked off into the surrounding forest.

After carrying her storm deer's tack into the well-appointed and extremely well-organized tack room, Piper was invited to grab her pack and follow Foster and Wileen to their cottage. She was still trying to get over her surprise that the two had just turned the three storm deer loose.

Foster and Wileen's cottage felt much larger on the inside than it had appeared from the outside. Though the furniture was simple in design and sparse, the cottage itself was warm and welcoming.

"You must be tired from your ride. I suspect yours is an interesting tale, but it can wait. Would you like to freshen up and then take a long nap?" Wileen inquired.

"Actually, I would like a moment to ask you some questions," Piper replied.

"Well, certainly. But first, by what name do you go?" Foster asked "We seem not to have gotten around to that yet."

"I am Piper of the clan Wynda, guardians of the southern pass."

"Ah, I know of your clan. Now then, Piper of the clan Wynda, what is it you need to know?"

"How did you find me? I mean, did you just happen to chance upon me when you were out in the forest? And how come you just happened to have a spare mount?"

"Wileen, would you like to answer Piper's questions while I go let Jing in? He is being quite persistent, and I think we might like that front door of ours to remain in one piece. Most unusual, most unusual," Foster muttered to himself as he crossed the room to unlatch the front door and let the mountain cat in.

"It was Jing who led us to you," Wileen explained. "He was most insistent. Since we didn't know the nature of his request, we came prepared. If it was an injured animal, we had healing supplies with us. If we needed to transport the animal back, the storm deer are very tolerant of passengers of all sorts. If it was a folk and injured, we knew we would need some way to get that folk back here."

"Yes, well, about the storm deer. I have never heard of anyone taming them, much less riding them," stated Piper.

"We neither train them nor tame them," suggested Wileen. "They seem to trust us and have offered us their services. I don't know any other way to explain it. Now then, a few questions for you. What brings you to our section of the forest?"

Piper had wanted to continue to ask questions, since she wanted to know more about the mountain cat, Jing, who was now lying at her feet, which was somewhat disconcerting. She decided it was only fair to answer Wileen's questions before she continued to ask her own.

"I'm on my way home after doing an errand for the Crown," Piper told Wileen and Foster, who had come back from letting Jing in.

Piper knew she was taking a chance by telling them who she had been working for. Nevertheless, it seemed only fair to warn them that she might still be being followed, and they may have inadvertently put themselves in danger by coming to her aid.

"It seems I have attracted the attention of folks who would like to delay my journey," stated Piper. "I awoke last night to the sound of voices and, after gathering my things, I tried to get away from what turned out to be two men who were not out in the forest for an evening stroll. Unfortunately, I had no other choice but to try to cross a rock slide in order to get away, and it collapsed under me, sending me to the bottom."

As Piper was telling about her tumble down the rock slide, she vaguely remembered, or thought she remembered, seeing a mountain cat and a strange arc of light. Being somewhat dazed and battered at the time, she was not sure if that had been real or something she had imagined. She decided not to mention the incident to Foster or Wileen.

"When I came to, I traveled as far away from the rock slide as I could. I don't know if the two are still following, and I hope I have not placed you in harm's way."

"Not to worry. We can well take care of ourselves and have a few friends in the area who would come if we called," declared Foster. "When you leave here, where is it you need to head next?"

"I was heading home. I've been away a long time, and I need to get some information to my folks. Mainly, I need to try to get home without any more incidents like yesterday's."

"Tomorrow will be soon enough," stated Foster. "I'm going to head along our back trail and see what I can find. I'll also try to contact the nearest foresters and ask them to be on the lookout for those who do not pass here by their leave. I'll leave you in Wileen's capable hands and see you in the morning."

When she looked out the front window of the cottage, Piper realized the truth in what Foster had said concerning him not being too worried about the two who had been following her. Lying on the front porch were the other two mountain cats who had accompanied them to the cottage. In addition, there was a brown bear and her cubs sleeping in the shade of a tree on the edge of the forest. When Piper went out back to use the privy, she was sure she had seen the silhouettes of several wolves slipping through the forest that bordered the meadow. When she returned to the cottage, she mentioned the wolves to Wileen.

"Ah, that's just Ulfred and his pack. They're a pretty peaceful group, unless threatened. Like Foster said, we have our ways of staying safe here."

*Oh yeah, just a few mountain cats, a mother bear and two cubs, and a wolf pack in the immediate area. Yup, those could be deterrents, should anyone appear threatening to Wileen and Foster*, Piper thought.

In the morning, after a hearty breakfast, Piper slung her pack over her shoulder and headed outside. She wanted to begin heading home as quickly as she could. When she stepped outside the cottage to say goodbye to her hosts, she was surprised at what awaited just off the front porch. Standing next to Foster was a young storm deer, and sitting next to the storm deer was one of the mountain cats, the one called Jing.

"I think before you go, we need to talk," Wileen suggested quietly.

Piper's heart sank just a tiny bit due to Wileen's words. Always before in her life when someone said "We need to talk," it usually did not turn out well for Piper.

"You have a slight look of dread on your face," Wileen said "The same one our daughter gets when we are about to ask her to do a chore she abhors, or when she has done something she feels she is going to get in trouble for. I'm sorry if I have caused you some concern."

Piper found herself more angry at herself than embarrassed, for usually she was much better at hiding her reactions. In many situations she had been in in the past, letting what she was feeling show on her face would have been very dangerous.

"I'm sure you have noticed that Jing has not been very far from you since we found you in the forest."

"Is that usual for him, this sticking close to someone?"

"No, it is not. What's more interesting is that he has been very adamant about it. He stayed in the cottage last night, something he has never done before, and slept on the floor by your bed. He only left just before you woke and, when he returned, he was followed by the storm deer you see here. Interesting," Wileen stated almost to herself. "The storm deer is not one I'm familiar with."

"Jing has always been an unusual one," suggested Foster, who had joined the group on the porch of the cottage and entered the conversation upon noticing Wileen had become distracted by the young storm deer.

"How so?" Piper asked.

"He's not of any of the litters of the mountain cats from this area. Mountain cats, as you know, are very territorial and, yet, the local mountain cats have not objected to him being here. He arrived as a very young kit in early spring. The other unusual thing about Jing is he has, well, it is not exactly a collar, but more like a necklace around his neck. He will not let anyone near enough to him to do anything like take it off or view it closely. It looks like a pendant on a sturdy chain, but it's hard to tell because it's mostly hidden by his fur. The pendant has a stone in it that I have seen only rarely, a firestar gem, such as the one in the bracelet you wear."

Piper took a good look at what she could see of the pendant on the mountain cat, Jing. Jing turned slightly and the sunlight hit the stone on the pendant, causing it to look like it was glowing. Piper then looked down at the stone on the bracelet that Collier had given her and noticed it too shone with a slight light. It then struck her that she was standing in the shade of the porch roof and so the light she saw was not because of the sun. She glanced up to say something to the two standing with her, but something held her back. When she looked back down, her firestar gem was dark. She wondered if she had just imagined the light within the stone. It took her a moment to realize that Wileen had picked up where Foster had left off and was speaking to her.

"Sorry, what did you just say? I must have been woolgathering," Piper said, still a bit distracted by the firestar gems.

"For that matter, he has never let anyone close to him, which makes his actions with you all the more unusual. First, his being insistent that we follow him. Then, his supporting your back out there where we found you, and practically scratching the cottage door down when we took you inside. Most unusual indeed, and now it would seem Jing has brought you transportation."

When Piper looked at her questioningly, Wileen pointed at the storm deer.

"I appreciate the gesture, but I don't have either a blanket saddle or a bridle."

"For some reason, I don't think you will need either. The storm deer are not difficult to ride bareback, and a simple rope halter with reins should be enough to get her to go the direction you want her to go. A soft tug on a rein should do. At the end of each day when you stop, you will need to remove the halter. There is no guarantee how long the storm deer will allow you to ride her. She needs to be set free each night," Wileen told Piper. "After all, the storm deer is neither a trained nor a tame animal."

"I would be grateful for even one day of riding, for it would, hopefully, put me ahead of those who would follow me. They could be a half day behind me or less."

"If they come here, we will certainly try to delay and misdirect them," Foster stated.

"Please don't place yourself in any peril on my behalf. You have been so kind, and I don't want you to get hurt. Tell them the truth if you need to."

"As I have said before, it would be at their peril should they threaten us. Our friends would not take kindly to us being harmed."

Just as Foster finished talking, Piper heard one wolf howl which was answered by several more. *Foster has a point,* Piper thought and felt better. Saying her thanks and farewells, Piper put the rope halter on the storm deer, mounted up, and turned the storm deer's head in the direction of home. The storm deer set off at a ground-eating pace. The mountain cat Wileen had called Jing kept pace with the storm deer.

The day passed by quickly. At first, Piper had been afraid of stopping for fear that once she dismounted the storm deer would leave. Each time she did stop, however, the storm deer waited patiently while Piper stretched her legs. Jing also stayed close, but on alert. As it drew toward evening, Piper began to look for a suitable place to camp. It did not look as though there was a storm on the horizon, and the sky was as clear as it had been all day. When her path crossed a small stream, Piper halted the storm deer and, spotting a stand of pines, turned upstream toward it. When she reached the pine trees, she noticed that others had the same idea before her and had camped there in the past.

Tired of having no one to talk to all day, Piper addressed the mountain cat and the storm deer. "Will this be a suitable stopping place, do you think?" Neither animal answered, but the storm deer stopped and patiently waited while Piper removed the rope halter. Jing, the mountain cat, sat and watched. Once Piper had a small fire going and was beginning to prepare a hot meal, for the evening had grown quite cold, both the storm deer and Jing left the campsite. Piper could only hope they were not gone for good.

# CHAPTER SEVEN

Piper found that she felt lonelier than she had in a long time. She had spent months away from home and had felt afraid, and at times terrified, but curiously enough, never lonely. Yet, when Jing left with the storm deer, Piper felt oddly bereft. No sense to it, she told herself, as she set about getting ready for the night. Banking the fire, she snuggled down into her blanket roll. Sleep was a long time coming.

The early light of dawn woke Piper. There was a stillness to the air, and the surrounding forest was quiet. Very slowly, Piper sat up and reached for her belt knife. As she looked out from under the pine tree where she had slept, she noted her fire had burned down and gone out. Suddenly, out of the corner of her eye, she caught movement to her left. It was the mountain cat, Jing, sitting calmly, licking his front paw, and then rubbing his paw across his left ear. Beyond Jing, the storm deer was grazing on the foliage.

Piper's feeling of relief that the two had returned was greater than expected and, she thought, just a bit embarrassing. *Here I am, someone who has braved the bowels of Farlig Brygge, for not just days but weeks, someone who has served in the southern mountains on border patrol, someone who has spent months on her own in various dangerous places working for the Crown, feeling overjoyed because a mountain cat and a storm deer returned. This is just not making any sense*, Piper thought.

The next thought that occurred to her was to question why the mountain cat was even there. Then she wondered if he responded to his name, or if that was just a name Wileen or Foster had given him to distinguish him from the other mountain cats that seemed to be quite comfortable with the couple, which was unusual in and of itself.

"So, Jing," Piper started, and was somewhat surprised when the mountain cat looked up and looked attentive. "So, ah, thank you for returning, I think." Piper wondered if she should also address the storm deer and thank her. She turned and did so, just in case she should.

Jing stood up and walked toward Piper, who had a fleeting moment of panic. He came to a stop directly in front of her and sat. Piper sat very still for a few moments before curiosity overcame good sense. Slowly and cautiously, she reached out her hand and began to gently scratch along Jing's jawline, just as she would if he had been one of the domestic cats that lived at the keep. Piper almost drew her hand back when she heard a rumbling sound coming from the mountain cat, until she realized what she was hearing was his very soft, deep-throated purr.

With Jing sitting so close, Piper could see that Foster had been correct about what Jing wore around his neck. It was not a collar, but indeed, a pendant on a short chain. Both the pendant and the chain looked to be made out of the same material as the bracelet that Collier had given her. In addition, the pendant that held the firestar gem had a design carved into it that looked almost identical to the design carved into her bracelet.

Piper took a chance and slid her hand down Jing's neck to his chest and picked up the pendant. Jing continued to sit still and purr softly. When she took the pendant into her hand, the firestar gem lit up from within. When she glanced at her bracelet, the firestar gem set in it also lit up from within. Piper felt both the pendant and the bracelet begin to warm slightly.

"It seems we have the same taste in jewelry, cat," Piper said to Jing. "Looks like your pendant and my bracelet were made by the same hand."

*Is it just serendipity that our paths crossed, the two of us with firestar gem jewelry by the same maker, or something more?* Piper wondered. *It seems too much of a coincidence. Wileen said that Jing had come to their cottage just that spring, and he was not all that old when he arrived. That means he had to have acquired the pendant within the last year. Had he somehow accidently slipped his head into the chain that was what…? Just hanging from a branch? Unlikely. Had someone put the pendant on the mountain cat? Possibly, but why? The pendant is finely crafted and probably quite valuable. Who would put a valuable pendant on a wild mountain cat?*

Since asking Jing these questions did not seem like it would get her any answers, Piper got up, packed up, stuffed a piece of trail biscuit in her mouth, and, after fastening the rope halter on the storm deer, took the reins and mounted.

The days passed by quickly, if not the miles. While traveling by storm deer brought Piper closer to home faster than if she had been walking, she began to be concerned about the weather. With each passing day of fall, the chances for freezing rain or snow, even in the lower mountains, was always a risk. Just as Piper was beginning to relax a bit, for they had moved into territory very familiar to her, Jing turned south off the path they had been following. The storm deer turned and followed.

"Jing, no, that's not the way to my home. That direction will lead us higher into the mountains."

The mountain cat continued to walk up the path. When Piper tried to turn around, the storm deer shook her head back, just missing grazing Piper with her antlers, and picked up her pace. Piper decided that jumping off a moving storm deer while she was traveling at a fast clip up a heavily tree-lined path was not going to be a good choice. When the storm deer slowed down and finally stopped, Piper was not sure she would be capable of walking anywhere. Despite the smooth gait, riding for hours and hours without a rest had caused her muscles to become very stiff. With a soft moan, she slid from the storm deer's back, but needed to lean against her for a few moments before attempting to step away. When Jing walked up and butted his head against Piper's leg, he almost sent her sprawling. She was glad the storm deer had not shied when she fell against her. Jing head-butted her leg a second time, but this time she was steadier on her feet.

"Now you just quit that," Piper admonished. "I'm not getting back on the storm deer until I've had a chance to stretch my legs, get something to eat, and …." *And try to figure out what is going on*, Piper thought. She was aware that, between the mountain cat and the storm deer, if they were working together and determined, she had very little hope of changing the direction they were presently traveling. That the two animals appeared to be working together was disconcerting enough. That Jing seemed to be leading Piper purposely somewhere was more than a little unnerving. That the mountain cat had ceased head-butting and was now sitting with an air of patient waiting about him was also unsettling.

"I don't suppose you will let me turn around and walk back down the path we just traveled, will you?" Piper asked, addressing Jing. "Would it help to know that I have been away from home for quite some time and wish to go there now?"

Jing's only reply was to stand up and start toward Piper. She tried to back away, only to bump into the storm deer who had shifted in behind her.

"Well, that answers my question." *Or at least one of them*, Piper thought, as she remounted the storm deer.

The higher the trio climbed, the colder the temperature and the grayer the sky became. Brooding storm clouds began to gather at the heights, and Piper thought she smelled a hint of snow in the air. She was certainly not prepared to travel much higher up the mountains. The clothes she had worn and brought with her out of the lowland marshes surrounding Farlig Brygge were made of thin material and certainly not adequate to keep the bone-penetrating chill out. She wished she had thought to ask Foster or Wileen if she could acquire a warm cloak from them, but then she had not known she would be heading this high up into the mountains.

It was with great relief when Piper dismounted after Jing finally halted for the day. He had chosen a fairly sheltered area near a small streamlet. There was plenty of dry wood available. Piper set about scraping a spot clear of leaves and gathering rocks to form a fire pit circle. The old adage about how she who gathers wood warms herself twice came to mind as Piper broke dry branches off nearby trees and built herself a substantial woodpile. She knew that she would not be alone this high up in the mountains, for it was hunting territory for a number of forest dwellers, most of whom she would be just as happy not to meet on a dark night.

Wrapped in her blanket roll, holding a cup of tea, and with her feet to the fire, Piper felt warmer. Neither the storm deer nor Jing had left her this night. Jing was lying alert on the other side of the fire. The storm deer was not all that far away, nibbling here and there on the foliage. She too had an aura of alertness about her. Piper was not sure if they sensed something she could not, or if this state of alertness was normal for one or both of the animals. After finishing her tea, Piper built the fire up and settled into her blanket roll. She knew from experience, it would be a long night, for she would need to sleep lightly. It would not do to let the fire go out.

The next morning, resigned to the fact that neither the storm deer nor Jing were going to let her go back down the mountain, Piper settled herself on the storm deer's back and tried to make the best of it. Unless they turned off the path they were now traveling, it looked like Jing was heading her up and over the mountain. She knew from experience that there was a rugged valley between the tree-covered mountains they were traveling and the rocky higher mountains.

It was said that there were other small high mountain passes that one could travel through by foot to get to the other side, but she had never traveled on one. Her family's keep guarded the only mountain pass through the high southern mountains that could be traversed by wagon. Trade by sea was much easier between Sommerhjem and Rullegress, the country to the south, than over the mountains.

Piper's family, from time out of mind, had guarded the southern mountain pass, for there had not always been peace between the folks of Sommerhjem and Rullegress. Rullegress was a country quite different from Sommerhjem. A flatter land of gently rolling hills covered with grass, there were few trees in the unrelenting landscape. Not a land Piper had ever aspired to dwell in. She hoped they were not heading there.

Once over the tree-covered mountain, Jing headed straight south across the narrow valley between the low southern mountains and the rocky, high mountains beyond. Piper once again questioned the wisdom of not just jumping off the storm deer. Something held her back, besides the possibility of imminent damage to herself should she land badly. Jumping off moving animals had never been included in any of the training she had ever had during her several years with the border patrol. In addition, Piper had become intrigued by the compelling focus that the mountain cat had maintained since she had begun to follow him.

Once they crossed the valley, Jing began to follow a path that started up the high mountain. The path was fairly wide and easy going, climbing between tall pines. As they moved higher, the trees began to thin out. Although not yet above the tree line, the air had grown colder and thinner. It was difficult to see what was ahead, but Piper soon realized that the light was rapidly fading, even though it was just midday. She had been concentrating so hard to maintain her seat on the storm deer, for the stretch of path they were currently traversing had headed sharply downward, that she had not looked up at the sky. When she did, Piper became aware that very dark, turbulent storm clouds were hanging low overhead.

Her attention was drawn sharply back to the path ahead by a low snarl that was answered back by a thunderous bellow from the storm deer. Ahead in the center of the path was a huge grevling, an animal that was both vicious and fearless, in addition to being very territorial. It did not matter that this grevling was facing the very lethal and dangerous antlers of a storm deer or the teeth and claws of a mountain cat, it was not about to let the trio pass.

Trying to stay seated on the storm deer, who was tossing her head, caused Piper to either duck or lean back. Her erratic movement on the storm deer's back was causing the storm deer to shift sideways and buck a little. Piper also noticed Jing's back hairs were standing straight up, and he was crouched, looking like he was ready to spring.

"Wait, Jing. We can turn around and go back up the trail. Let's take another path."

Just at that moment, the storm deer tipped her head back and then turned it toward Piper, catching her in a glancing blow that sent her flying off the storm deer's back. She landed hard on the ground, knocking the wind out of her. Lying there trying to catch her breath, she could only watch in dismay as the storm deer and Jing both charged the grevling. Growling, hissing, and thunderous bellowing filled the air and echoed off the mountainside. At the same time, the clouds that had been threatening most of the day fulfilled their promise, and snow began to fall in huge swirling flakes. It was hard for her to see exactly what was happening as the snowfall became thicker, and the wind picked up. At times the swirling snowflakes obscured her vision. Wiping the snow from her eyes to see better, Piper saw the storm deer standing silent and still, sides heaving, steam rising off her haunches.

Piper hurried to the storm deer and quickly checked her over. She did not seem to have sustained any injuries from confronting the grevling. Piper looked down the path and into the surrounding woods, but could see no sign of the grevling, nor could she see Jing. She was torn as to what to do next. Finally, she grabbed the rope reins of the storm deer and led her farther down the path. The snow had settled into a steady light fall, and the wind was no longer causing the snow to swirl and obscure the landscape.

When Piper and the storm deer reached the bottom of the down slope, she saw Jing lying just off the path ahead of her. Quickly tying the storm deer's reins to a nearby branch, hoping she would stay put, Piper rushed to where Jing was lying. The mountain cat had a shallow gash across his left shoulder. More worrisome, however, was the deep gash on the top of his head. She was relieved that she could see Jing's side move up and down in steady breathing. She knew she could not leave him lying there so, as gently as she could, she picked Jing up and carried him back to the storm deer. Draping Jing carefully across the storm deer's back, Piper mounted up behind him.

*What do I do now?* Piper wondered. *Do I turn around and try to make it back to Foster and Wileen, or do I move on in the direction Jing had been leading me?*

# CHAPTER EIGHT

No matter what direction Piper chose, one thing was for certain. She needed to find shelter and find it quickly. The wind had begun to pick up again as had the snow. The cold had increased with the wind and snow, and the air was very damp. Daylight was fading. Piper was not sure how much longer she would be able to stay on top of the storm deer, or direct which way she should go. Her hands were so cold, she was having trouble holding onto the reins and Jing. She had chosen to follow the path Jing had been leading her on. She had no rational explanation for why she had not turned back.

Piper lost all track of time. Even though the snow had finally stopped, she was so numb she was not sure if her eyes were playing tricks on her, or if she had actually seen a light in the distance. Reaching up, she brushed the ice crystals off her eyelashes and peered ahead. There did seem to be a light ahead. For good or for ill, the light suggested there might be shelter not far ahead. Thumping the storm deer's sides with her boot heels, Piper urged the mount forward. The storm deer too seemed to sense shelter ahead, for she picked up her pace. It was all Piper could do to stay on and keep Jing from slipping off.

Moments later, the trio rode into a clearing that held a small stone cottage. Light shone in the windows, and smoke drifted lazily out of the chimney. Just as she pulled the storm deer to a halt in front of the cottage, the door swung open, spilling light onto the covered porch.

Silhouetted against the light was the figure of a woman. Even more surprising to Piper were the two mountain cats that rushed swiftly down the porch steps. Piper stayed very still, as did the storm deer. One of the mountain cats stopped directly in front of them. The other one circled around them once and then hurried back to the woman on the porch. Just as swiftly, the mountain cat returned to where the other mountain cat was sitting. The woman followed.

By this time, Piper was so cold her entire body was shaking and her teeth were chattering. It was hard to get her words out. "P-P-P-Ple-Please, we, ne-ne-need your he-he-help."

"Hand the little one down to me. Can you dismount on your own?" the woman questioned.

Piper just nodded, for talking took too much effort. When she slid off the storm deer, she did not embarrass herself by falling to the ground. She did, however, have to steady herself against the storm deer for a moment.

"Follow me. Let's get you and this little one out of the cold and wind."

The woman led Piper not to the front door of the cottage, but to the back where the barn was attached to the cottage. The woman suggested it might be best if Piper, the mountain cat, and the storm deer started their warm-up there. The woman told Piper that the animals in the barn kept the barn quite warm, but not as warm as the cottage. The heat in the cottage might be too warm right away, she explained. After Piper had taken the rope halter off the storm deer, she thanked her for her service and released her. She was surprised when the storm deer moved further into the barn and began to graze on a stack of hay. Turning back to the woman, Piper asked what she could do to help.

"Do you see that pile of blankets on that shelf to the left of the door?" the woman asked. "Grab a couple, if you would, please."

Piper nodded toward the woman and did as asked. She could hear the woman murmuring to Jing, but could only catch a word here and there.

"Ah, little one … you … well. … so sorry … hurt."

When Piper approached her with the blankets, the woman told her to wrap herself up in one. She laid another blanket out on a stack of hay and gently settled Jing on it. Piper noticed that the two other mountain cats had followed them into the barn. When both of them approached Jing, the woman asked them to wait.

"Mosi, Namir, wait. I need to look your little one over first." Turning to Piper she asked, "Are you injured also?"

"No, ma'am."

"Please, call me Antini. And you are?"

"Piper."

"How did this happen?"

"Jing, the one you refer to as little one, anyway, I call him Jing, well, um, he tangled with a grevling. The grevling was on the path that Jing was insistent on traveling, and so ...." Piper's voice trailed off.

"Very brave, but somewhat foolish. Let's see what we can do." Antini motioned to the two other mountain cats that they should come forward from where they had been patiently sitting. "Curl up beside your kit, but be gentle. I will be right back." Turning to Piper, she told her to wait in the barn.

Several minutes later, Antini returned carrying a small clay jar. Scooping a greenish salve out of the jar, Antini cupped her hands around the salve. As her hands began to warm the salve up, the aroma of fresh growing spring plants after a rain filled the barn. Antini then placed both hands on the deep gash on Jing's head, holding them there. When she moved her hands, the gash had closed up, and Jing began to stir.

"Come along, Piper, I have done all I can here. The little one's family will take care of him now."

Piper could see that the woman who called herself Antini spoke the truth. The two other mountain cats were now cleaning the shallow gash on Jing's shoulder. Piper found herself torn between following Antini into the warmth of her cottage and remaining with Jing.

Once Piper and Antini had settled into the two chairs next to the fire, Antini turned to Piper and said, "I wish to thank you for bringing the one you call Jing home. Many would have just left him after he had been injured. It would seem he chose well."

Piper was now even more confused than she had been since Jing had turned them south and headed them up into the higher mountains. *I did not understand then and, now knowing he was heading back to his family, I do not know why he had insisted I follow him. Was he always heading back to his family?* she wondered. *Did I just assume he would not let me go back? Was I just fooling myself that he would have stopped me if I had tried to head east toward home? What exactly is going on here?*

The questions that were going around and around in Piper's head abruptly stopped circling when a new question popped in. *What had Antini meant when she had said Jing had chosen me, and in addition, just what has he chosen me for?*

"Excuse me, but you just said Jing had chosen well, that is, he had chosen me. Just what do you mean?"

"You must be hungry. I have a pot of stew warming on the fire. Would you care for some?" Antini asked, avoiding Piper's question.

"I'm very hungry for food, but equally hungry for answers. Jing led me this direction. It would seem he was leading me here. Why?" Piper had trouble controlling the tone of her voice and knew she sounded peeved.

"Sorry, I live here alone in the high mountains because I find most folk bothersome. It would seem I have forgotten how impatient younglings can be. I will answer your questions, although it is just as easy to have a civil conversation over a warm and filling meal. Your choice."

"My apologies. I'm normally not rude and ungrateful. A warm meal sounds very good indeed."

After the meal, once the two were settled in chairs by the fireplace, a scratching sound came from the door that led from the cottage to the barn.

"If you will excuse me," Antini said, getting up to open the door and let the three mountain cats into the cottage.

Jing was a bit wobbly as he crossed the room to Piper. Once he reached her, he put his head in her lap and let out a sound that sounded suspiciously like a sigh to Piper. She tentatively reached out a hand and stroked his back. She had been worried that Jing's family might object, but they had arranged themselves in front of the fireplace and were dozing.

"I don't understand any of this," Piper exclaimed. "I don't understand why Jing got Foster and Wileen to come find me. I don't understand why he brought a storm deer for me to ride. I don't understand why he has led me here. Mountain cats, to the best of my knowledge, don't normally come anywhere near folks, and yet twice now I have met folks who are at ease with them. Just what is going on?"

"Perhaps I should start at the beginning. I grew up an only child on a small estate. My father and mother both were scholars and historians, and the income from the estate allowed them to pursue their interests. A good manager ran the estate while I was young. While I enjoyed learning as much as my parents, I also enjoyed wandering the estate. I especially liked the animals there. I discovered in my solitary walks through the woods and fields of the estate that the animals, both domestic and wild, seemed drawn to me. I found over the years that I really preferred animals to folks. As time went by and my parents became more and more wrapped up in their research and writing, I took over managing the estate. It was a good life for a while."

Piper settled more comfortably in her chair by the fire. She guessed getting the answer to her question was going to take a while.

"A number of years ago, a man representing the Crown, or so he proclaimed, came to my parents asking them to use their knowledge and skills to find out more about the Gylden Sirklene challenge and the oppgave ringe. My parents began to split their time between the estate and the capital. As the time moved closer to the coming of age of Princess Esmeralda, more pressure was put on them to find and deliver more and more information about the challenge, and especially about the oppgave ringe. The Crown, it seemed, had an urgent need to discover who had the nine pieces of the oppgave ringe."

At the mention of the Gylden Sirklene challenge and the oppgave ringe, Piper sat up straighter. She was surprised, to say the least, that Antini would talk so freely about either the challenge or the rings.

"My parents began to become concerned because what had at first seemed like an honor to be asked to do work for the Crown gradually became a frightening and terrifying experience. By this time, they had discovered that they were not working for the Crown as they had thought, but were working for the Regent. It had become clear to them that the Regent was not asking them to help Sommerhjem, but to help him for his own gains. When my parents had tried to quit, they were kept virtual prisoners at a townhouse in the capital. At one point, they managed to convince their keepers that they needed to return to the estate. Told their keepers they thought they had an obscure reference they needed in a scroll or book at the estate."

By then Piper was so caught up in the tale Antini was telling that she had forgotten her original question.

"Late on the first night of their arrival back at the estate we managed to have a private conversation. They suspected that the Regent wanted them to find information that he could use to prevent Princess Esmeralda from taking over the rule of Sommerhjem. He also wanted information so he could circumvent the calling of the challenge. Those who had escorted my parents back to our estate had told them that some of them would remain behind to manage the estate, and that I would be going back to the capital with them. My parents feared the Regent would use me as leverage to motivate them to dig deeper and work harder. You see, they had been finding things out. However, they had not been passing all of the information on, just enough to avoid suspicion."

"What happened then?" Piper asked. "Did you have to go to the capital?"

"No. That night my parents gave me the information they had held back from the Regent. Unbeknownst to their keepers, they had gotten a message to me that they were coming and that I needed to be prepared to leave the estate on a moment's notice. Before they had arrived, I had packed for travel. After talking to my parents, I slipped out of the manor house and made my way through the woods to a loyal tenant's cottage where I had left my horse and supplies. I was long gone before it was discovered I had left."

"They must have sent someone after you," Piper suggested.

"I'm sure they did. With a great deal of luck, a lone rider traveling on fairly well-traveled roads can move across Sommerhjem swiftly. My parents had a great many contacts who were loyal to the Crown and also helped. In addition, I had a destination. My parents had indeed discovered what they thought might be the location of one of the pieces of the oppgave ringe. I set off to find it. I found much more than I bargained for." Antini trailed off and was silent for several minutes.

It was all Piper could do not to leap out of her chair and demand Antini tell her what she had found. Finally, she addressed Antini. "And …?"

# Chapter Nine

"Sorry, I was lost in thought," stated Antini. "I have never gone back home, and I've had little contact outside these mountains. I'm aware of what happened this summer at the Well of Speaking. Foresters stop here from time to time to check on me and bring news from outside this place. They also bring some supplies I can't provide for myself. I haven't been able to find out what happened to my parents or our estate. I could not leave here before now, however."

"Why not?" questioned Piper.

"When I left our estate in the middle of the night, my destination was always to come here. My parents had found a very obscure reference that alluded to a hermit's cottage here in the mountains. The reference suggested that traditionally a woman hermit dwelled here. It also suggested she may have been the keeper of one of the pieces of the oppgave ringe. At first, I thought I was traveling on a fool's errand, since the last time the pieces of the oppgave ringe were in the capital was several hundred years ago. The hermit living here then would have been long gone. There was no guarantee the cottage would even be here, much less occupied by a hermit who had knowledge of one of the rings."

Piper could feel her heart sinking. She had become more and more excited as Antini told her tale. The possibility of one of the pieces of the oppgave ringe being here had been so unexpected, yet exciting. Now, it just seemed like a fine, impossible tale.

"When I arrived here, I was amazed to find a cottage just where my folks had indicated it would be. Even more surprising was to find it occupied. The woman who lived here was quite old and frail. Oftentimes, she was more centered in the past than the present. Whenever she had lucid days, however, I learned a great deal. She was the one who sent Jing off. Said he would bring back the one we needed. I didn't really believe her until today. Unfortunately, she died several months ago."

"Why didn't you leave then?" Piper asked, before she had properly sorted through what Antini had just said. *What had she meant when she said Jing was to bring the one they needed?* "Wait, you think Jing was sent off to find me?"

"Yes. I was told that firestar gems, when worn by certain folk, and apparently by at least one mountain cat, will warm or glow or have a fire within when they come in contact with each other. The gems will do this, not the folk or mountain cats. Did something like that happen when Jing first approached you?"

"I thought I had imagined it," Piper said so softly that Antini had to ask her to repeat what she had said. "The first time I think I came in contact with Jing, an arc of light sparked between my bracelet and his pendant. I thought I had imagined that whole episode. But none of this is making sense. The bracelet only recently came into my possession."

"How did that come about?" Antini queried.

Piper told Antini about taking shelter in a shallow cave and discovering someone was trapped behind a cave-in. She told her how Collier had found the bracelet in the cave he had been exploring and had insisted she take it as thanks for saving his life.

"I can't be the one Jing was sent to find. I have been wearing the bracelet for only a very short time. Your hermit sent Jing off months ago. It must be coincidence."

"No, I don't think so. I think it does not matter how long you have worn the bracelet. What matters is that the firestar gem reacts for you and with Jing's pendant. The woman who lived here was convinced that Jing would find the folk who was needed."

"Needed for what?"

"Why, to locate the piece of the oppgave ringe, of course."

*Oh, of course,* Piper thought. *Is this woman balmy? Maybe living alone in the mountains for long periods of time has caused Antini to lose sight of the real world. Does she really believe that a very young mountain cat wearing a pendant holding a firestar gem would cross paths with some folk also wearing a firestar gem, and that folk would be just the one to seek out and find a piece of the oppgave ringe?*

"I don't mean to be rude, but this tale sounds like something a storyteller might make up to entertain wee folk," Piper replied to what she had just heard.

"I appreciate that the tale does seem very farfetched. Take a little walk with me, for I have something to show you."

Piper followed Antini out of the cottage, through the barn, and out the back. The three mountain cats followed. The group walked only a short way to a snow-covered mound. Piper recognized the mound as a cold cellar, the likes of which she had seen at home. Cold cellars were built in this fashion rather than below ground under a cottage in this part of the mountains because the bedrock was so close to the surface, making it difficult if not impossible to dig down very far. She watched as Antini lifted the bar off the door and swung the door open. Antini motioned Piper forward, and it was with some trepidation that Piper entered the cold cellar. She felt a little better when Antini followed her inside.

"This may look like a typical cold cellar, and for the most part, it is. This high in the mountains does not provide a very long growing season, so it is important to preserve much of the food that will be needed over the long, and sometimes harsh, winters. As you can see, I have stocked well for the coming cold season."

As Piper looked around, she could see that Antini had indeed put up a great deal of provisions for the coming winter months.

"What is not typical in this cold cellar is back here," Antini stated.

Piper looked toward the back of the cold cellar, and it looked very much like others she had been in. The walls and ceiling of the cellar were lined with fitted stone making the cellar more difficult for scavengers to dig or gnaw their way in. The floor was also made of fitted stone to keep animals from tunneling in.

Antini crossed the small room and moved several small barrels that had been stacked one on top of the other. She then did something Piper could not see, and a section of the back wall of the cold cellar swung inward. When Piper reached the opening, Antini had already stepped through and was heading down narrow stairs.

"Tread carefully, for the steps are shallow and very steep," Antini called over her shoulder. "I'll get a light lit when I reach the bottom."

Piper placed her hands on the walls on each side of her. Sliding her left foot forward, she located the edge of the first step and stepped her other foot down. Once she had both feet on the second step, she repeated the pattern, moving ever cautiously downward. Suddenly, a light flared and then steadied at the bottom, giving Piper enough light to move more quickly down the stairs. When she reached the bottom, she looked up and saw she was now standing in a small irregularly-shaped natural cave.

Piper was surprised when she took in what she saw before her. The small cave held a bed, a desk, and a bookshelf lined with books of all sizes and coverings. Some were leather bound and some were cloth bound. All were plain.

"It looks as though one could live here," Piper commented.

"I think, from what I learned, that this was indeed the dwelling place of one of the early hermits. It must have been a very hard existence. I think the cold cellar was originally built as a second room for living and then used as a cold cellar after the cottage was built."

Piper continued to survey the room, trying to imagine what it must have been like to live here in this cave. She found her attention being pulled toward the bookshelf.

Antini, seeing that Piper's eyes had been drawn to the bookshelf, commented, "That bookshelf is another reason I have not left here. Those are the journals of all of the hermits who have dwelled here over the span of several hundred years, and they contain a great deal of wisdom and history. My parents would have reveled in a discovery such as this. I find myself captured by what is here as thoroughly as they might have been. I have found numerous references to both the Gylden Sirklene challenge and to the oppgave ringe, which surprised me. Mind you, they are all somewhat cryptic. None of them comes right out and explains just what happens in the challenge, nor do they give any indication as to what to do with the nine pieces of the oppgave ringe. However ..."

*Oh, good, there is a "however," Piper thought. I hope it is going to be good news, because so far the news has not been very encouraging. I am skeptical about the whole idea that Jing was purposely sent to fetch someone, much less me.*

"... the journals are not what I brought you down here to see."

Once again, Antini did something Piper could not see, and the bookshelf swung toward her, revealing a hollow behind it. Antini reached in and pulled out an oilcloth-wrapped bundle. Moving over to the desk and nearer to the light, Antini motioned Piper closer. With some reverence, Antini unwrapped the bundle. Once the oilcloth was smoothed flat, Piper could see the bundle contained an elaborately-carved box. She was surprised when she realized that the carvings on the box were the same as those on the box Collier had taken her bracelet from. Indeed, the designs on both boxes were also very much like the designs on both her bracelet and Jing's pendant.

"Jing's pendant was housed in this box along with a small journal. I guess you could call it a pendant for want of a better term. The author of the journal indicated that she had been given charge of one of the pieces of the oppgave ringe after King Griswold had won the Gylden Sirklene challenge. She was a very old woman when the next hermit arrived with the news that King Griswold's daughter had assumed the rule and was now the Queen of Sommerhjem. Not knowing what the future would hold, but convinced that the challenge would be called again, they set about safeguarding the piece of the oppgave ringe. They could have had no idea that it would be such an exceptionally long time before the challenge was called again."

"How did they go about safeguarding the piece of the oppgave ringe?" Piper asked, now totally caught up in what Antini was telling her.

"I must confess that, from the first, I have been very doubtful about what the journal writers stated they did. Your being here with Jing and wearing that bracelet has certainly lent a great deal of weight to the writings."

"What did they say?"

"The two women enlisted the aid of a Günnary gem cutter. They, the two women hermits, had found a firestar gem somewhere in these mountains. They do not specify where. It apparently was quite a large one, as firestar gems go. The Günnary gem cutter took the stone and divided it into four gems. Apparently there are different types of firestar gems, and this one was one of the rarest. Firestar gems are reputed to choose who wears them."

Piper gave Antini a questioning look.

"I realize it sounds implausible. Try something for me, if you would. Try to take the bracelet off and hand it to me."

Piper thought of Antini's request. She found herself surprised that she had not thought to take the bracelet off in the time she had worn it. She also found herself reluctant to take it off now, very reluctant. Piper reached down to take the bracelet off, her hand hovering over it for a long moment, and then she dropped her hand.

"I just can't seem to make myself take it off," Piper stated, surprised by her own reaction.

"I'm not sure you could, even if you tried. I do know that it would be impossible to try to take the pendant off Jing. I know, I tried, and I have the claw marks to prove it. But back to the discussion about the firestar gem. The particular stone the two women hermits gave to the Günnary gem cutter had a unique feature. While most firestar gems will somehow let a wearer know if another wearer is of good heart.... I know, I know, that sounds fanciful, but I have come to believe the writer of this journal knew what she was writing about. Anyway, while the bracelet you wear will do that, it also has one other property. It will seek out its other parts."

Antini let that statement hang in the air for several moments before going on.

"One of the four pieces of the firestar gem that the Günnary gem cutter fashioned was placed in the pendant that Jing wears. A second part of the gem was placed in the bracelet you wear. The third part of the gem resides within this box, which is why I think Jing was drawn back here."

Antini reached into the box and drew out a pouch. She tipped its contents into her hand and quickly set it on the desk.

It was an arm cuff made of the same strange material as Piper's bracelet, carved in the same design, and embedded in it was a firestar gem. Arcs of light passed between her gem, Jing's gem, and the gem on the cuff. Piper had not even been aware that Jing had followed them down the steps into the cave.

"What just happened is described in great detail in the journal," Antini stated. "It would seem the journal writers knew what they were writing about. They said that your two gems would be drawn to this third one."

"What of the fourth piece?" Piper asked.

"I don't know, for the hermit hid it along with the oppgave ringe."

# Chapter Ten

Hearing that the hermit had hidden a piece of the oppgave ringe with the fourth part of the firestar gem caused Piper's heart to sink. The tale that Antini was weaving kept getting Piper's hopes up, only to dash them again.

"I don't suppose the hermit left a detailed map as to where to find the ring?" Piper asked.

"Not in the sense that there is a paper and ink copy waiting to tell you directly where to go, no," Antini answered.

"I guess that really would be too much to ask for."

"While the hermit who wrote the journal may not have left a map, she did leave directions."

Hearing that there were directions on where to find a piece of the oppgave ringe caused Piper's spirits to rise once again.

"It would be great if the directions were as easy as walk twenty paces northeast from the cold cellar, then head fifty paces to the east to the boulder shaped like a sleeping mountain cat …. Well, you get the idea. However, the directions are neither that simple nor that straightforward. It would seem the firestar gems are the key," stated Antini.

*Of course, it could not be that simple*, Piper thought. *The whole journey from Farlig Brygge to here was filled with unexpected twists and turns. Why would I ever think the directions for finding the piece of the oppgave ringe would be simple?*

"According to the directions, three of the firestar gems need to be together to guide the wearers to the fourth."

"That's good then. We now have three of the gems together. You, Jing, and I, or Jing and I, can now do what the directions tell us to do next."

"Wait. I'm afraid it's not that simple."

"Of course not," Piper remarked, discouraged.

"What happened when you put the firestar gem bracelet on?" Antini asked.

"It felt warm when it should have felt cold, and there was a glow within the stone. At least, I thought there was a glow."

"When I put the cuff on, one, it does not fit my arm. Secondly, the cuff feels cold and is just a dark stone to me. According to the directions from the hermit, the cuff should react to its proper wearer like yours does to you."

"So what does that mean?" Piper asked.

"Again, according to the writer of the journal, the two firestar gems you and Jing wear have drawn you both toward the third stone. You need to take this cuff and find its proper wearer. Once that's done, the combination of the three stones should give you the direction to head to find the fourth stone and the piece of the oppgave ringe."

"Let me see if I have this straight. Jing was sent off to find the wearer of the bracelet, which happens to be me. The combination of the two stones, Jing's and mine, led us here. Now that we are here, we need to take the cuff holding the third stone, and then Jing and I are somehow supposed to find the folk who should wear the cuff. Once that simple little task is accomplished, the three of us wearing the jewelry with the firestar gems embedded in them will be led to the fourth gem and the oppgave ringe. Have I got the sequence of what is going to happen right?" Piper inquired.

"That's about it in a nutshell," Antini replied.

"Oh, no problems then. Easy-peasy," Piper retorted, her voice laced with sarcasm. "Just how am I supposed to find the one who is supposed to wear the cuff?"

"According to the hermit's journal, the firestar gems will react to other firestar gems with an arc of light if the wearer is one who walks for the good of Sommerhjem. I think what the writer meant is that only those who in their heart want what is best for Sommerhjem can wear firestar gems. Wait,

I'm not explaining this properly. I'm loyal to the Crown and want the best for my country, but the firestar gems do not respond for me. I think the firestar gems respond to only a select few. If I were wearing the cuff, yours or Jing's would still be drawn to it, but you would note that there would be no glow from within."

"If Jing or I were to cross paths with someone who was wearing a firestar gem who was supposed to have it, we would notice a glow within the stone?"

"After the arc of light, yes, at least according to what I have read. Also, your firestar gem should warm to it or other objects of power. I think you can assume that a folk who is wearing a firestar gem is a friend not a foe."

"That's good to know, should I cross paths with another wearer of a firestar gem, but that doesn't help me find the folk who is supposed to wear the cuff. Winter is fast approaching and, while not long, other than here in the mountains, traveling about Sommerhjem in search of who knows who is going to be difficult. Meanwhile, time is not going to stop. All nine of the pieces of the oppgave ringe must be in the capital by the time of the capital's next summer fair.

"True enough. Yet, the task might not be as difficult as you are imagining. The writer suggests you will be drawn to the one you seek."

"Am I just supposed to wander around Sommerhjem hoping I'm drawn to some passing stranger?" Piper asked.

"No. Just as you and Jing were drawn back here, you will be drawn to the one you seek. Let me ask you a question. Since you have been in the presence of the cuff, have you begun to feel restless? Have you begun to feel like you need to get on with your journey?" Antini probed.

Piper had to think about Antini's question. First she settled her body, and then tried to still her mind, as she had been taught in her border patrol training. At first, she did not know if she was just imagining a feeling of restlessness, or if she was really feeling restless. Was she feeling restless because Antini suggested she might be? Piper's instincts had always been good, so she tried to listen to what they were telling her. Not only was she feeling restless, but she was also feeling a sense of urgency. In addition, she felt a pull away from here. If she followed the direction of that pull, it would lead her not home, but north and a little farther east.

"Piper?" Antini prompted.

"What? Sorry. Now that you mention it, I am feeling more restless than usual."

"Here is what I suggest. Stay the next few days here. That will give Jing time to fully heal after his encounter with the grevling. It will give you time to read through the hermit's journal. It should remain here, but I think you will find the information within helpful. Also, I have compiled a small booklet of information I have copied from the journals and writings left in this room by past hermits dwelling here that pertains to the Gylden Sirklene challenge and the oppgave ringe. I would have you take it with you when you leave. It may be information that the Crown doesn't have yet. I'm sure that our former regent and the folks who backed him have not given up wanting to find any way they can to seize back the rule," suggested Antini.

"I should take time to read that also, in case for some reason the booklet becomes lost or stolen during my journey."

"Excellent idea. I don't know about you, but I'm getting a little chilled. Cold cellars are good for keeping food from spoiling. However, since we are neither carrots, apples, onions, nor any other type of fruit or vegetable, I suggest we head back into the cottage, and you can read by the fire," Antini said with good humor.

Piper was more than willing to move back to the cottage and spend the rest of the day reading and talking with Antini. The next several days passed quickly. For the first time since she had left Farlig Brygge, Piper had a chance to catch her breath, sort through and repack her pack, and become more comfortable with not only Jing, but also the other two mountain cats.

With each passing day, however, she felt the pull to leave and head north. She hoped that those who had followed her out of Farlig Brygge had long ago lost her trail. When she had left the seaport, she had hoped no one had discovered who she really was, which was one of the reasons she had felt comfortable heading home. Piper had thought she would be able to avoid being caught before she reached home territory. Once there, she had known she would have a better chance to make it to safety. Now, though, she would not be heading home. She would need to head back over the forest-covered mountains and down into the foothills to start with, unless the one she was looking for was just conveniently waiting for her on the other side of the mountains. Piper did not think she could be that lucky.

Early on the morning of the fourth day since her arrival at the hermit Antini's home, Piper bid farewell to Antini and the two adult mountain cats. The storm deer stood quietly as Piper mounted. Jing approached each of his parents and briefly touched noses before turning and starting up the trail they had arrived on.

"Thank you for your hospitality, and for all the information you have gathered. If I'm successful and get to the capital, I will try to find out what happened to your parents and to your estate and send word back."

"Or come back yourself. You will always be welcome here. Safe journey."

The trek back across the mountains was not as difficult as the one over had been. The weather, while cold, had remained calm and neither snow nor rain fell. Piper was certainly better prepared for the journey, for Antini had insisted Piper accept the gift of a warm wool sweater, wool pants, fur mittens, and a warm fur-lined cloak. Having the right clothing allowed Piper to stay in the mountains rather than heading down into the foothills right away. Antini had also suggested that the storm deer would most probably not wish to leave the forest-covered mountains, so Piper had concluded that the longer she could ride rather than walk, the faster she would get to wherever she was being pulled. Though she felt pulled to head north and east, the longer she could avoid the more populated areas the better, so she chose to head east first before turning north.

Piper had never had an animal companion before. There were dogs and cats at her home keep, though she had not been close to any of them. They were working animals who herded, guarded, or kept the vermin down. Piper discovered she liked having the mountain cat around. She found herself talking to him at night. He would lie with his head resting on his crossed paws, blue eyes gazing directly at her, listening intently. She wondered if she was just fooling herself, thinking he understood what she was saying.

There came a time when heading east no longer felt right. The trail they had been following had been heading east, but also gradually down the mountain. They had come to a place where another trail crossed the one they had been following and headed more steeply down the mountain in a northerly direction. At the junction of the trails, Piper dismounted to stretch her legs and think about what to do next. The storm deer began tossing her head and scraping it against the side of a tree. It looked to Piper as if the storm deer was trying to remove the rope halter.

"Hold, please," Piper told the storm deer. "I will take the halter off."

The storm deer stopped her scraping and stood still, allowing Piper to remove the rope halter. Dropping the rope halter to the ground, she placed her hands on either side of the storm deer's head and, looking directly at her, thanked the storm deer for her service. Once she had released the storm deer's head, the storm deer nodded once, turned, and crossed over to where Jing waited. The storm deer bent her head down and touched her nose to Jing's nose before turning and heading back up the mountain.

"Well, my friend, it's just you and me now. I think we should travel down this path that heads steeply downhill. It's time to get off this mountain and back to civilization. I'm getting a wee bit short on supplies. I had hoped to restock at home, with both supplies and a bit of coin, which I'm very short on. Coin that is. Looks like I will need to make a living for the two of us if we are to continue to eat and pay for lodging when needed. Who knows how long it is going to take us to find the folk who is supposed to wear the cuff?"

Piper knew that this time of year was the beginning of harvest festivals. Both big towns and small villages held gatherings to celebrate what hopefully had been a good and plentiful harvest. Traveling players, musicians, and other types of entertainers could make good coin playing at the festivals. She also knew she could earn some coin playing the mountain flute at small village pubs. And, if not coin, she could get food and lodging for the night. It would keep the hunger pains at bay at least. Piper had been playing the mountain flute since she was a wee lass. She had won numerous prizes playing the mountain flute and other wooden flutes at summer fairs and other festivals. This would not be the first time she had made her way about Sommerhjem playing for her supper.

What Piper was not sure about was whether Jing would follow her into a town or village. How would he react to not being in the forest? Would he come with her at all, once they left the quiet and seclusion of the mountains? What would she do if he would not go with her, despite the pull of the firestar gems? She could not live completely off the land, especially with winter coming, as Jing could.

*Well, I will know shortly, for in just a few more days, we will reach the first village.*

# Chapter Eleven

Piper was very relieved that Jing showed no intention of abandoning her when they approached their first village. Jing adapted amazingly well to being in among a larger number of folks. Before walking into the first village, Piper had a short talk with Jing.

"Now Jing," she had said, "we are about to walk into a village which will be filled with folks we don't know. They, living so close to the mountains, will probably know of mountain cats. However, they will only know that you are a fearsome wild cat not to be tangled with. They are going to be surprised, concerned, and a bit to a lot afraid of you. Nevertheless, we need to earn a living, or more correctly, I need to earn a living. Anyway, there are some rules you need to follow. It would probably be best if you did not capture or eat one of the villager's cats, dogs, chickens, geese, or other livestock. That would get us in trouble. While I feel like I'm insulting you by telling you this, you should probably not harm any of the wee lads or lasses either."

Jing had just cocked his head slightly at the suggestion he might harm the village children and opened his mouth to yawn widely.

Piper felt more than a bit foolish at that point. She set off at a brisk pace, deciding that just boldly entering the village with Jing at her side as if a folk coming into the village accompanied by a mountain cat was no more unusual than one entering a village accompanied by a border dog. Other than one mother snatching her wee lad up and running into the house screaming upon Piper and Jing's approach, it had gone amazingly well. Arrows had not been nocked, knives had not been drawn, and they had not been threatened by flaming torches.

When Piper had approached the pub keeper and asked to provide an evening's worth of mountain flute music in exchange for a meal and a place to sleep, he had been agreeable. He had also not even blinked an eye in surprise upon seeing Jing.

"Had me a traveling storyteller here a few weeks back. He was tellin' about folks he'd met or heard about that's was traveling with uncommon animals. Heard tell there's a rover lass that travels with a hunting cat. Heard me from the storyteller about this lad that had a most uncommon animal. Said the lad had a halekrets. Don't recall hearin' about a halekrets ever. So I guess it don'ts surprise me none that someone might travel with a mountain cat. Long as he don'ts harm any of the payin' folk, he can come in. Now that restriction might not apply to those who would be freeloaders this night," the pub keeper had suggested with great good humor.

The pub keeper told Piper she could put her gear in a small room just off the kitchen. He had told her it used to be his cook's room. It was empty at the moment, since his cook had married and moved into a cottage in the village. Once Piper had stowed her pack, she set up on a stool near the pub's main fireplace. She placed a floppy-brimmed hat at her feet, top side down, to give the patrons a place to pitch a coin or two if they wished. She had been worried about what Jing would do, but he just curled up beside her stool with his tail over his nose and went to sleep. Some of the folks had glanced curiously at Jing. No one had approached her about him, however.

Word spread quickly that there was a visiting musician at the pub, and some of the village folk came with fiddles and other instruments. Soon Piper found herself playing lively tunes so familiar that she felt just a twinge of homesickness wash over her. The rest of the evening passed by uneventfully. Piper thought the folks who came to the pub had liked her music.

When the pub closed its doors for the night, the pub keeper bid Piper a good night and asked if she might stay a day or two.

"I thank you for your kind offer. Yours is a good crowd, and I enjoyed playing for and with them. Still I think I best be getting along on the

71

morrow. Hoping to head north and hit a few of the late harvest festivals. If I get back this way, I'll be sure to drop in again."

Piper and Jing left the next morning. As the days passed into weeks, Piper began to despair that she would ever find the folk who was supposed to wear the cuff holding the firestar gem. She often questioned whether she was just on a fool's errand. One morning, she got up and decided enough was enough. It was time to turn back and head home. Piper slung her pack over her back and called to Jing, who was sniffing about the wood pile behind the inn where Piper had played the night before. She set a brisk pace heading south and got no more than five minutes down the road before the pull north became overwhelming.

"Well fuddle muddle," Piper exclaimed, as she turned around and began walking north once again. "I guess we're not going back home today, Jing. I wish this darn firestar gem would make up its mind as to where exactly we are to go. We always seem to be heading north, but sometimes it's northeast and sometimes it's northwest. Sometimes it's due north."

Once Piper said what had been happening out loud, it occurred to her that whoever was to wear the cuff was probably not staying in one place, which would have certainly been more convenient. That idea had just not occurred to Piper before. Now that she really thought about it, she had no idea why she had thought this little trek she and Jing were on would be that straightforward.

Fall passed, and the harvest festivals were long over. The lowland cold season had begun with bitter winds, icy rain, and occasional snow. Sometimes Piper and Jing were able to hitch rides with long haulers or traders that were going their direction. Several times, rovers had given them a lift. Many days were spent walking, however. Piper's patience and funds were both getting very low. Over the last several weeks, there had been very little work.

"Our life has become what feels like a game of tug o' war. We are being pulled east, and just when I think we might have gone east far enough, we get pulled west. At least we are always being pulled north. I hope this constant zigzagging ends soon. What do you think, Jing?" Piper asked the mountain cat. He did not reply. "At least this night we should be warm and snug, for we should reach a fairly large estate by late afternoon. I'm hoping we can talk our way into the manor house and be invited to play. I would settle for a hot meal and a warm barn to sleep in. It's about time our luck changed."

Just as Piper finished addressing Jing, the bracelet on her arm warmed. When she looked at the pendant around Jing's neck, she saw a soft glow from within the firestar gem. Looking at her own firestar gem, she noted that it was also glowing. While the pull to head north had been steady, now it was much stronger, and getting stronger by the minute.

*Curious*, Piper thought. She began to wonder if the folk she and Jing had set out to find was either at the estate she was heading toward, or heading there.

When Piper arrived at the manor house, she went to the back entrance. If she was arriving as Piper, representative of the clan Wynda, guardians of the southern pass, she would have called at the front door and been given the courtesy due her rank and position. Of course, if she had been traveling representing her clan, she would have, at the very least, arrived on horseback and would certainly have been dressed in much finer clothing.

Knocking on the kitchen door, Piper waited patiently for someone to answer. She hoped it would be the cook. If no work was to be had, the cook might take pity on her and invite her in anyway. A fine icy drizzle had begun, which did not look like it was going to abate anytime soon. Much to Piper's relief, it was the cook who answered her knock.

"Begging pardon, mistress, but I'm looking for shelter. I'm a traveling musician and am more than willing to play for my supper."

"Get you inside here, now, before you let all the heat out. Dog can come in too, as long as it stays out from underfoot."

Piper was not going to correct the cook that Jing was not a dog before she got both of them safely inside. She could understand why the cook might have thought Jing was a dog, since it was very dark outside, and she probably only saw his general shape. Once through the door, and with it safely shut behind them, Piper introduced Jing. It took a little persuasion to convince the cook that Jing was harmless. Piper told herself she would need to remember to apologize to Jing later, when no one was within hearing distance, since the mountain cat was anything but harmless.

"You've come on a good night. The family above is celebrating the return of their second son to Stein Hage. He's been gone nigh on two years now. Traveled across the sea to far distant lands on a trading ship. Did quite well for himself. We're all glad he's home." The cook then lowered her voice and leaned toward Piper. "It's a good thing, too. The estate here was hard hit by the taxes and levies imposed by the former regent Klingflug. Had it in for the folks here, because they were loyal to the Crown and very vocal about what they thought of the former regent's rule. The second son being successful in seeking his fortune is surely going to help."

Piper was glad that she had chosen to try to enter the manor house the back way. Cooks, housekeepers, and others who worked for an estate often were founts of information. She wondered if this returning son was the one she was seeking. It might explain why she had been pulled on such an erratic course. He might have been finishing up business from his voyage, delivering or selling goods. She was anxious to see if her speculations were correct.

"Now, I have a question for you," the cook stated.

"Yes."

"Do you traveling musicians have some way of letting each other know when or where a celebration is happening?"

"No, not that I know of. Why do you ask?"

"Another traveling musician arrived at my kitchen door not more than an hour before you. Now, don't you worry none. There'll be plenty of work for both of you. This celebration will be going on until the wee hours of the morning, I'm sure. Let me have one of my helpers take you up to where you will play. You can store your pack in the pantry. It will be safe there. I'll make sure you and the other musician have vittles throughout the night, don't you worry. Your Jing will need to stay here. I think I can rustle up some meat scraps for him, to keep him content."

Piper put her pack in the pantry, and when she returned, the cook handed her the meat scraps she had promised. Piper took the scraps over to the corner where Jing had settled himself. She talked quietly to Jing, asking him to remain in the kitchen. The cook called one of the kitchen helpers over, and Piper was escorted to the back stairs. On the second floor, a balcony ran around three sides, overlooking the manor house's great room. On the opposite side from where she stood was the other musician. He was playing a lively tune on a set of pan pipes. Piper felt a great deal of relief that she was familiar with the tune. Since she could not really see much of the musician's face, she did not know if she had ever met him. He had his head tipped down, and his long hair covered the side of his face that was turned toward her. What she could see of the lower part of his face was covered with a beard that could use a trim.

Adjusting the strap on her flute case, Piper squared her shoulders and began to walk around the balcony. When she arrived, she sat quietly next to the musician and waited until he finished the tune he had been playing.

"They call me Piper, for I'm the best from my small village. I play the mountain flute."

"Do they now," said the musician, who looked up.

"Aaron?" Piper whispered, shocked to see who she was sitting next to. She had met him once or twice briefly at her home when he had traveled there with his uncle. In addition to sitting next to someone she knew, she found herself uncomfortably aware that the bracelet she was wearing was becoming painfully hot.

Just as she was about to speak, she saw a flash of color that moved rapidly through the door she had entered the balcony from. It could only be Jing. The fact that the mountain cat had left the kitchen and followed her was worrisome.

When Jing arrived at her side, she looked at the pendant hanging around his neck, which was now glowing quite brightly on his chest. Her bracelet was also glowing. Piper realized her hip was getting uncomfortably warm too. *The cuff*, she thought. She reached in and pulled it out, for it had grown so warm she was worried it would catch her clothing on fire.

Piper began to look about, thinking the reaction of the three firestar gems must be signaling that the folk who was to wear the cuff was surely close. She peered over the balcony to see if there was anyone in the great hall, but it was empty. She looked around the balcony to see if anyone else was there with her and Aaron, but nobody was.

"Ah, Piper, I don't know if you have noticed, but several things have just happened. We have been joined by a mountain cat, which in and of itself is quite something, but in addition, you two are wearing or holding three pieces of jewelry containing firestar gems, and in designs I have only recently seen someplace else. Can you explain what's going on?"

Before Piper could say anything, she found herself placing the cuff on Aaron's wrist. *Not the returning second son then*, she thought, *but Aaron Beecroft*. After she placed the cuff on his wrist, she watched a myriad of emotions cross his face. Before she could say anything, folks began entering the great hall.

"We had best play. Here I'm known as Beezle. We will talk later, Piper from the small village. Meanwhile, let's see what you can do. Try to keep up."

# Chapter Twelve

It was not until the early hours of morning that the celebration in the great hall began to wind down. Piper was beyond weary and was certain her fingers would most probably fall off if she had to play another song. All the while she had been playing, she had been trying to puzzle out just what the man she knew as Aaron Beecroft was doing disguised as a traveling musician. They had no time to talk during the long hours of playing, in part because at times they had been joined by other musicians who lived and worked on the estate. The one time they had a break and Piper had wanted to question Aaron, he had immediately shushed her. In a whisper, he had explained that the walls probably had ears. Piper had to muffle a laugh because of the mental picture she got in her head of walls having multiple pairs of ears. She did not think it was appropriate at the time to share that image with anyone, however.

Jing had chosen not to go back to the kitchen and, much to Piper's relief, no one who came to play music with them had seemed to pay him any mind. They may not have actually noticed him, since he had curled himself into a small ball under the bench Piper was seated on. It also helped that the floor made of local stone, upon which Jing was sleeping, was the same color as Jing's fur. Piper was grateful not to have the added distraction of folks inquiring about the mountain cat who accompanied her.

When the signal was given to cease playing, it was just Piper, Aaron, and Jing on the balcony.

"Not bad wooden flute playing, Piper. I can see why you are considered the best from your small village."

"Thank you, Aar … ah, Beezle. You're not so bad yourself. Glad you could keep up with me on the mountain reels," Piper said with great good humor.

*Truth be told, Beezle here, and I have to really begin to think of him as Beezle, kept up quite well on the mountain reels, as if he had been playing them all his life. Well, maybe he has been,* Piper thought. She really did not know much about him other than he came from a minor estate and was the nephew of Lord Hadrack of Glendalen Keep. He and his uncle had visited her home and had spent a number of hours in the last several years in private conversation with her parents and the captain of the border guard.

"Where have they put you up for what is left of the rest of the night?" Beezle asked. He then lowered his voice. "We need to talk, but not here. I need an explanation for what happened earlier."

"I don't know. You?" Piper replied, answering his first question and nodding her head acknowledging his statement about their need to talk.

"They directed me to an empty room over the stables. I think the grooms are quartered there. Now, I'm not so sure I want to stay. For some reason, I'm feeling very uneasy, as if I need to move on from here. Odd."

*Maybe not so odd,* Piper concluded, since she was feeling very restless, even more so than she had over the last few weeks. She wondered if it had something to do with finally finding who was to wear the cuff with the firestar gem in it.

Piper was drawn out of her thoughts when Beezle again asked her what her plans were.

"I, too, am feeling a great need to move on."

"Did you come by horse?"

"No, foot. You?"

"Horse. I also have a pack horse. We'll throw your gear on the pack horse and put you up behind me. My horse can handle a second rider for a few hours. I don't know what it is, but I'm feeling a great urgency to leave now. Do you feel it also, or is it just my imagination?"

"No, it's not your imagination. Once we are on the road, I'll try to explain."

Beezle turned, reached up, did something with the wall sconce that Piper could not see, and a panel of the wall swung open. "Why don't you go pick up your gear? I'll meet you at the stables," Beezle stated as he slipped through the opening.

Piper nudged Jing gently with her foot and suggested it was time to move out. They both climbed back down the stairs and headed toward the kitchen. When she arrived, there was no one there. It looked like the cook and her helpers had all gone to bed. They would be up soon, she imagined. It did not take her long to grab her pack and leave the kitchen. Under normal circumstances, it would have taken her longer to locate the stables in the dark in a strange place. Jing, however, seemed to know just where they should go, for he set off at a brisk pace. Once Piper started off, she too knew what direction to head. *It must be the firestar gems*, she thought. Thinking a bit more as she followed Jing, Piper realized that she felt two pulls now. One strong and one faint. She really did not have much time to think about it, for she and Jing had arrived at the stables and found Beezle waiting.

Once they were on the carriageway leading away from the manor house, Beezle spoke up. "Our host was very generous, and I took the liberty of accepting for both of us. We have an invitation to return any time. I explained our leaving at this hour as being too wound up to sleep. I suggested you had heard of a place to find work a bit over a day's ride south of here."

"Very clever explanation with just one exception. We need to head …."

"North. I know. There were several folks standing within hearing distance of my conversation with our host. They seemed much too interested in our exchange, more than I would have liked. I thought it might be best to give our curious friends some misdirection. We are not too far from one of the royal hunting preserves. Hopefully, we can lose anyone who might be overly curious about us there, if indeed someone does try to follow us. Also, we might be able to pick up a mount for you, which would make our travels easier. Now then, would you please explain to me what happened back there on the balcony?"

Piper was certain Beezle would not find it funny if she told him that they had been playing flutes on the balcony. She knew his question referred to the cuff containing the firestar gem she had placed on his wrist. Piper then proceeded to tell Beezle a condensed version of what had happened to her since the time she had rescued Collier from being trapped in the cave to the present. She told him about meeting Jing, and her time with the woman hermit. As she told her tale, it sounded very farfetched even to her, and she wondered what he thought about what she was saying.

Piper did not have a chance to ask Beezle, for the moment she finished her explanation, she heard a shout from behind her.

"There they are. Get them!"

"Hang on," Beezle shouted over his shoulder, as he spurred his horse into a gallop while trying frantically to untie the lead rope of his pack horse from his saddle. His pack horse was trained to follow, so if they could get away, they would still have their gear. That was the least of his worries at the moment. While his mount was strong and fast, it carried the burden of two riders and would tire more quickly. A quick glance over his shoulder showed him they were being pursued by three riders who were gaining on them.

Piper gripped Beezle around the waist and held on for dear life. She was glad she was holding on so tight when Beezle abruptly swung the horse to the left and down a steep incline. Fortunately, they reached the bottom of the slope still astride the horse and without the horse having broken anything. The pack horse also made it safely down. One of the three pursuing them had not been so lucky, for he had been thrown off his horse about halfway down. Unfortunately, the other two men had made it down the steep slope safely. While moving off the road had slowed those chasing Beezle and Piper, not being on a road or lane had also reduced the speed by which they all now traveled. The quick swerve off the road had really only reduced the number of folks chasing them.

Unfortunately, weaving around the sparsely scattered trees and shrub brush at a fast speed was beginning to take its toll on Beezle's horse, who was now covered in sweat and was beginning to wheeze.

"We are going to have to find a spot to take a stand," Beezle shouted over his shoulder to Piper. "My horse is not going to make it much farther. Keep a lookout, if you can, for someplace we can stop that might give us some protection."

Piper did as Beezle asked, looking both right and left, trying to find someplace, any place, that might give them some measure of safety.

"There, to the right," Piper called. "There are two huge pines grown together. Their combined trunks should give us some protection for our backs."

"Hold on," Beezle shouted back, so his voice could be heard over the pounding of the horses' hooves.

Reaching the twined pine trees, Piper quickly slid off the horse, followed by Beezle. Beezle handed the reins of his horse to Piper. Just as the pack horse trotted by, Beezle lunged toward it and grabbed its reins. Tying the pack horse to the nearest branch, Beezle unhooked his short bow and quiver from the back of the pack. Piper had secured Beezle's horse and had drawn her knife from her belt. Both Piper and Beezle squared themselves up with their backs to the twisted pine trees.

The two men chasing them halted their horses about twenty feet away from them. Neither dismounted. One at a time, each man reached behind his saddle and grabbed his short bow, each nocking an arrow and resting the bow and arrow on his lap.

"You really are quite severely outdrawn, you know. It would be best if you just dropped your bow and knife. This does not need to be violent," one of the pursuers said.

When the man finished speaking, it occurred to Piper that she had lost track of Jing. A part of her was relieved that he was nowhere near them and so might not be harmed. Another part of her worried that he had already been harmed. Part of her wondered if he had abandoned her, and she felt a swift wave of sadness at the thought. She did not have time to dwell on what had happened to Jing, however, and needed to pay attention to her present situation.

"What is it that you want?" asked Beezle.

"We noticed that the lord of the manor where the two of you played was very generous. Since we are in need of extra coin, we thought to relieve you of yours."

*There is something else going on here*, Piper thought. The man who was speaking was both too well-spoken and too well-dressed to be an ordinary highwayman. His horse and tack was of good quality, as was that of his companion.

"If you just toss any pouches of coin you have toward us, dump your saddlebags and packs, we will let you ride off on your horses. Don't want to be taken for common horse thieves, now do we? I suggest you comply. After all, you get to ride away with your lives. Oh, and that bracelet and cuff you folks are wearing can be added to the pile, too," the man added, as if it were an afterthought.

"These are not common thieves," Piper whispered to Beezle.

"Noticed that, did you?" Beezle whispered back.

"I think we might just have a standoff here," Beezle told the two mounted men. "While we only have one bow and you have two, odds are that one of you is going to be seriously hurt before you can get to me. Which one of you wants that honor?"

"A better question might be, how important is the lass standing next to you? She could come to great harm," the man volleyed back.

"Take your best shot. Never met her before last night," Beezle answered, with a nonchalant air and a shrug of his shoulders.

Piper looked outraged and swung her knife toward Beezle, letting it come to rest against his side.

Addressing the two men on horseback, she suggested that maybe they could come to some sort of understanding. Under her breath she cautioned Beezle to play along.

"I have no vested interest in this fellow musician, since he was quite quick to sacrifice me to save his own sorry hide. What will you offer me if I just dispatch him?"

Beezle began to worry that he just might have been too convincing about his not having a care about Piper's wellbeing. How well did he really know her anyway? Should he trust that she knew what she was doing?

# CHAPTER THIRTEEN

Piper hoped Beezle would not try to do something either heroic or stupid while she was holding a knife to his side. She was hoping to distract the two men so they would not notice Jing had stealthily crept up behind them. He had kept himself very low to the ground and was now in a crouched position.

"Be ready," Piper whispered to Beezle under her breath and then addressed the two men again. "I think we should be able to make some type of deal that doesn't leave me standing here with nothing, don't you think?"

"Well, well, well. It would seem our two musicians are no longer in harmony," the spokesman for the two on horseback stated, and then laughed at his own pun. "Actually, I have no reason to harm either of you. I just want your coin, jewelry, and anything else you might have of value. Hand that over and you will be free to go."

"I think not," Piper stated, just as Jing sprang from his crouched position behind the horses, landed on the rump of one horse, used it as a springboard, twisted sideways, and landed on the rump of the next horse. In a flash, he jumped off the second horse just as it reared.

The prick of Jing's claws as he landed and pushed off had startled the horses. Neither man had been prepared for his horse to rear. Both men were thrown and landed hard, knocking the wind out of them.

"Quick, before they get their breath back," Piper urged Beezle, as she ran toward the downed men.

"Actually, you only need one of us at this moment," Beezle declared.

"Get this cat off of me," the well-spoken man wheezed, since he still did not have his breath completely back, and his chest was occupied at the moment by a mountain cat, who yawned with great distain at his request.

As Beezle held his short bow ready, Jing continued to sit on the man.

"Oh, I think Jing should just stay right where he is. He looks quite comfortable," Piper said in response to the request. "Do you have any rope in your supplies?" Piper asked Beezle.

"Yes. Here, take my bow so our other would-be highwayman will think twice about whether to stay down or get up. I would suggest you stay down," Beezle advised. "If I recall, flute playing is not the only thing my fellow musician has won awards for at festivals and fairs."

While Piper and Jing kept the two supposed highwaymen under control, Beezle swiftly returned with sturdy ropes. He had the men remount and bound them to their saddles. He then grabbed the reins of both horses and tied them to his pack horse. He and Piper once again mounted and started off, the pack horse tied to Beezle's horse. Jing brought up the rear.

In a quiet conversation with Beezle, Piper asked if they should return to the Stein Hage estate where they had played the night before.

"Probably not a good idea," Beezle replied quietly. "It would be one thing if we had arrived there as ourselves. However, since we came in the back door as traveling musicians, whose word do you think they are going to take? Probably that of the well-dressed gentlemen behind us. We also need to worry about the third man who was unhorsed earlier. I didn't wait around long enough to see if either he or his horse was all right. If he and his horse were undamaged from their falls and have reunited, either he might have gone back to the estate to sound an alarm, or he could be trying to catch up."

"You make several good points. Where to, then?"

"I have friends camped not too far from here. I suggest that there is safety in numbers. In addition, seven heads will be better than two in figuring out just who these folks are, though I have my suspicions."

The night was beginning to wane, and the sky was filled with the red-gold light of dawn before Piper, Beezle, Jing, and their captives arrived at the campsite where Beezle's friends were camped. Piper was surprised to see two rover homewagons and two small tents. One homewagon's exterior was painted in a pattern that could have been designed by the same hand that had created the bracelet she wore. Even more surprising was the hunting cat that bounded down the steps of that homewagon and headed straight toward Jing. When Piper would have jumped off Beezle's horse and rushed to get between the hunting cat and Jing, Beezle put a restraining hand on her arm.

"Wait," was all Beezle said, continuing to hold firm to Piper's arm.

"But …."

"Trust me. No harm will come to Jing."

Piper learned Beezle was right. Jing stood still when the hunting cat approached, and the two cats touched noses. Then the hunting cat sat down next to Jing, who also sat. Piper's attention was drawn back to the rover homewagon the hunting cat had come from. A young rover woman was now quickly descending the stairs, hastily drawing a cloak over her shoulders.

"Beezle? So what kind of trouble have you gotten yourself into this time?" the rover woman asked. "And who are your friends and your not-so friends?"

"Nissa, the lass behind me is Piper, who travels with the mountain cat, Jing. The other two men accosted us early this morning. I'm hoping the seekers might know of them."

As Beezle swept his arm forward to point at the two small tents, his sleeve slipped back, revealing the cuff with the firestar gem, just as Nissa arrived next to his horse. Arcs of light shot out from the three firestar gems that Beezle, Piper, and Jing wore. Nissa stood very, very still, since the arcs of light had centered on the ring she wore.

"I ask again, Beezle, what kind of trouble have you gotten yourself into this time?" Nissa inquired, once she recovered from the shock of seeing three arcs of light come her way.

"Before we try to answer your question, for most of the answer is not mine to tell, I suggest we get these two would-be highwaymen settled. I think we need to move this discussion out of earshot. Ah, Seeker Eshana,

Seeker Chance, I'm so glad you are both still here," Beezle stated, addressing the two folks who had just emerged from the tents.

Piper could not help but stare at the small ring-tailed animal sitting on one of the seeker's shoulders. *This cannot possibly be the same lad and animal that the pub keeper told me about, but they sure fit the description the pub keeper had been given by the traveling storyteller. For that matter, was this Nissa, the rover with a hunting cat, he had also mentioned?* she wondered.

"Piper, this is Seeker Eshana and his apprentice Seeker Chance. That small fuzzy rascal sitting on Seeker Chance's shoulder is Ashu. Be sure to watch your plate if you have fruit or nuts on it and Ashu is around."

"Now, Beezle, Ashu would never be that impolite," Seeker Eshana said, with a slight chuckle in his voice.

More introductions were made when two more rovers climbed out of their homewagon.

"Piper, this is Shueller and Tannar. More later, my friends," Beezle suggested, when he got an inquiring look from Shueller. "We had best get these two men off their horses and secured before we talk."

A lean-to was quickly erected to shelter the two captives from the wind. It was built far enough away from the homewagons and fire pit to allow Piper and the rest of the party to talk quietly without being overheard. The men's blanket rolls, after being inspected for hidden pockets that might contain anything that would aid in an escape, were placed over them to keep them fairly comfortable. The fire in the fire pit was quickly built up. A kettle of water was put on, and the seven settled in to talk. Both Jing and Carz, Nissa's hunting cat, curled up next to the fire.

"Well met, Piper," the rover Shueller said. "I'm most anxious to hear your tale, and I hope it informs me of where you came by the bracelet you wear."

"I suggest you take a closer look, Shueller," Nissa stated. "Piper here is not the only one who wears a firestar gem. I'm most curious to hear how Beezle has come by the cuff he now wears on his wrist, not to mention that the mountain cat, Jing, also wears a firestar gem."

"What, this little bobble?" Beezle said, looking down at the cuff.

"Could you extend your arm this way, so I might take a closer look at your 'bobble'?" Shueller asked. "And Piper, would you be so kind as to do so also?" Shueller took his time examining both pieces of jewelry, which he made no move to remove from either Piper's or Beezle's wrists. "Is the mountain cat, ah, Jing, willing to have someone look at what he wears?"

"I'm not sure. He has, as far as I know, only let me close enough to really look at it. I can tell you that his pendant looks like it was made by the same hand that made both my bracelet and Beezle's cuff."

"Let's not disturb him then, for that answers my question. I think the pieces you all are wearing are very, very old," Shueller suggested. "I would like to hear the tale of where they came from."

"I, too, am most curious," Seeker Eshana stated.

"Are you sure those two men we have tied up over there can't hear what we are about to discuss?" asked Piper.

"If it would make you feel any better, we can move this discussion into Shueller's wagon. That is, with your permission, Shueller," Nissa said.

"It's obvious to me that Beezle trusts all of you. The tale I have to tell involves more than the jewelry and should really not be heard by those who might not be on the side of the Crown," Piper replied.

"And also not heard by those who might seek to profit from the information," added Beezle. "Which brings up a question I have been meaning to ask the seekers. Do either of you recognize either of the two men we arrived with?"

"Unfortunately, yes," remarked Seeker Eshana. "I imagine you recognized one of them also, didn't you, Seeker Chance?"

"Unfortunately, I did. I had hoped never to see that gentleman again, and I use the term 'gentleman' loosely."

"The man, who I assume was in charge," continued Seeker Eshana, "is one called Blaxton. My apprentice, Seeker Chance, and I had a very uncomfortable encounter with him earlier this year. He is certainly not a fan of the interim ruling council, and we are fairly convinced he is working for Lady Farcroft, who in turn was and still is a staunch supporter of the former regent, Lord Cedric Klingflug. I imagine he stopped you and tried to rob you. That seems to be his method. I can't quite figure out if he is a gentleman who likes pretending he is a highwayman, or a highwayman who likes pretending he is a gentleman. Regardless, if you have information that you do not want those Blaxton represents to know, we would be wise to move farther out of earshot."

"Ashu and I will stay outside and watch the two men, though you have them trussed up better than a feast bird," Seeker Chance told the others. "Besides, unless both Carz and Jing are going to crowd into Shueller's homewagon with you, I had best stay outside and make sure Ashu does not become too fond of Jing's pendant."

All heads swiveled to look at Jing. He was sitting, being very patient, letting Ashu look at the pendant around his neck. When Ashu reached out his small hands and pulled the pendant toward him for a closer look, Jing continued to sit quietly. Ashu turned the pendant this way and that, examining it quite thoroughly before he released it. Giving Jing a pat alongside his jaw, Ashu turned and scampered back to Seeker Chance, swiftly climbing up to Seeker Chance's shoulder, and settling in.

Piper shook her head in wonder as she climbed the steps of rover Shueller's homewagon. As she was waiting for everyone to get settled in, she had time to reflect on what little she knew about the folks in whose company she found herself. She felt she could trust Beezle. His uncle and aunt, Lord and Lady Hadrack, had been very outspoken against the taxes, levies, rules, and underhanded maneuverings of the former regent. Beezle and his uncle had visited Piper's family's keep several times, and her parents had certainly had nothing bad to say about Beezle or his relatives. Her father had once remarked that Lord and Lady Hadrack were two of the greatest assets that the Crown had during the troubled times before the former regent was forced to step down.

Piper had also heard a bit about Nissa. She knew Nissa had brought the first two pieces of the oppgave ringe to the capital. Piper did not know the other two rovers. She was aware of the reputation of seekers and knew that they had been asked by the Crown to find any information that might lead to finding more pieces of the oppgave ringe. She felt she might be able to trust them with the information she had about locating at least one of the pieces that had not been found yet. In addition, they might just be the ones to pass the other information on to, the information the woman hermit had copied from the journals she had found in the cellar room.

"It's a bit cramped with all of us in here," suggested Shueller, as everyone found a place to sit in his homewagon. "We should, however, be able to hear what Beezle and Piper have to tell us without being overheard."

Piper had just finished up explaining to those gathered how both she and Beezle had ended up at the same estate posing as traveling musicians, and how they had played until the wee hours of the morning, when a commotion could be heard outside the homewagon.

# CHAPTER FOURTEEN

Since Nissa was the closest to the door of the homewagon, she got up to look out to see what was causing the commotion. What she saw caused her some concern. Seeker Chance had moved to the bottom of the steps of the homewagon and was standing facing a group of five mounted men, four of whom were very well-dressed. The fifth man's clothing was quite the worse for wear, as if he had been wrestling in the dirt and leaves and had lost. Nissa also noticed that the two cats had moved to flank Seeker Chance. They were sitting, but were very alert. One of the well-dressed men was demanding to know why the men in the lean-to were tied up and being detained.

"Seeker Eshana, Shueller, Tannar, I think you might want to go outside and handle this," stated Nissa. "It might be best if the others of us stay inside here, but ready. Piper, would you stand here at the door with me, since our cats are out there and on alert?"

When the men had left the homewagon, Piper asked Nissa why they had all not just gone out to confront the men.

"You know as well as I do that in your present disguise, I guess you would call it a disguise, your word against someone of higher rank or supposed higher rank is going to be questioned. More to the point, however, is that if you wish to continue to travel across Sommerhjem as a traveling musician, it would be best not to give away who either you or Beezle are. In addition, seekers are known for truth-telling, and Shueller has a few tricks in his pocket. Between the three of them, I think they can straighten this out without you or Beezle having to be involved."

90

With a better understanding of what was going on, Piper settled in out of sight, just inside the homewagon, to listen to what was taking place outside.

When Seeker Eshana arrived at the bottom of the steps of the homewagon and was joined there by Shueller and Tannar, he sent Seeker Chance off to get their staffs. As Piper watched, she was surprised to see a transformation come over Seeker Eshana after Seeker Chance handed him his staff. Actually, she was surprised to see the transformation come over both of the seekers. They seemed to grow taller and have a more commanding presence. Even the little halekrets took on an air of dignity.

Seeker Eshana then stepped forward and addressed the mounted men. "How may we be of assistance to you gentlemen?" Seeker Eshana asked.

"We demand to know just why you have Blaxton and his companion tied up. These gentlemen you have detained are quite highly regarded by my father. They volunteered to go after a pair of traveling musicians whom they accused of having taking something that belonged to Blaxton. It was our estate that the musicians played at, you understand. I demand you untie these two gentlemen and, if they are here, turn over the two traveling musicians to me, so justice can be served."

"Well, we have a problem then. It would seem the other side of the story is the one the traveling musicians tell. They said they spent hours entertaining at your estate. They left in the wee hours of the morning and had not gone very far when they were accosted by three men. One of the men fell when he and his horse tried to take a steep slope too fast. I presume that was you," Seeker Eshana stated, looking directly at the disheveled man.

The man nodded, acknowledging that he was indeed the one who had been unhorsed. He looked decidedly uncomfortable and sputtered a denial about accosting Piper and Beezle.

"So, who do we believe?" Seeker Eshana questioned.

"Just turn the two musicians over to us, and we will take them back for a trial before the magistrate of our district. We will certainly be able to get to the bottom of what happened."

"I have a simpler solution," said Seeker Eshana. "This gentleman standing next to me is the rover Shueller. You may or may not have heard of him. The one thing I do know, if you do not, is that he is very highly regarded by the interim ruling council. He was invaluable in getting the former regent to step down. How, you ask? By being in possession of a very rare gem known as a truth stone. If you tell the truth while holding the stone, nothing happens. If you do not tell the truth, it can be quite painful. I suggest we simply need to place the truth stone in your companion's hand and ask him a few simple questions."

"You, you, you can't possibly be thinking of going along with what the Seeker suggests," sputtered the disheveled man.

"If you have told the truth to these fine gentlemen, then there should be no problem," Seeker Eshana suggested back.

"It seems like the easiest way to settle this matter, Kabos," said the gentleman in charge of the group. "If what you have said is the truth, there should be no problem."

"I'll not stand for this. I'm insulted you would not take my word, the word of a gentleman," Kabos spat out, as he wheeled his horse around and galloped off.

"I suggest that some of you go after him and bring him back," Seeker Eshana said, with a ring of authority in his voice that had the remaining four racing off after Kabos.

"So, whose turn is it to cook breakfast this day?" Seeker Eshana inquired. "It might be a while before those five return, and I think our discussion with Beezle and Piper might need to wait."

"I agree. Now, if I recall correctly, it's your turn," Nissa told Seeker Eshana, as she came down the steps of Shueller's homewagon.

The group was just finishing up breakfast when the riders returned with the man called Kabos. Beezle and Piper hurried up the steps into the homewagon when they heard horses' hooves pounding up the lane.

"We would have been back sooner, but we thought we would have a private conversation with Kabos before we returned. My apologies to the traveling musicians. It would seem you were correct, Seeker. There were two sides to the story. Kabos, here, was more than willing to tell us everything, hoping to gain leniency. He said he was talked into going along with Blaxton's scheme when he had been told by Blaxton that the musicians had something on them which would bring all of them great wealth. He did not know just what they were going to find when they tried to rob the musicians, however."

"I will tell you from experience that this is not the first time Blaxton has tried to rob innocent folks. I think it is time to put a stop to his thievery, however. By your leave, I would like to make sure Blaxton, that fellow Kabos, and the other man be placed in the proper custody. There is a royal guard station several days' ride from here where I can find help to escort these men back to the capital. Do you wish to accompany me?" Seeker Eshana asked.

"I would be most relieved to hand the whole matter over to you. With my brother just returning from being gone for so long, I'm anxious to return home. Now that we have some funds, we can begin to put the estate to rights."

Before the group from the estate left to head home, Seeker Eshana spoke to them and asked that they not mention anything about their adventure, other than it was a misunderstanding and had been settled. He suggested that if others inquired, they could tell them that Blaxton and the others had headed south, and that he was unaware of what had happened to the traveling musicians. Seeker Eshana had suggested that this might allow his party to get the highwaymen to the authorities without mishap. "You never know if there are others of this gang nearby," Seeker Eshana had told them.

Once the folks from the estate left, Kabos was secured with the others in the lean-to. The men Kabos joined in the lean-to were none too happy that he had ratted on them. Shouting and loud muttering could be heard coming from the lean-to as Seeker Chance and Tannar cleaned up the breakfast pots and dishes.

Finally, with Seeker Chance and the two cats once again on guard duty, the rest of the group gathered inside Shueller's homewagon. Earlier, Piper had talked to Beezle privately, which had helped ease her mind as to who these folks in the homewagon were. All had had a part in getting pieces of the oppgave ringe to the capital. All were extremely loyal to the Crown.

"Why don't you start at the beginning again?" suggested Nissa.

*Which beginning?* Piper wondered. *The one that explains what I was doing in Farlig Brygge, or the one that explains where the jewelry containing the firestar gems came from? I will start with the firestar gems. What I was doing in Farlig Brygge for the Crown is something best kept to myself. The less folks know, the less they can tell others.*

Piper told the folks gathered in the homewagon about what had happened prior to her arriving at the estate where she and Beezle had played the night before. When she told them what had happened on the balcony concerning the cuff that Beezle now wore, Beezle chimed in. Once Piper finished, there was a long period of silence before anyone spoke.

"I can understand why someone might be after Piper, since she holds the key to another piece of the oppgave ringe, but how would Blaxton and his cronies have known?" asked Shueller.

"Very good question," stated Seeker Eshana. "How might anyone have known you had a lead on one of the pieces of the oppgave ringe? Do others know about the particular properties of the firestar gems you folks are wearing?"

"Other than Beezle, Antini the hermit, myself, and Jing, the answer would be no, not as far as I know. I didn't even discuss it with Beezle until we were on the road," answered Piper.

"I quite frankly don't think they were after Piper. I think they might have been after me," Beezle declared. "I have been crisscrossing this part of Sommerhjem for the past month, following up one lead after another concerning pieces of the oppgave ringe. I have been using the traveling musician disguise, for it gives me entry to places that the nephew of Lord and Lady Hadrack might not have been able to go. I'm sure others have been following the same leads. The former regent has very loyal followers who are looking as hard for the remaining pieces of the oppgave ringe as we are. Blaxton might have seen through my disguise, for it's not much of a disguise. I could speculate he saw an opportunity to see if I had anything of worth on me that might give him a clue as to what I know. Piper, unfortunately, may have simply been in the wrong place at the wrong time. There is another possibility. We didn't think anyone saw the arc of light between the two firestar gems when Piper gave me the cuff on the balcony, but it is possible that someone did and alerted Blaxton."

"That makes an odd kind of sense," said Nissa. "The question now is what do we do with the three men tied up in the lean-to? Also, how might we help you and Piper?"

"As I told the men from the estate, there is a royal guard barracks two days' ride north of here. We could take our captives there and ask that they be transported to the capital. All of us traveling together will give us some safety," commented Seeker Eshana. "We could tuck them away inside Shueller's homewagon, so when we pass others on the road, they will not wonder what we are doing with tied-up men. Beezle and Piper, you two can ride in Nissa's homewagon, if that is all right with you, Nissa."

"Piper is most welcome, as is Jing. I guess I can put up with Beezle, if it is only for a few short days," Nissa replied with a twinkle in her eye.

Beezle just laughed, and Piper could see that he was very comfortable with Nissa's teasing.

"After we remove the tack from our reluctant guests' horses and store it in one of the homewagons, we can tie the horses behind one of the homewagons. I also suggest we pack up and move out of this area. I really was not telling tales when I told those from the estate that Blaxton could have others in his employ who might come looking for him. So, will heading north work for you, Piper, and you, Beezle?"

"For the moment, it seems to be where the strongest pull is coming from. Do you feel it also, Beezle?"

Bode was very reluctant to knock on Lady Farcroft's study door. Two messenger birds had arrived at the keep roost. Often when messages arrived at the keep and did not bring the news Lady Farcroft wanted to hear, life became very difficult around the estate for the next several days.

The two dwellings on the Farcroft land were very different as were the two personalities of Lady Farcroft. At the manor house, Lady Farcroft presented an image of a silly dithering dowager, as one more interested in the latest court fashions than what was going on in Sommerhjem. At the ancient keep high on a hill overlooking the manor house, the Lady Farcroft who held clandestine meetings there was a woman who was strong-willed and commanding. Lady Farcroft had worked tirelessly behind the scenes on behalf of the former regent. When Regent Cedric Klingflug had been forced to step down, all her planning and plotting to keep him in power had been thwarted. Bode knew Lady Farcroft's rage simmered just below her civilized veneer. The news he was bringing was not going to improve her mood. At his knock, he was commanded to enter.

"What is it, Bode?" Lady Farcroft asked.

"Your pardon, m'lady. Two messenger birds arrived this morning. One carried a message from one of your sources in the south. I'm afraid it's not good news. Blaxton and two others have been apprehended and are being transported to the capital under royal guard."

"Are you sure you translated the code right?"

"Unfortunately, yes. The message did not include much detail. It just said that Blaxton and two hires had been detained for attempting to rob two traveling musicians."

"That stupid, stupid man. I have warned him a number of times that playing highwayman was going to get him in trouble. His usefulness has run out. Make arrangements to eliminate the problem once they arrive in the capital. A long sea voyage should be in all three of their futures. Make it happen."

"It will be done, m'lady."

"Now then, what was the second message?" Lady Farcroft inquired.

"Ironically, it was from Blaxton. However, the messenger bird was delayed for some reason. Blaxton sent the message off before he was captured, but the bird arrived only this day. He had been tracking Lord Hadrack's nephew. What was his name again?"

"Aaron Beecroft, I believe."

96

"Yes, Aaron Beecroft. Blaxton's message was not very specific, but seemed to indicate he was very sure this Beecroft fellow might have discovered something important. Blaxton was going to follow up and send more information later."

"I will need to contact Lord Klingflug. It is unfortunate that Lord Klingflug will probably enlist the aid of Lord Braeden, for he is the most logical one to look for this Beecroft fellow, his estate being in the area where Beecroft was last seen. Quite frankly, I do not trust Lord Braeden. He has pretentions of being the Raven's successor, but is pretty ineffectual. He also is not as loyal to our cause as we would wish, I think. I am concerned, especially if he gets wind that Beecroft might have knowledge of where to find one of the rings, that Lord Braeden might use that to his own advantage rather than to ours."

# Chapter Fifteen

The royal guard barracks were located in a fair-sized town. After dropping Blaxton and his cronies off there, the group Piper was traveling with split up. Seeker Eshana and Seeker Chance had decided to accompany the royal guard to the capital with the prisoners. The rovers Shueller and Tannar were heading west, for they had a commission at an estate near the coast. Nissa and Carz were heading north and west, for she wanted to get to her father's house before the worst of the winter cold set in. None of the groups were heading the direction Piper and Beezle felt they needed to go next.

Before she parted ways with the seekers, Piper drew Seeker Eshana aside to ask him a favor. Beezle had assured her that she could trust both of the seekers with any message, information, or confidences that she chose.

"Seeker Eshana, I would ask a boon of you," Piper said.

"What is it that you need?"

"Actually, to be more accurate, I need two boons. The first is to procure a horse for me, for Beezle and I cannot continue to travel double. We talked it over and the sooner we leave the area the better. Even though you requested those from the estate not to say anything to anyone else about what really happened to either Blaxton and his men, or the two musicians, we don't know if they will follow through. We cannot be sure who might still be interested in either Beezle or me, or the two of us together. When I left the estate, I was traveling on foot and Beezle was on horseback. If I were someone looking for me, I would be on the lookout for a traveling musician who recently purchased a horse."

"You make a compelling argument for my getting you a horse," Seeker Eshana replied.

Piper found herself blushing, for she realized it sounded like she had wanted Seeker Eshana to buy her a horse, instead of her wanting him to buy a horse for her with her coin.

"I have the coin for a horse. I didn't mean to imply you were to purchase one for me. Well, yes, I want you to purchase one for me, but with my coin."

"I know that, lass. Now, what was your next boon?"

Piper looked around to make sure no one was within hearing distance. She then leaned in closer to Seeker Eshana and said in a whisper, "I carry with me several things that I think need to get into either a seeker's hands or the hands of some scholar at the capital. The hermit, Antini, sent with me a small booklet filled with information concerning the Gylden Sirklene challenge and the oppgave ringe that she had gleaned from the journals of previous hermits. The information is somewhat cryptic. None of the journal writers come right out and explain just what happens in the challenge, nor do they give any indication as to what to do with the nine pieces of the oppgave ringe. However, it might include information the Crown doesn't have."

"I would be honored to both take a look at the booklet and to take it to the capital to share with others who are studying all the information we can gather about both the challenge and the rings."

"Before my travels veered off course, I had been heading home with some information I picked up while in Farlig Brygge that also needs to get to the capital. I would have you take that there, too."

"Farlig Brygge, you say," commented Seeker Eshana.

"Yes. I would appreciate it if you did not mention this to anyone else, with the exception of either Lady Celik or her son Elek. Could you let them know that I'm no longer there? Perhaps they in turn could get a message to my parents, who are probably getting worried about now."

"I would be happy to do as you have requested." Not much caused Seeker Eshana's expression to change, but the mention of Farlig Brygge,

Lady Celik, and Elek gave him pause. He had to school his features. *This young lass, Piper, gets more interesting by the moment*, he thought.

"Well, I don't know," Seeker Eshana replied. "We now seem to be up to four boons, and you only asked for two."

Piper was about to come back with a retort, or an apology, until she saw the Seeker was teasing her.

"I would be honored to take care of all of your requests. I had best be off to find you a horse, so we can all be on the road sooner rather than later. I will send Seeker Chance off to find a used saddle."

Seeker Chance returned first with a well-used but well-made saddle and bridle. Piper spent the time awaiting Seeker Eshana's return cleaning up the saddle and tack. She had just finished when Seeker Eshana walked into the barracks stables, leading a mud-brown-colored, shaggy-coated horse that would not have won any prizes for beauty.

"He may not look like much, and you may think he is a bit long in the tooth, but this here fellow is of sound wind. While not the speediest horse in Sommerhjem, he will travel for hours without tiring. He is just old enough and plain enough that I think he would suit a traveling musician of limited means. What do you think?"

"I think he will do quite nicely," Piper told Seeker Eshana, as she ran her hands over the horse.

The horse stood patiently while Piper inspected him. When she was about to back away, the horse reached down and pushed his head against Piper's pants pocket.

"Besides picking a horse who can travel long distances, it would seem you picked an intelligent horse, too. Yes, yes, you can have the treat in my pocket, you clever fellow. Thank you so much, Seeker Eshana. Did I give you enough coin?"

"More than enough. In fact, I have some to return to you. Here," Seeker Eshana said as he gave Piper her change. "It is time Seeker Chance and I travel on. Are you and Beezle heading out this day?"

"Yes. The pull of the firestar gems is growing stronger. I'm also feeling a strong sense of urgency, and Jing has been pacing for the last hour."

"Lord Klingflug, Lord Braeden is here as you requested."

"Yes, yes, send him in," stated Lord Cedric Klingflug, briefly looking up from the papers scattered in front of him. The papers had not contained the news he had wanted to hear. So many leads on where to find pieces of the oppgave ringe had been false or dead ends. Time was running out. Six pieces of the oppgave ringe had already arrived in the capital. Only three more needed to get there. Preventing even one of the rings from getting to the capital and being placed in the vesteboks in the Well of Speaking would provide an opportunity for him to take the power back that he had when he was the regent for the Princess, now Lady Esmeralda. Lord Klingflug was drawn out of his ruminations by a discreet knock on the study door.

"Come."

"Lord Klingflug, I am here as you requested," said Lord Braeden. He was not quite able to keep the slight whine out of his voice, as if being summoned by a man he was supposed to be loyal to was a great imposition.

*Something will need to be done about this pompous fool who is operating under the delusion that he has taken the Raven's place,* Lord Klingflug thought. *He may have been an opportunist and swooped in to take over the Raven's land after the Raven's untimely demise, but he barely holds control over those few of the Raven's men who are left. Lord Braeden, up to now, has been useful to me, so I have been of a mind not to dispose of him quite yet. This interview may change my mind.*

"I've had word from Lady Farcroft," stated Lord Klingflug, "that Blaxton was not successful in stopping that upstart Beecroft and has not found out what he knows. The information I have received suggests he may know the location of one of the rings. He has certainly led her agents on a merry chase across the countryside. Unfortunately, Blaxton has been apprehended by the Crown. Fortunately, another one of her informants was able to get information to her. Lady Farcroft's last message indicated that Beecroft may have acquired an object of power. Beecroft was last seen leaving the Stein Hage estate where he was posing as a traveling musician.

He was also traveling with another musician, a lass. He was on horseback, but she was on foot. They will either continue as traveling musicians, or he may revert to being himself. It is hard to tell."

"What do you wish of me?" Lord Braeden interrupted.

*Ah yes, this sniveling, pompous, pretentious, blowhard needs to be gone soon*, Lord Klingflug thought, trying desperately to keep hold of his temper. *If I were still the regent, he would think twice before interrupting me.*

"I want you to send some of your men out to inquire discreetly of horse traders in your area whether they have sold a horse to a young woman of late and, if so, get a description of both the woman and the horse. See if they can find out if she was traveling with anyone, and where she or they might be headed."

"But I was not headed back to my estate at this time," Lord Braeden lamented.

*That is it*, Lord Klingflug thought. *I have had enough of this.* "If those loyal to the Crown are successful in bringing all nine pieces of the oppgave ringe to the capital, the challenge will most likely happen. Our chance of controlling the outcome of the challenge is slim to none. The new queen or king of Sommerhjem most certainly will not look kindly on those who have tried to prevent his or her choosing. How long do you think you will be able to hold onto the land you acquired by less than legal means, or your own estate for that matter?"

"But I, I ...." started Lord Braeden, only to be interrupted by Lord Klingflug.

"But nothing. Do you really think that those men who were loyal to the Raven are going to be content just sitting around your estate? Has it even occurred to you that, while you are off socializing and doing whatever you want, they are likely back on your estate either robbing you blind or just plain plotting to take over?"

The look on Lord Braeden's face was one of abject horror, for it had never occurred to him that those roughhewn men he had left back on his estate were not completely loyal to him.

"I think you now understand that you need to head home at once. I will send a group of my men to escort you home and make sure everything is all right on your estate," asserted Lord Klingflug in a voice that brooked no objections from Lord Braeden. "Be ready to ride within the hour."

Lord Klingflug waved his hand in dismissal and turned his attention back to the papers on his desk. Lord Braeden stood there, stunned by his abrupt dismissal.

The door to the study opened, and several of Lord Klingflug's men entered. One invited Lord Braeden to follow him for refreshments before traveling off to his estate. The second man remained after Lord Braeden left the study.

"I take it you heard all of that, Dubhlainn," said Lord Klingflug, directing his attention to the man who stood before him.

"Yes, sir."

"If I was not convinced before this last meeting with Lord Braeden that he is a completely self-centered buffoon, I am now. His hold on both his own land and that of the Raven's is tenuous. It would not do to have his holdings taken over by anyone other than someone completely loyal to us. It would also not do to have the Crown move in, should there be trouble there. We do not want their attention drawn in that direction. You know what needs to be done."

"Yes, sir. Our best information suggests that Lord Braeden's second son is young and not satisfied with his current position. Seems he had hopes of being given the Raven's land when his father acquired it, but so far his father has put him off."

"Much as I would like to eliminate Lord Braeden with a very untimely death on his way home from here, he still, unfortunately, has his uses. You need to gain control of what is left of the Raven's men and send them off in search of Beecroft. You also need to convince Lord Braeden that his second son should be placed in charge of the Raven's former holdings. Tell him that you will stay and help keep the Raven's men under control when they return, since they will be assigned to his second son. Convince him he would, then, no longer have to worry about them taking over his estate, and he would be free to travel again. He is so self-centered and self-absorbed, he might accept this plan. It would get his second son, who is a pain in his posterior, out from underfoot, and remove the Raven's men. I think the second son will be more than ready to follow your lead, for it gets him some of what he wants and out from under the control of his father."

"An excellent plan, sir. I will take care of it."

"See that you do. We are going to need to use the Raven's tower when we get hold of Beecroft and several others we are looking for. It's time to gather up Lord Braeden and be on your way."

# Chapter Sixteen

Piper, Beezle, and Jing had been traveling for over a week since they had parted company with the others. The pull of the fourth firestar gem was drawing them ever north. They had not stopped at any villages or estates along the way, but that would need to end soon, for they were both traveling very light and were running out of the meager supplies they had. With harvest well past, other than the game Jing caught, there was little to be scavenged in either the woods or the fields they traveled through.

"We are going to have to do something about earning some coin and restocking our staples," Piper said to Beezle. "Now, I like rabbit stew as much as the next folk. However, the last shriveled carrot and the last dried mushroom went into the stew this night. Plus, we cannot always count on Jing to provide the meat."

Jing looked up from where he lay by the cook fire, and Piper thought he looked insulted, that is, if mountain cats can look insulted. Just in case, Piper directed her next comment to him.

"I apologize, Jing. I'm more than aware you have provided something each night for our meal and will continue to do so."

"You are right about having to resupply. We could try to find a farm that might want some help and maybe get a meal and an offer to sleep in the hayloft. That will get us farther away from the Stein Hage estate, but it does not solve our needs in the long run. Have you noticed that our direction has changed since we left there?" Beezle asked.

"Yes. I still feel the pull to travel north, but realize that we are being pulled more northeast than true north. Each day as we travel northward, we angle more and more east. Am I right in thinking that this direction will eventually put us in the foothills of the eastern mountains?"

"More than likely."

"All the more reason to gather supplies, then, if we are going to end up there. I wish I knew where we were really going. It would make it so much easier to plan."

"What, and take away all the mystery and adventure?" queried Beezle.

"Quite frankly, I could do with a little less mystery and adventure at this point. Always being on alert, always having to be very cautious with everyone we meet or come in contact with, is wearing. But that one of us could have just found a map or directions as to where to find the oppgave ringe piece, travelled directly there, and then had a clear danger-free path to the capital. Now that would be nice," Piper suggested with a sigh.

"Based on the tales told by the others who have brought pieces of the oppgave ringe to the capital, none of their journeys have been risk-free, or easy, for that matter. I wonder if that is because it has been several hundred years since the last challenge was called, and the pieces of the oppgave ringe, or their importance, were lost over time, making it more difficult to gather them now."

"That's an interesting thought. When King Griswold died, if the challenge had been called as it should have been, those holding the pieces of the oppgave ringe would probably have known what they possessed. Folks would have known what to expect. It was a way to choose a ruler that had been in place for time out of mind. A way accepted by folks and designed, I think, to prevent intrigue and fighting," said Piper.

"As the events have unfolded this summer and fall, with six pieces of the oppgave ringe now in the capital, the word has spread, and more and more of the folks of Sommerhjem are growing to accept that the next ruler should be chosen through the challenge. Of course, there are those who still see themselves gaining power and wealth by backing the former regent in his pursuit to regain control. He knows he cannot take the throne by force, for too many would oppose him, but he still thinks he can take power back by preventing the Gylden Sirklene challenge," Beezle stated disgustedly. "There is a slim possibility that he could finagle such, and that is more than worrisome."

"Then we had best leave early in the morning and cover as much ground as we can before stopping. Let's try to stay at farm houses for the next few days, but then I think we need to earn our keep somewhere. Perhaps small wayside inns would be best. We would get a meal and a warm place to sleep, which would be especially welcome if we are heading into the foothills of the eastern mountains," suggested Piper.

As they headed north and ever more east, the land became more rugged and the weather colder. Villages were farther and farther apart. The pull now was so strong that it was difficult to stop at the end of each day, and nights were less than restful. Soon they moved into the foothills and found some relief in a forester village. Beezle had risked revealing his true identity to the head of the forester clan and had asked for assistance, hoping that this clan was still loyal to the Crown.

"We owe a great deal to Lady Esmeralda and the interim ruling council, for they returned us to our home here. Whatever we can do to help you will be gladly given," Arberie, the head forester, told Beezle. Glancing over her shoulder to where Piper and Jing were sitting surrounded by a number of the village children, Arberie asked Beezle about the mountain cat.

"I think you will really need to ask Piper about him."

"I will, once I can pry them both away from the children. We see the occasional hunting cat, but we have never seen a mountain cat this far north. I hope that will not be a problem for you folks. The hunting cats are territorial. But enough of this seriousness. You both look like you could do with rest and a good meal. Will you stay with us a while longer?"

"I thank you for your kind offer of hospitality, but we are on urgent business for the Crown. It's important that we keep moving, for we have a task to complete. As for the hunting cats, Jing has made the acquaintance of one already, and it went smoothly. I'm more worried about two-legged predators. We suspect there are folks looking for us who would be most happy to prevent what we would do. Any help you might be able to give us in preventing the curious from finding out which way we go from here will be helpful. That and supplies, for we are very short. Also, might it be possible to leave most of our gear here, including our horses? I think we will be in need of a pair of your sturdier mountain horses."

"It will be done," stated Arberie, as she turned and began walking toward Piper.

"Lord Klingflug, several messages have arrived this morning, and both with good news."

"Well, what do they say?" Lord Klingflug asked impatiently of his second-in-command.

"Dubhlainn sent a message by courier saying that all has gone well. Lord Braeden has been convinced to turn the Raven's former holding and tower over to his second son, who is more than willing to take his cues from Dubhlainn. He is an ambitious one, unlike his father or his older brother. He will bear watching, but, for now, he is content."

"That is good news indeed. And what of the other message?"

"It's from your contact within the forester clan near the eastern mountains. Said two folks have entered the forest his clan oversees. The man spent quite some time with the head of the clan, and the woman arrived with a mountain cat, which struck him as unusual."

"A mountain cat, you say?"

"Yes, sir, a mountain cat. Is that important?"

Lord Klingflug began shuffling through the papers scattered on his desk. "I just had it here a moment ago. Now what did I do with it? Ah, here it is. Yes, a lass traveling with a mountain cat is significant. A follow-up note from Stein Hage said the female traveling musician was accompanied by a mountain cat. There cannot be too many folks traveling about Sommerhjem with a mountain cat. Does the message say anything more?"

"Only that our contact said they were alerted to look out for anyone who might be following or interested in the two, well three, to be accurate. He will try to follow them and see where they are headed."

"Finally, a break. Chances are fairly good that the pair with the mountain cat are Aaron Beecroft and his companion. Have we got someone we can send who will not cause the foresters to become concerned?"

"Yes, sir. I will see to it right away."

When his second-in-command left the study, Lord Klingflug leaned back in his chair and ruminated on the news he had just received. Having the forester Bradwr beholden to him had certainly paid off.

Piper was glad they had the good fortune to gather more supplies from the forester clan. The pull of the fourth firestar gem was now so strong that, other than stopping to rest the horses and stopping for the night, the three of them had been traveling steadily, drawing ever closer to the higher foothills of the eastern mountains. The trees had become sparser, growing in between rocky outcrops. Despite the urgency, travel became slower as they maneuvered themselves up narrow trails that often had sheer drop-offs to one side.

The higher they climbed, the more worried Piper became. She knew from her experience growing up in the mountains that the weather could change quickly, and with disastrous results. A heavy snowfall, high winds, or both, could spell disaster for them on the narrow path they were following. She had been watching the buildup of dark gray clouds all through the morning. She could smell snow in the air.

When they reached a place at midday where the path leveled out onto a wide stretch of land, Piper called a halt, in order to rest the mountain horses and stretch her legs. The pull of the fourth firestar gem was so strong now it was all she could do not to leap right back on her horse. Jing was pacing, over and over, up the trail and back to where Piper and Beezle stood.

"Jing, settle down, please. We will move on in a minute. You are going to wear your paws out if you keep going back and forth."

Jing did not heed Piper's warning, but paced back up the trail.

"He feels it, too," suggested Beezle.

"I know. The pull of the gem is almost unbearable. We must be getting close. I'm worried. Those clouds overhead are getting darker and more ominous."

"I guess we need to hope the land ahead stays like this, and we don't have to travel on any more narrow paths."

"Here's hoping," Piper called over her shoulder, as she remounted her horse.

Unfortunately, hoping did not prevent the snow from starting just after they had moved onto a narrow trail that hugged the side of a cliff to their right. There was no room to turn around and go back. They could only move forward. Soon the snow began to fall more rapidly, and the wind picked up, causing the snow to swirl around them and making it so they could see no more than a foot in front of them.

*This is not good*, Piper thought, as she pulled her horse to a halt. She had seen in a break in the swirling snow that she had reached a spot where the trail widened just a bit. Calling back to Beezle, she told him she was going to dismount and lead her horse. Once off her horse, she began to walk slowly forward, shuffling her feet, trying to detect the path ahead. It was slow going, bent against the wind and snow, and very frightening. Visibility was only intermittent, and it did not look as if the trail they were on was going to widen out any more.

*This is the second late fall snowstorm I have been in over recent weeks*, Piper thought. *This one is even worse than the last. I have lost sight of Jing, and I can only hope Beezle is still behind me.*

What seemed like hours passed as the trio picked their way along the trail, which had become dangerously slippery. Piper swiped a mittened hand across her face, trying to wipe away the frost that was forming on her eyelashes, obscuring her vision. Despite the warm clothing she was wearing, her head covered with a woolen cap and the hood of her cloak tied with a scarf that covered most of her face, Piper was becoming numb. Her feet and hands had lost most of their feeling, and she was worried that soon she would not be able to feel the reins of the horse she was leading.

Piper began to despair. She was not even sure Beezle was behind her. He could have fallen off the trail and she would not have known, for the wind was howling so loudly it was hard to even think. She was so tired. It took her a moment to figure out that something had changed. Her wrist was becoming unbearably hot. So hot that she reached down and pulled back the sleeve of her coat. A light shot out of the firestar gem, lighting up the swirling snow.

# CHAPTER SEVENTEEN

Through the swirling, blinding snow, Piper could just make out a glow of light low to the ground ahead of her. The firestar gem on the bracelet on her wrist continued to glow.

"Beezle, can you hear me?" Piper shouted over her shoulder.

"Yes," came a muffled reply.

Piper was filled with relief, just knowing Beezle was still behind her. Before she could tell him to push back his sleeve to expose the firestar gem on his wrist cuff, an arc of light shot over her head.

"Jing is ahead of me, and his pendant is sending out a steady glow, which I can see between gusts of wind. My firestar gem is also glowing steadily. How about yours?"

"Yes. It … glo … stead …. What do … think … means?"

"I don't know. Jing!" Piper called, frantic because she could no longer see the glow from his pendant ahead of her. Had he fallen off the narrow trail they were walking on? Had the trail curved abruptly to the right? As Piper kept cautiously walking forward, straining her eyes, trying to find even a glimmer of light ahead of her, she felt the panic she had been holding at bay begin to rise up.

Looking down at her wrist, she could see that the firestar gem on her bracelet continued to glow. Carefully shuffling her feet along the trail and sliding her mittened hand along the wall to her right, Piper began to inch herself along once again. It was a good thing that she was moving slowly, for her next step found nothing to place her foot on. She stood frozen with one foot on the trail and the other dangling. She stepped back quickly and backed into the nose of her horse, who snorted and also took a step back.

"Beezle, you need to hold. I just ran out of trail directly ahead."

"Holding."

Cautiously, Piper felt along the wall on her right with both her hand and her foot. She realized she had not felt the ending of the wall because she had led with her foot. Had she moved her hand just inches forward, she would have felt the ending of the wall before she felt the ending of the trail. Peering around the corner, she could once again see the glow of Jing's firestar gem ahead of her.

"The trail turns to the right, and I can see the glow of Jing's firestar gem. The trail is very narrow rounding the corner, so be careful," Piper shouted over the roar of the wind, hoping Beezle heard her. "Did you hear me?"

"Yes, trail … very narrow … careful."

Lowering her head against the wind, gripping the reins of her horse as tightly as she could, Piper carefully moved around the corner with her horse following safely behind. She was not sure if the wind now blowing into her side was any better than when it had been blowing directly at her. It was still hard to see. She was relieved when she heard Beezle shout that he was around the corner.

As the three moved slowly forward, the trail began to widen. While the wind did not lessen, the snow tapered off, and it became easier to see where they were going. The wind also scoured the snow off the trail so that they did not have to add walking through deep snow to the already dangerous cold.

Piper had been concentrating so hard on putting one foot in front of the other, that she almost bumped into Jing, who suddenly appeared before her. He turned and ran a few yards ahead of her, and then returned, repeating the pattern several times.

"Look, Jing, I can hardly feel my feet, they are so cold, and you want me to move faster. I'm doing the best I can."

Jing apparently did not think Piper was truly moving as fast as she could, for he came back and literally nipped at her heels.

"Now you quit that, you hear me. I ...." Piper suddenly stopped, for she was sure she had just caught a whiff of wood smoke. *That's not possible*, she thought. It was then that it occurred to her that they had been heading down for the past little while. She had been trudging along following Jing, so cold and tired that she had not paid any attention to the fact that the landscape had changed. Walls were now on two sides of the trail. *You would have thought I would have noticed the lack of wind*, Piper thought.

"Beezle?"

"Still here, but barely. It's a good thing the reins of my horse have frozen to my mitten, or I would not be able to hold on, my hands are so cold. I hate to mention this, but we need to find shelter soon," stated Beezle through chattering teeth.

"I know. I think I just caught a hint of wood smoke, but that might just be wistful imagining. Jing is really anxious that we move on, so I will try to pick up the pace, not that I have much choice. Do you feel the pull of the firestar gem? It's almost overwhelming. I don't think we could stop right here even if there were a convenient inn with a roaring fire within."

"At this moment, it is all I am really feeling. The feeling in my hands, feet, and face left hours back," replied Beezle.

Emerging from the walled passage, Piper, Jing, and Beezle found themselves in a long valley. While there were trees on the hillsides of the valley, the valley floor was covered with rows upon rows of cultivated bushes, now leafless, but covered with nets. Still clinging to the branches of each bush were bunches of berries. In the center of the valley stood a sturdy log cottage with an attached barn, and multiple outbuildings.

Beezle had drawn up alongside Piper and stared at the view ahead of them.

"Do you know where we are?" asked Piper.

"The eastern mountains?" Beezle replied.

"Funny, very funny. No, what you are looking at is a terte isen berry patch, or maybe farm would be more accurate. I have heard of these, but their locations are kept so secret. Have you ever tried terte isen berry syrup on a griddle cake?"

"Way too rich for my purse."

"I think we should be prepared for a hostile greeting rather than a warm welcome. We really have no other choice than to approach. None of us are going to last much longer in this cold, and the pull of the firestar gem is almost painful," Piper stated, as she began to move through the snowdrifts toward the cottage.

When the three came to the front gate of the fence that surrounded the log cottage, Piper called out. "Hello in the cottage. We would ask for hospitality."

Piper could see smoke was rising out of the chimney. No one, however, answered her call. The windows were shuttered against the cold, so they could only see a slight bit of light, shining out from the gap where the two shutters met.

"I don't see any fresh tracks coming down the path to this gate. Light and smoke would seem to indicate someone is here. Maybe someone is in the barn," suggested Beezle.

Just as they were about to head around the back of the cottage toward the attached barn, Jing stepped in front of Piper and Beezle, his hackles standing straight up. From around the corner of the cottage came two huge snow-white mountain dogs, barking and snarling. They halted just ten feet away from where Jing, Piper, and Beezle stood.

The figure that rounded the corner following the dogs was bundled against the cold. Piper did not know if they faced a man or a woman, for the folk's features were obscured by a hat pulled low and a scarf covering the face, all but the eyes.

"Yas, Yepa, hold. Now you folks just need to turn around and head back the way you came," stated a gruff voice.

Taking a chance, holding her hands out as a sign of peace, Piper said "We mean no harm to you and yours. We have not come to steal your crop. I beg hospitality, for if you turn us back, we will surely freeze to death."

When Piper held her hands out beseechingly, her coat cuff slid back from her wrist. The firestar gem began to glow brighter and brighter. It also began to warm up to the point that it was becoming uncomfortable. She looked up to see the man standing before them frantically trying to get his left mitten off. Finally, he shook his hand and the mitten flew from

115

it. An arc of light shot out to be met by three arcs of light. All just stood there for a few moments, trying to get their sight back after the intense burst of light.

"Who are you?" the man whispered, hunkering down to wrap his arms around the two mountain dogs, who had slunk back and were huddled at his feet.

"We would like a chance to explain, but do you think we could do it out of the wind and cold?" Beezle asked gently. "We truly mean you no harm. Actually, at this point I'm so cold that if you were to hit my arm, it would probably crack right off and land in the snow."

Gathering his composure around him like a warm cloak, the man gestured the three should follow him and bring the horses. He led them around the cottage and into the attached barn. Just the little warmth of the barn was a welcome change from the bitter cold outside.

"Settle your horses. I will take the dogs inside," the man stated as he turned, walked to the door of the cottage, and went inside.

"So, Beezle, do you think he means us to stay out here, or are we to follow him once the horses are settled?"

"Hard to tell. We'll find out when we have the horses settled."

It took a while to remove the tack from the horses, for the leather straps were stiff with cold, as were Piper's and Beezle's hands. They took the time to make sure the horses' hooves were clear of ice, brushed the snow and ice off their bodies, and settled them into a stall with water and hay. After the horses were settled, Piper walked to the cottage door and knocked.

The door was opened by a man much younger than Piper had expected. He was not much older than she was. He gestured that they should divest themselves of their icy and snow-covered outer wear, and then enter the cottage quickly, so as not to let the heat out. *Such a warm and welcoming fellow*, Piper thought, and then chastised herself for her unkind thoughts. The rareness of terte isen berries, and the profit made from the sale of the syrup made from them, would certainly be attractive to many unscrupulous folks. Add that to what had happened outside with the firestar gems, and he had a right to be wary.

"I thank you for your kindness and the warmth of your cottage. We would not have survived much longer without shelter. I'm called Piper, and I travel with the mountain cat, Jing. I don't think he will harm your dogs."

While Piper was addressing the young man, Jing took it upon himself to slip by her. He headed directly toward the two dogs who were lying near the fire.

"Jing, wait!" Piper exclaimed. *Just what we need*, she thought, *a dog and cat fight in the middle of the cottage.*

Jing, however, paid Piper no mind and walked straight up to the two mountain dogs. For a moment there was a great deal of sniffing going on, and then all three animals settled down near the fire.

"Well, that went better than expected," commented Beezle. "I am called Beezle, and I also thank you. By what name do you go?"

"Pyry. I'm called Pyry. Why are you in my valley?"

"I think it's because we have been drawn here to find you," Piper replied. Piper's explanation came to an abrupt halt when a door burst open, and a young woman stepped out, leveling an arrow nocked in a short bow at them.

As the woman pulled back the bow string, Pyry called out, "Snezana Tula, no!"

The woman lowered her bow but remained alert. "I was so worried. I couldn't stay hidden any longer."

"I know, beloved, I know," Pyry said gently. "Before we act rashly, I think we need to find out more." Turning to Piper and Beezle, Pyry introduced his wife. "Before you made your heroic and dramatic entrance, I think Piper here was trying to explain why they are in our valley."

Piper glanced at Beezle, and he gave her a nod of encouragement. They had talked previously about what they might say if and when they found the fourth firestar gem, should it be in possession of someone rather than just lying about.

"Do you mind if we sit down? This might take a while to explain," Piper asked. When all were seated, she continued and told them about being given the bracelet by Collier, about being rescued by Jing, Foster, and Wileen. She told them about her venture into the high mountains and meeting Antini, the hermit, and what she had learned there. She told of finding Beezle, and of their difficulties with Blaxton and his men. Finally, she suggested that the ring he wore on his hand held the fourth piece of the firestar gem, and what might be with it.

Beezle contributed at the end, telling what he had seen happen at the Well of Speaking at the great summer fair in the capital, and what had happened four times since, with others bringing in pieces of the oppgave ringe. He emphasized how important it was to find the piece that was supposed to be connected to the firestar gems they all wore.

"The ring I'm wearing was my father's ring and has been passed down from father to son or daughter for several generations. My grandfather, Poppa, gave the ring to my father. When Father left the valley, he and Poppa decided I should have the ring. My father and my mother left here several years ago to go and help my sister and her family out. She married into a family that has a small vineyard at the base of the foothills of the southern mountains. They were hard hit by the former regent's special licenses and taxes. I don't know anything about the ring really, other than I should keep it safe. I'm sorry, but I know nothing about this piece of the oppgave ringe that you speak of."

Piper's shoulders drooped. Was she on a fool's errand, risking life and limb for nothing? Jing, sensing her change of mood, came and laid his head in her lap. It also struck her as ironic that if Pyry's father had taken the ring with him, she might have come upon it before she had even left the southern mountains.

"Wait, we might not know about this oppgave ringe piece you have described, but Poppa might," suggested Snezana. "I'll go fetch him."

# CHAPTER EIGHTEEN

Snezana returned to the cottage's great room not with just one folk, but with several more. She was accompanied by an older man and an older woman carrying a small child.

"This is Poppa and Ganna, Pyry's grandparents. Ganna is holding our son, Qannik," Snezana said.

"I couldn't stop that fool wife of yours from rushing off to defend you," stated Poppa gruffly.

"Oh hush now, Poppa. You know I would have done the very same thing if I thought you were in danger, even if you had told me to hide. Besides, Snezana knew you would take care of the little one and me. Now, where have our good manners gone? Come, Snezana, help me get a warm meal started. Pyry, you take Qannik for a while," admonished Ganna.

"Ah, Poppa, these folks have a question for you," said Pyry.

"Questions can wait. Hungry babies cannot." Qannik emphasized Ganna's point by beginning to fuss loudly. "You, Poppa, we need more wood."

After the meal, when all had pushed back from the simple but filling fare, Ganna was about to direct a question to Beezle and Piper when Snezana leaped up from the table with a horrified look on her face.

"Qannik, your mountain cat, oh no," Snezana sputtered.

Everyone turned to see what she was looking at. Qannik was lying all curled up, nestled against Jing, using his side as a pillow. Jing had a resigned but patient look on his face.

"It's obvious to me that your son has very good instincts. He has found a very safe and warm place to nap," Piper suggested, trying to bring some calm into what could otherwise become a tense situation.

"I just didn't think. We always let him down after a meal. The gate around the fireplace keeps him out of harm's way," said Snezana.

"Sit back down now, Snezana. The boy is fine. Now then, Snezana said something about a ring you were looking for, but not the one Pyry wears. Maybe you should start at the beginning," Ganna proposed.

Piper repeated what she had told Pyry and Snezana, with Beezle chiming in here and there.

"We are pretty isolated here. By choice, mind you, so we have heard little from the outside. We sell our syrup through a trader we trust. We knew the Regent was no longer in power, and the interim ruling council was no longer requiring special licenses to do what our family has been doing for generations. Heard that some sort of challenge had been called, but don't know all that much about it. Never heard of this thing called an oppgave ringe," Pyry's Ganna stated. "This story about the firestar gems all being linked seems a bit farfetched to me. Besides, we don't have time for this nonsense. We have a harvest to bring in. The early snow has frozen our berries, and they should be just right for the picking. A bit early this year, but the time is now. Now, you two can just sit there by the fire toasting your toes, or you can help. Pyry, get the lanterns. This batch of berries ought to be extra sweet, since we will be picking them by the full moon."

With that said, Ganna got up and began pulling on warm leggings and other warm outer gear. Pyry and Poppa got up swiftly, and they too began dressing for the cold out-of-doors. Snezana bustled out of the room, saying she was going to put the babe down for the night.

When the room was empty, Beezle turned and looked at Piper. "I think Poppa knows something. When you were describing the piece of the oppgave ringe, I thought I saw a look of recognition cross his face. He also looked like he was about to speak when Ganna got up and began ordering us all about."

"The firestar gems led us here. The almost unbearable pressure to get here has stopped. Yet I still feel something. Maybe the four gems being together again is what is causing it, but I don't think so," Piper told Beezle.

"I know what you are saying. It's like you can almost hear or feel something, but not quite. I don't know how to explain it. After seeing Nissa's firestar gem react to ours, I asked her to tell me what she knew about them. She told me that when the firestar gem is near an object that is more than what it seems by its outward appearance, it grows warm. Mine hasn't felt warm. Has yours?"

"No."

"Nissa also said that if someone is wearing a firestar gem, and is someone of good intent, it will arc, of like to like. It is a way for one to know friend from foe. If someone is not of good intent, the gems will neither arc nor glow. Based on that information, it would seem that Pyry is someone we can trust."

"Speaking of trust. Maybe we can gain either Ganna or Poppa's trust by going out and helping with the berry harvest. I think they were skeptical about what we told them. If a piece of the oppgave ringe is here, it is imperative to find it and convince them that it has to get to the capital. I'm not looking forward to going back out in the cold, since I have just now warmed up from our trek here," groused Piper.

"I agree with you on both counts. Let's get bundled up and head out. How hard can berry picking be on a cold snowy night?"

Hours later, when Piper and Beezle stumbled into the cottage once again, they knew just how hard picking terte isen berries was. Jing had been outside with them the whole time and seemed ready to go out again.

"Go ahead, cat, be full of energy. You have just been frolicking in the snow with those two big lumbering dogs and chasing rabbits with them. You have not been bent over picking berries, or hauling basket loads to the hut where the kettles for cooking down the berries into syrup are, not to mention hauling wood for the fires. No wonder terte isen berry syrup is so expensive. Pyry informed me that they will be working in shifts around the clock until the last berry is picked and cooked down into syrup. He suggested it would be all done in about a week. A week!" Piper grumbled.

As the days and nights blended one into another and time blurred, both Piper and Beezle tried to strike up conversations with the two older folks. Neither had much success learning anything more about the possibility of a piece of the oppgave ringe being anywhere in this isolated valley. Both, however, still felt that strange feeling they had talked about.

Finally, Piper found herself alone with Poppa in the hut where the berries were cooking down into syrup. She took the opportunity to try once again to get any information she could from Poppa about the piece of the oppgave ringe. She, like Beezle, had come to the conclusion that, if he did know something, he was reluctant to talk about it. What she did not know was if his reluctance came from not trusting Beezle or her, or if he had other reasons. Since he had asked her to address him as Poppa like the other younglings, as he called Pyry and Snezana, Piper did so.

"Poppa, I have the feeling that you know more about a piece of the oppgave ringe than you have been willing to discuss," said Piper, having decided that coming right out and making this statement might get her more answers than beating around the bush.

Poppa looked at her and paused in what he was doing. "Here, stir the syrup," he stated briskly. He then went and opened the door to the hut and stepped out. He was gone for several minutes. Upon returning, he took over the stirring.

Piper stepped back and patiently waited for him to speak.

"I was married before to Pyry's father's mother. She died a number of years ago. The woman he calls Ganna is my second wife. The ring Pyry wears with the firestar gem in it comes from my first wife's family. She gave me the ring upon our marriage. She always wore a pouch of golden pine spider silk around her neck which contained ...."

The door to the hut opened, and Ganna stuck her head in, interrupting the conversation.

"Piper, would you be so kind as to come with me? I need your help."

Piper was loath to leave the hut and the conversation she was having with Pyry's grandfather, but she could not come up with a reasonable excuse to stay, so she reluctantly followed Ganna.

"I need some help moving some heavy barrels in the storage area," Ganna explained.

Ganna led Piper to another outbuilding, which was made of stone and round in shape. Once through the door, Piper saw that the entire interior of the building was just a wide spiral staircase leading down. She reflected that it was like being at the top of a round tower, if the tower was set deep in the ground. She also noticed that on one side of the stairs was a shaft, which Ganna explained allowed a rope and pulley system to lower barrels of the syrup down to the underground storage area.

"Once we are far enough underground, the rooms stay cool but do not freeze. There are several levels of storage rooms. I think this shaft we are climbing down was intended to be a well, but whoever dug it hit bedrock before they hit water. Works well for storing all sorts of things," Ganna explained. "Those barrels I want moved are on the lowest level."

Piper could see little of her surroundings in the dim glow of the lantern Ganna carried. The light was barely enough to see the stairs. Once Piper reached the bottom of the stairs, she could see the edges of a few barrels. Ganna had indicated that they were not the ones she wanted Piper to help move, so Piper followed her into a side room.

"I'll be right back. I'm so forgetful," Ganna exclaimed, as she backed back out the door, taking the lantern with her. Once she was through the doorway, she swiftly swung the door shut and set the bar across the two metal brackets on either side of the door, locking Piper in. "That ought to hold you, you and that cat of yours. Now, to go take care of that meddlesome man you are with."

Piper could not believe what had just happened. The old woman had locked her in a storage room, which was completely dark and very cold. Piper was thankful she was still in her warm outdoor clothes, for she had enough to worry about without having to worry about freezing to death. *What prompted the old woman to lock me up?* Piper wondered.

Just as she thought that, two things occurred to her. First was that Ganna had said the room ought to hold both Piper and her cat. Second was that Ganna had said she was now going to take care of Beezle. Piper did not like the sounds of the second thought and wondered just what Ganna had meant by her statement about Jing.

"Jing? Jing?" Piper whispered, and then wondered why she was whispering. Who else did she think was locked in this room with her anyway? It also occurred to her to question just how Ganna was going to explain her disappearance. The old woman was obviously not quite right. Did she think either Beezle or she was going to steal the terte isen berry syrup? What other explanation was there?

While all these thoughts were swirling around in Piper's head, she had not been aware that the bracelet on her wrist was growing warmer and had begun to glow, until her attention was drawn to the very dim light leaking out from under her coat cuff. Once Piper noticed both the warmth and the light, she pushed back her coat cuff, and the light within the firestar gem began to glow brighter. Not moving from the spot where she was standing, Piper turned slowly in a circle. When she had turned about three quarters of the way around, she noticed a very faint light close to the floor not far from her. Moving cautiously forward, Piper drew closer to the dim light. It was when she was almost next to the light that she realized what she was looking at was the glow from another firestar gem.

Dropping to her knees, Piper reached out, and her hand touched soft fur. "Jing," she called, shaking him gently. Her efforts were rewarded by a quiet snore. Shaking Jing less gently produced a louder snore, but Jing did not wake. Running her hands over Jing's body, Piper could not discern any cuts. His limbs felt strong and whole. *Now, if only he would wake up. Ganna must have fed him something that had a sleeping draught in it,* Piper surmised.

Squatting here, continuing to run her hands over the sleeping mountain cat, was not going to get them out of the locked room, so Piper stood up and felt her way back to the door. Yanking on the handle did not work. She considered yelling at the top of her lungs, but thought better of the idea, realizing that no one was likely to hear her. When she ran her hands over the door, Piper discovered a small, high, barred window in the door. Even standing on tiptoes and reaching her hand through the window down the outside of the door, she could not reach the bar across the door.

Unbuttoning her coat, Piper reached under her sweater and unbuckled her belt. She hoped she could slide the belt out between the bars of the small window and catch the bar on the hook on her belt buckle. Slowly, she slid the belt out the window in the door. She let it slide down the outside of the door. She heard the belt buckle hit what she thought was the wooden bar. Easing the belt back a little bit, she flicked it out while simultaneously letting it down. Letting the belt go a little farther down, Piper paused to let the belt settle in close to the bar. Then with great patience, she began to draw the belt upward. As she drew it upward, the hook on the buckle did not catch on anything. Time and time again she tried. Beginning to think her idea was not a good one and becoming discouraged, she was about to quit when the hook on the buckle caught on the bar and held momentarily, before it slipped off the bar and the bar settled back.

Over and over, the hook on Piper's belt buckle would catch on the bar holding the door locked, and over and over it would slide off. All the while trying to maneuver the buckle to catch onto the bar, Piper kept repeating in her mind a message to Beezle to beware of Ganna. She had little hope about her message. She had some hope her belt buckle would catch onto the bar and stay hooked.

# Chapter Nineteen

Beezle could not remember a time when he had felt this cold. He was glad that the berries were almost harvested. If he ever heard anyone complaining about the high price of the syrup made from terte isen berries, he was certainly going to enlighten the grumblers. Straightening up and pressing his hand against the small of his back to ease the ache, Beezle looked around and noticed he was alone in the berry patch. It took him a moment to remember that Pyry had taken a sled loaded with berries back to the cooking hut and said he would return shortly. The snow that had been threatening all day had finally begun to fall. Beezle hoped Pyry would return soon.

The next time Beezle looked up, he could see the horse-drawn sled approaching. It was difficult to see who was driving due to the increasingly heavy snowfall. When he could make out the driver, he noted that it was not Pyry but Ganna. She pulled up alongside and called down to Beezle.

"Toss those last few baskets of berries on the sled. Then, can you climb up and grab the tarp? Just unroll it as you back up toward me. Doesn't do to let the sled bed and berries be covered with any more snow than is needful."

Beezle did as asked and unrolled the tarp toward the front of the sled. When he was almost to the driver's seat, he felt a blow to his head, and then everything went black.

Piper's arms were beginning to ache, and her knees almost buckled when Jing staggered against them. She was soaked to the skin from working so long and so hard trying to get the bar on the door free from the metal brackets holding it place. Piper had long since taken off her cloak and warm coat. When she stopped to steady Jing, she could feel the chill air of the storage room beginning to seep in.

"I'm so glad you're back with me. I'm very worried that we are stuck here, and I'm worried about Beezle."

With even more determination than before, Piper slipped her belt out the window of the storeroom door. This time, however, she tried something new. Instead of trying to catch the bar in the middle, Piper had moved the belt to the far right side of the small barred window on the latch side of the door. Once she lowered the belt down, she could feel it bump into the wooden bar that held the door closed. Moving the belt outward and down, she let it come to rest below the bar. Easing the belt upward, she felt the hook catch, as it had so many times before. Holding her breath, she began to pull the belt very slowly upward. This time, instead of feeling the hook slip off the bar, she felt resistance. Tired and frustrated by her earlier attempts, Piper was tempted just to jerk the belt upward, but refrained. Slowly, ever so slowly, she inched the belt up. The belt hook continued to hold. When she felt one side of the bar slip free of the bracket, Piper, holding the belt in her left hand, slowly reached down and cautiously turned the latch holding the door closed. Quickly, she pushed the door open. She heard her belt drop to the stone floor, but did not bend down to try to locate it right away. She just leaned against the door jamb for a few moments to settle herself before she moved forward.

After retrieving her belt, coat, and cloak, Piper inched forward, trying to locate the stairs that would take her up and out of the storage building. She felt a great sense of urgency, for she did not know how long she had been locked in, and was now more worried than ever about Beezle.

When Piper and Jing reached the top of the stairs, Piper cautiously cracked the door open and looked out. She was surprised to discover that, while she had been trapped down in the storage room, it had begun to snow heavily.

"Come on, Jing, we need to find Beezle," Piper whispered. "I hope we're not too late. I know we certainly can't trust Ganna. I don't know about the others. Perhaps we can trust Pyry. His firestar gem responded to ours, and according to what we have been told, if he were not a good man, it would not have done so."

As quickly as visibility in the swirling snow allowed, Piper and Jing crossed over to the hut where the syrup was being cooked. Peering inside, Piper was relieved to see that Pyry was the only one in the hut. Still completely unsure where Pyry's allegiance would be concerning Ganna, Piper asked if he knew where Beezle was, but did not tell him Ganna had locked her in the storage building.

"Poppa just headed out to the berry patch to pick up the last of the berries. He was going to bring Beezle back with him. They should be returning any moment. Snezana is supposed to come here to relieve me. Did she send you instead?" inquired Pyry. "Do they have a pot of soup going? I'm beyond tired at this moment, and very hungry."

*He thinks I have been at the cottage. How do I explain what is going on?* wondered Piper. *Do I just blurt out that I have no idea if the soup is cooking because I have been locked away by Ganna, and I am very worried she might have harmed Beezle?*

Before Piper could say anything, Poppa stuck his head into the hut. "I couldn't find Beezle. He's not at the cottage, and he is nowhere to be found at the berry patch. I didn't see him along the way to or from the berry patch. I was supposed to pick him up along the way. Your Ganna took the longest time to get back from the berry patch, and then the snow started in earnest as I headed out. I can't imagine where he has gotten to."

"Maybe Pyry and I need to go back out to the berry patch and look again. He might have fallen and, with all the snow, you might have missed him," Piper suggested, trying to keep her voice calm, when inside she was feeling anything but calm. "You look like you could use a bit of warming up, Poppa."

"I won't argue with you about needing to warm up. That chill wind out there cuts straight to the bone. I'll unload the last few baskets of berries.

You two go on. I certainly might have missed Beezle when I was looking for him."

With each passing minute outside, Piper became more and more anxious for Beezle. The icy wind seemed to find any opening in her clothing, no matter how tiny, causing her to feel uncomfortably cold in just the short time they had been walking. Piper checked the right side of the path, and Pyry checked the left. Jing ranged back and forth between the two. The light was already dim due to the lateness of the afternoon, and visibility was even more limited by the swirling snow. When they reached the terte isen berry patch, they rested for a minute and talked over what to do next.

"I'll take this row, and you take the next," Pyry shouted to Piper over the howl of the wind.

When they came to the end of the first two rows, they moved over to the third and fourth rows and headed back down. Both were bone cold by the time they had searched half the patch. When Piper stopped to catch her breath, it suddenly occurred to her that perhaps they were going about looking for Beezle the wrong way. Holding her lantern aloft, she waved at Pyry that he should join her.

"I'm about half frozen from my toes all the way to my head and overtired to boot," Piper stated. "I think that's why my mind has been only half working. Jing and I found Beezle the first time because of the firestar gems. Beezle, Jing, and I found you because of the firestar gems. I wonder if we concentrate on them, if they will give us some indication as to where Beezle might be?"

"Do you think that might work? If he is out here and hurt, every minute counts. I can't imagine what happened to him. When Ganna returned with a batch of berries, she said Beezle had decided to walk back, but we did not see him along the way, nor did Poppa. What should we do with the firestar gems?"

"I really am not all that sure. I suggest you meet me at the end of these rows. Jing, with me, please."

All three moved quickly down the rows. When they met, they turned their backs to the blowing snow and hunkered down.

"I don't know very much about firestar gems," Piper said. "When I was looking for Beezle before, and then when we were trying to find you, I felt a pull. I don't know any way else to describe it. Maybe if we link hands, put a hand on Jing, and concentrate on Beezle, his firestar gem might respond to ours. Just think as hard as you can on Beezle."

Taking Pyry's hand in her right hand and placing her left hand on Jing's back, Piper bowed her head, closed her eyes, and concentrated on Beezle. *Where are you, Beezle?* she thought over and over. Piper was pulled out of her concentration when Jing jerked under her hand. Looking up, she saw him move away and was surprised to see he was not moving back into the berry patch or toward the cottage and outbuildings. Instead, he was moving east toward the mountain side of the valley. Piper did not jump up from her crouched position right away. Instead, she stilled her breathing and quieted her mind.

"Do you feel it?" Piper asked Pyry. "Do you feel the pull?"

"Yes, and it's strong, but also in a direction I did not expect. Your cat is heading toward the mountain side of the valley, toward the new berry patch. What would Beezle be doing there? The patch is so new that the bushes would be covered by this last snow. Also, it's in a very small valley that branches off this one. How would he even know to go there? This doesn't make any sense. I think maybe we should go back to checking the rows here."

Rather than arguing with Pyry, Piper asked how far it was to the new berry patch. "I'm going to follow Jing and the pull," Piper called over her shoulder. As she moved off down the row after Jing, the pull in that direction became stronger with each step. When she came to the end of the row, she glanced back and felt better when she saw Pyry following her.

Once out of the berry patch, the snow became deeper and the occasional drifts slowed all of them down. Finally, they entered the smaller valley.

"That's odd," Pyry remarked.

"What's odd?" Piper asked distractedly, for she was trying to keep the snow-covered Jing in sight. The mountain cat had increased the distance between Piper, Pyry, and himself.

"See there?" Pyry pointed. "Sled tracks in the snow in the lee of that drift."

"Why is that odd?"

"There is no reason for a sled to have come this way since the snow started, especially since we have all been so busy picking berries and boiling them down to syrup. I just don't understand it."

"The tracks seem to be going in the same direction as Jing. Hurry," Piper urged.

It did not take long for Piper and Pyry to catch up to Jing, who was frantically digging in a mound of snow.

"This isn't a natural drift. Someone has piled the snow up," Pyry told Piper, as he knelt down and began to dig in the snow alongside Jing.

Piper joined the two and frantically began moving snow, for she had been overcome with a sense of urgency. As the snow flew from her mittened hands, she became more and more convinced that following the pull she had felt had been the right thing to do.

"Stop!" cried Pyry. "I see something."

Piper looked over and watched Pyry gently brush the snow away.

"That's Beezle's jacket," Piper exclaimed.

"From the feel of it, there is a Beezle still inside of it," Pyry replied.

"We need to hurry, but be careful," Piper said, as she began to brush away more snow. "I'm on his head end, so I will work my way upward and try to clear the snow from his face. You work on clearing the snow off his body."

Pyry nodded and began moving snow, a grim look on his face. The snowfall that had slacked off for a while was back, with huge heavy flakes falling. He was worried about a number of things. *What had a sled been doing in this side valley? It had to be their sled. Who had been driving it? More importantly, had Beezle been brought here on that sled?*

Piper was moving snow as quickly as she could. She too was worried. She had briefly placed her hand on Beezle's chest to see if she could feel it rise and fall, but her hand was so numb with cold and he was wearing so many layers, she could not be sure she had felt his chest move. Finally, she had the snow moved off his face. He was very pale. Piper felt a great deal of relief when she saw a puff of breath leave his mouth.

"He's alive! Beezle, Beezle," Piper called, but Beezle did not respond. Piper brushed away more snow. As she moved the snow away from the side of his head, Beezle moaned.

"Leave him covered," Pyry suggested. "The snow will hold what little body warmth he still has. We're going to need the sled to move him back to the cottage. I'll go get it. I'll hurry."

Jing, who had been sitting close to Piper, moved in and lay next to Beezle. Piper settled in on the other side of Beezle to wait for Pyry to return. Time, she was sure, had slowed down as the snow began to fall more heavily. Suddenly, Jing rose up and faced away from Beezle toward the mountain slope, hackles up. From a distance, a howl echoed over the valley, to be answered by another.

# CHAPTER TWENTY

Piper was already worried, since Beezle lay so still. The howls she had heard were followed by yet another howl and added to her concerns. With the snow increasing and visibility decreasing, the area around Piper had become eerily quiet, so quiet that she could hear the snow falling. That eerie silence was only broken occasionally by the howls that were drawing closer and closer. Piper thought she could possibly get back to the safety of the cottage, but she could not leave Beezle, even though she had little to defend herself with. *A torch would help, a blazing bonfire would be even better*, she thought. *My lantern is not going to be much of a defense.*

As the howling grew closer, Piper began to despair. She did not dare leave Beezle to find wood for a fire, not that she would be able to quickly find any under the snow at this point anyway. Beezle had been dumped and buried under the snow too far away from the new berry patch, so Piper could not even break off a few branches to try to form a makeshift torch. She could only hope Pyry would arrive back soon, though she was not sure the horse-drawn sled could outrun a pack of wolves, if indeed those were wolves who were howling.

The snow tapered off and a break formed in the cloud cover. Moonlight lit up the landscape, revealing that Piper and Beezle were in much more trouble than Piper had thought. There were four wolves ringing them. Low to the ground, they began to slink forward. Jing had moved to the opposite side of Beezle, and Piper could hear a steady low growl coming from his throat. The wolves came closer and closer and began to circle, tongues lolling out of their mouths, breath coming out in puffs of steam.

"Hold steady," Piper cautioned Jing. "Pyry may yet get here and scare them off. I think at the moment those wolves are toying with us."

Suddenly, the wolves stopped their circling. *Here they come*, Piper thought. Much to her surprise, they did not continue toward her but turned their backs to her, and in unison howled a challenge, shifting their attention away from Piper, Beezle, and Jing. They moved together swiftly, forming a tight pack facing the mountain slope. Their chorus was answered by a very commanding deep-throated howl. Leaping over the tallest snowdrifts came one of the great night wolves, which were so rarely seen they were more myth than real to most folks. Black as midnight, the tips of his hair sparkled silver in the moonlight, like the stars on a crisp dark winter night. The four wolves who had been threatening Piper, Beezle, and Jing, upon seeing the night wolf coming toward them, tucked their tails between their legs and ran off.

Once again, Piper cautioned Jing to hold, but he did not heed her warning. Instead, he leapt over Beezle and headed toward the great night wolf.

"No, Jing, come back!" Piper yelled.

Jing did not stop his forward rush. When he was within several feet of the night wolf, he skidded to a halt in the snow, and then held himself very still.

Piper held her breath, her heart pounding, fearful that something very bad was about to happen to Jing. She could not understand why he had run toward the night wolf, much less what was happening now. The great night wolf dipped his head to Jing, who then turned and headed back toward Piper. The night wolf followed.

When Jing arrived where Piper was crouching, he placed himself between Piper and Beezle. The night wolf padded up to where Beezle lay. When Piper made a move toward Beezle, Jing sounded a warning growl. He was not warning the night wolf away, but her. She could only watch in horror as the night wolf lowered his massive head down, ever so slowly, toward Beezle's neck. The night wolf sniffed Beezle, and then lifted a paw and placed it on Beezle's chest. Jing reached back and gently grabbed Piper's hand in his mouth, pulling her up to the night wolf. Jing pulled

Piper's hand down so it was resting on the night wolf's back. He then moved to the other side of the night wolf and placed his paw on the night wolf's paw. The three held still in this strange tableau.

When Piper looked at the night wolf, he swung his head her way, and she found herself caught in the pale ice-blue of his eyes. Slowly, Piper felt the bracelet on her wrist begin to warm. Breaking eye contact with the night wolf, she looked over at Jing and could see the firestar gem on his chest begin to glow. She could not tell if it was her imagination or real, but she felt like warmth was flowing from her to the night wolf. She did not understand quite what was happening, but was heartened when Beezle began to stir.

At that moment, a number of things happened all at once. Jing removed his paw from atop the night wolf's paw, the night wolf stepped back so Piper removed her hand from his back. Beezle sat up, his back to the night wolf so he did not see him, just as Pyry drove the sled over the rise and entered the valley. Piper turned toward the night wolf, but he was already moving away at a fast pace toward the tree line.

"Thank you, I think," Piper whispered after the retreating night wolf. Turning her attention back to Beezle, she was relieved to see him sitting up. Color had returned to his cheeks.

"Piper?" Beezle questioned, looking confused. Bending over and holding his head in his hands, he moaned. "Oh, my head!"

Before Piper could ask what had happened, Pyry pulled the sled alongside and jumped down.

"Piper, is Beezle all right?" Pyry asked.

"No," Beezle stated, as he struggled to pull himself out from under the snow. "I'm definitely not all right. My head hurts, my ears are ringing, and I'm very cold. More than that, I'm very confused. I remember loading the last few berry baskets on the sled and getting on it to unroll the tarp as Ganna asked. The last thing I remember is getting hit on the back of the head. Where's Ganna? Was she hurt too?"

"Ganna seems to be missing. I would have been here sooner, but I had to hitch up the horse to the sled. Ganna had settled this horse in her stall. My family is looking for her now, but a set of skis is missing. Poppa found ski tracks heading out of the valley. None of us understand what is happening. Come on, let's get you both on the sled and back to the cottage. I thought I heard wolves howling. Did they get close?"

"Way too close for comfort. I think you scared them off," Piper replied.

Piper did not know why she did not tell Pyry about the night wolf and what had happened between the night wolf, Jing, Beezle, and her. Something held her back. Instead she asked a question.

"Are wolves a problem here?" Piper asked, as she helped Beezle climb onto the sled, since he was a bit unsteady on his feet.

"No, actually it's very unusual to see them here in our valley. They pass through every once in a while, but rarely linger," replied Pyry, snapping the reins to get the horse moving.

When they arrived back at the cottage, Piper helped Pyry settle the horse and stow the sled. Then all of them entered the cottage, shedding their outdoor gear and settling Beezle by the fire.

"Has Ganna returned?" asked Pyry.

"No, lad," answered Poppa. "You didn't see her out there, any of you?" he asked, looking from one to the other.

Piper was reluctant to begin. She knew what she had to tell them was going to cause concern and possibly heartache. Before she could start, Pyry spoke up.

"Poppa, we found Beezle in the side valley. He was knocked out and buried under a snow pile. Our sled had been in that valley this day. Did you drive it there? Did you, Snezana?" Pyry asked his wife. When both of them answered in the negative, Pyry went on. "That's what I feared. The last thing Beezle remembers is being directed by Ganna to pull the tarp over the berries on the sled. He said he was hit on the back of his head and can't remember anything after that."

"I really don't want to add to your worries, Poppa, but do you remember when you and I were in the hut and Ganna came in?" Piper asked. "She asked me to come with her. Said she needed my help."

"Yah, I remember."

"She led me to your storage building and down to the very bottom. We went into one of the storage rooms, for she said she needed help

136

moving some barrels. Once I was in the room, she told me she was so forgetful, suggesting she had forgotten something. She stepped out the door, taking the lantern with her. Then she swung the door shut and dropped the wooden bar across it, locking me in the storage room in the dark. I discovered that she had earlier brought Jing down and left him in the room. She must have fed him something to knock him out, for I could find no physical harm had been done to him. Why would she lock Jing and me in a storage room?"

"Jealousy, I think," Poppa said sadly. "She is my second wife and always seems to have been jealous of my first wife, though they never met. Part of what just happened is my fault. When my first wife came with me to this valley, she brought with her two items that had been in her family for as long as she could remember. One was the ring I gave to you, Pyry. The second was what she kept in a golden pine spider silk pouch she wore around her neck. It contained an oddly shaped gold ring. She explained to me that the second ring was important to Sommerhjem. She didn't know why, only that it was. Said her family held it in trust. Said not to let anyone who came asking about it have it."

*So what the hermit in the southern mountains told me was true. The firestar gems are linked to a piece of the oppgave ringe,* Piper thought.

"My wife had asked me to guard both items well, if anything happened to her, and pass them down to whomever I thought would guard them well after me. Obviously, my son and I agreed Pyry was to be the keeper of the firestar gem ring. Something has held me back from passing on what the pouch holds."

"But Poppa, that doesn't explain Ganna's actions today or what her jealousy has to do with anything," commented Pyry.

"After your father left, I put the firestar gem ring away until you were a little older. When I got the firestar gem ring out from where I had put it for safekeeping to give to you, your Ganna saw me and questioned what I was doing. We talked about the two items. She suggested then that she would be happy to take care of the pouch and its contents. I know her feelings were hurt when I refused her offer. It just didn't feel right to hand over the pouch to her."

*Was that what all this was about today?* Piper wondered. *Was I locked in the storage room, and Beezle knocked out and left buried under the snow, so Ganna could get the ring? Had she succeeded?*

"Have you checked to see if she took the golden pine spider silk pouch with her?" asked Beezle, asking the question that was on everyone's mind.

"Sadly, she did indeed take the pouch and what you tell me might be a piece of the oppgave ringe. I am so sorry. I should have said something earlier."

Piper's heart sank, and she bowed her head. To have come so far and gone through so much, only to have what she sought ski out of the valley with Ganna.

"My first wife had warned me that the ring, what you say is a piece of the oppgave ringe, would cause physical harm to any who would try to touch it and should not possess it. When I once opened the pouch thinking to tip its contents out into my hand, something held me back, and I don't think it was just my first wife's warning. I passed that warning onto Ganna. Once, when she didn't know I had started to enter the room where the ring was hidden, I saw her start to tip the ring out of the pouch, hesitate, and then close the pouch up. She never did touch it. Now she has taken the pouch from its hiding place and left us," Poppa stated sadly. "She left me," he said softly, putting his head in his hands.

Several feelings went through Piper, sorrow for Poppa and anger toward Ganna.

After Poppa's pronouncements, all in the room sat in silence, all lost in their own thoughts. The only sounds were the crackle and snap of the fire in the hearth and the increasing howl of the wind. After several minutes, Poppa pulled himself together, raised his head, and spoke.

"I'm worried about Ganna in this storm," Poppa said. "I'm also worried as to what she intends to do with the piece of the oppgave ringe she has taken."

Piper had been mulling over the same questions but had taken it one step farther. "I can appreciate your worry about your Ganna. The snowstorm that has been hitting here off and on is certainly one I would not like to be out in."

"She was born in these mountains and left well-prepared for the storm. Ganna is a very skilled cross country skier. She knows the trails well. Also, two valleys over is the village of Mellomdaler. Once she reaches there, she will have shelter and a number of ways to leave the area. Come morning, I will head that direction. Trying to follow her this late in the day would not be a wise decision. Her ski tracks most certainly would be covered by the blowing and drifting snow by now."

"We need to head out now," Piper insisted. "She already has quite a head start. Besides being concerned for Ganna's wellbeing, I'm also concerned about who she might talk to concerning what is in the pouch she took, and what might happen once it is discovered she has a piece of the oppgave ringe. I know, Poppa, that you want to follow her and find her on the morrow, but that might be too late."

"If Ganna had just taken the pouch out of some misguided sense of jealousy and fled our home, I think I could forgive her. I can't condone what she did either to you, Piper, or to you, Beezle. Both of you could have died because of her rash actions. As hard as it is to think about, she needs to be found and brought to justice. I know her best and need to go after her. Unfortunately, it really is too late in the day to try to follow her now. Listen to that wind. The storm has picked up, and it is already dark," Poppa stated with conviction.

Silence once again fell over the room. How long it would have gone on was anyone's guess. Suddenly, Jing rose and stood at alert, facing the mudroom door. A short while later, the sound of someone stomping snow off boots could be heard from the mudroom.

"Who could that be coming here in a raging snowstorm?" Pyry asked, standing up and walking cautiously toward the door, followed closely behind by Beezle, who had grabbed a split log from the stack of firewood next to the fireplace.

"Wait, let's be smart about this," Beezle whispered to Pyry. "I'll take one side of the door, and you take the other."

Pyry nodded and did as Beezle had suggested. Beezle flattened himself against the wall in a position where he would be hidden from sight once the door swung into the room. The others remained quiet. Jing remained on alert. Slowly, the door swung open.

# Chapter Twenty-One

A snow-covered figure stumbled through the doorway and headed straight toward the fireplace. In the heat of the cottage, the snow and ice clinging to the figure's clothing began to fall off in clumps, leaving small wet pools of water where it lay melting.

When the figure flipped the hood back on her cloak, Piper realized, as did the others, that they were looking at Ganna, whose face was as white as the snow melting off her clothing.

"I can't go back out. You have to keep it away from me. I can't, I just can't, can't, can't …." mumbled Ganna over and over. "It's after me. It won't let me go."

"After what you have done this day, I should just throw you out in the snow and let it, whatever it is, have you. You just couldn't be satisfied with the life we had. These two could have been grievously harmed," Poppa said angrily, gesturing toward Piper and Beezle. "Whatever were you thinking?"

"Mercy, I beg you, mercy. You can't send me out to face that, that, that …." Ganna sputtered to silence.

"Poppa, none of us is happy with what Ganna did, but she is not going to tell us anything coherent with you towering over her and yelling. Let's get her out of her wet cloak and wrapped in a warm blanket by the fire. Maybe she'll stop shaking, and I'm sure we'll understand what she's saying better when her teeth stop chattering," Snezana suggested, as she tried to gently move Poppa away from Ganna.

Piper's attention was pulled away from the scene near the fireplace when she noticed Jing was pawing at the mudroom door. She was torn

140

between wanting to hear what Ganna had to say and Jing. Getting up, she crossed over to the mudroom door, but before she could open it, she heard Ganna screech.

"Don't open that door. It will get us all. I beg you, don't open that door," Ganna beseeched, sobbing.

Piper, who in most situations was very patient, moved swiftly over to Ganna. Trying to rein in her impatience, she knelt down and took both of Ganna's ice cold hands in her own hands. It was hard not to want to shake this woman who had locked her in a cold dark storage room, knocked Beezle over the head and left him buried in a snow pile, and taken what might be a piece of the oppgave ringe. Taking a deep breath, Piper addressed Ganna.

"You need to calm down and let us know what it is you fear," Piper stated. What she really wanted to ask was whether Ganna still had the golden pine spider silk pouch and its contents.

"I-i-it's huge and da-da-dark as midnight. A looming monster with ice for eyes and huge te-te-teeth. It wouldn't let me go t-t-to Mellomdaler. It blocked my way. Any direction I tried to go but back here, it blocked my way. What if it's still out there? We can't go out. You can't open that door."

"Ganna, did you take the pouch with the ring in it?" Piper asked.

"Ye-ye-yes."

"Do you still have it?"

"Yes," Ganna replied in a slightly steadier voice.

"Ah, Piper," said Beezle. "Jing is going to scratch through that door if you don't do something."

While Piper wanted to continue her conversation, she left Ganna and crossed over to the door, admonishing Jing to stop. Jing did not heed Piper's words and continued his frantic scratching at the door.

"I'll let him out and be right back," Piper said over her shoulder.

Piper closed the door behind her when she entered the mudroom and crossed over to the outside door to let Jing out, but he blocked her way. Reaching up with a paw, he knocked her cloak down. As Piper reached for it, Jing swatted her boots out from under the row of hanging cloaks. He then turned and began pawing at the outer door.

"Why yes, yer royalness, I'd be happy to go outside with you where a monster may be waiting. Your wish is my command."

Jing ceased his pawing of the door just long enough to look over his shoulder and give Piper a look that knocked any more sarcastic remarks right out of her.

Quickly pulling on her boots, throwing her cloak over her shoulders, and grabbing her hat and mittens, Piper opened the outer door and stepped outside. A light snow was still falling, but the clouds had parted, allowing bright moonlight to shine down. With the moonlight reflecting off the snow, it was almost as bright as day. A quiet stillness had settled over the valley. Everywhere Piper looked, the valley was covered with fresh snow and snowdrifts. She could see nothing threatening, and yet she found herself holding her breath. Jing stood quietly beside her.

Piper caught movement to her left when what had looked like a shadow under a towering pine tree stood and shook off a light dusting of snow. With great dignity, a night wolf approached Piper and Jing. He first bowed his head toward Jing, and then he turned his ice-blue eyes on Piper. Piper found she could not look away. Minutes passed. Finally, the night wolf nodded his head to Piper, nodded once more to Jing, turned, and walked away.

"Thank you," Piper called out after the retreating night wolf.

"Was that what I thought it was?" inquired Beezle, causing Piper to jump.

"Oh, Beezle, you scared me."

"I scared you? You stood mere feet from a huge night wolf and didn't flinch, and I scared you?" questioned Beezle.

"Let me rephrase, you surprised me, and while that was a night wolf, we are now old friends," Piper said. Though her voice held steady, she felt her knees shaking in a delayed reaction.

To postpone any further questions, and to get inside and find a place to sit down, Piper turned and headed toward the door. Beezle moved aside so she could enter the mudroom. He continued to look out the door for several long moments.

"Old friends?" Beezle asked.

"It's a long story and I will tell you all about it later, but right now I would like to get inside, get warm, and talk further with Ganna."

When Piper entered the cottage, she noticed Ganna was sitting comfortably by the fire, drinking a cup of steaming liquid. Piper found herself getting irate once again. She had to take several deep breaths to calm herself down.

"Did I miss anything?" Piper asked.

Ganna looked up and asked Piper if the horrible monster was still out there.

"Just a light snow and moonlight. No, no night comers out there now," replied Piper, giving the night wolf the name folks often call things that go bump in the night or hide under small children's beds or in wardrobes. Piper did not look at Beezle, hoping he would give nothing away.

"Ganna has given me back what she took. No, that's not right. She has returned the pouch, but she took more than that when she left. She took the trust I had in her, and I don't know what I'm going to do about that. One thing I do know is she will not be leaving this valley any time soon, even if I have to lock her in a storage room," stated Poppa, and there was both conviction and sadness in his voice.

"I'm glad the pouch with what we assume is a piece of the oppgave ringe inside has been returned," Piper said. "The question is, which one of you is willing to try to get it to the capital? It's important that it get there. Poppa, you seem to be the most logical one, since the pouch was placed in your care for safekeeping."

"No, no, I can't. I need to stay here and make sure Ganna stays put."

"Then what of you, Pyry?"

"I can't leave my wife and small son. I'm sorry, but a journey to the capital would take me away from home for too long. Poppa, were your instructions from Grand-mére to give the ring to Father or me specifically, or to pass it onto someone you felt should have it?"

"She said I should pass it onto someone I felt would guard it well. I guess I always assumed it would be a family member, but now …." Poppa paused and looked thoughtful.

"The firestar gems have brought these three here, Poppa," Pyry stated. "Maybe one of them is supposed to take the ring to the capital."

"A good suggestion, Pyry. I think you're right. The firestar gems are somehow connected to the ring. I don't think these three showed up here by chance. But which one should take it?" Poppa asked.

"Beezle should take it," Piper responded quickly, "if you are willing to let one of us take it."

"Why me?"

"Well, because … because you're, ah, because …."

"That certainly makes it clear. Would you all excuse us? I think Piper and I need to talk, compare notes, and try to figure out whether either of us is the right one to take the ring to the capital," Beezle stated.

"Why don't you folks head out to the cook hut and check on the fire? It may need to be stoked and have some wood added. I was cooking down the last of the berries, and with Ganna returning, it quite frankly skipped my mind. I hope this last batch is not ruined," Poppa said.

"We would be happy to do that," Piper told Poppa, as she headed to the door, followed closely by Beezle and Jing.

Once all three were in the cook hut and had stirred up and added wood to the fire, Beezle gave the syrup a stir and then turned to Piper.

"Maybe we should start with the fact that you and a night wolf are old friends."

"Old friends might be a bit of an exaggeration. When we found you buried under the snow pile, you were very still and very cold to the touch. Pyry left to get the sled so we could get you back to the cottage. While he was gone, wolves began to howl, and soon four of them had us surrounded."

"You should have left me, tried to get away."

"Is that what you would have done?"

"Well, no …."

"As I was saying, four wolves surrounded us, and just as they were slinking closer, a night wolf came leaping over the snow. The other wolves scattered. Jing went out toward the night wolf …."

"So, Jing saved us from a night wolf? He's some protector. You told me about how he fought a grevling."

"Yes, well actually, Jing greeted the night wolf and led him back to us. I don't know how to describe what happened next, but Jing, the night wolf, and I placed our hands, or paws as the case may be, on you, and the firestar gems glowed and warmed. I felt like the night wolf was drawing warmth from Jing and me, or the firestar gems, or all three. Soon you were stirring, and your color began to return. At that point, the night wolf left."

"Do you think it was the same night wolf who herded Ganna back to the cottage?"

"Yes."

"Amazing. Next question. So, why do you think I should be the one to take the piece of the oppgave ringe to the capital?" asked Beezle.

"I guess because your uncle sits on the interim ruling council, and, well …."

"Actually, I think it is my aunt who is sitting on the council at the moment, but that is neither here nor there. Near as I can tell, being on the interim ruling council, or whether you are a large land holder or not, has nothing to do with whether or not you can handle one of the pieces of the oppgave ringe." When Piper looked to interrupt, Beezle went on. "Look who has brought in the previous six rings. A rover brought two. Then a street boy and a messenger bird merchant brought the next two. A seeker and a librarian brought in the last two. Besides, I don't think we get to pick. From all that I have heard about the pieces of the oppgave ringe, the rings pick the folk and not the other way around. I appreciate that that might sound a bit like an old granny's tale."

"So, are you suggesting we should let the ring pick one of us?"

"Pretty much."

"You do realize then that the ring could pick Pyry, Snezana, Poppa, or even Ganna. It would not necessarily pick either you or me."

"There is much truth in what you suggest. If it picks one of the others, then our job will be to try to convince that folk to get the ring to the capital and to assist in that endeavor."

"We had best get back to the cottage then," Piper stated, as she put several more logs on the fire.

Once back at the cottage, Piper and Beezle told the others what they had discussed about the piece of the oppgave ringe.

"Let's form a half circle around the fireplace. After that, Poppa, you could tip the contents of the golden pine spider silk pouch out onto the hearth. We should probably make sure this really is a piece of the oppgave ringe," Beezle suggested. "If it is, then one by one, we could each make a decision as to whether or not we want to try to pick it up. I must remind you that according to what I have heard, we do so at our own peril."

Poppa did as Beezle had suggested, but what happened next, no one could have imagined.

# Chapter Twenty-Two

Poppa had no sooner tipped the ring out of the pouch when several things happened simultaneously. All four firestar gems began to warm and glow. Then three arcs of light shot out, all aimed at the fourth gem, the one on the bracelet Piper wore.

"I don't know about the rest of you, but I might take what happened as a sign," said Beezle, looking at Piper, who had a stunned look on her face.

"Sign?" Piper questioned.

"Since the beginning, when you were given the bracelet with the firestar gem, you have been drawn from one firestar gem to the next, all once part of a whole. That journey has led you here. I find it interesting that the very moment what looks to be a piece of the oppgave ringe was placed on the hearth, three of the firestar gems reacted, all pointing to you."

"But that doesn't, I mean, it wouldn't necessarily ...." Piper protested.

"First, you seem to think Poppa should be the one to take the ring to the capital. Then, you suggested I should be the one. Three arcs of light pointing to you seem to be a pretty strong indication that you are the one to take the ring. At least, that is my guess as to why the firestar gems reacted the way they did when Poppa tipped the ring out onto the hearth. Why are you so reluctant to think it might be you?" Beezle asked.

Piper sat down abruptly. She wondered why she had thought someone else, anyone else besides her, should take the ring to the capital. She had been so focused on finding information on where to find pieces of the oppgave ringe, and then finding the piece that was connected to the firestar gems, that it had never really occurred to her that she might actually be the folk who would take the ring to the capital. And was that what the arcs of light from the firestar gems were really indicating? Maybe there was some other explanation.

"Piper, are you all right?" Poppa asked gently. "Did the light hurt you?"

"I'm fine, thank you. Just a bit surprised," Piper replied.

While others were focused on Piper, Ganna began to inch forward toward the hearth. Jing moved between her and the hearth, a low menacing growl coming from his throat.

"It would seem that Jing agrees with me, Piper," suggested Beezle. "Somehow I don't think he is going to let anyone even close to the hearth, except you."

"Maybe he is just protecting the ring from Ganna," said Piper. She did not say it in a very convincing tone.

Pyry then made a slow move, as if he were going to approach the hearth, and Jing blocked his way, too.

"I think Beezle has the right of it, lass," Poppa concluded. "The pouch and its contents were given into my safekeeping. I have done what I was asked to do. I feel no driving need to either pick up the ring or deliver it to the capital. Do any of the rest of you?"

"You foolish old man. You, who have wealth from the sale of the terte isen berry syrup, are content to stay in this valley, only spending coin for equipment or fencing. You could drape us in fine garments, or build a fine house, or buy us a fine carriage so we could travel in style. We could take that ring, and demand a high price from the highest bidder, and live in grand style for the rest of our lives. I expected much more than this living way beyond the beyond in a humble cottage when I married you, the wealthy syrup merchant," spat out Ganna bitterly. "So typical of you, to be willing to just give the ring away."

"I was always honest with you, when I was courting you, about my life here in the valley and what cost it takes to produce the syrup. You also know that what coin we have put away has always been so we would not starve or lose our land due to bad fortune such as drought, fall frost coming too early or too late, or any of the other natural disasters that can cause the crop to fail. It was a good thing too, since, without the coin we had put away, we would have lost our land to taxes and special license fees under the former regent."

Ganna sat with her arms folded, a frown on her unhappy face, as Poppa went on.

"I have put coin away to save for a rainy day, or days without rain, as the case may be," Poppa said. "When it comes to the ring, a folk is only as good as his or her word, and I gave my word to my first wife that I would keep the ring safe. Putting it up for grabs to the highest bidder is not going to keep it safe."

"And you think giving it to this lass here is going to do that?" Ganna asked bitterly.

"For reasons I cannot explain, yes, I think Piper will do her very best at keeping the ring safe, and that she has boon companions to help her," Poppa answered. "Lass, I think it's about time you go pick up the ring and relieve Jing of guard duty."

It was with some trepidation that Piper walked past Jing to the hearth. Even though the pull to go and pick up the ring had been getting stronger and stronger as Poppa talked, Piper was still reluctant to bend down and pick it up. She stood for a long moment staring at it. Being swatted across her backside by a mountain cat's paw brought her back from wherever she had gone in her thoughts.

"Well, that was rude, Jing," Piper admonished. "I'm getting to it now."

Piper reached down and picked up the ring. It certainly was not a ring of great beauty, a misshapen gold ring with deep scratches on its surface. She did not know what she expected to happen, yet she was surprised when the ring was only slightly warm. She had expected the ring to be hot, having sat for many moments right near the fire. What also surprised her was the feeling of peace and calm that came over her the moment she picked up the ring. She felt a rightness at having it in her hand. *So much fuss over such a small object*, Piper thought.

Piper reached back down and picked up the pouch of golden pine spider silk, opened it, and put the ring inside. She then placed the cord of the pouch over her head and tucked the pouch under her shirt. Turning back, she spoke to those gathered.

"I thank you for your trust in me. I'll do my very best to get this ring to the capital and place it where it belongs. Poppa, you have done Sommerhjem a great service by keeping this piece of the oppgave ringe secure."

The group broke up a short while later, for it had been a very long and trying day for all of them. Piper and Beezle wanted to leave early the next day. They took time to talk over their route. Going back the way they had come seemed risky. While they knew they needed to head back to the forester village where they had left their horses and some of Beezle's gear, they determined it would be easier to go to Mellomdaler on a better and easier lane, and then head back along the base of the foothills to the forester village.

Piper thought she might have trouble sleeping, for she was aware of the importance of the object she now carried and thought that it would weigh heavily on her. Surprisingly, she felt lighter than she had in a long time. That lightness quickly faded when she came from her sleeping quarters to breakfast.

"We are so sorry, Piper," Snezana said. "We thought Ganna was settled in and was resigned to her fate. We thought she would be contained in the back bedroom, but somehow she slipped out. Poppa and Pyry have gone after her, but she has several hours head start. Another storm is heading this way also, so I don't know how long they will be able to stay after her. They promised me they would turn back if the snow started coming down heavily, or the wind began to pick up. They know they cannot risk being out there in a winter storm. I need them to be safe and home. Beezle is out in the barn, preparing your horses to ride."

"It's not your fault that Ganna left, so there is no need for you to apologize. All folks make their own choices. We cannot prevent them from making them, nor can we be responsible for the choices they make. Which way did she head?" Piper asked gently.

"She headed out of the valley toward Mellomdaler once again. She has family there. If she makes it that far, they will hide her. Poppa and Pyry will not be able to find her then."

"That's worrisome news, especially considering she is none too happy with not getting the ring."

"She's also none too happy with not being able to get her hands on our savings either. Poppa moved it from where he usually keeps it. He is feeling much betrayed at the moment and very sad."

"I can only imagine. This does complicate things quite a bit, however. We had intended to leave here and ride toward Mellomdaler and beyond, but that now would seem to be a risky route. Going back the way we came is not going to be easy."

"Sadly, you are right on both counts," Snezana said. "The way you came into the valley is never easy, and very treacherous this time of year, especially with a storm brewing. While you might run into Pyry and Poppa on your way out of the valley heading toward Mellomdaler, who knows who else you might run into? I'm also worried that whatever chased Ganna back here is still out there and might harm you or the others."

"I think I can put your mind at ease about Ganna's 'monster.' It was a night wolf. Jing and the night wolf, ah, met, and the night wolf left. Well, I'm not sure how to explain it, but I don't think the night wolf has any interest anymore in any of your family," Piper said.

Piper did not know why she did not elaborate and tell Snezana about what the night wolf had done concerning Beezle, or that she suspected the night wolf had herded Ganna back because she had stolen the piece of the oppgave ringe. *The less known about what happened in this valley over the last few days the better*, she thought. *The tales Ganna would tell would be bad enough should Pyry and Poppa not catch up with her. Better there was a monster lurking than have the villagers hunting for one of the rare night wolves.*

"I know you might think I'm spinning a yarn about the night wolf. I truly believe I saw one, and I truly believe it will not harm you or yours. I also think it would be wise not to mention this to anyone else for fear that others might try to hunt the night wolf down."

"With all else that has happened since you folks arrived in our valley, I'm inclined to believe you. I'll do as you ask and not mention the night wolf," Snezana replied.

Further conversation was cut off when Beezle entered the cottage. After a brief discussion, it was decided that leaving the valley the way they had come was the best course of action. Piper and Beezle bid farewell to Snezana and thanked her for her help. They asked that she thank the men when they returned.

"Stay safe, Snezana. If anyone comes to the valley asking about us, if they threaten you, tell them the direction we have headed. We don't want anyone in your family harmed on our behalf," Beezle said.

"But what of you?" Snezana asked.

"We will do our best to stay out of harm's way."

"Wait, before you go, Pyry and Poppa talked it over and thought you folks should take the ring with the firestar gem with you. Both felt its time with our family is ended. Neither could explain, but felt it best, especially in light of Ganna leaving again."

"I think you should take it, Beezle. That way each of us are carrying one piece of what has been kept safe in this valley. I realize that while that might not make any sense, it does feel right."

"All right. Snezana, please thank Poppa and Pyry for us. We had best leave," said Beezle.

Travel across the valley was difficult, for the path they followed was drifted over in places. Once they started up the mountain path, however, it was easier, for the dense pine trees blocked the wind, and drifts were at a minimum. When they reached the narrow cliff-side trail, the path was clear of snow, having been scoured by the wind. Fortunately, the wind was light this day, as was the falling snow. Nightfall found them down out of the foothills and settled in a sheltered area next to a blazing campfire.

"I figure we have a day to a day and a half head start at the most, if Ganna got to Mellomdaler and alerted anyone who might have an interest in us," Beezle suggested.

"I'm worried that this way might also hold trouble. While the foresters were willing to cover our back trail and would have watched out for strangers, that doesn't mean those who might have been looking for either of us, or the two of us together, aren't still waiting where we are heading."

"We will certainly need to be extra vigilant. We had best add some more wood to the fire and try to get some rest this night. Do you want to take first watch?"

"Jing and I will take first watch. While you are settling in, I'll gather more wood."

Piper was actually grateful that she had first watch. It gave her time to think over all that had happened in recent days and try to sort out how she felt about it all. Wrapped in her warm woolen cloak, her back to a tall rock, her feet to the fire, and Jing snuggled up against her, she was warm enough. She had never expected to be the carrier of one of the pieces of the oppgave ringe. She did not quite know how she felt about it. She thought she should feel honored, but mostly she just felt confused. Shaking off her thoughts, Piper began to think about the best way to get the ring to the capital. On the morrow or the next day, they would arrive at the forester village and that should be safe enough. From there, they could plan what to do next.

# CHAPTER TWENTY-THREE

Piper was relieved to be out of the snowy mountains and back into the lower, forested foothills. For once, the sky was a crystal clear blue, and the sun was shining brightly. She could almost forget the harrowing trip they had taken along the windswept mountain path, hoping it would not rain before they reached the shelter of the trees. Just thinking of that journey now caused Piper to shiver.

They had arrived late in the day at the forester village. The news they received upon arrival was not good news. After they had left, the foresters had several inquiries as to whether any traveling musicians had passed through the forest.

"It would probably be best if you do not go back the way you came into our forest from the south. It is obvious that you should not go the mountain route either. Heavy snow this early is unusual, but certainly not unheard of," the head forester stated. "Bradwr, here, has offered to escort you on a safer way out of the forest. If anyone is still looking for you, they're probably thinking you will be farther north or else will come out where you entered our forest. The way Bradwr will take you will have you traveling south, but farther down than where you originally came into our forest. You will be traveling through quite dense woods, which will slow you down if you are in a hurry. Hopefully, the path will bring you out in a place where folks won't expect you. You will want to leave early on the morrow, I expect."

It was on the evening of the fifth day of travel, while Bradwr was off gathering more firewood, that Piper drew Beezle aside. "Do you feel we have been traveling in circles?"

"The trees are so dense. It's hard at times to get a feel for what direction we are traveling," replied Beezle.

"I am sure we have been by this outcrop we're camped next to before. What do you think?" Piper asked Beezle.

"Now that you mention it, that rocky ledge over there to your left does look familiar, but then when you look at trees and rock formations for days, it all blends together. I must admit the sameness of the dense trees, and the monotony of following your horse, has had me drifting off from time to time, so I have not paid much attention. I am sorry. I seem to have let my guard down, and I should not have."

"Another thing, does Bradwr seem kind of jumpy to you? Most foresters I have ever met are always alert and cautious, which I think would be natural, considering they live in the wilderness. Bradwr's jumpiness seems more than that."

"Shush, I hear Bradwr coming back. We will both be more watchful on the morrow," said Beezle in a whisper.

The next day was more of the same. They rode on a narrow path that wound through the dense trees. It was midday when they finally left the dense forest and forded a fairly wide shallow river.

"Had a fire here a number of years back, which the river fortunately stopped. Mostly new growth from here on out. We should reach a fire lane in about an hour, and suppertime should bring us to a young quirrelit grove. We can camp there for the night," Bradwr told Piper and Beezle.

Bradwr, Beezle, Jing, and Piper had just come in sight of the quirrelit grove when six horses and riders came charging out of the surrounding woods from behind.

"Piper, go, flee!" Beezle shouted as he whirled his horse around to face the oncoming riders.

Piper did not hesitate to follow Beezle's directions, but did so with a heavy heart. While she knew that what she carried in the golden pine spider silk pouch hanging around her neck was important to the future of Sommerhjem and worth any sacrifice, she was loath to leave Beezle behind. She was also not all that sure she would be able to outride any who would follow her. While her horse had been great for her disguise as a traveling musician, he was neither a young horse nor the swiftest. That did not stop him from taking off at a gallop.

Piper glanced quickly over her shoulder and saw four of the riders had surrounded Beezle and Bradwr. Two riders had broken off and were chasing her. Looking ahead, she saw that Jing was racing toward the quirrelit grove. Though it was a young grove, the tree trunks were large and unevenly spaced. Piper zigzagged between and around the trunks. She could feel her horse begin to strain with the continued effort. The riders behind her were swiftly closing the gap.

Dodging left around a huge tree trunk, Piper's horse stumbled, throwing her out of her saddle. She rolled as she had been taught to escape injury. Scrambling to her feet, she was hit in the face by a knotted rope. With few other options available, and out of sheer desperation, not even questioning where the rope had come from, Piper grabbed it and swiftly climbed up into the dense foliage of the quirrelit tree, pulling the rope up behind her. She hoped her horse was all right. She did not have time to worry about him now, for she could hear the riders chasing her, yelling to each other below. In addition, she could hear something moving in the quirrelit tree above her.

Piper hoped she could not be seen from below. She really wanted to climb higher before the men who were trying to find her rode beneath the quirrelit tree in which she was hiding. The rustling sound from above made her hesitate. Looking up, trying to see what was above her, she saw Jing peering down at her.

"I don't even want to know how you got up here before me," Piper whispered to Jing, as she joined him on an upper branch. "I'm just glad you are safe."

The two men who had been chasing her rode past where she and Jing were hidden several times. On their last pass beneath her, she heard them discuss going back and joining the others. While she was glad they did not have her horse in tow, she also worried she might not be able to recover him. Being on foot would be a definite disadvantage. Just when she was feeling a little safer, however, she heard the sound of riders approaching.

Taking a chance on parting a few leaves so she could get a better view of those beneath her, Piper was relieved to see that Beezle was none the worse for wear. Tied up, but intact. The party stopped below where Piper was hidden, so she could hear their conversation.

"You're sure her horse ran off without her?"

"Yes, sir. When we's rounded this tree, we's could see her horse, but it was carryin' no rider. We's searched all around here, but couldn't find nary a trace o' her. It's sort o' creepy. No footprints, no sign she ever touched the forest floor. Asin' you can see, there's no ways she could o' reached any o' the branches on these trees even if'n she was standin' on her horse. I can't explain where's she's gone."

"Regretful that we could not capture them both. It's also too bad that forester fellow gave us the slip when we were rounding up Beecroft and chasing after the lass. Our Lord will be pleased that we have the Beecroft fellow, however. Most pleased. Let's get out of this quirrelit grove. Never did like them. We'll travel for about another hour and then set up camp."

Piper waited until she could no longer hear the riders who had captured Beezle before she shifted. She was just about to climb lower when she felt a slight brush of fur on her right cheek. She looked to the right, thinking it was Jing. It was not. She could see he had moved farther out on the branch and was on alert. Even his tail was not close enough to touch her.

Piper was distracted from her thoughts when she saw Jing slip down to a lower branch. It was then that she heard what had alerted him. She too could now hear the sound of someone moving slowly through the quirrelit grove on horseback.

"Piper, are you here? It's me, Bradwr. I got away."

Several things happened at once. Jing settled in on the lower branch, still alert, but not moving farther down. A soft brush on her cheek happened again, the firestar gem in the bracelet began to warm, and Piper felt a wave of warning wash over her. Carefully, she looked around, but could still not spot anything in the quirrelit tree with her besides Jing.

Bradwr called out again, as he moved on past Piper and Jing. Piper remained frozen in place, heeding the warning. She had been feeling a bit mistrustful of Bradwr for several days. She could not put her finger on just what it was about him that bothered her. That feeling that he was leading them in circles had persisted. *Had he been stalling them?* she wondered. *Had he been working with the men who captured Beezle?*

"Come on, lass. If you are here, I can help you," Bradwr called out.

Piper remained silent. Long moments passed. Several times Bradwr had ridden past the quirrelit tree where she sat hidden. On his last ride through the grove, he stopped just under the branch Jing was lying on. Piper could only hope Jing remained where he was. She froze where she sat. Bradwr continued sitting on his horse, and Piper could feel an air of expectation about him, as if he were waiting for something or someone. *Did he really expect me to just show up? Well, perhaps he did*, she thought, *for he does not realize I do not trust him.*

Piper did not know how much longer she was going to be able to sit frozen in place, especially since her nose had begun to itch. She did not dare move her hand up to scratch the itch, and it was beginning to drive her just a little crazy. Glancing down to where Jing lay, she noticed his ears had perked up, as if he were listening intently. Moments later she heard the sounds of a single horse approaching. Piper wondered if it was her horse wandering through the quirrelit grove. She had mixed feelings about the idea that the horse she now heard quite clearly might be her horse. *It would be good to have my horse close,* she thought, *but not so good if Bradwr caught him.* When a horse drew up next to Bradwr, Piper was surprised to see it was ridden by one of the men who had been chasing her.

"Any sign of the lass?" the newcomer asked.

"No, I haven't seen a thing move since you folks were here. It has been almost eerily silent. Not even a bird singing, nor any rustling in the grass or leaves. Like I said, it's been very eerie," Bradwr said. "Quirrelit groves are normally quite peaceful and welcoming. This one is no longer that."

"You foresters are an odd lot, thinking trees and whole forests feel one way or the other."

"It matters not what you believe. Trust me when I tell you this grove no longer welcomes us. It's time to leave. Tell Lord Klingflug I have done as he has asked and feel I have paid my debt. I just want to head back home."

"The lass could be anywhere by now. She's on foot, so it will take her some time to get to anyone and report Beecroft has been taken. By then, we will have him locked up tight in the Raven's tower with none the wiser. I'll roam around these woods for the next hour or so, and then camp here for the night. I have another errand to do several days' ride from here, so I will leave in the morning. Wouldn't mind company. But you go on, if the woods are scaring the big brave forester," the man said with a sneer in his voice.

"I'm not afraid of the woods. I just said they were unusually quiet and that is not the only strange thing going on. I followed that lass's horse's hoof prints and they lead through the quirrelit grove, but then just disappear," Bradwr told the man.

"That's just not possible."

"Come see for yourself."

After the two men who were hunting her rode off, Piper moved her stiff limbs and finally was able to scratch her nose. Jing leapt up and settled in beside her.

"Doesn't look like we'll be going anywhere soon, Jing. It's going to be a very long night, so we had best get comfortable. If you need to hunt and find food for yourself, go on ahead. Be careful though. I wish I had the ability to move along tree branches and glide quietly through the woods like you do. I don't think I should leave the shelter of this tree until our searchers out there are gone in the morning."

Jing took her word for it and departed. Piper moved several branches higher in the quirrelit tree and settled in on a gently curved branch that allowed her to stretch out. It was not long before the events of the day caught up with her and she dozed off. She awoke a while later to see Jing resting at her feet. Just as she was about to stretch to get the kinks out, she looked down and saw several quirrelit leaves were lying on her lap. Even more astonishing were the mounds of nuts and berries placed on each leaf.

"Ah, Jing, have you added gathering nuts and berries to your hunting talents?"

Jing just looked up at the sound of Piper's voice and then went back to washing his paw.

159

When Piper's stomach rumbled, she decided not to question where the food had come from. Though not a great feast, it certainly tasted like one. Night fell quickly and Piper dozed off and on. When dawn arrived, she was more than ready to stand on firm ground, but caution prevailed. It was midmorning before Piper and Jing started climbing down out of the quirrelit tree. Their progress came to an abrupt halt when Piper heard the sounds of a single horse approaching.

# CHAPTER TWENTY-FOUR

*When I fell off my horse, I must have hit my head, or been dreaming, or something,* thought Piper. *First, a knotted rope appears for me to climb, just when I needed to hide from the men chasing me. Then, I awaken and find food neatly laid out on two quirrelit leaves, when I have no food nor am I able to go gather food. Now this. My horse, who ran off yesterday, is quietly standing below me, calmly eating grass.*

Piper pinched herself to see if she were dreaming. She discovered to her discomfort she was not. When she climbed down out of the quirrelit tree, she saw that not only had her horse returned, but he did not look any worse for wear. His saddle was clean of road dust and forest debris. *He looks the same as always,* she thought, and then did a double take. *Well, except for the flowers braided into a strand of his mane. Just where had he been overnight?*

Piper shook off her questioning thoughts, for she had more pressing concerns now that she could leave the quirrelit grove. Before Beezle and she had reached the forester village, they had discussed how they might get the piece of the oppgave ringe to the capital, and what they should do if they were to become separated, or if one or both of them were to be captured. Of course, at the time, when they were discussing "what-ifs," both of them hoped they would never need to use any of their plans.

Beezle had insisted that if they were separated, no matter what the circumstances, Piper's first and only duty was to get what she carried in the pouch around her neck to the capital. *It is one thing to talk about what you think will be the right thing to do, and quite another when you actually have to make a choice,* Piper concluded. *Now I am torn. Beezle is most certainly in very deep trouble. He has become a friend since we played flute together at the Stein Hage estate all those weeks ago. How can I just abandon him to his fate? I should try to help him. Friends look out for friends.*

In trying to rescue him, however, Piper would certainly put herself in harm's way. She too could become captured, and that would put the piece of the oppgave ringe in the wrong hands. Putting herself in harm's way was one thing, but losing the ring to the wrong sort would have disastrous consequences for all of Sommerhjem.

Beezle had gently suggested that neither one of them would want to go down in history as the one who caused the challenge not to be completed. When they had been debating whether Piper should head to the capital or try to find or rescue Beezle should they become separated, Beezle had said, "Think about it. Do you want to be the one who gave the former regent or others any chance to stop the Gylden Sirklene challenge from happening? You and I and others have spent months and risked our lives to make sure the pieces of the oppgave ringe are found and returned to the capital. Is either one of us any more important than that? One or the other or both of us need to get what you carry to the capital and safely placed in the vessteboks in the Well of Speaking. If anything happens to me, you have to get to the capital as fast as you can."

Those words had made sense to Piper when Beezle and she had been discussing them. Now that she found herself in circumstances where she really had to choose, the choice was so much harder than she had thought it would be. It was with great reluctance that she turned her horse onto a path that led in the direction of the capital and not in the direction the men had taken Beezle. Jing, sensing Piper's mood, stayed close.

As the hours passed, Piper tried to take stock and sort out how she was going to get to the capital safely. Other than her blanket roll tied to the back of her saddle and some meager supplies in her saddle bags, she had very little with her. Most of their supplies and equipment had been on Beezle's pack horse, which had been captured along with him. Piper still had her mountain flute and, normally, could at least earn a meal and a place to stay for the night. That did not seem like a safe option now, however, for the word might have gone out to be on the lookout for a traveling musician lass of her description.

Another option might be to find a royal guard station, appeal to its commander to give her an escort to the capital, and ask to have a patrol or two sent to rescue Beezle. A good idea as far as it went. It was difficult not to choose that option, but Piper was wary. It was hard to know just who she could trust during these difficult times. Just as she was trying to decide what would be best, Piper chanced upon a crossroad sign. She had thought she knew where she was, but had not been totally sure if she really did know, or if her idea was only wishful thinking. The sign at the crossroads confirmed she had been right. Now, however, she really was at a crossroads in more ways than one. From where she had halted, she could head south to her foster brother Elek's estate, or she could head west toward the capital.

"What do you think, Jing? South or west?"

Jing sat, yawned a huge yawn, and looked up at Piper.

"No opinion then? Leaving it up to me, are you? If I head west, which may be the most expedient thing to do, we will get to the capital if all goes well, maybe, assuming we can find food and shelter. If I head south, I think I will be able to find help for us, and perhaps Beezle, but it will delay my arrival at the capital and may put us more at risk. I also don't know if either Lady Celik or Elek are at home. There should be someone I know on the estate who would help. At least, I think so. Listen to me, Jing, I'm trying to talk myself into heading south instead of west. It could be the best solution. We can get help and supplies for us, and maybe help for Beezle. I'm really worried about Beezle. Still no opinion, huh?"

Piper sat at the crossroads arguing with herself, going over and over the consequences of each choice. She was exhausted, having spent the night in a quirrelit tree getting very little sleep. Her emotions were in turmoil. She was pulled this way and that between wanting to do what was best for Sommerhjem and loyalty to her friend. In the end, having weighed all the possibilities, she turned her horse south. She had concluded she need not carry her burdens alone.

Once Piper determined which direction she wanted to go, she pushed on past all of their limits, and then some. Seeker Eshana had been right when he had told her that her horse would not win any races but could travel for miles on end. At times, however, she worried her horse had more heart than stamina. Each day, Piper had them on the road in the earliest light of dawn and did not stop until well past dark, when they were all staggering with exhaustion.

While Jing and her horse had been able to find food, Piper knew she could not travel much farther on the meager amount she had been able to forage. She was not yet ready to eat raw rodent or grass, but knew she would need more food soon. She hoped she would not have to sneak up on anyone any time soon, for her growling stomach would give her away. Already she had to put another hole in her belt to tighten it to fit.

Day passed into night. Piper was barely holding herself erect in the saddle when her horse stopped. It took Piper several moments to pull herself out of the stupor she had fallen into and realize she was no longer moving. Looking up she saw a stone arch spanning the side lane she had instinctively turned onto. Carved into the pillars on each side of the arch were beautiful trees, their limbs reaching out to form the arch. Seeing the stone arch, Piper realized they had finally reached Cliffmoor Manor, home of Lady Celik and her son. She was relieved to see the gate was open.

As Piper traveled down the lane leading up to the manor, she thought about her approach. She could go to the back door and hope to talk with one of the servants, or she could boldly approach the front door and announce herself. Stating her name and rank might get more attention at the front door, so she headed there. Rapping smartly on the door knocker, Piper waited patiently with Jing. She was sure, knowing a little about Lady Celik, that her approach and presence at the front door of the manor had been duly noted and reported within, probably the minute she passed through the gates.

Piper did not know what type of reception she was going to get by boldly going to the front door, looking as she did. She knew she looked a mess. Her clothes were more than worse for wear, her hair was windblown and tangled, and she was standing there with a mountain cat at her side. Piper heard footsteps approaching and began to prepare herself. The door swung open and before Piper could announce herself as Piper of the clan

Wynda, guardians of the southern pass, she was lifted off her feet and pulled inside the hall. She held onto enough of her wits to tell Jing not to attack.

"Piper, lass, you are a sight for, well, you are a sight," exclaimed Elek.

"Thanks ever so much. Now put me down, you brute, before I tell Jing to have you for a snack."

It was then that Elek took a good look. He very carefully set Piper on her feet and backed away several steps, hands out. "Jing is it? I mean Piper no harm," Elek stated. "I can hardly wait to hear where you have been since I last saw you in Farlig Brygge."

"I'll be happy to catch you up. It's important, however, that you get me out of this hall and to a quiet place so others don't know I'm here. Also, I have left a horse tied up outside. Is your mother at home?"

"Follow me. And yes, Mother is here in residence."

Elek swiftly turned into the first door on the right of the entrance, which was the library. Heading directly to a wall of bookcases, he caused one of the bookcases to swing open.

"In here, and quickly. I will get one of our trusted servants to take care of your horse and alert mother you are here. It will take a little while for us to get back to you. We have guests, and not ones either Mother or I are very fond of or trusting of, if you get my meaning. I was on my way to the library to retrieve a book when I heard your knock. I need to get back to them, for I have been gone too long. Thankfully, they are in a room that does not have a view of the front of the manor. They should not be aware that you arrived."

Piper and Jing did as asked and moved through the opening as quickly as their legs would carry them. Once the bookcase swung closed behind them, Piper was relieved that there was light from an upper window. The room they were hiding in was a small one.

"Ah, look, Jing, all the comforts of home," Piper whispered. "A soft chair, a braided rug, and a chamber pot. How grand. Well, at least the chair is not moving and looks more comfortable than my saddle. You must be exhausted, and your paws must be sore. I'm sorry I pushed us all so hard."

When Piper eased herself down onto the chair, Jing walked over to the rug and flopped himself down with a sigh. In minutes, both were asleep, even though Piper had tried to stay awake. The long ride and the events of the last week had taken their toll. A short while later, Piper was roused from her light doze by the sound of Jing's soft growl.

"Hush now, Jing," Piper whispered, moving quietly closer to the back of the bookcase. As she listened intently, she could hear two folks talking. *They must be standing just on the other side of where I am*, Piper thought.

"What have you found out? Tell me quickly, before our host and hostess return," one of the voices asked. It sounded like a man's voice to Piper.

"Not very much, I am afraid." This voice sounded female. "Lady Celik is never very forthcoming about anything, nor are the cooks or the maids. Are you sure she is the one who has this vast band of informants and loyal coteries spread across the land?"

"Yes, yes, we are sure," the man said impatiently in a lowered voice. "You have been here for a fortnight now, and yet you have observed nothing? No comings and goings at strange hours, no unexpected house guests?"

"No, it has been almost too tranquil for my tastes. Lady Celik certainly runs the estate. She spends part of her day overseeing all aspects of it. She has been available each afternoon to share a long tea with me. Her son has been here this last week, and he has spent time with me, taking me riding about the estate …."

"Did you see him receiving or exchanging information with anyone on your rides?"

"No, Father. He would stop and talk to the crofters and others on the estate, but always about estate matters. I am sorry, but what you sent me here to find either is not happening here or is very well concealed." The daughter's voice now sounded distraught to Piper.

"I know you tried. Lord Klingflug is not going to be pleased, but that is hardly your fault. If we could just get our hands on one of Lady Celik's informants or infiltrate her group, we could gain valuable information. We will have to try … Ah, Lady Celik, what a delightful library you have here. I was just commenting to my daughter about what a lovely collection of books you have concerning the history of the region. I see some of your predecessors were prolific writers. Are you continuing the tradition?"

Piper did not hear the answer, for the two who had been speaking moved away from where she stood. For a while, she could hear the murmurs of conversation, but the folks speaking were soon too far away. Soon even the murmurs stopped, and she moved back and settled into her chair. Once again exhaustion overcame her, and she sank into a deep sleep. She did not hear Jing's soft warning growl when the bookcase silently began to swing open.

# CHAPTER TWENTY-FIVE

"It's just me, Jing. I will not harm Piper. She is my friend, too. Hey, foster sister, could you have your guard mountain cat stand down?" Elek requested.

"Ah, hum-m-m, what?" Piper mumbled, trying to shake off the sleepiness that threatened to pull her back into slumber. She was slightly embarrassed and mad at herself for allowing anyone to catch her with her guard completely down. Shaking herself, she focused in on Elek. "Quick, close the door."

Elek raised an inquiring eyebrow but did as asked, stepping in and closing the bookcase behind him. "Is there a problem?"

"Earlier I heard two folks talking, a man and his daughter I think. They are definitely not on the side of the Crown. The female has been here for several weeks. The male might be newly arrived."

"Ah, yes, them," Elek said. "Mother has taken them on a ride to the village. If you will follow me, we will get you settled in. By the time they return, you will have just arrived, so to speak. Mother has put a travel pack in your room containing what you probably would carry with you on the road. She hopes she got your size right."

"And why am I visiting?" Piper asked.

"Do you even need an excuse to visit your foster brother?"

"No, but then how would I know you were here and not gallivanting about the countryside on behalf of your mother or the Crown?"

"Very good question. How about you just happened to be in the neighborhood and dropped in?"

"That would be about as good as me visiting you unexpectedly," Piper replied.

"Let us think on it while you get a hot bath and a change of clothes. The clothes mother put in your pack are befitting your station. Do you have any sentimental attachment to the clothes you are wearing? From the looks of them, they would be best suited for the rag bag. No offense."

"None taken. A bath sounds lovely, so lead on, foster brother. A bit of a nosh for Jing and I would not be turned down either, or is dinner soon?" Piper asked. Her grumbling stomach echoed the question.

"Dinner will be fashionably late, although I think it is a strange fashion to wait until you and your guest are beyond hungry to sit down to the evening meal. Mother had something sent up when she had the hot water taken up for the tub. You had best hurry before the bath water gets cold. I will stop by your rooms in about an hour. Will that suit you?"

"That will be fine. Though I do not need any help dressing, you might want to bring a trusted maid along to maintain propriety since you have guests, and I presume they are in the same wing as you have put me."

"Good point. I will fetch Themba when I come."

"Yes, your old nanny will be perfect."

"Here we are," Elek stated, as he opened the door to the sitting room of Piper's rooms. "See you in an hour. I am glad you are here. Much as I would like to linger and talk, for I think there is a tale to tell and I am anxious to hear it, our guests will be back soon."

Piper so wanted to talk to both Elek and his mother right away, but she knew it might not be safe to discuss openly what had brought her to Cliffmoor Manor. Both Beezle's fate and the piece of the oppgave ringe were of urgent importance. It would not do to jeopardize either by blurting out to Elek her concerns while standing here in the hall. She needed to be patient.

After Elek left, Piper checked out the rooms she had been assigned. Even though she was among friends in a place she considered safe, old habits die hard. The work she had been doing for the Crown had taken her to some strange and dangerous places over the last few years. She had learned to always have an escape route and contingency plans in place.

Jing, too, wandered the room sniffing here and there. Finally satisfied with her inspection, Piper grabbed an apple and headed toward the tub to enjoy a good soak.

When the water began to cool, Piper finally dragged herself out and rummaged through the travel pack Lady Celik had provided. She found it fascinating that Lady Celik would have clothes her size that were in the style and material favored in the southern mountains. When Piper thought further on it, she concluded that maybe it was not so surprising that Lady Celik was prepared. The woman had been in the intrigue business for the Crown for years.

"She probably stays up late at night just thinking about how to be prepared for any contingency. What do you think, Jing?"

Jing was finishing his own ablutions, so with one last lick of his fur, he turned to face the door and ignored Piper's question.

"Someone coming, Jing?"

A knock at the door answered Piper's question.

"May we come in, dear?" called out Elek's former nanny, Themba.

Piper strode to the door and opened it. "It is so good to see you again, Themba. Please come in. Oh, and you too, foster brother."

"How very gracious of you," Elek said, lifting an imaginary hat off his head and making a low bow.

"Ach, get on with you, you rascal," Themba said, making shooing motions with her hands. Reaching out, she took both of Piper's hands. "It's so good to see you again, though you are looking way too worn and gaunt."

"Thank you so much," Piper said with a hint of humor in her voice. She knew Elek's former nanny was not saying anything to be mean. Turning to Elek, she asked if he had figured out any reason she might be visiting.

"Well, because you have not come to visit my charming self, I thought you could be here on an errand for your father. Something vague to do with clan Wynda business. We can hope our other guest will not be so uncouth as to ask you just what that business is. I, however, am going to be very uncouth and ask what you are really doing here."

"How secure are these rooms?" Piper asked.

"As secure as we can make them, but let me check," Elek replied. "Themba, will you check the hall while I check elsewhere?"

Themba did as asked while Elek opened the wardrobe and disappeared through an opening in the back. Moments later he returned.

"All clear, Themba?" Elek asked.

"All clear."

"So, what brings you to our door, Piper?" Elek asked.

"The short version is I have a piece of the oppgave ringe with me, and Beezle, Aaron Beecroft, has been captured and is being taken to the Raven's tower. I, I, I …." Words failed Piper. She still was not sure she had made the right choice coming to Cliffmoor Manor and not traveling directly to the capital.

"You did the right thing coming here. I am sure we can get you to the capital safely, and …" Elek hesitated for a moment before continuing. "… and I will leave it to mother to tell you about what we can do to help Beezle. Meanwhile, the dinner hour has been moved up. Our other guests have decided they need to leave very early and, wishing to pack and be early to bed this night, have asked to eat at a less fashionable hour. Cook is grumbling. She will, I am sure, rise to the occasion."

The dinner meal was a quiet one. Piper was introduced and tried not to yawn throughout the meal. She participated in the small talk when required. Jing had stayed back in her assigned rooms, for she and Elek felt it was better that the other house guests were not aware of him. After the meal was over, all of them moved to the library for a hot drink before retiring for the evening.

As they stood, Lady Celik turned to her visiting guests and said, "I am so sorry, Lord Mislykket, that you and your daughter will be leaving so soon. I do understand, mind you, the need to be on top of what is happening on your estate. I am fortunate that my son will be here, since I need to return to the capital again three days hence."

"And what of you, Piper?" Lord Mislykket asked.

"I'm going to take up Lady Celik's gracious offer to stay several days. It has been a long ride from home. Having a chance to rest before I head back home is welcome. It was nice to meet you both."

Piper headed up to her rooms. She had no sooner sat down to give Jing a scratch behind his ears when a soft tap came from the wardrobe. The back silently swung open, and Lady Celik stepped through.

"It does cause one to wonder about our ancestors that they built so many homes and keeps with secret passages. I'm sure your family home is riddled with them, too. Certainly comes in handy now and again. Just wanted you to know you should be ready to leave right after Lord Mislykket and his daughter leave tomorrow. We will let them get far enough along the road toward their home, which is to the south, before we head out. We will go by carriage with an escort. The sooner we get you to the capital, the better," stated Lady Celik.

"What of Aaron?" Piper asked.

"I know you are anxious about your friend. Will you trust me that help is on the way? I will explain more when we are in the carriage and on the road."

Piper was so tired and, she realized, cranky, that it was all she could do not to stand up, stamp her foot, and demand that she be told right away what was going to be done to help Beezle. She had to draw in a deep steadying breath to curb her impatience.

Sensing Piper's agitation, Lady Celik tried to assure her that all would be well. She wished her a good night's rest, slipped back through the wardrobe, and closed the panel behind her.

Piper fell into an exhausted sleep and did not awaken until the upstairs maid knocked on the door to announce breakfast. Pulling herself out of bed was especially hard. Asking Jing to be tolerant for a little while longer, Piper headed down to partake of the morning meal. It was a great relief to be able to wave goodbye to Lord Mislykket and his daughter.

Piper wondered what Jing would do once she entered Lady Celik's carriage. *Would he travel alongside, would he be willing to ride within, or would he refuse to go with her?* She need not have worried, for the minute she had settled herself on the carriage seat, and before anyone else was able to enter the carriage, Jing swiftly climbed aboard and settled himself on the seat cushion next to Piper, as if he had been riding in carriages all of his young life.

Before the wheels of the carriage had hardly made one revolution, Piper asked Lady Celik about the plans to rescue Beezle.

"We have been aware of Waldron Keep, which is now more commonly called the Raven's tower, for a very long time. My son, as you know, had infiltrated the Raven's cadre and was quite high up. He spent some time at the tower and was partly responsible for the Raven's fall from power, literally. When Lord Braeden took over the Raven's land and position, the Crown made plans. Know that who enters and exits the tower is well observed. Word has been sent concerning Beezle."

"I have heard of the Raven's tower. It is a formidable fortress. Mounting an attack on the tower will have dire consequences. It could cause a great deal of trouble among those for the Crown. It would give those who are still loyal to the former regent, Lord Klingflug, reason to cause an uprising."

"I am sadly all too aware of the consequences of too bold and blatant a move, lass," sighed Lady Celik. "The former regent and his ilk are playing a desperate and dangerous game by capturing Lord Hadrack's nephew, who we fondly know as Beezle. However, plans have been in place for quite some time, should the tower once again be used to hold someone against his or her will. I really cannot tell you more. Please trust me that others will do all in their power to help Beezle." When Piper began to protest, Lady Celik went on. "It is always true that the more folks are in on a secret, the more chances there are that others will find out. What you do not know, you cannot accidently let others know. As I said, I hope you will trust me that all that can be done to help Beezle is being done. He would not want us to divide the country over him by rashly storming the Raven's tower."

Piper knew Lady Celik was right. It did not make her feel any better. She worried about her friend even though she knew that her decision to get help for both of them had been the right one. She and the piece of the oppgave ringe were safely on their way to the capital. Lady Celik's assurances that help was on the way for Beezle would have to do for now.

Piper spent the rest of the trip to the capital switching back and forth between her worry about what was happening to Beezle and anxiety about what was going to happen once they arrived at the capital. Lady Celik had assured her that she had nothing to worry about concerning placing the piece of the oppgave ringe in the vessteboks. Jing, sensing her mood, tried his best to comfort her. Piper was grateful for his continued presence at her side.

Once settled into Lady Celik's townhouse, no time was wasted gathering members of the interim ruling council and others for a meeting. Piper was introduced to Master Clarisse, who took Piper aside for a private talk after the meeting ended.

"Let us go sit in the warm sunshine in Lady Celik's garden. It is both quiet and private," Master Clarisse suggested. "I want to talk to you about what is going to happen tomorrow at the Well of Speaking."

"I really would like to skip all of that and just go now and deposit the ring. I don't really know what I can do to help Beezle. I do know, however, that I'm feeling the pull of the firestar gem to head his direction, just like I was before, when I set off to find him to give him the cuff. With each passing moment, the pull gets stronger."

"I know this is hard," soothed Master Clarisse. "Most folks talk a good game about how if push came to shove, they would rise to the occasion and do what is right for their country. It is quite another thing to face real decisions like you have faced these last few days. You want to rush off and help Beezle, for he is a friend and you are very loyal to your friends, I think. And yet, you hold a major piece of Sommerhjem's future in a small pouch hanging around your neck. I appreciate that you want to just place the ring where it belongs, grab the swiftest horse you can find, and ride off toward where Beezle is being held."

"You are right about that," Piper said, glad that at least one folk understood the turmoil she was going through. "Can I leave right after I place the ring in the vessteboks?"

"Much as I would like to say 'yes' to that plan, I am afraid you are not going to like my answer. Of course, no one will hold you here at the capital without your consent, but ..."

"I need to find that swift horse then," Piper said, starting to rise.

"... but it is imperative you stay through all the falderal that follows. Folks need the reassurance that the Gylden Sirklene challenge is truly what needs to happen. They need the meetings and celebrations after each one of the rings is placed in the vessteboks. Yours is the seventh ring. The cold winter months are going to hamper travel, then spring will come all too soon, and then summer. There are still two more rings to be found by the end of summer. This year is rushing by too swiftly, and the former regent's followers are getting bolder and more desperate. We need to show a united front here in the capital. We need to show we are not at all worried. If you leave right after the ceremony, many might question your swift departure. It could put Beezle in even more jeopardy."

Piper was not all that happy with Master Clarisse's logic, but could not find a decent argument against it. She resigned herself to staying in the capital a few days and enduring the falderal.

The next morning, Piper, with Jing at her side, was escorted to the Well of Speaking by members of the interim ruling council, including Lady Esmeralda. When she reached the top of the stairs leading down into the amphitheater, she was astonished at the crowd of folks seated below.

"Do you wish for someone to walk down the stairs with you?" Lady Esmeralda asked kindly.

"No, thank you. Jing is with me. I will be all right."

Taking a deep breath, Piper made her way down the stairs. She was met at the bottom by Master Clarisse, who had coached her the day before as to what she should do and what she might expect. Upon reaching the vessteboks set into the stone wall, Piper tipped the ring out of the pouch and placed it in the vessteboks. At first, nothing happened. Then an arrow-shaped column of silver light shot out of the box and headed directly inland. Had the sky not been darkened by approaching storm clouds coming in from the sea, it would have been hard to see the silver column.

A buzz of conversation followed as folks rose to leave. Piper was not sure how she felt. Relief mostly. On the other hand, the descriptions by Master Clarisse as to what had happened to the other ring bearers had led her to expect more than a swift silver arrow of light.

Piper endured the next two days of receptions and gatherings. By the end of the second day, the pull of the firestar gem had become almost unbearable. It was with great relief when the morning of the third day arrived and Lady Celik greeted her with the news that a horse, supplies, and a few loyal folks awaited.

"Be safe, lass," said Lady Celik. "I have arranged for changes of horses along the way. Those you ride with will get you where you wish to go. I would trust any one of them with my own life."

"I thank you for everything, Lady Celik. Hopefully, whatever plan you have in mind will succeed, and we are not too late," said Piper, as she moved swiftly down the stairs to join the waiting group.

# PART TWO

# CHAPTER TWENTY-SIX

Lord Klingflug was not a happy man. He had received news that another piece of the oppgave ringe had been placed in the vessteboks, bringing the total in the capital up to seven of the nine pieces. Though it was still fall, he felt time was running out. What was really sticking in his craw was the fact that his agents, if they had only known, had almost had their hands on the lass who had placed the seventh ring. She had been with Aaron Beecroft, of all folks. Sometimes, Lord Klingflug felt if he did not have bad luck, he would not have any luck at all. Some of his most loyal supporters were beginning to question his leadership.

The information Lord Klingflug had been given by his agents was that Beecroft had found or acquired something of importance. The agents felt he either had a piece of the oppgave ringe or knew where to find one, so they had captured him. They had thought the lass with him was just a traveling musician who happened to be in the wrong place at the wrong time.

*They had not thought she was anything other than part of Beecroft's disguise,* Lord Klingflug thought with disgust. *All of the focus had been on capturing Beecroft in such a way that did not reflect back on me. That much was good anyway. Since the lass had run off, she would not know where Beecroft had been taken, or who he had been taken by. Once they were done wringing any information to be had out of Beecroft, no one would ever find out what had happened to him.*

Having the Raven's tower under his control was a stroke of genius. Should anyone find out that Beecroft was being held in the Raven's tower,

Lord Braeden or his son would be blamed. Lord Klingflug would regret the loss of the tower if that happened, but not the loss of Lord Braeden. Since Beecroft was sitting in a stinking cell in the very lowest depth of the tower, he might be more than willing to talk to Dubhlainn when he returned with the lad, Lom. Now Lord Klingflug could just hope that the lad was what his agent in the capital suspected he was.

Lom could not quite figure out what was happening. His head hurt, and he was trussed up like a midwinter feast goose ready for roasting. He could not see anything due to a hood pulled over his head. He was aware he was on the floor in some type of wagon or carriage. He did not understand why. *What would anyone want with me? There must be some type of mistake. I am a nobody. They must have grabbed the wrong lad,* he thought. *After all, I only work in the royal palace gardens as a laborer under the assistant to the assistant to the assistant royal palace gardener. I weed, carry mulch, pluck dead flowers off plants, rake, hoe, and do other odd jobs. Once they figure out I am not who they want, they will turn me loose, or at least I hope they will.*

This time of year was Lom's second favorite, for he tended the greenhouse plants, watering and weeding. In addition, he planted the seeds in small pots for the early spring blooms. He liked the repetitive work, the smell of the rich dark earth, the quiet. Lom did not much like being around lots of folks. He preferred working alone.

Lom's other favorite time of year was anytime fresh flowers bloomed. Because he was dependable, the folks who cut and arranged the flowers trusted him to get the flower arrangements to the proper rooms in the royal palace. Delivering the flowers was not what Lom liked best, but rather being able to wander all about the palace and see the beautiful items housed there. Some of the items stored in glass cases in the long corridors and halls of the palace called to him. If he had been inclined to tell anyone about what he felt, that is how he would describe the feeling. Certain items called to him. He never would have dared to open any of the cases or touch any of the items. He would have been summarily dismissed from his job for that. Just knowing that some bauble or knickknack pulled at his senses was enough for Lom.

Lom knew he had not done anything to displease those he worked for. He had not broken a vase nor spilled a bag of dirt. He had always been at work early and had always been willing to stay late. He just could not understand what was happening to him. When the wagon jolted to a stop, throwing him up against something hard, Lom's concern rose higher than it had been already. When rough hands grabbed him and dragged him out, he felt extremely frightened.

"Now, lad, you listen, and you listen well," said a gruff voice. "I'm going to untie you. The hood over your head stays on. Do you hear me?"

"Yes," Lom replied, nodding his head. "Why …?"

"No talking. Don't try to run or get away, or things will go very bad for you. Now move."

Lom was barely able to keep his balance due to the hard shove from behind. It was difficult to walk without being able to see where he was going. The path he was walking on was very uneven and strewn with rocks and tree roots that he kept stubbing his feet on and tripping over. Finally, someone grabbed his arm and began to steer him along. When they came to a halt, he heard the creak of hinges on a door being opened. Lom was unprepared for the shove that sent him stumbling forward and slamming against a wall. He heard a door slam behind him.

"These are your quarters for the night. You can take the hood off now. If you feel around, you should find a water skin and a few bits of jerky. Have a nice evening," the voice said mockingly.

Lom quickly pulled the hood off his head and tried to take a good look at where he was. He could not see much, for there was very little light seeping in from the outside between the cracks in the boards. He thought he was in a small storage shed. As he began to feel about the floor for water and food he realized it must be close to dusk. He had wanted to ask the man who had shoved him into the shed what was going on. He wanted to tell the man he must have snatched the wrong lad.

All too soon, the few bits of jerky were gone along with the water in the water skin. Lom was glad, if he was going to be kidnapped, he had been taken off the street, rather than taken from the greenhouses, for he was wearing his cloak. The night had grown quite cool. Lom wrapped his cloak tighter around himself and curled into a small ball, trying to stay warm.

Lom was roughly awakened the next morning by a pounding on the door. He was told to turn around and put his hands behind his back. The hood was placed over his head, his hands were tied, and he was dragged down a path. When they came to a halt, he was lifted up and thrust into the back of a wagon. He could hear the tailgate being shoved in place, and what sounded like rope lashing the cover over him. Lom could tell by the feel of the ride that he was in a different wagon than the day before.

Each day was the same. He was tied up and hooded in the morning and pushed, lifted, or shoved into a wagon, cart, or carriage. Each night he was locked up in some small, dark shed or room and given a bit of food and water. He was not allowed to talk, and no one talked to him. His imagination was running itself in ever-more-frightening circles. Soon he lost track of time. He was so exhausted, hungry, and thirsty that he found it hard to even think.

It was well past dusk when the current wagon Lom was lying in rolled to a stop. He was barely aware that the wagon had halted until he heard the tailgate drop open and found himself being pulled none too gently out by his feet.

"Douse that lantern, you idiot. I suspect there are watchers out there, even if we never seem to be able to find them. We don't want anyone to know our business. Someone just lift the lad up and get him inside quickly."

"I'll take him," said a gravelly male voice.

Lom found himself unceremoniously tossed over someone's shoulder, knocking the wind right out of him. He heard a door close behind him and felt the man who was carrying him move quickly down several flights of stairs. When they reached the bottom, the footsteps of the man carrying him sounded hollow. Lom heard the man greeted by another man, keys rattling, and a door opening. He was then dumped on a hard floor. The rope tying his hands was cut off, nicking his wrist, causing it to sting.

Footsteps quickly retreated. He heard a door swing closed, and the turn of a key in the lock.

Pulling himself upright, Lom pulled the hood off his head. From the light coming in through the small barred window in the door, he could see he was in a very small room made entirely of stone. Next to the far wall, which was slightly curved, was a pallet on the floor that had a rough blanket tossed on it willy-nilly. A wooden bucket completed the furnishings. He thought he might be in a tower or turret, but had no idea where he really was.

Lom cautiously made his way to the door and looked out. In the dim light of the lantern hung on the opposite wall, he could see very little. Across from him was a stairwell leading both up and down. To both the right and the left he could see several other doors similar to the one he was looking through. He had a very long time to contemplate his situation, for no one came to where he was being kept. Finally, Lom went and curled up on the pallet, wrapping his cloak around him. He awoke some time later and pulled the scratchy blanket over him. When he awoke a second time, he realized he had awakened to the sound of a door closing. It took a few moments to realize a tray with food and drink had been placed just inside his door.

Time dragged. Lom was not sure if it was day or night. No one came to speak to him, so he could not tell them he was sure they had the wrong lad. It was hard for him to be in the dirty, dank, tiny room. He felt like the walls were closing in on him. He had always preferred the out-of-doors to being in a building. Now he wanted to see the blue of the sky and feel the sun on his back more than ever. Finally, he heard someone coming down the stairs.

"You, lad, stand back," commanded the gravelly voice Lom had heard before. "You need to do as I say, or it will not bode well for you. Do you understand?"

"Yes, but …."

"Silence. You will talk only when asked a question. Do you understand?"

"Yes."

"Good, now follow me."

The man led Lom to the stairs. Instead of leading him up, he gestured that Lom should move down the stairs. Once they reached the bottom, Lom was directed to go and sit at a small round table placed in the middle of the room. He was struck once again by the thought that he was in a round building or a tower. Besides the stairwell opening, there were three open doors which led into rooms similar to the one Lom had been kept in. A fourth door was closed. Lom wondered what was behind the fourth door. His contemplation was interrupted when he heard what sounded like folks coming down the stairs.

Two more men entered the room. One was a young man who reminded Lom of a number of young folk he had seen in the capital. They came from landed gentry and had too much time on their hands. Because they felt they were entitled and privileged, they did not feel the rules applied to them. He had seen too many of them disregard even common courtesy when it came to those who worked for a living. When they would idly wander the royal palace gardens, they would disregard the signs that asked them to stay on the paths. Often they would just cut a flower off here and there, sniff it, and then toss it aside. Lom often wondered if they were so stiff with importance it prevented them from bending at the waist and smelling the flowers on the plant.

It was the other man who concerned Lom more. It was more than clear to him that this man was the one making the decisions, even though the younger man's swagger suggested he thought he was in charge.

"So Dubhlainn, this is the lad who's supposed to ...." the young man started to say.

"Perhaps, Girvin, it might be best if we don't discuss our business in front of the lad. I, for one, wish to find out if he is worth all of the trouble to bring him here," Dubhlainn suggested.

"Begging your pardon, kind sirs, but I can't for the life of me think of what you would be wanting of me. You must have the wrong lad." Lom had tried to talk calmly, but no one in the room could have missed the shakiness in his voice.

"No talking unless told to do so," Girvin said menacingly, stepping forward with his fist raised.

"Hold," Dubhlainn said very quietly. That was all it took to stop the young man from advancing farther. "No sense in harming the lad, now is there?" Turning his attention back to Lom, he continued, "We just want you to do a few chores for us. I'm sure you will be most cooperative, now won't you, lad?"

Lom had no doubt in his mind that not cooperating with Dubhlainn would be very painful, so he nodded his head in the affirmative.

Dubhlainn pulled a chair out from the table, turned it around, sat down, and rested his arms on the back of the chair. "So, you work in the royal palace gardens I hear."

"Yes, sir, but I'm just a laborer. I'm not even an assistant to the assistant royal palace gardener. I know my plants, sir, but …."

"I, er, we did not have you brought here for your knowledge of plants, lad. It's your other special skills we are more interested in."

"I don't have any particular special skills, sir."

Lom was wrenched from his chair abruptly and shaken by Girvin. "Don't you lie to us," Girvin said, throwing Lom to the ground. Standing over Lom enraged, Girvin swung back his foot.

# Chapter Twenty-Seven

Girvin found himself dangling off the ground just as his foot swung forward, barely missing Lom's ribs. "Put me down. You put me down. How dare you manhandle me? I'm in charge here, not you. I'll be the one to decide how to proceed."

"I would suggest to you that you are here at your father's forbearance, and because Lord Klingflug suggested it. You have other brothers and a sister or two who would gladly take your place. One word from me, and you are back home playing second fiddle to your older brother. Now get yourself under control," Dubhlainn stated very, very quietly as he set Girvin down. "Perhaps some fresh air would do you some good."

Between the actions of Dubhlainn and the conversation that had just taken place, Lom had little doubt he was in very deep trouble. That a subordinate would send the one who was supposed to be in charge out of the room so dismissively was enough to increase the rising fear inside of Lom. The fact that he had fallen into the hands of folks loyal to Lord Klingflug, the former regent, caused a wave of sheer terror to wash over him.

"Now then, let us begin our discussion once again," Dubhlainn suggested as he reached down, lifted Lom up, and none too gently set him back in his seat. "You work in the royal gardens, is that not correct?"

"Yes, sir."

"You are one of those who bring fresh flowers into the palace, is that also not correct?"

"Yes, sir."

"Good so far. Now, it has come to our attention that you sometimes linger in the halls and corridors while delivering the flower arrangements. Is that not correct?"

"Yes, sir. Why?" *Is that what this is all about? I have been taking too much time delivering flowers?* Lom thought. *I have not even been delivering flowers these past few months. I have been assigned to the greenhouses to clean up from the fall and get pots ready for the spring. Someone had me picked up off the street and brought here just to tell me that I had lingered too long in the palace last fall? This does not make any sense.*

Not answering Lom's question, Dubhlainn asked "Why do you especially linger in the corridor that is lined with glass cases?"

"I like looking at the curious and beautiful things on the shelves, sir."

*What did this man want?* Lom knew he was often drawn to some of the curios in the cases. He had never told anyone about this feeling. He sometimes felt something peculiar about someone who passed by him in the gardens when he was working, too. He really did not know what that was all about either. That was the only thing odd or different about him. Lom often thought it was merely fanciful imaginings on his part.

"You have been observed lingering by the same cases often. Why is that?"

"I don't know, sir. I wasn't aware I …."

"You can stop lying to me now."

"I'm not lying to you, sir. I just liked looking, that's all. No one at the palace ever had any complaint about me that I know of. If someone didn't like my work, they just could've told me. You all didn't have to go to all this trouble just to scare me so I wouldn't stop to look and take time away from my work," stated Lom sincerely.

"Interesting," murmured Dubhlainn. "You weren't snatched up off the street because you dawdled occasionally."

"Then why?"

"It's because those items that you found yourself going back to look at time and time again are small objects that hold some power within. I imagine you felt something like a pull, or tingle, or something when you came near them."

Try as he might, Lom could not keep himself from looking swiftly up at Dubhlainn. *How could Dubhlainn know?*

"Ah, I see I struck a correct chord. Ah, Girvin, you're back. Can I trust you not to harm this young man while I fetch our other guest?"

If looks could kill, Dubhlainn would have dropped to the ground dead the minute he turned his back on Girvin.

"You move an inch from that chair, you give me any reason at all, you'll be sorry," Girvin whispered to Lom.

Lom sat frozen in his chair, barely daring to breathe, his head down, hands clenched on his lap to keep them from shaking. He heard a key turning in a lock and a door swinging open. He felt the table in front of him lurch as someone was thrust into the seat across from him. Raising his eyes, he saw a very dirty man. His hair was matted and his beard a mess of tangles. The man's clothing was filthy, and he smelled as if he had not bathed in quite some time. The man's eyes were clear and bore straight into Lom's.

Lom's first impression of the man was quickly replaced by two new impressions. First, Lom felt he knew the man. He needed to really concentrate. He rarely forgot a face. He knew he had seen this man's face before. *Ah, Aaron Beecroft, the nephew of Lord and Lady Hadrack. Oh, this could not be good if they were holding Aaron Beecroft captive*, Lom thought. *Both Lord and Lady Hadrack are very powerful folk, very involved with the interim ruling council. I am now even more confused and more afraid than I was before.*

The second impression that struck Lom was he was having that same feeling he often felt when he was near some of the items in the cases at the royal palace. Something was pulling at his senses. He was pulled out of his contemplations when he heard the sound of something hitting the top of the table.

"Pick it up," Dubhlainn commanded.

Lom looked down at the top of the table. Lying there was a ring with a dark stone inset in the band. Next to it was a golden pine spider silk pouch. He felt a great need to pick up the ring. Not wanting to appear too eager, with great effort, he held himself in check. Slowly reaching out,

Lom picked up the ring and the pouch. The ring felt very warm against his skin, which struck him as odd. Before he could be questioned further by Dubhlainn, the sound of footsteps pounding down the stairs could be heard.

"Now what?" Dubhlainn said angrily.

"My apologies," stated Girvin's servant. "Your father is waiting above. Said he wished to speak with you and Dubhlainn. Something about a disturbance on the border between the two properties."

Dubhlainn directed the gravelly-voiced man, whom he addressed as Yarrow, to lock up both Lom and Aaron Beecroft. "Once you have them locked up, stand guard at the top of the stairs. Don't let any of Lord Braeden's folks down here."

Yarrow nodded, drew a sharp knife from his belt, and grabbed Lom. Directing his comments to Aaron Beecroft, he said, "Now, unless you want this young lad's blood on your hands, you will get up and walk into your cell. I need you to stand by the far wall. And you lad, Lom is it? You need to stand very, very still, and hope this gentleman values your life."

Lom did not need to be asked twice. He stood frozen in place, the ring in one hand, the golden pine spider silk pouch in the other. Once Aaron Beecroft was in his cell and next to the far wall, Lom was none too gently shoved forward into the cell with him. The door swung closed behind him and locked. He could hear the sounds of retreating footsteps climbing the stairs.

"Lom is it?"

"Yes, sir."

Before the conversation could continue, Lom felt the ring he was holding becoming almost unbearably warm. He opened his hand, prepared to put the ring in the pouch, when an arc of light shot from his hand toward Aaron Beecroft to be met by one coming from Aaron Beecroft's wrist. Lom almost dropped the ring. Somehow he managed to hold onto it. Thinking his first instinct to put the ring in the golden pine spider silk pouch had been the right one, he surprised himself by not doing that. Instead, he slipped the ring on his finger. The ring cooled almost immediately.

Whatever remark either Lom or Aaron Beecroft was about to make was halted when they both turned toward the back wall of the cell, having heard the sound of stone moving on stone. As they watched, first one block of stone moved back out of the wall to be followed by others, forming an opening in the wall. A short young man covered in stone dust stepped through the opening.

"You Beezle?"

"Yes."

"Good. We need to be quick. Name's Collier, and there's a lass at the other end of that opening named Piper who will have my hide if I don't get you out of here. Wasn't expecting a second folk. We'll have to take him with us though. We can sort it out later," Collier said in a whispered voice. "Is there a guard in the room on the other side of this door?"

"No, I think he's stationed one landing up. He is there more to prevent anyone from coming down here."

"Good. Let me take care of that lantern. If he does come down here to check on you as we are getting you out, he will find the room dark, and what we are doing will be harder to see."

Without so much as a by-your-leave, Collier stepped around both Lom and Beezle. He pulled a slingshot out of his back pocket, fitted a stone to it, pulled back, and let the stone fly. It hit squarely on the lantern, shattering it, plunging the center room and the cell into darkness.

"If you will follow me, please. I want to get you two out of here and have the wall closed up before anyone is the wiser. We don't have much time. My breaking the lantern may have alerted the guard. It's a chance I felt I needed to take. Darkness will help us and slow down any who enter the outer room."

Lom wondered how they were going to see where they were supposed to go, when he noticed a pale red glow outlining the opening in the wall. While he did not know what would happen next, he figured that following Aaron Beecroft through the hole in the wall and out of the cell was better than staying where he was. As he stepped through the opening, he realized there were others waiting on the other side of the wall.

"Hady here will lead you out," Collier said in a very quiet voice. "She will get you away safely."

"What of you and the others?" Beezle asked.

"If all goes as planned, we will follow you shortly. We need to clean up any indication of how we got you out of here. We may want to disappear another prisoner another time. Go quickly now," Collier said, as he turned to reenter the cell.

"Keep your heads low, for this tunnel is not very high. It is also very narrow in places. Just follow my light," Hady said.

Lom saw that she held a small red-globed lantern which gave off barely enough light to see where he was going. The tunnel they hurried through changed from being carved out of stone to timbers shoring up dirt walls and back to stone more times than he could count. He could not imagine what a tremendous amount of effort and time it had taken to construct their escape route. *Who were these short folks who rescued me?* he wondered.

It seemed like no time at all before Lom was directed to climb up a ladder. After dousing the light of her lantern, Hady followed both Beezle and him out. It took Lom several moments for his eyes to adjust to his surroundings. He found they had stepped out into a dense wood. He caught movement off to his right and was just about to say something when a lass slid out of the shadows.

"Follow me please," the lass said. "We need to be away as quickly as possible. Glad to see you are still with us, Beezle."

"Pretty glad to see you too, Piper. Did you …?"

"Plenty of time to catch up once we're away. We did not expect two of you. Do we need to do something about the lad with you?"

"Check your bracelet, but don't uncover it. He is wearing Pyry's ring, and it seems to suit him." When Piper gave him an inquiring look, Beezle said, "Long story."

Lom wished he knew what they were talking about. It did not seem the time to ask at the moment, since they had begun to travel through the woods at a dangerous pace. He did not know how the lass leading them knew where to go, for there was not much light. Finally, they arrived at a lane where there were others waiting with horses.

"Did they get him out?" asked a male voice.

"Journeyman Evan? What are you doing here?" Beezle asked.

"Someone had to make sure you had swift horses. Who better than me?" Journeyman Evan replied. "Let's mount up and be on our way. Hady, will you and the others be all right?"

"We should be away shortly. We'll scatter in different directions to confuse the trail, should anyone follow. We are very good at not being followed," Hady suggested. "Tell Lady Celik's son the debt is paid. Know we are always, and have always been, at the service of the Crown."

Lom mounted up on the horse Journeyman Evan directed him to and prepared to ride. He could only hope he had not jumped from the griddle into the fire.

# CHAPTER TWENTY-EIGHT

The party Lom was with rode for several hours before halting at a farmhouse. He was so happy to be out in the cool night air and away from where he had been held captive, he would have been willing to ride all night. When he saw Aaron Beecroft stumble with fatigue after he dismounted, Lom was quickly off his horse and at the man's side, lending support before he could think to do otherwise.

When Piper noticed Lom had moved so swiftly toward Beezle, she immediately started toward them at a rapid pace. She halted when Beezle held up a hand and spoke to her.

"It's all right, Piper. Seems this young man has a kind heart and is only helping me not fall flat on my face. Thank you, Lom. My legs seem to be a bit wobbly at the moment. Probably the kindest thing my young friend here could do would be to help me over to the horse trough and dump me in. I am filthy and must smell atrocious. Some really strong soap would be welcome."

"Ach, I think we can do better than that, lad. I'm Farmer Karel. I take it that your mission went as planned, Piper?"

"Yes, it went surprisingly well."

Redirecting her remarks to Beezle, Farmer Karel suggested that, while he and others were welcome to bathe in the horse trough, they might prefer the bathhouse. She suspected the water might be just a wee bit warmer there.

"There should be fresh towels left. I and mine will stand guard to make sure no unwanted intruders come onto the farm."

During this conversation, Piper had walked back to her horse and removed a saddlebag. She walked up to Beezle and handed the saddlebag to him. "I'm sorry we could not recover your horses and packs. There are clothes in here that should fit. Glad you are all right, or mostly all right. We'll talk once you have had a chance to clean up."

"Thank you, Piper. For the clothes, and for the rescue."

"I wish I could take responsibility for the rescue. The plan was in place long before I ever got to the capital, much less the Raven's tower. Seems after the rover Shueller was held there, a plan was put in place to dig that tunnel. The Günnary almost had it completed before you were taken there. Now go. I'm standing downwind, and it's not pleasant."

It was not until everyone had a chance to get cleaned up and partake in the simple filling fare that Farmer Karel had laid out that conversation could occur about what had happened since Piper and Beezle had become separated.

"Before we begin," Piper said, "perhaps you could formally introduce me to your fellow prisoner."

"I would really like to give you a full background on the lad sitting across from us. As it happens, we just met. I have some suspicions, however. I heard him addressed as Lom."

"Have we brought one of the former regent's agents with us?" asked Piper, alarmed.

"I would suggest you pull your shirt sleeve back. Jing might consider sitting up from his sprawled position in front of the fire."

Piper did as Beezle had asked, as did Jing. Before she could comment on either request, an arc of light shot out from the ring on Lom's finger to be answered by an arc of light from Piper's bracelet, Beezle's wrist cuff, and Jing's pendant, startling Lom.

"You could have warned me," Piper told Beezle.

"What, and miss all the fun, which has been sorely lacking these last few weeks."

Journeyman Evan took that moment to enter the farmhouse to find Beezle filled with mirth, Piper looking a tad miffed, and Lom looking confused.

"Did I miss something?" Journeyman Evan asked.

"It would seem you've rescued a good lad here," Beezle replied.

When Journeyman Evan gave him a questioning look, Beezle explained what had just happened concerning the firestar gems and their properties. "So you see, Lom has to be of good heart for the firestar gems to respond as they did. It also suggests that the ring has chosen him. I know of no other way to put it. Now the next question is, just what was he doing in the Raven's tower? What did Dubhlainn want with him? We were interrupted before we found that out. Why were you there, Lom?"

"I don't know. I'm just a laborer in the royal palace gardens. I weed, and mulch, and deliver flowers. I pot, and plant, and ...." Lom's voice trailed off. He just did not know why everyone seemed so interested in him. He also did not understand why he could not seem to take the ring with the firestar gem off his finger, which he had been trying to do in these last few moments.

"I overheard Dubhlainn questioning you about your attraction to items in some of the cases in the palace. He also wanted you to check out the ring you now wear. I imagine you are unable to remove the ring now, is that right?" Beezle asked.

Lom looked up, startled, and wondered how this man, Aaron Beecroft, who others here referred to as Beezle, would know that.

"You can remove the ring no more than Piper, Jing, or I can remove what we wear that holds the firestar gems. My wrist is still sore from when my captives tried to remove my cuff." Turning to address Journeyman Evan, Beezle asked him if he remembered Siri, the herbalist on the Deaver's farm.

"Yes. Why?"

"She suggested to Nissa that there are some folks who are sensitive to items which hold some sort of power, like the oppgave ringe pieces and other such items. Nissa and I discussed it once when we were discussing the properties of golden pine spider silk. I wonder if Lom here was snatched because those who Dubhlainn works for suspect Lom is a sensitive and want to use him."

*Was that what all this has been about? I was kidnapped and taken to the Raven's tower because I can tell if an object holds some type of power?* wondered Lom. *The idea that I might be what they called a sensitive is almost a relief. It explains so much. It suggests that I am not moonstruck, or imagining things.*

"Lom," Beezle said very gently. "Know that you do not have to say anything. No one here will cause you any harm. Know that you are free to leave here at any time. Yet, I would like to ask you a few questions, if I may."

"Yes … yes, all right."

"Siri told Nissa that some folk could sense power in an object. She knew when she touched Nissa that Nissa carried an item that held power. Actually, it turned out Nissa was carrying two pieces of the oppgave ringe. Nissa did not know that at the time, however. It was Siri who gave her a golden pine spider silk pouch to put the rings in, for golden pine spider silk can prevent someone from knowing you carry something that holds power. Do you follow me so far?"

"I think so," replied Lom.

"What attracts you to certain objects in the glass cases in the palace?"

Lom did not answer right away. He needed a moment to really think through what Beezle had told him about the firestar gems, and about his possibly being what Beezle called a sensitive. He also needed to think long and hard as to whether he could trust these folks.

Lom wished he had paid more attention to what had been happening in the capital since the summer fair. All that had been changing in Sommerhjem as to who ruled had not interested him much. He was just trying to do a good job, so he could afford the small room he rented in a boarding house and get a decent meal every day. He had been one of the fostered children taken care of along with their own children by a croft family on a very large estate. He really did not know who his folks were. His foster family did not talk about them, other than to say they had been good folks who had been unable to care for him.

His foster family had only a very small croft, which under the former regent's rule could no longer support such a large family. The landlord his foster family was beholden to had passed some of the fees and taxes down to them. Lom had left home to try to be on his own and not be a burden. The job at the royal palace had been literally a lifesaver.

Lom knew that this man he knew as Aaron Beecroft, nephew of Lord and Lady Hadrack, was an important noble. He knew that this Nissa who Beezle talked about had brought the first two pieces of the oppgave ringe to the capital. He concluded that these folks must be working for the Crown, and he could probably answer the questions Beezle wished to ask, if for no other reason than he might put in a good word for Lom when they got back to the capital. He hoped his job would still be there when he got back. He needed these folks to explain why he had left so suddenly. He did not want the head royal palace gardener to think he had just walked away.

Having made a decision to trust these folks, Lom said, "I'm not sure I can explain it. It's just a feeling I get when I'm near certain objects. I guess it's like a pull. Sometimes I feel the same way when certain folks pass by me."

"It sounds like someone in the palace noticed Lom's attraction to certain items. We can also conclude that the same someone had some knowledge of what those items were," suggested Piper.

"That is a worrisome thought on two fronts. That there is someone who must be in the palace employ, or a frequent visitor, who knows about the properties of some of the items in the cases in the palace and who, on observing Lom, took it upon himself or herself not to let the Crown know, but instead to get word to the former regent," stated Beezle, a worried frown on his face.

"We can't solve that problem from here. It does, however, create another problem," said Piper. "It is obvious to me that Lom will not be safe if he returns to the capital. If his particular attraction to items that may have some special qualities to them caused him to be captured by those who do not favor the Crown, what is to prevent them from capturing him again?"

A silence settled over those gathered, each lost in her or his own thoughts. Lom began to feel a rising panic. It was sounding like he could not go back to the capital. If he did, he would not be safe and might be recaptured. He could not return to his foster family, for it might put them in danger. Besides, they had enough burdens trying to put food on the table and survive. He had nothing with him to be able to take off on his own. No clothing, no supplies, no coin, no water skin, not even a knife. He wondered how he would survive.

Even if he took to the road and tried to find work, work was certainly scarcer in the winter months. During the second half of the winter, folks became even more conservative with what they had stored in their root cellars. Game also became scarcer and harder to find. Folks just did not go on walkabouts in the middle of winter.

Another thought occurred to Lom. *What if these folks decide they too want to use me? Will they lock me up somewhere too?* Lom could not stand the thought of being locked up, unable to see the sky or walk in the fresh air. He felt himself becoming short of breath just thinking about that happening. He began to feel flushed and had an overwhelming need to rush out the door and away from these folks.

It was Piper who first noticed that Lom was flushed and looking panicky. "Lom, are you all right?"

"No, I, ah, I need fresh air," Lom said, as he stood up and bolted toward the door.

After he left, Piper suggested that one of them should probably go after him. She started to rise when Journeyman Evan volunteered.

"Why don't you let me go? Here we were talking about how he can't return to the capital, and then all of us went silent. I can imagine a whole mess of things that must be going through his mind," Journeyman Evan suggested. He stood up, grabbed his cloak off the back of a chair where he had thrown it, and left the room.

Once outside, Journeyman Evan was relieved to find that Lom had not gone far. He found him seated on the farmhouse porch steps, one of the farm cats settled on his lap. He gave Lom a few moments to become aware that he was there before he spoke.

"Would it be all right if I joined you on the steps? Sometimes being inside gets just a bit stuffy for me too. I could use a bit of fresh air."

"Yah, sure, all right," Lom answered somewhat reluctantly.

"I apologize for all of us. We were certainly being rather insensitive to the position you now find yourself in. I can only guess as to what must have been going through your mind. The first and foremost must be, just what happens to me now? Or, what are these folks going to do to me, or expect of me? Are they going to ask me to do what those at the Raven's tower wanted me to do? Are they going to lock me up too and use me?"

Lom was startled by how accurate Journeyman Evan was about the thoughts that had been swirling around in his head.

"Unlike the former regent's followers, and others who would like the Crown to fail to bring the Gylden Sirklene challenge to fruition, those who serve the Crown would never ask anyone to do something against his or her will. I think all of us in there were silent because we were trying to figure out a solution to keep you safe. You have a skill that would be best not to fall into the hands of the Crown's enemies. Let's sit out here for a bit, and then, when you are ready, let's go back inside. Let me tell you what I think might be a great solution to the dilemma you find yourself in."

# CHAPTER TWENTY-NINE

Lom had been following Journeyman Evan for several days. The horse he rode was strong and swift, taking them farther and farther away from all he had known. He was still not sure he had made the right choice. After Journeyman Evan and he had discussed Journeyman Evan's plan while sitting on Farmer Karel's porch, they had reentered the farmhouse. All Journeyman Evan had told the others was he had a plan, and they should trust him to get Lom to safety. It had not struck Lom as odd at the time that Journeyman Evan did not tell the others just what his plan was. Lom did wonder about that now. Everything had happened so fast. After a short night's sleep, they had left before dawn.

Lom's head was still spinning as to how fast everything had transpired after Journeyman Evan had announced he had a plan. Farmer Karel had taken over and dragged Lom off to the attic of the farmhouse to look through several trunks.

"Never throw anything away around here," Farmer Karel had informed Lom. "Waste not, want not, my ol' granny used to say. You'll be needing several changes of clothes, warm socks, and other necessities. Should be able to find something here in your size. You'll also need a blanket roll. Have you got a good knife? No? Well, remind me to find you one when we get downstairs."

Before Lom had a chance to even catch his breath, he was loaded down with items he was to try on or pack. Once that was done, he was sent off to get some rest. He was sure he had just shut his eyes when his shoulder was being shaken to awaken him. After a quick breakfast, Lom had mounted up. The days that followed had been filled with long hours of riding and short hours of sleep.

About midafternoon, Journeyman Evan slowed his horse down so that Lom could draw his horse alongside.

"I think we're getting close," Journeyman Evan said.

Lom looked at Journeyman Evan with a worried look on his face. Journeyman Evan had told him he knew of a place way off the beaten track where Lom would be safe. He had told him that he had been there once and was sure he could find it again. Lately, Lom had not felt very reassured. He wondered if he might have made a mistake. After all, he really did not know this Journeyman Evan fellow. Who knew where he was really being taken? An additional worry was the strange feeling he had had over the last few days that there was something out there keeping pace with them, and watching them.

When they stopped for the night, they camped on a hill that had a really good view. They had been traveling upward for several days. Lom had not realized they were so close to the foothills of the eastern mountains, for they had been traveling mostly through dense forest. The feeling of being watched had persisted all day and was becoming worrisome.

"I think it might be a good idea if we gather more firewood. I have had the feeling that we are being watched," Journeyman Evan stated. "I know that might sound fanciful. I would rather err on the side of caution, however. We might also want to take turns at watch. Just as a precaution, mind you."

Lom had mixed feelings. He felt relief that he was not just jumping at shadows, since Journeyman Evan also felt they were being watched. On the other hand, he was not sure he had wanted the feeling of being watched confirmed. That might mean something was really out there watching.

In the middle of the night, Journeyman Evan woke Lom up to take watch. The cloud cover, which had been blocking the sky for several days, had broken up. Above him the night sky was filled with stars. The half-moon added its light. Lom placed a few more logs on the fire and settled in, trying to keep his eyes open. Yawning, he reached for another log and froze when he heard movement in the trees beyond his fire. It sounded way too large to be the rustling of a small animal.

Slowly, ever so slowly, Lom reached to his left and picked up a branch that Journeyman Evan had rigged as a torch, just in case. Gripping it tightly, Lom pulled it toward himself. He did not light it. Minutes passed. Whatever had been moving in the trees had either moved away, or had stopped and was standing deep in the shadows. Lom was not sure if he should light the torch, wake Journeyman Evan, or continue to sit still. He chose to sit still a while longer.

Quite some time went by. Just as Lom was beginning to relax his tight grip on the torch, a hunting cat boldly walked out of the surrounding darkness. Lom began to surreptitiously draw the torch closer. He halted when the hunting cat lay down.

"Just make yourself comfortable, why don't you?" Lom murmured very quietly under his breath.

The hunting cat did so, settling in and licking her paw. Once the hunting cat had settled, Lom moved the torch a bit closer. The hunting cat did not pay him any attention. Feeling a bit less threatened, he loosened his white-knuckled grip on the torch, only to tighten his fingers once again when two slightly smaller hunting cats slipped out of the shadows and proceeded to lie down on either side of the larger hunting cat. Lom realized his small torch and a dying fire were not going to be of much use. It might hold one hunting cat off for a while, but it would not hold off three. He knew he should alert Journeyman Evan as to the change in their situation. He was afraid, however, to make any noise, for fear he would draw attention to himself.

When the faint light of dawn began to lighten the sky, Lom could no longer feel his bottom, for he had been sitting in the same position all through his watch. The three hunting cats had not moved from their spots across the fire from him. They had taken turns sleeping. At one point, Lom almost wished the cats would advance so he could at least go down fighting. When he heard Journeyman Evan begin to stir, Lom whispered to him to hold still.

"What?" Journeyman Evan said, far too loudly as far as Lom was concerned.

"Hold still. Hunting cats," Lom whispered. "Three."

"Three?"

"Yes, three."

"Vadoma?" Journeyman Evan said quite softly, after turning his head to look at the three cats arranged quite comfortably across from him.

The largest of the cats rose, stretched, and then with an impatient look over her shoulder, wandered to the head of the path leading away from the campsite.

"It is always nice to know that even in these unsure times, some things stay the same," Journeyman Evan groused as he crawled out of his blanket roll.

"You, you, you know this hunting cat?" Lom asked.

"Yes, and she has not learned patience since the last time I set eyes on her. So, Vadoma, you will have to wait for us feeble folks to get a bit of food before we mount up and follow you."

"We're going to follow a hunting cat?" Lom was beginning to feel very foolish. He had sat frozen in place, afraid the hunting cats would pounce at any moment, and it turned out that Journeyman Evan knew these hunting cats and was prepared to follow at least one of them. Here he had been blindly following a young man he barely knew to who knew where, and now he was going to follow that young man following a hunting cat? *Can life get any stranger?* he wondered. How Lom longed to be back weeding in the royal palace garden.

"Come on, Lom, don't just stand there. Stir that fire back to life so we can cook a hot meal before we travel on. We should reach our destination in a day or two."

By noon of their second day together, the hunting cats led them into a pasture that had the lushest grass Lom had ever seen. In addition, there was a shed and a single horse in the pasture. Journeyman Evan directed Lom to stow his horse's tack and saddle in the shed and grab his saddle bags.

Lom could not figure out just where they were going, since they were headed back along the path they had arrived on. They had passed through a clearing on their way to the pasture. There had been nothing there but a vine-covered mound that, oddly enough, had a chimney sticking out of it. It occurred to him that there had also been smoke coming out of the chimney. Now that he had a chance to really observe the vine-covered mound, he noticed the vines were constantly moving, yet there was little to no wind.

The larger hunting cat, the one Journeyman Evan called Vadoma, led them toward the vine-covered mound.

"So, Vadoma, you brought him back again, did you?" called a booming voice from the mound. "And how serendipitous, since I have need of someone who knows how to handle glass panes."

Lom heard Journeyman Evan moan. He did not have too much time to wonder what the pained moan was about. He was thoroughly distracted when the vines covering the mound pulled aside to reveal a porch. Even more surprising was the man standing on the porch. Very tall and rail thin, with long shaggy hair and skin the color of pine bark, the man more resembled the trees surrounding his cottage than the folks he faced. He was certainly one of the oddest looking men Lom had ever seen. The oddness was not due to the very tall height of the man, nor his thinness. Rather, it was the fact that the man standing on the porch was draped in leaves, or to be more accurate, twined in vines, which started out of the tops of his boots and extended upward until they threaded through his beard and hair.

"Good to see you again, Ealdred. Not particularly glad you need help with glass panes," quipped Journeyman Evan.

"So, are you going to introduce me to your traveling companion? Please do me a favor and tell me his real name the first time, if you would."

"This is Lom, recently a worker in the royal palace gardens. I have a boon to ask of you concerning him."

"Do you now? Well, you had best come on in. I've been expecting visitors for about a week now. I expect you are them."

Lom looked at Journeyman Evan, and his concern was evident. *How could this strange man have been expecting us?* Before he could ask Journeyman Evan, the man called Ealdred hollered that they needed to get their feet moving. The midday meal was on, and they certainly would not want it to burn. Upon entering the cottage that had been hidden by the vines, Lom saw that the table was set for three. He turned to head back out the door, only to find it blocked by the three hunting cats.

"Now, Vadoma, let the lad by. If he needs to hit the privy and wash up before he eats, who are we to stop him?" admonished Ealdred. "Living alone, sometimes I forget those niceties. I'll just give the pot a stir. The meal can wait a few more minutes. A bit of a scrub-up wouldn't hurt you either, Journeyman Evan."

The three cats, who had been blocking the doorway, moved farther into the room and settled themselves into various places, leaving a clear path to the door. Lom walked out as far as the porch and then halted. *Where do I think I am going to go?* he wondered. *How far can I get on foot? I would never think of taking the horse I was riding, since it is not mine. How did this strange man know to expect two visitors and prepare for their arrival with a warm meal and the table set? As far as I know, Journeyman Evan did not tell anyone where we were heading. He asked the others to trust him. He kept our destination secret so that others could not inadvertently give it away. How then did this Ealdred know we were coming?*

"Are you all right?" Journeyman Evan asked, as he joined Lom on the porch. "Ealdred may have a somewhat strange appearance. He is, however, a very good man and very loyal to the Crown. I think you will be safe here."

"I was only a little surprised by his appearance. That is not what concerned me just now." Lom stopped speaking, for he found he was very embarrassed and reluctant to tell Journeyman Evan his thoughts.

"Go on," Journeyman Evan suggested gently.

"How did he know we were coming? Did you see the table? He had three places set out."

"I don't know. I just know that I would trust the man with my life. I already have once, and I would do it again. Come on, let's get washed up, and then head back in."

The meal was of simple fare and a quiet one. Afterwards, Ealdred showed both the lads around. Lom was fascinated by the greenhouses, which were kept warm even in the coldest months due to Ealdred piping hot water into them from the hot springs. Being in the small greenhouse, smelling damp earth and growing plants, reminded Lom of being back in the royal palace garden and planting. How Lom longed to be back there!

"Besides keeping the greenhouses warm and being able to grow vegetables in the cold months, the hot springs also provide warm water in my bath house. Why don't you go first, Lom? Take a good long soak while I consult with Journeyman Evan here about the problem I'm having with my newest greenhouse."

After showing Lom where the bathhouse was, Ealdred walked back to the cottage with Journeyman Evan.

"Is this another lad carrying one of the pieces of the oppgave ringe?" Ealdred inquired.

"Would that he was, but no. He is, we think, a sensitive, one who can tell if some object is one that holds power." Journeyman Evan went on to tell Ealdred what had happened at the Raven's tower. "So you see, it's best he be someplace where he might be safe. That is the boon I would ask of you. May he stay here?"

Before Ealdred could answer, all three hunting cats suddenly scrambled up and swiftly ran out the front door.

# Chapter Thirty

Lom took his sweet time washing up. It was the first time since he had been snatched in the capital that he was truly alone. Neck deep in the warm water, really clean for the first time in weeks, he wanted to savor the moment for just a bit longer before he returned to the vine-covered cottage. He was still having trouble coming to terms with what had happened to him and why folks thought he had some sort of special ability. Finally, Lom reluctantly pulled himself out of the bathing pool and dried himself off. It felt good to be in clean clothes, even though they were not his.

Lom glanced up at the sun when he stepped outside the bath house and realized he had spent more time soaking than he had thought. When he looked down the path to the cottage, he stopped dead still. Standing, blocking the path, was a huge wolf, a huge black wolf. Lom found he could not tear his eyes away from the wolf's ice-blue eyes, which seemed to be looking into him so very deeply that Lom was sure he would have had no secrets left, if he had ever had any secrets.

The wolf broke eye contact first when he tilted his head just a bit, as if he were listening. Lom caught a hint of movement out of the corner of his eye and was surprised when Vadoma and the other two hunting cats came flowing out of the forest surrounding the bathhouse. The two younger hunting cats flanked Lom. Vadoma moved to stand in front of him. Lom found himself afraid to breathe.

As Lom stood frozen in place, it struck him that the hunting cats and the wolf were not growling or hissing at each other. They seemed to be taking each other's measure. There was something timeless about this meeting between hunting cat and wolf. Lom felt he was witnessing something important. He just was not sure what. After a few moments, Vadoma nodded her head, and just as swiftly and silently as they had arrived, the three hunting cats melted back into the forest. The black wolf slowly advanced toward Lom.

For reasons he would never be able to explain, Lom did not immediately turn, grab for the door behind him, open it, and escape into the safety of the bathhouse. Instead, he stood frozen, his feet glued to the paving stones. When the black wolf was just a foot away from Lom, the wolf sat down. Lom did not know what to do. It was way too late to try to get inside the bathhouse. The wolf was making no threatening moves. Tentatively, Lom reached out his hand. He was not sure if it was a gesture of peace or pleading.

"Ah, um …." Lom started. He stopped speaking, for he did not know what to say. *Should I ask the wolf to move aside so I can go back to the cottage? Should I ask the wolf if I am about to be dinner? I am sure the black wolf can feel my fear.*

When Lom was thinking about what the wolf might do, it struck him that he was having that same feeling he had when near certain objects in the glass cases in the royal palace. Following that thought came a second one. He had a similar feeling when the hunting cats had first entered the campsite those many days ago. Lom had dismissed the feeling, for he had been concentrating on holding onto the torch and had been worrying about his and the journeyman's life expectancy.

*What is it about these animals? I know a hunting cat sometimes partners with a folk. What do I know about wolves? Somewhere in my distant memories is something about black wolves in particular. Night wolves, that is what they are called,* Lom thought. *I remember hearing of night wolves from a street storyteller I once stopped to listen to on my way home from work. I thought it was an old granny tale meant to scare young children. Surely, the black wolf sitting in front of me could not be a night wolf. They are the stuff of stories and legends.*

The wolf continued to sit patiently, waiting. Finally, he stood up and stepped forward, pushing his nose against Lom's outstretched hand, which he did not realize he had continued to hold out. Lom tentatively scratched the black wolf behind his ears, as he would have done if the black wolf were one of the dogs on his foster family's croft. A feeling of warmth and rightness spread over him. A little bit of the aloneness he was not even aware he had been feeling slipped away.

"So, what now?" Lom asked.

The black wolf turned and headed down the path toward Ealdred's cottage.

"Right, then. Back to the cottage it is," Lom said, somewhat bemused.

Ealdred and Journeyman Evan were standing on the front porch of the cottage flanked by the three hunting cats as Lom and the black wolf approached.

"Oh my," Journeyman Evan said.

"Oh my, indeed," Ealdred agreed. "If my eyes are not deceiving me, the lad is walking toward us following a night wolf. I've only ever once seen one, and only from a distance."

"On our journey here, off and on I had the feeling we were being watched. When we got closer to your place, I thought it might have been the hunting cats. Maybe not."

"Speaking of hunting cats, Vadoma and her companions don't seem to be too alarmed by the night wolf. The next minute or two ought to be interesting," said Ealdred.

As Lom and the night wolf came closer to the porch, the hunting cats lay down, relaxed, yet remained watchful. The night wolf stopped at the bottom of the stairs and sat.

"So, Lom, is the night wolf with you?" Journeyman Evan inquired.

"I honestly don't know. When I came out of the bathhouse, he was waiting. Then the hunting cats came. I think some type of communication went on between the hunting cats and the night wolf. The hunting cats left, and the night wolf approached me. I, I, I don't know why I didn't run. He seems to like me," Lom stated with a great deal of wonder in his voice. "I think his name is Taarig. I don't know how I know that."

"Well, lad, it would seem we could all stand here all day. A better idea would be for all of us to step inside," suggested Ealdred. "Would you like to come in, Taarig?"

The night wolf stood and proceeded up the short steps to the porch. Ealdred and Journeyman Evan stepped aside. Once the night wolf had entered the cottage, the rest followed. Lom took a chair by the fireplace, sitting down rather abruptly, since his legs were suddenly very shaky. Taarig, the night wolf, lay down beside his chair. The hunting cats each found their favorite spots and curled up as if they had not a care in the world.

"Now then, now that we are all settled, you might want to get your bath, Journeyman Evan," suggested Ealdred.

"Are you sure, sir?"

"Yes, yes, we'll be fine here." Eldred took a seat opposite Lom. "I should have suspected right away."

"Suspected what?" both lads asked in unison.

"Why, that Lom was Neebing blessed, of course."

Dubhlainn had been cooling his heels for over three hours, waiting for an audience with Lord Klingflug. He was dreading his meeting with the former regent, for he had no explanation for how he had let not one but two prisoners escape from the Raven's tower. One minute they were there, and the next minute they were gone. Several weeks later, a troop of royal guards had arrived at Lord Braeden's estate. They had taken Lord Braeden's son Girvin into custody and seized the Raven's tower. Dubhlainn had barely escaped, along with a few others. The Raven's tower was now a garrison for the royal guard. With the strong presence of the Crown in the area, Lord Braeden was of no more use to Lord Klingflug. To lose a strategic place and a loyal supporter all at one time was certainly going to be a blow to Lord Klingflug's plans. Dubhlainn hoped the former regent would not blame him for what had transpired. His thoughts were interrupted when a servant beckoned him to follow him to Lord Klingflug's library.

When Dubhlainn entered the library, Lord Klingflug immediately shouted, "Just what happened? How can folks just disappear? How could you let them get away, especially Aaron Beecroft?"

Having been given no indication that he was allowed to sit, Dubhlainn stood ramrod straight in front of Lord Klingflug's desk. "I don't have an answer for you, sir. We had just taken Beecroft out of his cell and given that lad Lom the ring Beecroft had on him when he was captured. One of the men came down the stairs and said Lord Braeden was at the front door demanding to see Girvin and me. We went up to find out what was going on. I had Yarrow lock the two of them up in Beecroft's cell. At some point they managed to knock out the lantern. Yarrow heard the breaking of glass and, looking down the stairs, could see that the lantern had gone out. He did not go down to check anything out. Said I had told him to guard the landing, and that's what he did."

"It is so hard to find intelligent help these days," Lord Klingflug said pointedly. "Go on."

"Turned out, two of the estate tenants were having a disagreement concerning a pig. Lord Braeden wanted Girvin to intervene rather than take care of it himself. Said it would be a good learning experience. I think he just wanted to know what was going on in the tower. It was easily taken care of. When we went back down and opened Beecroft's cell, it was empty. Yarrow swore that no one went past him. No one went past us out of the tower's only door to the outside either. I can tell you we searched that tower from top to bottom, looked in every nook and cranny, and could not find either Beecroft or the lad Lom. They certainly did not leave by getting past either my men or me. I'm sorry, sir. I just don't know what happened."

"What happened is Aaron Beecroft escaped and went running to his uncle, who in turn convinced the interim ruling council that the Raven's tower should be confiscated along with Girvin. While Lord Braeden is a pompous fool, he was still a loyal pompous fool we could count on. Now we have lost both him and the tower. Most of the large landholders who surround Lord Braeden's holdings are loyal to the Crown. Those who were leaning our way are less inclined now. This has been a costly and most grievous setback. Time is running out. We have to find at least one of the last two rings. Have you had any luck in tracking down what happened to the lad, Lom?"

*This is the second part of my report that Lord Klingflug is not going to like,* Dubhlainn thought. "No, sir. He did not return to the royal palace gardens to ask for his position back. He did not return to the croft where he grew up. He was not seen arriving at the capital with Beecroft. At one point we thought they might have sneaked him into the capital, but our informants have seen neither hide nor hair of him. It was noted that Beecroft arrived at the capital with the lass, Piper. When she left to head home to her family, who guard the southern pass, the lad Lom was not observed to be with her either. He has vanished into the countryside as completely as he vanished from the Raven's tower. My informants in the capital reported that Beecroft made no mention of anyone else being held in the tower or escaping with him. Yet, he was observed talking to the head royal palace gardener shortly after he arrived. No one was close enough to hear their conversation."

"Beecroft must know something. We cannot afford to have him picked up again. There has already been too much attention shown my way after Beecroft escaped the tower," Lord Klingflug said. "He is now surrounded by too many folks to attempt to get ahold of him again. Besides, his usefulness is done. He did not have a piece of the oppgave ringe as was thought. We will just have to keep track of him and have him followed, in case he knows where to find one." Lord Klingflug stated.

"Yes, sir. I already have folks in place to keep track of him."

"Good. You know what to do now. I trust you will not fail me in this."

"No, sir."

"Then go," Lord Klingflug said, with a dismissive wave of his hand. Once Dubhlainn left the room, Lord Klingflug sat back in his chair with a weary sigh, rubbing his hands over his tired eyes. Beecroft's escape and the loss of the Raven's tower was much more than an inconvenience. Folks who had been loyal to him were now beginning to question his leadership. There had always been other plotters. In the past, he had been able to control them by suggesting a united front would better serve all of them. Lord Klingflug knew all too well what happens when too many folks tried to gain power and position. It only weakened them all against the Crown. He needed to make something positive happen soon, before it was too late. He needed to locate the lad, Lom, or another like him.

# Chapter Thirty-One

Very few folks would have recognized the former royal garden laborer named Lom when he left Ealdred's home in late spring. While he would never be described as a strapping lad, he had changed from an underfed, gangly lad to a slim, fit, young man. His hair had grown to shoulder length, and he kept it tied back in a queue. He was quite proud of his beard, which he kept neatly trimmed, even if it was a bit sparse. With a full rucksack on his back, blanket roll tied on top, he looked like a typical youth heading out on a walkabout. What was not typical for an average lad his age on a walkabout was the fact that he was accompanied by a night wolf. From a distance, one might think he was accompanied by a rather large, dark-colored dog. Upon closer inspection, however, it was clear that he was accompanied by a night wolf.

While Lom certainly had changed on the outside, what folks looking at him would not see or know was just how much Lom had changed on the inside. All of his life, he had never felt he quite fit anywhere or had any real purpose in life. The closest he had come to having a feeling of belonging was when he had worked at the royal palace gardens. Yes, he had belonged to a group of workers, yet he had not really known any of them very well, nor had he let any of them really know him. He was often alone. He had felt it suited him. He had told himself that he was not lonely, he just preferred to be alone. Reflecting back now, he realized that he had been fooling himself.

Lom had come to the conclusion that being kidnapped had been one of the best things that had ever happened to him, strange as that sounded.

It had taken him to Ealdred's home. It had been difficult for Lom to see Journeyman Evan leave a few days after they had arrived at Ealdred's vine-covered home, for he was at least someone familiar. Ealdred, on the other hand, was not only a stranger, but, in comparison to many, would also be considered strange. While his size was unusual, it was not that which would make others do a double take should they see him striding down the lane. As Lom had noticed upon first meeting Ealdred, the man had vines twined about himself, rising up from his boot tops and ending up threaded in his beard and hair. What Lom had learned, to his great surprise, was that this was not a strange affectation of attire. Ealdred did not go out in the woods each day, cut fresh vines, and then drape them about his body. No, the vines that twined about Ealdred's body were living vines.

When Lom had finally had the courage to ask Ealdred about the vines, whether they grew out of his body, the man had thrown his head back and had roared with laughter. After he had pulled a large handkerchief out of his back pocket and wiped his watering eyes, Ealdred had responded. "Ach, lad, no, they do not grow out of my body. I just like having green living plants close. These here live on air, so no, I don't have dirt in my boots. But I can see more questions just bubbling in that head of yours."

Lom had been taken aback, for he was fairly good at hiding what he was thinking. Ealdred was right, he did have more questions. First and foremost was how did Ealdred manipulate the vines that covered his cottage? Also, how did he get plants that looked as if they were withered and almost dead to show new life? His questioning thoughts were interrupted when Ealdred addressed him again.

"Well, lad, now that you have shown you are curious, I think it is time to begin your lessons."

"Lessons?"

"Journeyman Evan said you were kidnapped by folks who thought to use you. They thought you were what is known as a sensitive, someone who is aware of things that others might not be. In your case, you can sense objects which might be more than they seem to most. I think that is probably true. In addition, I think you also have an affinity for living plants."

214

"Oh, sir, I don't know about that," Lom replied.

"Let me ask you something. When you were working in the royal palace gardens, did the head royal palace gardener ever assign you to an area that was especially damaged or neglected?"

"Yes, often. The former regent had not wished to hire the labor needed to keep up the royal palace gardens, so there were many areas like that at the bottom of the groomed part of the garden along the edge of the wild and neglected back area. The other workers often commented that they were happy they were not in the head royal palace gardener's bad graces like I was. They would ask what I had done to get the jobs they particularly disliked. 'Better you than me,' they would say."

"Were you in the head royal palace gardener's bad graces?" Ealdred asked.

"No, sir."

"So, how did you feel about being assigned those areas?"

"I didn't mind. I liked working alone. I liked cleaning up an area and finding what was hidden under the dead branches and leaves. Sometimes many of the original plantings were still there. They just needed to be given space to grow."

Ealdred let the lad continue to talk for a while, encouraging him here and there to talk more. He watched the lad's usual somber countenance light up as he talked about living plants. *Ah yes, there is more to this lad than others might notice*, Ealdred thought. Ealdred knew the head royal palace gardener and could speculate he had known what Ealdred had begun to suspect.

"Now about those lessons," Ealdred said. "I have been looking for someone to pass my knowledge about plants to. You seem like a likely candidate. Are you interested?"

Lom had not needed to think very long or hard before he answered "yes." He had not really known what he was getting himself into. The rest of the winter had passed by quickly. Each day included doing routine chores, book learning, work in the greenhouses, lessons with Ealdred, and spending time with Taarig. Lessons with Ealdred and time with Taarig had been his favorite parts of each day. Lom had been delighted when the night wolf had continued to stay with him.

All things living, Ealdred had told him, respond to forces of nature. And he had said, some living things respond to certain folk. Plants responded to him, if he asked nicely and did not ask them to do anything against their nature. At first Lom was torn, thinking Ealdred was quite mad. On the other hand, he had seen Ealdred do the unexplainable, like control the vines that covered his cottage. Ealdred explained he did not control the plants, merely asked for their help. In return, he tried to keep their environment in good condition. Ealdred suggested that Lom had a natural aptitude with plants, and he could teach him more. During their lessons, Ealdred had taught Lom about the nature and characteristics of hundreds of plants. He had taught him how to still his mind and listen. For the first time in his life, Lom felt he had some worth. Ealdred had become more than a teacher; he had become a friend over the course of the winter.

"Now, lad, plants don't really talk to you in clear, colorful sentences, mind you. It's more of a feeling you get. Be observant, listen carefully. You have been doing that all along, you know. When you worked in the royal palace garden and discovered those plants under all of the deadfall and trash, did you always know what they needed?"

Lom had to think about the question for a long while before he replied. While he had grown up on a croft, only a little of what he had learned there had been useful in the royal palace gardens. Though he had watched and observed others as to what they did, more often than not he acted more on instinct, he realized. The plants always seemed to flourish under his care.

"You have the instincts, lad. It is clear you have never been trained. Now let's give you the training. You are going to be working hard, mind you. Are you up for that?"

Lom had been more than ready for anything Ealdred taught him. Some of the lessons came easy. Some came hard. It never mattered to Lom if he got what Ealdred was trying to teach him the first time, or the second, or the third. He was fascinated and determined. Winter passed by quickly.

When winter finally came to an end, Lom had helped Ealdred with the spring cleanup and planting, putting things to rights after the cold months. With the coming of the spring rains and the continued warming of the days, the ferns and other forest groundcovers came up, and the trees began to open their leaves. There was a freshness to the air. However, with each passing day, Lom had begun to feel more and more restless. The discovery he had made in Ealdred's side room, which held books on plants, had made him more so.

It had been on the afternoon of a very rainy early spring day when Ealdred had told Lom to take the afternoon off. They had been working hard day after day and Lom deserved a break, he had said. Feeling at loose ends, Lom had gone into a side room of the cottage, which held an amazing number of books. He had not spent very much time in there, for Ealdred usually brought whatever books they might be using on any given day out to the kitchen table, where there was plenty of room to spread out and the light was good.

Lom had thought he would start at one end of the book room at the bookshelf closest to the door and work his way around the room. He had never really had the luxury of just looking at shelf after shelf of books. His foster family had been too poor to use what little coin they had on books. Lom had never found the time when he had lived in the capital to go to the royal library, though he had thought about it from time to time and wished he could.

Lom had been in Ealdred's book room no more than a minute or two when he heard a noise coming from the far left corner. Glancing over his shoulder, he noticed that Taarig was pawing at something under the bookshelf. It seemed odd to him since he had never seen Taarig pay much attention to anything in the cottage. Lom felt a bit of apprehension for some reason, but he could not put his finger on it. He dismissed the feeling at first. He thought it was just a bit of unease, maybe caused by the pounding rain, lightning, and the almost continuous loud rumble of thunder. The feeling persisted to the point that Lom needed to pay attention to it. Turning, he faced the far back corner of the room. He felt no surprise at seeing Taarig now sitting patiently by the bookshelf across the room and something lying at Taarig's front paws. The night wolf gave him an impatient look, as if Lom should quit his dawdling. When he reached Taarig, the night wolf pushed a very small, tied, cloth-bound bundle forward.

"I take it you would like me to pick this up?" Lom said. "Found this under the bookcase, did you? I had best show it to Ealdred."

Lom headed back into the main room of the cottage to find Ealdred in a chair by the fire.

"Ealdred?"

"What is it, lad?"

"When I was in looking at your collection of books, Taarig was worrying at something under the far left bookcase. I didn't pay much attention at first. He seems to have found this," Lom said, handing the bundle to Ealdred.

"Let's take it to the kitchen table and look at what he found. I certainly don't recognize it. It's not something I ever remember putting there, nor do I recall anyone giving it to me."

Ealdred lay the bundle down on the kitchen table. Very carefully, he untied the string that bound the bundle and began to fold back the cloth.

"Interesting that whatever is in here is wrapped in cloth made out of golden pine spider silk," Ealdred remarked.

The unwrapping revealed a small carved wooden box. Once the box was fully unwrapped, Lom felt that familiar pull, the one he had felt before when near some of the objects in the cases in the royal palace.

"Why don't you pick it up, lad?"

When Lom picked up the small carved box, he almost dropped it, for it felt like it had a heartbeat.

"What is it, Lom?" Ealdred asked, seeing the look that crossed Lom's face.

"I'm not sure." Lom felt flustered, for he was afraid of what Ealdred might think of him if he told him the box felt like it had a heart beating inside it. He thought he might have been mistaken, so he held the box out to Ealdred.

"It's an interesting little box," Ealdred said, looking at it after Lom had placed it in his hand. "You felt something, didn't you?"

"Yes, sir."

"I don't happen to have that talent. I've known others who do. You should not doubt what you feel. Let's take a look at what Taarig found. I have never seen carvings like these before. For some reason that I cannot explain, this box feels very old to me. I think it is made of quirrelit wood. Shall we see if something is inside?"

Ealdred opened the box. Inside was a tightly-folded piece of paper.

"I think this task calls for smaller hands than mine, Lom," Ealdred said, and handed the box back to Lom.

Very carefully, Lom removed the folded paper from the box. Taking care to unfold the paper without ripping or tearing it, he laid the paper down on the kitchen table and smoothed it out. Both sides of the paper were filled with spidery handwriting in a language Lom had never seen.

"This paper is written in the old language."

"The old language, sir?" Lom questioned.

"Yes. When our ancestors came here to Sommerhjem, the majority of the settlers spoke and wrote in the language we use now. A very small minority of the early settlers were of the Høyttaier clan, and they brought with them the knowledge of a very old language. The history behind the language has been lost over time. However, they felt it was important to pass down to future generations the knowledge of the language, both spoken and written."

"I have never heard of the Høyttaier clan," Lom remarked.

"No, probably not. What little is known of the distant past suggests that the Høyttaiers were often regarded as different. Because they were hardworking folks and stuck close together helping one another, they prospered. As often happens when times grow tough due to a downturn in weather or a change in rule, those who did not do as well were often jealous. As a result, sometimes members of the Høyttaier clan were persecuted. To help them survive, the members of the Høyttaier clan faded into the woodwork, as they say. They became secretive about who they were. However, they did continue to teach each new generation how to read and write in the old language."

Ealdred got up and lifted the tea kettle off a hook over the fire and brought it back to the table. He poured both of them a cup of tea before going on.

"You probably heard something about what happened at the capital during the great summer fair there, which caused the Regent to step down."

"Only a little, sir, and I really didn't understand or pay attention to much of it."

"The Lady Esmeralda, then the royal heir, called the Gylden Sirklene challenge. One of the elements needed at that time was the Book of Rules, which tells what must happen for the challenge to be called and fulfilled. It is written in the old language. Lord Klingflug knew that basically only a member of the Høyttaier clan could read the Book of Rules, so he had set about trying to eliminate members of the clan. Fortunately, members of the clan had been warned. Most escaped one way or the other and survived."

"Do you think this paper is important, then? I have the oddest feeling it is."

"Well, Lom, I would suggest you pour another cup of tea and settle back. I will read you what it says."

It was the contents of the paper and Ealdred's accident that had sent Lom off down the lane with only Taarig as a companion.

# Chapter Thirty-Two

As he continued to walk down the lane ever farther and farther away from Ealdred's cottage, Lom reflected on the last few weeks. Ealdred told Lom he could translate the paper. It took a moment for Lom to realize he was being entrusted with perhaps the most important of Ealdred's secrets. Ealdred was a Høyttaier. He had asked Lom to give him some time to translate the paper, for he had said he was a bit out of practice reading the old language.

Ealdred had spent several hours hunkered over the paper muttering and murmuring to himself, complaining about the author's very bad penmanship, not to mention how tiny the writing was. He had finally asked Lom to light the lamps, for the sky had darkened further with the increase of the storm overhead. When he had looked up, he had a bemused look on his face.

"Over the years, I have had a number of visitors, especially during the early times, the hard times, when the former regent was trying to hunt down members of the Høyttaier clan. We had a lot of help moving clan members from one location to another. A lot of folks who were loyal to the Crown took very great risks hiding members of my clan. My place was a sanctuary for a number of folks during that terrible time. I remember well the one who must have hidden the box here. She was a woman who had a great talent with plants. Perhaps she thought she might return here at some time. I don't know. Anyway, it was written by an elderly woman who lost her entire family during that dreadful time. Her name was Aldys. Only she escaped, for she had been out in the forest mushroom hunting.

When she returned home, she found her home destroyed and her family missing. I heard later that her family had survived. I think she died, however, before the family could be reunited. Fortunately, on the day her family went missing, her neighbors took her in temporarily and hid her. Others got her on her journey to a safe place. Mine was just one of the stops along the way."

"Is what this woman wrote on that paper important?" Lom asked.

"More than I would have suspected at the beginning. At first, it was just the ramblings of an old, terrified, grieving woman. She was quite frail, if I remember her rightly, and I heard she did not live but a few more months after she stayed here. It's what she wrote on the back page that is really important," Ealdred said.

"What is the back page about?" Lom inquired.

"It is about a piece of the oppgave ringe."

"One of the pieces everyone is still looking for?"

"I'm not sure. Who held the two Nissa brought in has been accounted for. A lad named Greer brought in the third ring. His family held the one he brought to the capital for a number of generations. The lass Meryl found hers in a hole in a cliff, so that one could be the one I just read about. I think not, however."

"Why not?" Lom asked, becoming even more interested in what Ealdred had to say. *For someone who lived away from most folks, he is very well-informed as to what is happening in Sommerhjem*, Lom thought.

"The way I heard the tale, that piece of the oppgave ringe was probably stolen by a tyvfugl bird. While they have a fairly wide range, I think where this woman traveled would have been out of the range of a tyvfugl bird."

"That makes sense."

"The fifth ring was brought in by a young man named Chance, and it had been in his family for a long time. A young woman named Yara brought in the sixth ring and, again, it had been in the possession of a member of her scattered family for several generations. Journeyman Evan told me that Piper, the musician traveling with Aaron Beecroft, brought the seventh ring to the capital. It also had been in the possession of a family for several generations, and so is not the one that Aldys wrote about," Ealdred said.

"So this piece of the oppgave ringe is either the one Meryl brought to the capital, or one of the last two pieces to be found," suggested Lom.

"You have the right of it, lad."

"Did Aldys take the ring with her when she escaped the former regent's agents?"

"According to what she wrote, yes. She wore it in a golden pine spider silk pouch around her neck, so had it with her when she was away from her home when the former regent's agents came. And before you ask, she did not have it in her possession when she came here, so she did not leave it here somewhere, or with me."

"Does the note she left in the box tell where she left it, or with whom?" Lom asked.

Ealdred took a moment to think. He knew if Journeyman Evan or Greer were sitting before him asking him that question, he would not hesitate, as he was now. He knew that Aaron Beecroft had entrusted Lom into Journeyman Evan's care to get him away from those who would use him. At least, that was the story he had pieced together. Ealdred thought his instincts were correct, and that Lom was indeed one of the Neebing blessed. Though he really did not know much about Lom, the fact that the night wolf had shown up and was sticking close to him supported his conclusion. Lom had proved to be an apt student of all that he had taught him during the winter months. *The plants certainly would not have responded so readily to one with evil intent in his heart*, Ealdred thought. Shaking himself slightly, he pushed away any concerns he had that Lom was anything other than what he thought he was and began to speak again.

"Aldys knew of the Gylden Sirklene challenge. She writes that she surmised that the former regent had gone after members of the Høyttaier clan for the very reasons he did so, to prevent the Book of Rules from being read. Aldys also knew what she carried. She knew it was part of the oppgave ringe, and was fearful she would be caught with it. Even more interesting, she knew why it was important. Unfortunately, she does not reveal that here. We have lost so much knowledge over the years," Ealdred said sadly.

"So, what did she do with the piece of the oppgave ringe?" Lom asked, as he absentmindedly scratched Taarig behind the ears.

"She left it in the royal forest near the capital, in a quirrelit grove of all places. I have been in the royal forest near the capital. Someone early in the history of Sommerhjem recognized the need to preserve large areas of forests and natural meadows near what would become the capital. Eventually these areas would be designated as parks or royal forests, and no attempt has been made to build or farm the land since time out of mind. The trees there are huge and ancient. Interspersed among the pines and other trees are quirrelit groves. Not one grove, mind you, but many groves. Unfortunately, Aldys does not specify just which grove she left the ring in."

"Can't you search out her family? They might know."

"Possibly, but I don't think she had a chance to tell them. Another problem is she does not say how she left the piece of the oppgave ringe. She does not tell whether she just hung it on a tree, buried it, stuck it in a hole in a tree, nothing. What might complicate finding the ring even more is the fact that Aldys, as I told you, had a great deal of talent when it came to plants. I learned much from her when she stayed with me. She might have used her talent to disguise the hiding place even more thoroughly."

"After all this time, how would anyone be able to find the piece of the oppgave ringe, if it is even still there?" Lom asked.

"A very good question, and one you already have an answer for."

"Me? I have the answer?"

"You are the answer, Lom."

"I don't understand."

"I think you do."

Lom did not want to understand what Ealdred was suggesting. If he did, he knew his time here was going to come to an end. He did not want to leave. He had grown to care a great deal for Ealdred, and he treasured learning from him. This place had begun to feel like more of a home than any place he had ever known.

*Let someone else wander the royal forest looking for just the right quirrelit tree where some old woman hid a ring*, Lom thought. *This story she wrote in her journal is just a bunch of twaddle. Just the ravings of a frightened old woman.* Even as he considered these thoughts, Lom knew he was only trying to convince himself that he was not the one to go. He could refuse. He was so lost in his own thoughts that he did not realize Taarig had moved his head from under Lom's hand and had taken that hand in his mouth. Lom was abruptly pulled out of his musings when Taarig nipped him.

"Ouch. What was that for?" Lom asked the night wolf.

Taarig placed a paw on Lom's knee. Lom looked down at the paw and then up into the ice-blue of Taarig's eyes. Suddenly, for some reason, Lom felt both ashamed of his selfish thoughts and, strangely enough, at peace with the idea of leaving Ealdred's place. A sense of rightness washed through him concerning the idea of going in search of the piece of the oppgave ringe. Taarig nodded his head, breaking eye contact. Lom looked up to see Ealdred watching them.

"Have you and the night wolf sorted it all through then, lad?"

"So it would seem," Lom answered ruefully.

"It'll take us a few days to close things up here so we can be gone for a while. I would suggest we leave four or five days hence."

"You, you, you want to come with me?" Lom asked, as a feeling of relief washed over him.

"Well, of course. Should be an adventure."

Everything had gone well until the day before they were going to leave. Lom had been out back behind the cottage splitting wood when he heard a crash and a bellow. Racing around the corner of the cottage, he spotted Ealdred lying face down just outside the door of one of the greenhouses, a broken clay pot and dirt scattered on the path beyond Ealdred's prone body. Lom had arrived at the greenhouse to hear Ealdred railing away about what a clumsy oaf he was. Interspersed between the complaining were heartfelt moans.

"I'll be needing your help to stand up, lad," Ealdred said.

Lom struggled to help Ealdred get to his feet. At one point, he suggested to Ealdred that he could get a large tree branch and try to lever him into a standing position, for Lom feared he would not have the strength to get Ealdred upright. Lom had always thought Ealdred was one of the tallest men he had ever encountered, which was part of the problem. Finally, he got Ealdred into an upright position, but their troubles were only starting. When Ealdred tried to put his full weight on his left foot, he found he could not. Placing his hand on Lom's shoulder, he managed to hop and hobble to the cottage.

Ealdred lowered himself into one of the chairs by the fireplace. Lom almost had to cut Ealdred's boot off, for his ankle had swollen to twice its normal size.

"Well, this could put a slight crimp in our travel plans," Ealdred said, and then grimaced as Lom lifted his leg and slid a stool underneath. "I don't think the ankle is broken. Just a really bad sprain, which will take a while to heal."

"I'll just go put my things back in my room. We can go when you are feeling better," Lom said.

"No, Lom, you need to be off. I have this feeling that it is necessary for you to go now, and not later when I can travel."

"We could put you on that horse that is getting fat and lazy on the thick green grass out in the clearing. I'm not going to leave you," Lom said.

"That horse has traveled its last trail ride. He is old, and deserves his final days munching on green grass. He and I would not make it more than a few days before we both collapsed. No, bring me paper and pen so I can send a note to my sister by messenger bird. She will come tend to me, and you can get on with what is really important, finding that ring."

Depending on how one looked at it, fate solved the issue of whether Lom was to stay or go before he had even fetched the pen and paper. Just as he stood up, Taarig had already done so and was facing the front door, very alert, ears perked forward. Suddenly, Vadoma flowed into the cottage, followed by the two smaller hunting cats.

"Check out the front door now, would you, lad? I'm thinking we are about to have a visitor," said Ealdred, "and someone the cats know."

When Lom peeked through the vines, he saw a small wagon approaching, driven by a slender woman who would be distinctive wherever she went, for her skin was translucent in appearance and her hair was the color of frosted glass.

"Hallo brother, are you home?" the woman called.

"Open the vines and let her know we are here, Lom. Help has arrived before we even needed to send for it," suggested Ealdred. "That is my sister, Master Opeline, the one I was about to send for. Saves me a messenger bird."

Lom was glad to note that, despite being in pain, Ealdred had not lost his sense of humor. He quickly got the vines covering the cottage to move the way Ealdred had taught him. Stepping out the door, he invited Master Opeline in.

"Your brother is inside. He had a slight accident just before you arrived and sprained his ankle. He was just about to send a messenger bird off for you."

"Good thing I arrived when I did, for I would not have gotten the message for several weeks," Master Opeline said, climbing the steps of the cottage. "And you are?"

"My apologies. I'm Lom. Please come in."

"Oh my. A hunting cat or two I have come to expect when I visit you, Ealdred. I never expected to see a night wolf in my lifetime, much less in your cottage!" exclaimed Master Opeline.

"Good to see you, Sister. I'm not responsible for the night wolf. Taarig is a friend of Lom's here."

Master Opeline raised a questioning eyebrow.

"It's a long story," Ealdred said. He went on to explain just how Lom had arrived at his cottage, and what had transpired over the late winter months. "If all had gone as planned, if you had come a day or two later, you would not have found us at home. What brings you my way anyway?"

"I can't rightly tell you. I was on glassmaker guild business west of here. Something seemed to be urging me in your direction."

"Glad you've come. Can you stay a while? Lom still needs to leave, and I would only slow him down."

"I would not have left until Ealdred could come along," Lom stated, directing his comment to Master Opeline.

"Is anyone going to explain to me just why it is so urgent for Lom to leave right away?" Master Opeline asked.

"Sorry, didn't I get to that part?" questioned Ealdred.

"No."

"Sorry. It seems that I have had in my possession for years clues to the whereabouts of a piece of the oppgave ringe, not that I would have known what the oppgave ringe was until recently. Lom here discovered the clues. Well, more correctly, Taarig discovered them. We were about to set off to the royal forest near the capital to look for the piece of the oppgave ringe when I tripped over the threshold of one of the greenhouses and severely sprained my ankle."

"Your accident might have actually been for the best," commented Master Opeline. When both Ealdred and Lom looked at her questioningly, she went on. "Brother, you are not exactly a plain, average-looking man who just blends in with other folk. Even without the vines growing willy-nilly about your body, you are a very tall man. Combine you with a lad and a night wolf, and you all would have been pretty noticeable and unforgettable. If you had thought the three of you could travel to the royal forest unnoticed, that would have been really pushing your luck."

"Ah, leave it to my sister to be the practical one and suck all the joy out of an adventure," crabbed Ealdred.

"Oh, pish posh. Let me take a look at that ankle of yours."

The three spent the rest of the evening talking over how to get Lom safely to the royal forest near the capital. One suggestion was to call on the same folks who had helped members of the Høyttaier clan escape the former regent's agents over the years.

"Don't know how many are still in place. It'll be chancy. Better than nothing, however," Ealdred had said.

# CHAPTER THIRTY-THREE

Spring was in full bloom outside the meeting room of Lord Klingflug's summer lodge. Now that the weather made travel easier, Lord Klingflug had invited his top advisors to gather. Summer was approaching way too fast and with only two more pieces of the oppgave ringe not yet brought to the capital, it was time to put their collective heads together if they hoped to have any chance at all of keeping the Gylden Sirklene challenge from happening. Each of the advisors and their top aides had circuitously and surreptitiously made their way to the meeting place.

"There has been no pattern as to whether the folks bringing a piece of the oppgave ringe to the capital have been male or female. Neither has there been any indication that rank or the way they make their living matters. All of these folks have little or nothing in common, nothing that makes them stand out," Lord Klingflug remarked.

"Insofar as male, female, rank, position, post, type of work, you are most correct that they have nothing in common," stated Lady Farcroft. "However, I think there is a pattern." All those sitting around the table turned to look at Lady Farcroft. "None of the folks who brought a piece of the oppgave ringe came to the capital unaccompanied."

"You are right. They always had the help of those who are loyal to the Crown. It is not very helpful knowing that, since we can't watch everyone we know who is loyal to the Crown," interrupted the man sitting to the right of Lady Farcroft.

Forcing down her anger at being interrupted, Lady Farcroft took a deep breath and continued. "Of course they were helped and accompanied by those loyal to the Crown. That is not the point. The point here is that each one of the folks who brought a piece of the oppgave ringe to the capital was accompanied by an animal, most of them uncommon animals, or ones rarely seen with folks."

Lady Farcroft felt a moment of satisfaction that she finally had everyone's attention. "That rover girl had a hunting cat. While Lord Avital's whelp had only a border dog, it was of a color rarely seen these days in Sommerhjem. That lass, Meryl, came into the capital with a griff falcon, and the librarian, Yara, a red bog fox. The lad, Chance, had the strangest animal of all. I think it was called a halekrets. The latest ring bearer, Piper, was accompanied by a mountain cat, an animal hardly ever seen outside of the southern mountains, much less in the company of a folk."

Lady Farcroft looked around the table at those assembled there, and could see their expressions change one by one as each realized what she was suggesting.

"Perhaps we need to be alert to anyone who is traveling about the countryside with an uncommon animal," suggested Lady Farcroft.

"Brilliant, just brilliant," said Lord Klingflug.

*Which is why I will be the next ruler of Sommerhjem,* Lady Farcroft thought. *I have already alerted my agents to be on the lookout for anyone traveling with an uncommon animal. They are not to apprehend them right away. No, try to befriend them, if possible. If not, keep track of them, and if they are heading toward the capital, intercept them.*

While Lady Farcroft congratulated herself on her forethought, Lord Klingflug issued orders to send the word out to those loyal to him to be on the lookout for any folk who might be traveling with an uncommon animal.

Lom took reluctant step after reluctant step, taking him farther and farther away from Ealdred's cottage and relative safety. He and Taarig were now off on their own on what many would see as a fool's errand. Ealdred and his sister, Master Opeline, certainly had more faith in Lom than he had in himself and his so-called abilities. As each hour passed, Lom trudged farther down the lane leading away from Ealdred's cottage and became more doubtful that he was doing the right thing.

"We should turn back, Taarig. Ealdred might need us. Who knows how long his sister can really stay? What if she gets called away before Ealdred's ankle is healed? We should go back. Besides, we are probably just kidding ourselves that we can find the ring."

Lom turned to head back the way they had come, only to find Taarig blocking his path. When Lom tried to move past him to the right, Taarig swiftly blocked his way. After several more unsuccessful attempts to get past the night wolf, Lom turned around and resignedly started once again to walk away from Ealdred's cottage. Taarig fell into step beside him.

"I know I was being foolish, Taarig. It's just that I'm scared and quite a bit overwhelmed. I mean, who am I to be responsible for finding a piece of the oppgave ringe? I was content to work in the royal palace garden. I was happy there with the green growing plants and the smell of dark earth. At least, I thought I was."

As Lom continued to walk, he thought about what he had just said and realized that it was true, he had been content to work in the royal palace garden. He wondered if he would still be content with his old life now that he had trained with Ealdred. He knew Ealdred had more to teach him. The one thought Lom was holding on to was that Ealdred had told him before he left that he was always welcome to return and to stay as long as it suited them both.

The days of walking were pleasant. The spring rains were mostly past. The warm sun shining down felt good on the cool days. The nights were still quite cold. Each night Lom had been fortunate to find a sheltered camping spot. Between the fire and Taarig's warm body nestled against him, Lom kept warm through the nights.

Lom, Ealdred, and Master Opeline had talked about what routes Lom should take, where he might seek help, and when his route would become riskier. He knew he should avoid the larger towns and villages. At some point, he would need to get more supplies and would have to risk going into a smaller village. He certainly could ask for a night's shelter and a meal at a farmstead or croft. Traveling with a night wolf was going to make him stand out. No one was going to mistake Taarig for an overlarge dog. Lom knew that, given a choice, he was not going to give up Taarig's companionship. He hoped Taarig would stay with him.

The landscape had been changing from dense forest to grasslands and large woodlands. Lom knew he was getting closer and closer to farmland. Soon the lane he was traveling down would bring him to fields that were being plowed and made ready for the spring planting. Folks would be out and about putting their gardens in. He was not going to be able to walk much farther without running into others.

Ealdred had Lom memorize the names of three individuals who had helped the Høyttaier clan in the past and who had once lived along the way he would be heading. Ealdred was not sure if they would still be on their lands. Many folks had been displaced by Lord Klingflug's edicts, rulings, and taxes. Ealdred's sister, Master Opeline, had talked about how hard the interim ruling council's judges were working to return displaced folks to their former lands.

It was midafternoon when Lom turned down a side lane that meandered through a large woodland. "If I remember the instructions right, a small farm beyond this woodland should belong to Farmer Parlan, that is if he has not been caught by the former regent's agents for helping the Høyttaiers. He could also have lost his farm due to the levies and taxes."

Lom realized he had begun to talk to Taarig over the last few days as if Taarig really understood what he was saying. *I have been on the road by myself way too long*, Lom thought. When he thought more about it, he realized he talked more to the night wolf than he had ever talked to folks.

He began to slow down when he saw that the trees were thinning. Motioning to Taarig, Lom moved cautiously forward. He wanted to have a chance to survey the farm before he approached it. Slipping from behind one tree to the next, Lom slowly made his way toward the edge of the trees that bordered the farm field across from the farmhouse and outbuildings. Sliding down the trunk of the tree into a crouch and slipping behind the low hedge that ran along the edge of the field, Lom cautiously raised his head and peered over the top of the hedge. He quickly ducked back down.

The man in the field behind horse and plow fit the description of Farmer Parlan that Ealdred had given him.

"I think we should watch for a little while," Lom whispered to Taarig.

Taarig settled in next to Lom, his ears pricked up, alert. Time passed. The scene seemed tranquil enough. Insects droned, and birds sang in the trees. Small animals rustled in the ground cover. The sun beamed down on the field, and the air was filled with the smell of newly-turned earth. Still Lom waited. Even when the farmer passed fairly close to where Lom and Taarig were hidden, Lom did not step out of his hiding place. A low growl from Taarig alerted Lom that something had changed. He scanned the field and spotted three riders moving across the field toward Farmer Parlan.

"You, Farmer …." one of the riders yelled when he was halfway across the field.

The farmer was frantically trying to wave him and his companions back, for their horses were tearing up a section of his freshly-plowed field. The riders did not heed his waving.

The first rider brought his horse to an abrupt stop inches from the farmer's horse, causing it to shy away, pulling the plow sideways out of Farmer Parlan's hands, and tipping it over.

"What do you think you are doing?" Farmer Parlan yelled, pulling on the reins of his horse to regain control. "You've no right to tear up my land and frighten my horse."

"You had best be keeping a civil tongue in your mouth. When our man becomes the next king, we're going to remember those who were not cooperative. I'm just here to warn you that a dozen or so folks will be walking through those woods yonder. We're looking for a lad who was reported entering the woods accompanied by a large black wolf. You had best be looking to your livestock if you know what's good for them. Heard tell the wolf is a killer. We're to wait right here until they flush him out."

Lom had heard enough. As quietly as he could, he drew back deeper into the woods, frantically trying to figure out what to do next. He could not go forward out into the field and, from what the lead rider had said, there were folks spread out coming his way looking for him. That they were looking for him was something Lom would need to think about later.

Right now, he had to figure out how not to get caught. He needed to move before the panic he felt rising within him froze him in place.

Taarig moved close to Lom and gently leaned against him. Just Taarig's presence calmed Lom enough that he took a deep breath, began to think, and swiftly moved deeper into the woods. He remembered seeing a small hollow that just might work, for there was a wild brambleberry patch growing there. If he could convince the brambleberry bushes to part just enough for the two of them to crawl into the center without being torn to shreds by thorns and then form a dense canopy over them, they might be safe for the moment.

When Lom reached the brambleberry patch he was very short of breath, and the panic he had felt before had risen again. He tried to remember what Ealdred had taught him. At that moment, his mind went blank. Once again, Taarig leaned against him, and Lom felt calmer.

*You can do this*, Lom thought. *You can do this. Take a few breaths, center yourself, and remember what Ealdred taught you.* Concentrating as hard as he could, Lom tried to block out the sounds around him and push down his fear. *Concentrate,* he told himself, *concentrate.* At first, he feared that he was not doing it right, for nothing seemed to happen. He lost his concentration when he heard folks in the distance shouting to each other.

Squatting down to make himself less visible, Lom closed his eyes, blocked everything out, and tried again. When he heard the rustling of leaves, Lom dared open one eye. The brambleberry plants in front of him had split, bending away from each other, forming a small opening just wide enough to crawl through. Getting down on hands and knees, pushing his pack in ahead of him, Lom moved forward, also asking the small ground cover he and Taarig had been walking on to stand back up all the way back into the trees to cover their passing. The brambleberry bushes continued to part for some distance ahead of them until Lom and Taarig arrived in a small open spot just big enough for the two of them to sit down. The brambleberry brushes closed in and formed an impenetrable bower over them, blocking out the sun.

Sitting there, Lom could only hope the folks scouring the woods would not find them, and that the brambleberry bushes would let them get out unscathed when the search was over.

# CHAPTER THIRTY-FOUR

Long minutes passed. Lom wished he had a way of commanding the bugs, which continued to buzz around both he and Taarig. Most were just annoying and, considering the circumstances they found themselves in, annoying bugs were a minor problem. It was the bugs that bit that were causing Lom's growing discomfort.

The voices Lom had heard were drawing closer and closer. He hoped the ground cover outside the brambleberry patch had done what he asked, and those folks coming closer would not be able to pick up his trail. He also hoped that he and Taarig were sufficiently hidden in the brambleberry patch. Soon, several of the searchers were close enough that Lom could hear their conversation clearly.

"When we gathered this day, I thought we'd be walkin' the woods to flush out game for Lord Madron's hunt. I didn't think we'd be lookin' for some lad and a wolf, for gosh sakes. Then that crofter Gnager comes rushing to the manor tellin' he's seen this lad and a wolf, all excited like. No one stopped to question why he was in this particular woodland, mind you. He was so excited lookin' for some type of reward that he didn't stop to think that someone might just figure out he was in the woodland poachin'."

"These nobles has the strangest ideas. I heard tell the crofter claimed the wolf was a night wolf of all thin's. There imman't any such thin'. Ever since Lord Madron got back from wherever he went durin' the last fortnight, he's been actin' odd. Askin' us to keep a lookout for anyone who was travelin' these parts with an uncommon animal. I asks you, isn't that just passin' strange?"

"Lots o' fuss an' bother if'n you asks me. Lots o' fuss an' bother. Won't put no meat in the pot either. An' whats is theys gonna do with the lad and the wolf, which I suspect is a dog most likely, anyway? Makes me rethinks let'n me son go on a walkabout. We's best move on. No one would thinks to try to get in the middle of a wild brambleberry patch. Would just plain tear thems to shreds."

Lom found himself holding his breath while he listened to the men talk. Finally, they moved on, and he gave a quiet sigh of relief. It was obvious to Lom that his troubles were very far from over. First, he had to get clear of the brambleberry patch. Then, he needed to get out of the woodlands without being detected. Beyond that, he needed to travel from where he was now to the royal forest south of the capital, find a piece of the oppgave ringe, and then get that piece to the capital without being detected.

"We might as well just stay here in the brambleberry patch," Lom grumbled quietly to Taarig. "Maybe you should go back to wherever night wolves live so you'll be safe. It would seem folks are now on the lookout for individuals who are traveling with uncommon animals. I don't want you to get hurt because you are with me." *I also really do not want you to go*, Lom thought.

Taarig just yawned and settled himself more comfortably, passing the time amusing himself by snapping his teeth at bothersome insects as they flew by.

While the two sat there, Lom tried to figure out what to do next. It was obvious to him that Taarig, at least for the moment, was staying with him. That was both a relief and a concern. With the night wolf at his side, he certainly fit the description of what those men were looking for. That was going to complicate traveling. He still had the option of trying to contact the farmer he had seen in the field. The farmer appeared to have no liking for those men who had ridden across his land. He did fit the description of the farmer Ealdred had told him about. Maybe the farmer would have ideas or know folks to contact who could help Taarig and him travel safely across the countryside without being apprehended.

Several more times folks passed by the brambleberry patch. The last two passed by after Lom heard the sound of a hunting horn. It was getting on toward dusk by that time, so Lom hoped the hunting horn was calling the searchers back. By the time full dark had arrived, he was tired, hungry, dirty, and itched all over from bug bites. He was also not as successful crawling out of the brambleberry patch unscratched as he had been going in. It was much more difficult to do in the dark.

It was with great caution that Lom headed back toward Farmer Parlan's farm. He tried to take his cues from Taarig, who was alert, but not overly so. When they reached the edge of the field, Lom halted. The clouds had moved away from in front of the full moon, making them more visible, should anyone be watching. He could see light spilling out of several main floor windows of the farmhouse. There was also light from a turned-down lantern in the barn showing through the main barn door, which was partially open. He could see the silhouette of several other outbuildings beyond the farmhouse and barn. Nothing was moving in the field or near the buildings. He figured the farm animals must be on the other side of the barn and outbuildings. His brief glimpse of the farm ended when the dark clouds once again obscured the moon.

"What do you think, Taarig? Should we chance it?"

Taarig slowly began to walk along the edge of the woods until he came to the end of the freshly-plowed field. Slipping under the fence, he headed across the meadow toward the farmyard. Lom followed, berating himself for a fool, for he would just have crossed the freshly-plowed field, leaving footprints in the soil. *Good thing Taarig is smarter than I am*, Lom thought.

Once they reached the farm buildings, they slipped quietly from shadow to shadow until finally Lom had his back pressed up against the side of the barn next to the partially open door. Slowly he poked his head around the door frame and quickly withdrew. There was someone sitting in the barn and, at the moment, he looked to be asleep. Whoever it was, he did not resemble the farmer in the slightest. The wicked-looking pike laid across his lap suggested to Lom that this might be someone who would be interested in finding Lom outside the barn, and his interest would not be good for Lom's health.

Lom stood there, trying not to make a sound lest he disturb the man in the barn. He was concentrating so hard he did not hear someone approach. He felt Taarig shift. He slowly placed a hand on Taarig's shoulder and found the night wolf was facing away from the barn door. Before Lom could even turn his head, a small hand lightly came to rest on Lom's shoulder.

"Sh-h-h," a voiced whispered. "I am Farmer Parlan's daughter, Lexine. We want to help. If Lord Madron's folks are looking for you, then you must be important to the former regent, whom we have no great fondness for. Would that be true?"

"I don't know. The former regent's agents snatched me once before. This time I don't think they are looking for me specifically. I overheard several of the men saying Lord Madron's folks were to be on the lookout for anyone traveling with an uncommon animal," Lom whispered back.

"The man in the barn is one of Lord Madron's searchers, and he bears you no good will. Turn and follow me. Quickly now, before his companion comes back from walking the perimeter of the buildings. I will take you and the wolf to a safe place."

Lom turned and followed Taarig, who was following the small folk ahead of him. Lom figured that the night wolf would not be blithely following someone unless his instincts led him to believe that it was all right. They stayed in the shadows, moving quickly away from the barn doors.

"We've been watching for you and hoping you would come to us. Here, duck down behind the woodpile and wait. I'll be back to get you. I need to let Papa know. He is going to cause a ruckus, and hopefully the two men will be drawn away for the time we need."

Minutes passed. Soon the quiet of the night was broken with the loud barking of dogs and mooing of cows. Lom could hear a man shouting. He was concentrating so hard, trying to hear what was being said, that he once again did not hear Lexine approach, until he caught movement out of the corner of his eye.

"Hurry, come with me," Lexine said.

The three of them traveled swiftly across the farmyard toward the farmhouse. When they reached the porch, Lexine moved aside the branches of a bush and ducked down close to the house's foundation. There she pushed hard at the foundation, and a section of it swung inward.

"Quick, get inside and close the wall behind you. The space is small, but you will find light and food. It is snug and dry. We never thought we would have to use the hidey-hole again. When it is safe, Papa or I will come for you."

Once Lexine backed out, Lom did as he had been asked and swung the section of the foundation closed. He felt his way forward and was relieved when his hands found a small lantern. He soon got a dim light burning. He was glad he did not have to sit in the small enclosed space in the dark. He was very grateful for Taarig's company, and that the night wolf was willing to be inside with him. Lom had wondered as he entered the hidey-hole whether Taarig would follow him in. Being trapped inside something was unnatural for the night wolf, he was sure. Lom also wondered if he had been smart to go into a hidey-hole without a question. He did not know if he could trust Lexine not to lock them in, trapping Taarig and him, only to turn them over to Lord Madron. He snuffed out the lantern, cautiously made his way to the front wall, and tested whether it would open. He was relieved when it did.

Time passed slowly. Lom had no way of telling if he had been hiding under the porch for an hour or longer. He eventually fell asleep. It was a fitful sleep, for he awoke at the slightest noise. Finally, he gave up, sat up with his back to a wall, and tried to contain his growing impatience and rising worry. Taarig did not seem to have the same concerns, for the night wolf slept soundly, his legs occasionally moving as if he were chasing something.

More time passed and Lom drifted into a doze, only to be abruptly awakened by the sounds of booted feet above him. He heard what must have been a fist pounding on the farmhouse door. It occurred to Lom that the sounds were quite clear, considering he was under the porch. He then realized that he was feeling a slight breeze. Holding the dim lamp aloft, he spied an opening near the top of the back wall. Very quietly, moving over to the small round opening, he took a closer look. He could not see very far in, so taking a chance, Lom reached in. The hole went in about half a foot before it curved upward. He surmised what he was looking at was a vent which had been cleverly built to allow fresh air to come in, yet prevent any light from being seen. A side effect was the fact that he could quite clearly hear the conversation taking place on the porch.

"Farmer Parlan, open up," a male voice commanded.

"You ride upon my land uninvited, you disturb my freshly-plowed field, you waste my time, you insist your men stay in my barn and wander my farmyard, and now you wake me before dawn?" groused Farmer Parlan. "What is it you wish now?"

"I told you before, you best watch your mouth, Farmer Parlan. You may think you got your land back free and clear. That may be true for the present ...." said the man, letting the implied threat hang in the air between them. "We are leaving for now. There will be folks watching. That lad and the night wolf could not have gotten by us, so our search is not over."

Lom heard the stomp of boots moving off the porch and down the steps. He also heard the farmhouse door close decisively. A short while later, he heard the door open again.

"Papa," said a voice Lom recognized as Lexine's. "I'm just going to sit out here on the porch and work on braiding a small rug. I will keep watch to see if anyone is about. I'll be quite all right while you go back to your plowing. I'll keep our guest company."

"Good idea. We need to look as if nothing is amiss. Just an ordinary day. Your mother and brother should be home later this afternoon. We will all put our heads together then and try to figure out what to do next. I hope this trip to get new seed for planting did not cost us too dear."

Lom could hear the worry in Farmer Parlan's voice. All too often under the former regent's reign, farmers and their families were forced off their land, and it either lay fallow or new tenants were placed on the land who misused it. If either had been the case here, Lom knew, there may not have been seed held over for this year's planting.

After Lom heard Farmer Parlan walk down the steps, it was quiet. Finally, Lexine spoke.

"If you can hear me, rap twice on the ceiling."

Lom did as she asked.

Lexine had tilted her head down over the cloth strips she was braiding. With her hair hanging down and hiding her face, Lexine started speaking again.

"We are still being watched. Papa and I need to keep things as normal as possible. Do you have enough food and water? Rap twice if that is so."

Lom rapped twice.

"Good. As you heard, the rest of my family will be back later today. Once there are more of us here, there will be more of us for them to watch. They can't keep watching our farm indefinitely."

Lom hoped those watching would soon decide he was no longer in the area. He could feel the walls closing in already.

# CHAPTER THIRTY-FIVE

Lexine talked to Lom off and on during the morning. In her second conversation with him, as she sat on the porch churning butter, she had suggested he should blow out the lamp and open the foundation wall a crack so he could get some fresh air. Just having the muted light from the outside coming in did a great deal to help him feel not so closed in.

During one conversation, Lexine asked, "Did you just happen upon our farm? The two men who were posted on our farm overnight are now gone, and I think those who are watching from the woods are too far away to hear us if you talk softly."

It seemed an innocent enough question, yet something told Lom it was not. He had to think a moment as to how much he really wished to reveal. He finally decided some of the truth was a place to start.

"I have spent the winter with a man named Ealdred, who was supposed to travel with me. On the day before we left, he hurt his ankle. His sister, Master Opeline, arrived shortly after he hurt himself and offered to take care of him, so he told me to travel on. He and his sister told me of some folks who might help me find a way safely to an area a little south of the capital. Your father was one of those folks."

When Lom had told Lexine this, she rattled something off very fast in a language he did not know or understand.

"I'm sorry. I don't understand what you just said. I suspect it is something in the old language, which I neither read, write, nor speak. I can barely read and write in the language of Sommerhjem, much less the old language. Never had much time for book learning. Head gardener at the royal palace taught me to speak proper. Was on me something fierce my first year. Told me I would never get anywhere in the world, or gain the respect of others, if I sounded like I hadn't had any schooling. Took me under his wing, he did."

Lom abruptly stopped talking when he realized he was babbling. He did not know why Lexine made him so nervous. Upon thinking further, he realized it was not Lexine who made him nervous. Rather the situation of continuing to be trapped in a small enclosed place and hiding from those looking for him was weighing on him.

Lexine must have sensed something for she said in a quiet, gentle voice, "I know of Master Opeline. I quite admire her. During the truly bad times, she risked life and limb to get folks to safety. You say she and her brother sent you to us?"

"Yes."

"I'll be back. I need to talk to Papa. It's time to call him in for lunch," Lexine had said. "I am sorry I cannot bring you more food other than the jerky and water I left you with last night."

Lom sat quietly waiting, becoming more and more anxious with each passing minute. He began to second-guess himself, wondering if he should have told Lexine as much as he had. Maybe these two were not really the ones Ealdred had told him about. Maybe they were, but were no longer loyal to the Crown. A short while later, he heard the sounds of two folks climbing the stairs.

"I'll just sit a spell here on the porch, Daughter. Would welcome our midday meal out here."

Lom heard the door to the farmhouse open. He also heard the creak of the floorboards overhead as Farmer Parlan rocked back and forth on the porch rocking chair. Moments later, Lexine returned.

"Now then, lad, I need you to describe Ealdred to me. Think carefully before you answer, for what you say in the next few minutes is either going to convince me we should continue to hide you, or I will pull you out of that hidey-hole myself and holler for the folks who are still lurking in the woods watching this place."

"Ealdred is one of the tallest men I have ever seen, sir," Lom began, "and thin. He is not much beyond middle years, I think. The most distinguishing feature, you might say, is the fact that he has green growing plants climbing up out of his boot tops and entwined in his beard. I spent the latter part of the winter with him. He is my friend and teacher." Lom continued on, telling Farmer Parlan how Ealdred had him memorize his name along with those of two others who could help him along his way.

"Yes, well, that sounds like him," Farmer Parlan said cautiously. "Others could have told you those things, and you could be trying to trick us. Tell me about his home."

"He lives in a cottage in the middle of a clearing. His cottage is covered with vines that hide it from view, except for the chimney. I could go on to describe his greenhouses, the hot springs, and of course, the beautiful meadow full of lush green grass. Those descriptions I could have been told by someone, of course. I think I can do something that might convince you that Ealdred truly is my teacher and my friend. Could you tell me please which way the wind is blowing? Is it blowing toward the porch or away? Is it blowing from the left across the porch as you face out or right?"

"It is blowing across the porch from the left. Why?"

"Just watch the bushes in front of the porch."

With that said, Lom centered himself, calmed his breathing, and concentrated on the bushes he knew were in front of the porch, for he had crawled through them. He had never tried to get plants he could not see to move before. He knew he needed something to convince Farmer Parlan that he did indeed know Ealdred, and that Ealdred had given him the information to find Farmer Parlan's farm.

"Stop. That's enough, lad. I believe you know Ealdred," Farmer Parlan said very quietly. "Do you know why you're being sought?"

"I don't think they are looking for me specifically, sir. I really am nobody. I think they are looking for folks who travel with uncommon animals, and again, before you ask, I don't know why that should be. Since I travel with a night wolf, I fit the general description of those they are on the lookout for. It's a little hard to travel with a night wolf in more populated areas without being noticed. We stand out a little bit, I would guess."

"A huge bit would be a better description. Night wolves are just stories and legends to most of us. Most of us think they are just tall tales made up by some long ago storyteller, and not at all real."

"So I thought, too, sir."

"We need to come up with a plan as to how to get you away from here.

Lom suggested he could try to get to one of the others in the area Ealdred had told him about. Perhaps they could help.

"The other two folks Ealdred told you might help you are no longer around. One," Farmer Parlan said, "left several years back and never returned. The other has moved in with her daughter, and is no longer able to help. It's too risky for her. Unfortunately, it would look suspicious if we sent you off in the farm wagon, since it will just be returning from a trip, hopefully by early afternoon. Let me think on it while I'm out in the fields this afternoon. Do you have enough food and water to hold you until then?"

"I'm fine, sir. Better now that I have the wall open a little bit."

Several hours passed before Lom heard the approach of a wagon. A woman's voice called out to Lexine to come and help unload. He heard Lexine's swift footsteps climb down the stairs, and then the footsteps of several folks climbing up and down the stairs. Finally, it was quiet for a while. When it was getting on toward midafternoon, Farmer Parlan once again sat on the porch and began to rock. His wife came out, brought him a refreshing drink, caught him up on what supplies and seeds she and their son had been able to secure, and told him she might have a plan to move their unexpected guest off the farm with none the wiser.

"Why," said Teca, Farmer Parlan's wife, "I heard tell that my niece was more than worried about the arrival of her first child when I was getting seed. She's right afeard and missing her momma something fierce. I'm thinking I ought to hitch up the horse and buggy and go be with her. No one's going to question me, the local midwife, about going to the aid of a relative. We've slipped folks off the farm in the buggy before."

"How will getting our guest less than several hours ride away from here help?" Lexine asked, having stepped onto the porch as her mother was telling her father her plan. "My cousin has no place to hide him and the night wolf. Also, do you think it's a good idea to bring more worries into her life right now?"

"I don't intend to take him all the way to your cousin's place. I intend to drop him off just beyond Tørkes Falls. There is that long stretch of forest along the river the foresters look out for. I know that group has no love for anyone who's opposed to the Crown. The former regent felt there was no need to have the foresters there and moved them all out. Without them there, folks almost ruined the forest, and certainly jammed up the river. It will take the foresters years to put that section back to rights."

"It's a good plan, dear. It will get him safely away from here and watching eyes," said Farmer Parlan.

"Excuse me," said Lom, "What happens if someone stops your buggy? Wouldn't a passenger, not to mention my night wolf friend here, be somewhat noticeable?"

"Well now, the night wolf is a bit of a problem. You, however, are not. There is a compartment built into the buggy where you can hide for a short ride. It's a bit tight, but you will fit curled up around your pack. As to the night wolf ..."

"I won't leave without him," Lom interrupted.

"... I suspect he is used to taking care of himself. If he is as intelligent as I think he is, and as loyal, he will find a way of staying with us without being noticed. Think about it, lad. He can't possibly be the only night wolf in existence, yet it's rare that anyone has ever seen one."

Lom thought over what Farmer Parlan's wife, Teca, had said. Journeyman Evan had thought Taarig might have been the same night wolf his friend Beezle had encountered in the eastern mountains. It was a guess on his part, to be sure. He thought it felt right, however. While he might be the same night wolf Beezle had encountered, Teca was probably right in concluding that he was not the only one in Sommerhjem.

Taarig had come to Lom early in his stay at Ealdred's and had been with him ever since. Ealdred had speculated that Taarig was meant to be with Lom. When he had left Ealdred's, Taarig had accompanied him. He wondered whether the night wolf would follow him if he climbed into and hid in the buggy. The thought of not having Taarig with him on this journey he was on was frightening to Lom. He had come to count on the night wolf's calm presence. The two of them had a good partnership. He did not wish to lose that.

Lom turned, took the night wolf's head in both hands, and gazed deep into Taarig's ice-blue eyes. "Will you follow me if I go in the buggy? Will you keep yourself safe? I don't want to go without you, yet we can't continue to stay here."

Taarig gave a slight nod with his head and pulled back, settling down into a comfortable position. Lom was not sure if Taarig had nodded agreement, or if he was just pulling away. He hoped the night wolf understood what he was asking.

"I know I can't continue to hide under your porch," Lom said, addressing the folks who were sitting above him. "I don't want to bring danger to your door, and my staying here will do that, I think. I will be ready to leave when you think the time is right."

"I will need an hour or so to do things here and pack my supplies. It will still be daylight, so I hope that night wolf of yours is as smart as I think he is," said Teca.

*You are not the only one*, thought Lom as he spent some time sorting and rearranging his pack in preparation for leaving.

"I'll be leaving in the daylight, so I hope you will stay and wait until the night hours," Lom told Taarig. "I'll be dropped off at the edge of the forest. I won't be able to stay there waiting for you. I'll have to keep moving. I know you'll be able to find me." *I hope you will find me*, Lom thought.

All too soon in Lom's mind, he heard the sound of what he assumed was the buggy pulling up in front of the porch. He was instructed to quickly move out of his hiding place. It took him a moment for his eyes to adjust to the brighter light as he was almost dragged by Farmer Parlan into a covered buggy. Farmer Parlan had the seat cushion pulled up and told Lom to climb into the small space underneath. Once Lom had squeezed himself and his pack inside, Farmer Parlan let the seat cushion drop back into place.

Lom felt the buggy shift as Farmer Parlan stepped out of it, and then shift again as his wife got on and sat down.

"Now don't you worry none, lad. I'll get you safely away. It won't be too long a ride. Knock twice if you are all right in there."

Lom did as she asked. While he was not very comfortable, the small space was bearable for what he hoped would be a short time. He also hoped the lane they were to travel on was a fairly smooth one.

"Lexine," her mother called out quietly. "While I have the buggy in front of the porch, why don't you go make sure the door to the hidey-hole is open enough so the night wolf can get out?"

Lexine ducked through the bushes covering the front of the porch, pushed the opening to the hidey-hole wider, and looked in. She swiftly backed out, stepped up to the buggy, and said, "He's gone."

"What do you mean he's gone?" her mother asked.

"He's not in the hidey-hole. He's gone."

# CHAPTER THIRTY-SIX

If Lom had been able to turn his body from his curled up position so he could place his hands and feet on the seat cushion covering him, he would have tried to heave the seat cushion up, Farmer Parlan's wife and all. *How could Taarig be gone? Was there anyone out there in the woodland next to the farm still watching? Did they see Taarig?*

"There's nothing to be done about the night wolf being gone. All we can do is hope that anyone watching the farm didn't see him leave. You had best be on your way, dear. The day is not getting any younger, and you need to get to your niece's farm before dark," Farmer Parlan told his wife.

"I'm sorry, lad," Teca said. "None of us saw him leave. He can well take care of himself. Get ready, we need to leave now. Brace yourself. Unfortunately for you, this is not going to be a comfortable ride. I will try to avoid the biggest bumps and holes."

With that said, Teca snapped the reins, and the buggy lurched forward. Lom was glad he was stuffed into the area under the seat, for he was not getting tossed about too much. He could not imagine what the ride would be like if Teca were driving just willy-nilly down the lane, hitting the big bumps and holes.

There was no conversation between Teca and Lom as the ride progressed. Lom had almost been lulled to sleep by the steady clip clop of the horse's hooves and the sway of the buggy when he felt it slow down, and then stop.

"Lord Madron."

"Farmer Parlan's wife, are you not?"

"Yes, sir."

Lom froze inside the area under the seat. He could feel the sweat trickle down his spine. Unfortunately, he could also feel a sneeze coming on.

"Out a bit late in the day, aren't you?"

"Couldn't be helped. My son and I just returned this afternoon with seed for the planting. My niece is with child, her first, and it's due any day now. I go to be with her. Babies, as you know, never come on a schedule, or at times that are convenient, most of the time."

Lom grew more and more tense as the need to sneeze grew stronger and stronger.

"You have been told to keep a lookout for any strangers who might approach your farm accompanied by an uncommon animal, have you not?" Lord Madron inquired.

"Yes, sir."

"We have had a report that a lad accompanied by a night wolf was seen near your farm."

"My husband told me your man told him that a lad and a night wolf were seen by Crofter Gnager. You know the crofter hasn't been quite right since he was thrown from his horse and hit his head. Sees strange things all the time."

"You could be right. Then again, this time he could have actually seen what he said he did," stated Lord Madron.

Lom sincerely wished they would finish their chat, for he knew that any moment he would not be able to hold the sneeze in.

"Why all the interest in folks wandering the countryside with uncommon animals?" Teca asked.

"Well, I will not keep you any longer and delay your travels," Lord Madron said, as he wheeled his horse around, told his men to follow him, and left Teca with her question unanswered.

Just as Teca was about to snap the reins, she heard a muffled sneeze coming from below her. *Luck seemed to be riding on our shoulders this day*, she thought. *Or maybe not.* Suddenly, she had the feeling that she was being watched. Looking carefully around, Teca could not spot anyone, so she started the horse moving. Alert now, she kept a wary eye out.

The sun was just hitting the treetops when Teca pulled the horse to a halt once again. She stood, stretched, and looked around. Again, she could not spot anyone. The feeling of being watched persisted. Knowing she could do nothing about whatever might be out there, she lifted the seat cushion up and helped Lom stand.

"I'm sorry we were delayed by Lord Madron. It is too close to dusk for me to be letting you off here. It can't be helped. We could not risk keeping you on the farm for very long. Lord Madron and his folk have been suspicious of us for a long time. I'm sure he is the one who had us moved off our land when the former regent was in power."

"I'll be all right," Lom said, trying to reassure Teca. "I'm pretty comfortable in woods and forests. I thank you and your family for your help. Please go on now and care for your niece."

"I'll be going. Just follow the path to Tørkes Falls and then follow the river upstream. It will take you the direction you want to go. Luck travel with you, lad."

Lom stood just inside the tree line and watched the buggy drive off. Then he turned and began following the path. He could hear the roar of the falls getting louder and louder the farther he moved into the woods. He hoped no one was around, for he could not hear much over the sound of falling water. He kept glancing back over his shoulder. There was never anyone there, which was somewhat of a relief. Not that he wanted anyone to be following him. He hoped when he looked over his shoulder, he would see Taarig coming up the trail behind him. Each time he looked, the trail remained empty.

Once Lom reached Tørkes Falls, he took a moment to stop and look at it. The water cascaded down a series of steps, tumbling over rocks, until it fell into a turbulent pool at the bottom. The trail he had been following turned inland, away from the falls. It was steep and rock-strewn, a bit slippery in places. Lom was relieved when he reached the top of the trail, for the sun was setting and it was getting more difficult to see. He began to look around for someplace sheltered to spend the night, for the wind had picked up. He knew he could not have a fire this night, since he was still too close to the lane where Teca had dropped him off.

Walking farther down the trail, Lom spotted a pine tree that might suit his purposes. Its lowest branches were full and low to the ground. If he really concentrated, he might persuade those branches to drop down lower to provide a windbreak and some shelter, should it storm. Once settled under the tree, it was a relief to take his backpack off and snuggle into his blanket roll. He was still close enough to the river to feel the damp, which made the air colder.

When he had lived in the capital, Lom had often been alone. He was rarely lonely. Now, huddled in his blanket roll, enclosed by pine boughs, he was more than aware of how alone he was, and how lonely. Lom missed Taarig. He knew the night wolf was a wild animal. He knew that he did not have any claim on Taarig, that he could not command him to stay with him. Lom knew all that in his head. It was his heart that was having trouble. He had hoped when Lexine had announced that Taarig was gone, that the night wolf would somehow wait close by and follow him. That did not seem to be the case.

Resigned to the loss of the night wolf, Lom tried to get comfortable under the pine tree. After a time, he settled into an uneasy sleep. Shortly before dawn, Lom found he was too warm and tried to throw back his top cover, only to find it was being held down by something. Slowly turning his head to the side, he saw Taarig snugged in next to him, which explained both why he could not move his top cover and why he had grown over-warm. Wrestling an arm out from under the covers, Lom rolled onto his side, placed his arm across Taarig, sighed, and slipped back into sleep.

Dawn came and went before Lom woke again. To his very great relief, Taarig was still under the pine tree with him. Just as he was about to speak, Taarig abruptly sat up, alert. Lom glanced around to make sure the pine boughs still hid them, and then froze, listening.

"We'll walk a little ways farther. I knows whats I seen. I'm a good enough tracker to know Farmer Parlan's wife's buggy stopped at the path into Tørkes Falls. Her horse was there long enough to graze. Also looks like someone walked on the trail recently."

"Yah, yer right. Lost the trail when they's climbed up by the falls."

"Well, you can keep going, but I's is turning back. No one's here now. Whoever it was is probably long gone. Probably a forester."

"All right, all right. Just didn't want Lord Madron saying we's not doing our job. I thinks Crofter Gnager was seeing things. A night wolf indeed."

Lom held still for quite some time to make sure the two men were really gone. Taarig had lain back down, which was some reassurance that it would be all right to leave the shelter of the pine tree. Before he did, he addressed Taarig.

"Thank you for finding me. I missed you. I'm glad you are with me again."

Taarig just nodded and, after stretching out his front legs, moved out from under the pine. He gave an impatient look over his shoulder.

"Fine, good, I'm coming. Just give me a minute to pack up my blanket roll."

All morning, Lom and Taarig continued to follow the river. As the day grew warmer, the smell of pine grew stronger, since most of the forest they walked through was made up of various types of pines that grew naturally. By midday, the forest began to change. Here the pines had been planted and thinned, standing in long rows of tall trees. It reminded Lom of rows of corn on a giant scale. Clearly the tree planting and trimming was the work of the forester clan in charge of this forest. This section of the forest would provide prime lumber a number of years hence. He could only hope that, if he ran into a forester, she or he would be on the side of the Crown.

The advantage of entering a portion of tended forest was the lane that ran through it. It certainly made walking easier than the trails Lom had been following. The disadvantage was that the lane and the more open forest left Lom and Taarig more exposed with fewer places to hide should they meet someone. He was very worried about how he was going to get to the royal forest south of the capital without being spotted by folks who were looking for folks who were traveling with uncommon animals, and not so as to help them out.

Late afternoon, Lom began to look for a suitable place to spend the night. The lane he had been following had led him back to and across the river to an area that was less tame than where he had been walking most of the afternoon. Looking around, he found a sturdy pole, attached a line and a hook to it, baited the hook with a juicy bug he had found under a rock, and settled in on the bank of the river, hoping for a fish. His food supplies had grown low, and fresh fish would certainly be a welcome change.

Lom had no sooner cast his line into the water than he felt a hit. He pulled his line in, delighted to find a fat fish about the size of his hand at the end of it. At the end of a half hour, he had eight good-sized fish.

"We'll be eating fine this night, Taarig. A fine fish stew for me and fish for you. Well, maybe not," Lom remarked, when he noticed Taarig was finishing up something that was now unrecognizable.

Lom determined he was going to risk a small fire. Others had camped by the river near the spot he had been fishing, and there was a fire ring. He set about building a small, nearly smokeless fire. When the coals were ready, he placed in the coals his small kettle filled with fish, water, and some spring greens. Leaving it to simmer, he made his way back to the river, found a quiet side pool, and washed both himself and the clothes he had been wearing for days.

By the time the sun had set, Lom was well-fed, clean, and now warm, wrapped up in his blanket roll. He had doused the fire and found a sheltered area to sleep slightly away from the campsite behind a concealing boulder. He was awakened at the crack of dawn by the sound of voices carried up from the river.

"Fish are running, so we should get a good amount, and be able to be back and open our shops before anyone is up in the village. Man can't live for work alone, you know."

"Yer right about that."

"What do you think about all this talk about a challenge to pick out the new king or queen?"

"At first, I was thinking it was just a bunch of nonsense, them folks at the capital just making something up to get rid of the Regent, not that I minded getting rid of the Regent, mind you. He didn't do any of us common folk any favors, that's for sure. Anyway, now that there have been those folks bringing in pieces of …. What's it called?"

"The oppgave ringe."

"Right, pieces of the oppgave ringe. The strange things that happened in the Well of Speaking, and the changes in the countryside when those things happened, have me a lot more convinced. Thought at first it was just a bunch of smoke and mirrors, but no longer. Saw the lights in the sky myself when the first ones were placed. Seen strange lights other times, too. I'm thinking maybe we forgot the old ways and need to go back to them. I'm not the only one either. Lots of folks here feel the same way."

"You've got the right of it. Had we followed the old ways, we wouldn't have had to suffer through years of the former regent. Now, I hear that seven of the pieces have been found. Only two more need to be brought to the capital by the end of the summer."

"On another note, what do you think about being asked to keep a lookout for folks wandering through accompanied by uncommon animals?"

"Considering who was doing the asking, if'n I saw someone like that, I'd warn them they's in a heap of trouble."

# Chapter Thirty-Seven

Lom was not hearing anything new from the two folks fishing by the river. He already knew, had known for a long time, he was in a heap of trouble. It was hard to think otherwise, since he had been kidnapped off the streets of the capital, taken to the Raven's tower by those loyal to the former regent, rescued, and then given the task of finding a piece of the oppgave ringe in the royal forest south of the capital. Other than that, his life was just sailing along smoothly. He remained still, listening to see if he could learn any more from the two who were sitting by the river and fishing.

"Makes you wonder why those folks are looking for folks who travel with uncommon animals, don't it?"

"Yah, they certainly weren't willing to explain. I think if I ran across someone traveling with, say, a hunting cat like that rover lass we heard tell about, I would offer to help them in any way I could, just so as them's that's asking can't get their hands on them."

The two men's conversation was interrupted by the sound of horses' hooves pounding over the bridge. Several riders pulled to a halt when they spotted the two who were fishing.

"You two," one of the riders called out, "have you seen anyone pass this way this morning? Anyone traveling with a nigh… large black dog?"

"Nope."

"If you do, let Lord Madron know."

"Why is this folk being looked for?"

"He, well, he stole the dog. If you see him, don't get too close. Just let Lord Madron know."

The riders left, leaving the two fishing deep in their own thoughts for a moment, and Lom more concerned than ever.

"Lord Madron may be the largest landholder around here, but we certainly don't owe him any loyalty. He sure as heck didn't help any of us in the village during the hard times under the former regent. Just filled his own pockets, took folks' land he had no right to, and set himself up as the tax collector over all of us."

"Yer .... Whoa, I've got a live one at the end of my line."

Lom continued to stay still, listening. He heard the two bantering back and forth about who had caught the biggest fish. Finally, he heard the two men pack up and head down the lane. When he thought they were far enough away, he rolled up his blanket roll, attached it to his pack, and headed out. He had gone no more than half a mile when a voice called to him out of the woods.

"You really should be more careful. You left both your footprints, and your companion's, on the river bank."

Lom was surprised by both the voice coming out of the shadows of the trees, and the fact that Taarig had not given any warning. A man well past middle years stepped out from behind a large tree, fishing pole casually resting on his shoulder, fishing creel strap crossing his chest.

"That's some large black dog. Seems he would be a bit hard to steal. Seems he's not exactly a dog either, is he?"

Lom did not know what to think of this man. He did not seem threatening. Taarig continued to stand calmly at his side, alert.

"Yer going to have trouble leaving this area. Lord Madron spread the word to be on the lookout for you. Those men who stopped by our favorite fishing spot earlier are not his men, but from around here. Couple of good-for-nothings always after easy coin. Why are they looking for you, lad?"

"I honestly don't know. I'm nobody important. Just on a walkabout. I haven't done anyone any harm. I haven't stolen anything from anybody. I just don't know."

"Yer not going to get out of this area without help, or a great deal of luck. Those two you overheard this morning are not the first as come looking for you. Would you be willing to accept some help from those as don't much care for Lord Madron or the former regent?"

Lom knew the man was right. He was going to have trouble leaving the area without help. He looked down at Taarig who had moved closer to him and was lightly leaning against his leg. Taarig still did not seem concerned with this man.

"Why would you help me?"

"Because during the bad times under the former regent's rule, I did nothing but protect myself while others suffered. I'm ashamed. I should have done something. You may not be important. Yet, you should not be hunted just because you have had the fortune to be companioned by what I think is the stuff of tall tales. That is a night wolf leaning against you, is it not?"

"Yes, sir. His name is Taarig. He is my friend."

"Well, I'll be. Old ways returning, and old tales being true. So lad, are you wanting help?"

"Yes, sir."

"First things first, then. Walking this lane will take you to my village, which will not be the best way to keep you hidden. I know these woods better than most so, if you will follow me, we will take the back way to the backside of the village. My cottage is right on the edge of the woods. You should be safe there for the time being. Tomorrow is market day, and folks from the surrounding area will be heading into the village. We might get lucky and find you a way out of here. By the way, folks around here just call me Cooper, for obvious reasons, since I'm a barrel maker. And you?"

"Lom."

"Well, follow me, Lom."

Lom could only hope that Cooper had been truthful about knowing the woods, for the path they followed was little more than an animal path and wandered its way twisting and winding over hill and dale, over small creeks, around huge tree trunks. Finally, Cooper held up his hand, motioning Lom and Taarig should halt.

"We're almost there, lad. Let me go ahead and make sure no one has dropped in at my cottage."

When Cooper left, Lom squatted down next to Taarig and put his arms around the night wolf's neck. "If anything happens to me, be prepared to run. Do you understand?" Taarig did not reply.

Cooper returned and motioned that Lom and Taarig should follow him. He led them to a small thatched stone cottage. "I need to head into the village. I'm the local coopersmith. I make fine oak barrels, if I do say so myself. Folks will be wondering if I'm not at my shop. You should be safe here for the day."

The day passed slowly after Cooper left. More than once Lom wondered if he should have taken his chances trying to move on, on his own. With each passing hour Lom's debate with himself became more and more heated, causing him to pace back and forth in the cottage. Finally, Taarig stood up, stretched, and went and stood directly in front of Lom, who stumbled to a halt.

"I'm sorry. Besides driving myself crazy, I must be driving you crazy, too. I just don't know what's best, Taarig. I don't know if I should trust Cooper, or if we should just leave. I'm not cut out for this, you know. I've lived such a quiet life. I've never wanted adventure. I've never wanted to go on a walkabout like so many young folks. I would be happy to just be back at Ealdred's, or at the royal gardens. Why did you come to me?"

Taarig just pushed his head under Lom's hand. Lom dropped to his knees and buried his face in Taarig's ruff, taking solace from the warmth and companionship of the night wolf. Moments later, Taarig stiffened and Lom lifted his head up. He heard the sound of a wagon approaching the cottage. Just as he was about to fling his pack through the back window and follow it out, he heard Cooper's voice.

"Just pull your homewagon in to the right of the cottage. There's a good level place there."

Lom heard another voice thanking Cooper for his kind offer of a place to camp after market day.

"'Tis an added benefit that seeking you out to mend our water barrel happened on your village's market day. Was able to sell a bit of my wares and barter for things we needed. Now then, you said you would barter the repair with me. What did you have in mind?"

"I think you had best come in and see for yourself. If'n I tell you, you'll think I'm drink-addled. Lom, it's a friend I'm inviting in."

Very quickly and quietly Lom lowered his pack out the window and placed it on the ground. If he still needed to make a hasty exit, he did not want to do so without his gear. Standing next to the window, he turned and faced the door. Cooper and a man who was obviously a rover entered.

"Lom, this is my friend Raahil, a rover. You can rest assured he has no love for anyone who would want to be loyal to anyone other than the Crown. I think he might be able to help."

Raahil stood stock still in the doorway, an astonished look on his face, watching warily as Taarig stood up out of the shadows where he had been lying and placed himself in front of Lom.

Addressing Lom, Raahil said, "That is not just a really large black dog, is it?"

"No, sir."

"Ah, I'm beginning to see the problem here. If we are going to have a talk about you and the night wolf, I need to get my wife, Nellwyn. She needs to be included in this."

Raahil turned and headed out the door, shaking his head, muttering about how it was not possible he had just seen a night wolf. He returned quickly, followed by his wife. It was decided to put off the conversation concerning Lom and Taarig until a meal could be prepared. After the four folks sat down to the hastily prepared meal and ate, Lom once again repeated what he had told Cooper.

"We have heard the rumblings about being on the lookout for folks traveling with uncommon animals. I think I may have an answer as to why you have become so important to find," Raahil stated. "It has come to the attention of folks, both for and against the Crown, that all of those who have brought a piece of the oppgave ringe to the capital have been accompanied by animals who rarely travel with folks. That might be just coincidence. Most of us don't think so. There have certainly been times in the past when someone might have a hunting cat as a companion. Rarer still might be someone who befriends a red bog fox or a griff falcon."

"I never thought of that," said Cooper. "To have seven such folks all arrive at the capital within the last year, I don't think that's just chance. So young man, are you on your way to take the eighth piece of the oppgave ringe to the capital?"

Lom did not know what he should say at this point. He was still trying to mull over what Raahil had just suggested, that he was being sought because some folks believed he had one of the pieces of the oppgave ring, or maybe that he might know where one was. He certainly knew where one might be. What he did not know was what he should say to these folks who were waiting so patiently for him to reply. He did not like lying, yet what part of the truth could he tell? For that matter, should he say anything at all?

"Now, Cooper," said the rover's wife, speaking for the first time. "Put yourself in the lad's boots. Would you answer that question to three strangers whom you have no reason to trust?"

"Yer right. Sorry to have put you on the spot, Lom."

"It would seem no matter whether the lad has anything to do with the oppgave ringe or not, he is being looked for by factions who would do him harm. What is it you need, Lom?" Raahil asked.

"Taarig and I need to get away from here without being seen. We need to head in the direction of the capital. No, I don't have a piece of the oppgave ring. I just want to get back to the life I had before I was kidnapped."

All of what Lom had just told the folks sitting around the table was the truth as far as it went. *Well, maybe not*, Lom thought. *Do I really want to return to the royal gardens? Perhaps. Or perhaps I might want to return to Ealdred's cottage and take advantage of his offer to continue my studies. That seems too far in the future for me to even really think about. The here and now is complicated enough.*

"I'm beginning to get an idea of the boon you wish to barter. You would like us to get Lom and Taarig out of this area," Raahil said to Cooper.

"Yes. Perhaps he and the night wolf could hide in your homewagon when you head out. No one would be the wiser."

"Well, lad, would you be willing to trust us to get you safely away from here?"

# Chapter Thirty-Eight

Lom knew walking out of the cottage and heading on his way was possible. Taarig would certainly not let any of the three looking at him harm him. How far he would get on his own was certainly a question. The rover couple was offering him a way to leave the area undetected. The question was, could he trust them?

Lom thought of what he knew about rovers. They certainly were a fiercely independent clan who individually or in small groups traveled about Sommerhjem in their homewagons plying their trades. They owed no landholder allegiance. He had heard the former regent had mistrusted them, and had tried to make them look bad in the eyes of the common folk. They seemed, as a group, to be loyal to the Crown, while not involving themselves in the goings-on in the capital. He knew one of the rovers was on the interim ruling council, for he had seen him at the palace.

"Lom?" said Cooper.

"Sorry, I was just thinking ...."

"Of course you were," suggested Raahil. "Know that my wife and I have no love for the former regent or any who would want to toss Sommerhjem into turmoil. We saw what happened all over Sommerhjem when the former regent and his followers were in power. That would not have happened, we think, if the old ways of choosing a ruler had been followed after King Griswold died. There is rover lore handed down that suggests that the land needs to choose our country's ruler. I don't know what that means. I know word has gone out for a gathering of rover elders to meet soon, hoping to combine what they know about the time before King Griswold, about the oppgave ringe, and the Gylden Sirklene challenge. But I'm rambling. Back to the question at hand. We leave tomorrow just after dawn. If you wish to go with us, be ready. Would that suit you?"

"Yes, sir."

"Then my wife and I will take our leave. It has been a long day, and tomorrow is not going to be any shorter."

With that said, Raahil and Nellwyn left the cottage. Cooper banked the cook fire and showed Lom where he could put his blanket roll. It was full dark by then. Once he had things settled, Lom stood and walked to the back door to go out to the outhouse one last time before settling in for the night. He had no sooner opened the door than Taarig rushed past him and disappeared into the shadows of the trees behind the cottage. Lom could only hope that the night wolf was off hunting and would be there in the morning. He worried that the past few days had held too much confinement for the night wolf. Lom tossed and turned most of the night.

It was almost a relief when dawn came. Lom had just finished putting his pack to rights when Taarig leapt in the window and began nudging Lom toward the front door. There was some urgency in his action.

"Listen, do you hear them?" Cooper asked.

"Hear what?"

"Baying. Someone has let loose tracking dogs. They are on a scent. I worry it is that of your night wolf, or it might be you they are hunting. Quick, into the rover homewagon."

"Won't they just follow the rover's homewagon?"

"We'll just have to chance it."

The three quickly exited the cottage. Fortunately, Raahil already had the horses hitched to the homewagon and was set to go.

"I heard the hounds," Raahil said.

"I don't want to create a problem for you," Lom said. "If the hounds have caught either of our scents, they will just follow the homewagon."

"Oh, I don't think that's going to be a problem. Dear," Raahil said, addressing his wife, "do we still have that jar of nyse powder?"

Lom saw a look come into Cooper's eye, and then the coopersmith started laughing. Seeing the confusion on Lom's face, Cooper explained. "It's the crushed-up, dried leaves of the nyse flower. It blooms abundantly in the grassy plains in the fall. It doesn't smell bad when in bloom, and has little or no smell once the flowers are dried and pounded into powder. Then it becomes not so nice. It causes massive sneezing, and certainly messes up one's sense of smell for a while if sniffed in. Those baying dogs have their noses to the ground while tracking. Once they get here, they are going to get some of this nyse powder up their noses and will be worthless for quite some time for tracking anything other than their own tails."

Raahil was holding a jar of brown powder. "We keep a bit with us to discourage especially skunks from becoming too friendly, too close to our campsite. Why don't you and Taarig walk in a zig-zag pattern down the lane for about ten feet. Sprinkle the nyse powder behind you. We will pick you up in the homewagon. That way we will also spread the powder, for some will get moved by the horses' hooves and the homewagon's wheels."

After Lom retrieved his pack, he handed it off to Raahil. He took the bottle of nyse powder, asked Taarig to join him, and walked in the zig-zag pattern as Raahil had suggested, spreading the powder out behind him. He called his thanks to Cooper as he climbed up into the homewagon, followed by Taarig. Once inside the homewagon, he settled himself at the table across from Raahil.

"I'm worried about Cooper. If those hounds were indeed following Taarig's scent, it will lead them straight to Cooper's cottage, to his door, and also his back window."

"He will have his place shuttered and locked. When you went back in for your pack, he told me he was going to let it be known in the village he was heading to the next town to visit his daughter and would be back in a few days."

"That's good then. Those folks tracking us, if they are indeed even tracking either of us, what's to keep them from following your homewagon?"

"In less than an hour, we should be on the royal road. Our tracks should just be lost in all the other tracks. There is a lot of movement on the royal road, with the fair season starting."

Raahil was right about the traffic on the royal road. Luck seemed to be with them as they pulled onto the royal road right behind several other wagons going the same direction they were. Neither Lom nor Taarig minded riding inside the wagon. Taarig had made himself at home, and napped on and off the whole day. Lom sat out of sight behind Raahil and his wife so he could talk and listen to them without being seen. He learned a great deal during the day about how the pair made their living, and what they had observed during their last month on the road.

"Things aren't perfect, mind you," Raahil had said, "but all in all, the country seems better off now that the former regent is gone. Folks are back where they belong, the taxes are once again reasonable, and folks don't seem so desperate. We're hoping the summer fairs will be more profitable this year, with folks more willing to part with their hard-earned coin."

"Or have hard-earned coin to part with," Nellwyn added.

"Ayup, yah have the right of it," Raahil said.

The three spent some time discussing how far south they thought they could get Lom and Taarig before they had to part ways.

"We would take you as far as you needed to go, lad, if we could. We need to make our regular stops and attend as many market days leading up to the big town fairs," Raahil stated regretfully.

"I understand, sir. You need to make a living. I'm so grateful for your being willing to take us at all."

Lom and Taarig traveled for three days with the rovers before they parted ways. Each night Raahil had chosen a campsite that was off the beaten path, which allowed both Lom and Taarig to get out of the wagon and stretch their legs. Each night the night wolf would disappear from the campsite to hunt. Each morning, he would be waiting at the homewagon.

On the last day before the rovers needed to turn east, they met up with several other rover families who were heading the way Lom needed to travel. He reluctantly bid farewell to Raahil and Nellwyn. For the next week, Lom and Taarig travelled with rovers, sometimes for a few hours, sometimes for a few days. Each passing day brought him closer and closer to the capital. He hoped his luck would continue to hold. He knew he could not count on it holding, and so would need another plan, for the land as they drew closer to the capital was less forested, more open.

Finally, the day came when the rover family he was riding with was going to stop and spend several days in a village a half day's ride from where they had camped overnight. He knew he and Taarig could not continue on with them. It was too risky. Someone in the village was bound to notice that there was someone with the rovers. It is hard to keep secrets in a small village, where everybody knows each other and each other's business.

After the rover family left, Lom knew he could not just boldly start down the lane. He had determined he needed to find a place to spend the day and await nightfall before he headed out. Traveling by night would certainly slow him down. Hopefully, it would be safer than traveling during the day. He also now knew of different possible routes to take that might allow him to meet up with other rover families who might help him. Taarig and he rode with the rover family for several hours before they were dropped off at an abandoned mill.

"This old mill has been falling down for as long as I can remember. I can't imagine anyone disturbing you here while you wait until nightfall. We are so sorry we can't take you any farther."

"I thank you for getting me this far," said Lom. "Safe travels."

"Safe travels to you, too, lad."

The mill was way past seeing better days. What was left of the waterwheel lay rotting and broken on its side; the creek that had run it had long since dried up. Any wood left in the window frames was gray and splintered. The roof was long gone, and vines covered the crumbling outer walls. Once Lom was inside, he discovered that the vines covered the inside walls as well. Stepping across broken rock and what was left of the floorboards, he carefully made his way to a corner of the building dark with shadows. There he cleared a spot so he could sit down to wait out the rest of the day.

A soft low growl roused Lom from his dozing. Finding it dark, he realized he had slept the day away. Instantly alert, he listened intently, trying to figure out what had disturbed Taarig. Standing, he placed his pack on his back, and was prepared to move when he was blinded by the light of a torch thrust through the open doorway. A second and then a third blazing torch were thrust through two of the windows. When Lom's eyes finally adjusted to the light, he found he was facing a man holding a nocked arrow pointed right at Taarig and him.

"Well, well, well, what do we have here?" asked the man still pointing the arrow at Lom. "You were right to come to me with what you overheard the rover saying," the man told the folk now climbing in the window, "about how sad they were to have to leave a lad at the old mill, the lad and his wolf. Lurking in shadows listening so as folks don't know we are there has made us many coins over the years. This one might be the best listen ever. Now, lad, you and your wolf are going to move out of that corner."

"Run, Taarig, run!" Lom shouted, hoping against hope that the night wolf would do as he asked.

Taarig spun and headed toward an open window, sprang, and was followed through the window by an arrow. Lom heard a yip and then silence. He started to move when an arrow thudded at his feet, causing him to freeze.

"Now, what did you have to go and do that for, lad?" the man pointing an arrow at Lom's chest asked in a deceptively calm voice. "You two, go see if you can find that wolf. Be careful. Either he is lying dead outside that window, or I wounded him."

Lom found he could not breathe. The thought of Taarig dead or wounded was more than he could bear. He felt a great pressure building inside of him.

Both of the two other folks returned after a few minutes.

"Well?"

"He's not anywhere near. You must have hit him, for there's blood. No good trying to track him in the dark."

"We'll look for him in the morning. Now lad, I want you to walk toward me. I'll not hesitate to shoot."

The anger that had been building inside of Lom at that moment broke loose. The vines that covered the walls began to stir, detaching themselves from the walls and, swinging wildly, they wrapped themselves around anything near.

# CHAPTER THIRTY-NINE

Lom stood in the center of the swirling maelstrom of writhing green vines. He did not know how he had gotten to the center of the mill. Trying to calm himself, he took several deep breaths. The vines slowly stopped moving and settled back against the walls. It was dark inside the mill now, for the torches had gone out. Other than the rustling of leaves, there was only the sound of muffled moaning.

What had he done? Lom was against harming any living thing. He even hated to hurt the bugs that were not good for the garden. More often than not he would just pack them up and move them away from the royal garden, rather than harm them. He needed to get some light to see what he had done. Going more by smell than by sight, he stumbled across one of the torches. With trembling hands, after a few attempts, he lit it. Holding the torch aloft, Lom saw the vines which covered the interior walls of the old mill had settled back into place, with the exception of three areas where the vines bulged out from the walls. The moaning was coming from those three mounds. Through openings in the vines he could see bits and pieces of the three folks who had accosted him. Those three folks were trussed up tight, held to the mill walls by the vines.

Lom concentrated and asked the vines to hold until daybreak those who would have captured him. Out loud he told those held by the vines that their wait would be more comfortable if they ceased their thrashing. They would be released at dawn. *At least I hope so*, thought Lom. He would make sure someone knew the three were at the old mill as soon as he was able, after daybreak. They were not his main concern. Taarig was.

Holding the torch aloft, Lom climbed through the opening Taarig had left the mill by. He found the small droplets of blood that had been reported. He was so frightened for Taarig. Lom did not know how he was ever going to find the night wolf in the dark. He certainly was no tracker. Taarig could be anywhere. He would not necessarily have run down an established path into the fields beyond the mill. He could have run down the lane or through the fields themselves. Lom did not know which way to go.

Lom knew he could not stay where he was, turning in circles. He also knew he would see better if he put the torch out. Once his night vision had adjusted to the darkness, he realized it was brighter outside than it had been in the old mill. The stars were out in the clear night sky, and there was a half moon. Now that he could see what was around him, he noticed a grove of very tall trees across the meadow. Something seemed to be urging him to head toward the trees.

With no better idea of where to go, Lom headed off across the meadow toward the trees, making no effort to hide where he was going. Finding Taarig was his most important and urgent need. Nothing else mattered right now. The folks held to the wall of the old mill did not matter. Finding the piece of the oppgave ringe did not matter. Only Taarig mattered. Lom hoped the night wolf was all right. He hoped that the arrow had only grazed him. He hoped.

Lom arrived at the grove of trees much sooner than he had expected. He found himself entering a young quirrelit grove. Winding between the huge tree trunks, Lom softly called Taarig's name. He heard nothing. He walked a little farther into the grove and called again. This time he thought he heard a soft bark. Heading in the direction he thought the bark came from, Lom rounded a quirrelit tree trunk and found himself in a small clearing. Lying in the clearing was Taarig.

Rushing forward with little caution or heed to any possible dangers, Lom was soon at Taarig's side.

"Are you all right? Are you hurt anywhere? I need some light."

Lom took off his pack and frantically dug around until he located a candle. Lighting it, he held it aloft so he could see Taarig. At first, he could see nothing. No wounds, no fur missing. Then he noticed two things. There was a dark wet-looking spot on Taarig's shoulder, and there was a thin braid of very small wild flowers around his neck. Upon closer inspection of the wet spot on Taarig's shoulder, Lom recognized it from its smell as a salve used on cuts and wounds. It was used to seal the opening and heal it.

Quickly, Lom jumped up and, turning in a circle, realized he had taken no precautions at all when he had rushed into the clearing. He could see no one. *Who had helped Taarig?* he wondered. Crouching back down, Lom gently ran his hands over Taarig to make sure he had not missed anything. Taarig lay patiently, resting.

"Can you travel? We can't stay here. Those folks who were after us in the mill will only be held until morning. At least I hope that is true. We need to be away from here."

Taarig slowly stood and took a few steps before lying back down again with a quiet whimper.

Lom sat down beside the night wolf, gently stroking Taarig's head and murmuring reassuring words, which masked the rising panic he was feeling. They were not safe where they were and, yet, Lom could not just leave the night wolf there and head out on his own. Wrapping his arms around his drawn up knees, Lom laid his head down and let the tears of frustration and fear flow. Finally, exhaustion overtook him and he slipped into a fitful sleep. A soft shake of his shoulder awoke him.

Lom opened his eyes and then closed them quickly again, thinking he was seeing double. Rubbing his eyes to get the sleep out of them, he opened them again. *There really are two night wolves in front of me,* he thought. *One was Taarig. Who was the other night wolf?*

When he lifted his eyes a bit farther, Lom could see the new night wolf was not alone. He could just make out the silhouette of someone sitting near the night wolves. He thought it was a woman.

"I am sorry to wake you, wolf friend. The night is half over. Dawn will bring danger."

"Who, who are you?" asked Lom, stumbling over his words. "Are you the one who took care of Taarig's wound?"

"I am Theora, wolf friend to Tala here. No, I did not help Taarig. It looks more like the work of the …." Theora became silent and alert. Both of the night wolves also became alert. "We must go, and quickly. Follow Tala, I will bring Taarig."

Before Lom could even question his rising and following Tala, he found his feet moving. Looking over his shoulder, he saw Theora gently lift Taarig up with little or no effort, which was quite a feat since Taarig was not a small animal. As fast as the darkness allowed, they moved through the quirrelit grove, arriving finally at what was little more than an opening between the trees, wide enough for a small horse-drawn wagon.

"Do you know how to drive a wagon?" Theora asked.

"Yes, ma'am."

"Good, then give the horse its head, and drive us out of here while I get the night wolves settled."

Now that Lom had a moment to think, he began to wonder if he had made the right choice to follow the other night wolf, ending up in a small wagon with a woman he did not know. He did not have time to ponder the questions long, for they did not travel far before the two wagon ruts they were following joined a larger lane.

"We have come to a T in the road. Which way should I turn?" Lom asked.

"Turn right. It will head us south," Theora said, as she climbed into the driver's seat, sitting alongside Lom. "Taarig is resting comfortably. I took a close look at his shoulder. What caused the wound?"

"Arrow."

"I thought so. The arrow caused a gash which will heal fairly quickly. I am sure you have been sitting up here with questions circling around in your head, like who is this woman? Can I trust her? Why would she help us? Is she helping us?"

Lom wondered if she were a mind reader.

"No, I'm not a mind reader. These are just the questions I would be asking if I were in your boots. I'm a watcher, a member of the border guard who watches the high eastern mountain passes. Most folks in Sommerhjem are aware that there are two passes, one each through the northern and southern mountains. Very few are aware that there are also two places you can get through the eastern mountains. Neither are easy passages, and neither would allow even a small wagon to pass through. Nevertheless, it is always important to be aware of what is coming in your back door. It is a cold and solitary duty. We rotate out every six months."

While this information was useful, it did not really reassure Lom he had made the right decision to follow this woman and her night wolf.

"A while back, when my duty was over, I was headed down out of the mountains and had set up camp for the night when Tala came out of the woods and just set herself down next to my fire. Scared the daylights out of me, I can tell you. Was pretty insistent as to just where I was going to head to. That brought us to you."

"Why did you think we needed help this night, other than Taarig's wound?"

"There was this little matter of three folk I found trussed up in vines in an old ruined mill. They spun me this tale about a huge night wolf and his evil companion."

"Did you cut them down?"

"Nah, they seemed unharmed, if a bit angry. One had managed to get his mouth uncovered. I wonder if those vines tasted any good, but I digress. He should take to the road as a storyteller. That man spun me such a tale. Tala became impatient, so I left him and his tale hanging and followed her. She led me to you. However, just as we were exiting the mill, I heard riders approaching. I stuck around for a few moments outside the mill to see if the riders stopped."

"And did they?" asked Lom, finding himself pulled into Theora's tale.

"They did indeed. Seems they were friends of those you left behind in the mill. That was you, wasn't it?"

Lom remained silent. He did not know how he had done what he did back at the mill and knew even less how to explain it.

"No matter. At any rate, the new arrivals had come looking for their companions. Wanted to know what had hung them up. Sorry," Theora said laughing, "I just couldn't resist that. Anyway, they were starting to try to cut their partners down when I left. The vines appeared to be a bit uncooperative until one of the new folks suggested they just burn the vines. I left at that point, for all of them were shouting and arguing at the same time. Now then, was I wrong to invite you to go with me? Are you a great evil one?"

"No, ma'am. Not even a little evil."

"So, why are those folks interested in you?"

"For the same reason they would be interested in you. You are traveling with a very uncommon animal, a night wolf, as am I. It seems there is a great deal of interest by those loyal to the former regent in folks who travel with uncommon animals," Lom went on to tell Theora. "How have you not come to the attention of the same folks who have been after me?"

"When we were traveling in the high hills and more forested land, Tala would disappear should we be happened on by folks. No one ever saw her or, if they caught a glimpse, they either thought she was a large wild dog, or didn't believe what they saw. Once we got to more open spaces, the grasslands or farms, she began to ride in the wagon. After what you have told me, it would seem that, besides the night wolf, luck has also been riding with me."

The two rode in silence for a time before Theora spoke up. "Night wolves are the stuff of legends. I thought maybe this last time as a watcher had driven me a little crazy, that I was just seeing things. Of course, I soon learned that was not true. One never expects to ever see a night wolf, and now I have seen two. Hard to believe."

Lom and Theora talked for a little while longer before she suggested he head back into the wagon and catch a nap. Once she mentioned he get some sleep, Lom realized how exhausted he was. When he climbed into the wagon, he was surprised at its interior. From the outside, it had looked like a typical covered wagon with its waterproof sailcloth cover. The inside was more like a rover homewagon. It had a bed, a small stove, washbasin and water jug, a table that slid out from under the bed, and cupboards for storing gear. The interior was plain in design and very functional.

Lom stepped over the two sleeping night wolves. He stopped, turned, and checked on Taarig, who seemed to be doing fine. His wound was already healing, which surprised Lom. Once Lom was settled, he had time to think about all that had happened since the day before. He knew being in the wagon with Taarig was certainly keeping them from the view of anyone they passed by, which was a good thing. The ride was certainly taking them farther away from Lord Madron's folks and territory, which was also a good thing. He wondered, however, if now traveling with two night wolves was better than traveling with one, or if it would cause more trouble.

# CHAPTER FORTY

Feeling refreshed after a short nap, Lom got up, checked on Taarig, and then called out quietly to Theora. "Do you want me to take over the driving?"

"I don't think quite yet. Those who are after you might still be trying to find where you went. It will have taken them some time to round up their horses, since I cut their reins, and Tala urged them away when we left the mill. She can be a pretty effective herder, I found out," Theora stated with a chuckle.

"Another question?"

"Yes."

"Where were you heading before Tala found you?"

"Eventually, to see my family. Mostly, I was just going to wander my way there. They live on the coast, south of the capital. Own a pub and eatery. You ever get down that way, they make some of the best clam chowder in Sommerhjem."

Lom could hear the pride in Theora's voice. As they rode along, he asked her other questions, such as why she would join a border guard patrol that spent six months isolated up in the cold, snowy, eastern mountains.

"Pays double, and serving time is half. Times were tough for my family when the former regent was ruling. My pay helped my family survive during the hard times.

"But you changed your plans to go home after Tala came to sit by your fire?"

"She can be pretty insistent. I still do not know why she led me to you, or if it was you she led me to. Maybe she led me to Taarig," Theora said.

Before Lom had fallen asleep, he had been thinking about what it meant that Theora had been led to Taarig and him by a second night wolf. *If Tala had just wanted to find Taarig, she would not have needed Theora. Why had Tala chosen to find and redirect Theora? Just why had Taarig chosen to find and stay with him?*

Ealdred believed that there was a reason Taarig had sought out Lom. Lom felt it may have had something to do with the firestar gem in the ring he wore. Ealdred did not seem too convinced it was the firestar gem that had attracted Taarig to Lom, however. He felt it had more to do with destiny. He told Lom he felt the night wolf was there because Lom was supposed to search for a piece of the oppgave ringe. If that was true, was Theora supposed to be looking for a piece of the oppgave ringe, too? Lom needed answers. He needed to sort through what he should do next.

From what Lom knew and had been told by Journeyman Evan, who had learned it from Aaron Beecroft, the man he called Beezle, a night wolf had been part of the adventure Beezle and a lass called Piper had in the eastern mountains. The night wolf seemed to have prevented a piece of the oppgave ringe from falling into the wrong hands. For animals that were so rarely seen as to be thought only tall tales, night wolves seemed to be overrunning Sommerhjem at the moment.

All of this thinking had brought Lom around full circle to the questions that were foremost in his mind. He wondered if Theora being accompanied by a night wolf meant he could trust her. Was she also seeking a piece of the oppgave ringe? He knew he had to determine if he could trust her before he could discuss anything about the oppgave ringe with her. That she had gently carried Taarig to her wagon, and so far had not betrayed them, went a long way toward convincing Lom he might be able to trust her. That, and the fact that she traveled with a night wolf who Taarig was aware of and had not challenged. Rather, when Lom looked over his shoulder, the two night wolves were curled up together, asleep.

Lom's thinking was interrupted when Theora asked, "So, now that we are away from those men who seemed to have an unhealthy interest in you, what next? Where are you heading?"

Before he could answer, he felt a cool, wet nose pushing at his hand. Looking down, he saw it was Taarig. Lom glanced down and saw the area where the arrow had cut a gash on Taarig's shoulder was completely healed. Taarig was standing steady, despite the sway of the wagon. Lom came to a decision. He did not think he would make it to the royal forest south of the capital if he tried to do it on his own. He could certainly use some help. Theora and Tala might be the help he needed.

"Anyone ahead of us on this lane?" Lom asked Theora.

"No, and I have a pretty clear view for a long way."

Lom moved to the back of the wagon and peered out. He could not see anyone following them.

"I need to get to the royal forest south of the capital without anyone the wiser. I …. Well, you see, I'm looking for a piece of the oppgave ringe there."

Theora was silent for a great long while. Finally she spoke. "Were those folks who were detained in the mill aware of what you are seeking?"

"I don't think so. They were just looking for folks traveling with uncommon animals."

"So why do you think there is a piece of the oppgave ringe in the royal forest south of the capital?"

*In for a copper, in for a silver,* Lom thought. "Maybe I should start at the beginning," said Lom. He started with being abducted from the capital and why. He went on to tell Theora about his rescue, his stay with Ealdred, and what they had found. He did not tell Theora that Ealdred was a Høyttaier, or that the note was in the old language, for that was not his tale to tell. Lom also had tried to breeze past the part where others thought he was a sensitive. That, however, did not work.

"So let me see if I have this straight," Theora said. "This note you found suggested that a woman had hidden a piece of the oppgave ringe in a quirrelit grove in the royal forest?"

"Yes."

"She didn't leave a map or give specific directions as to which quirrelit grove, did she?"

"Unfortunately, no."

"Do you know how many quirrelit groves there are in the royal forest south of the capital?"

"More than can be counted on both hands," Lom said.

"I've been there. There are ancient groves, which have been there since time out of mind, that have withstood fire and fierce storms. Then there are the newer, younger groves. While the groves are young, they still would have been there when the note writer put the ring there. Why would she leave such a cryptic message?"

"I don't know. She thought she had lost her entire family at the time. She was also in fear for her life. She wanted to leave a clue, and yet not give the information straight into the hands of those pursuing her, should she be caught. Maybe she hoped to return, retrieve the note when she safely could, and then retrieve the ring. She died before she could do either."

"So now you have set off to find a very tiny object in a very large forest. Do I have the right of it?"

"Yes."

"And you expect to be successful because you are drawn to objects that hold some sort of power?"

"Yes." Lom thought what Theora just said sounded so ridiculous and daft. He had a hard time believing in what he was doing, so how could he expect anyone else to?

"Well," Theora said, "we had better get you to the royal forest south of the capital with none the wiser, then."

Lom let out the breath he was not aware he had been holding. "Just like that? No more questions?"

"Tala led me to you for a reason. You have given me a reason. I don't believe fate would have sent night wolves to each of us just on a whim. I'm honored such a rare and powerful animal as Tala has chosen to join her life with mine. She is a boon companion."

"So how do you suggest we get to the royal forest with two night wolves without being caught by the likes of Lord Madron's men?"

"I certainly have had the advantage of having a wagon to travel in, and have been able to travel during daylight hours, since Tala seems content to travel in the wagon. When we have camped in sites where there have been others, I always tried to pick a spot that was either away from others or close to trees. Once we are camped, she often leaves me to hunt, at least I think that is what she is doing. She leaves after it's full dark and returns before first light. So far no one has spotted her. I suggest we find an isolated spot this night and see what happens. Eventually, we are going to have to camp where there are others."

Theora's plan seemed reasonable to Lom, so he asked again if she wanted him to drive the wagon.

"I think for today, since we are still not so far from the mill, it would be best for you to remain hidden from view. We are bound to pass others on this road. They should only be able to say that they saw a wagon pass, driven by a lass. Actually, I might stop and put on my border guard uniform. I don't have to wear it when I'm off duty. It might, however, act as a way to confuse the issue even more since, when I was in the area where I found you, I was dressed much like others there. If they are looking for a lass passing through, they might get thrown off if the folks we pass this day say yes, they saw a lass driving a wagon. If they are asked to describe me, they will say they saw a border guard pass by."

When Theora found a dense woodland lining the road they were on, she pulled over to the edge of the road. Both she and Lom climbed down from the wagon to stretch their legs. Both night wolves came down out of the wagon and silently slipped into the woodlands. Lom stayed outside, while Theora went back into the wagon to change into her uniform.

Lom was surprised how much the uniform changed Theora's appearance. Gone was the relaxed lass, changed into a somewhat stern, alert, border guard. While Theora had not grown taller in the brief moments she had been inside the wagon, she nonetheless looked taller and older.

Straightening her collar, Theora remarked, "I had hoped not to put this back on for another few months. Ah, well, it can't be helped. Tomorrow, you can drive, and I will ride. That will confuse any who might still be looking for a lass who might have been seen in the vicinity of the old mill."

Theora suggested she would wear her border guard uniform for the next week. After that, she would pack it away again.

The days passed by quickly. Each morning, they set out on the road shortly after sunrise, stopping every few hours to give the horse a rest. They would stop at noon for a cold lunch, and then around the time of the evening meal begin to search for a place to camp for the night. Each night, one or both of the night wolves would leave after dark and return before first light.

Lom and Theora had discussed what route they should take. The royal road would certainly be a quicker route to the royal forest, they concluded one night, after spending several hours poring over maps Theora had in the wagon, but there would be too many folks traveling on it heading to and from the major summer fairs. While it might take them longer and not be as smooth a ride, they concluded the smaller roads and lanes would be safer for all of them.

Lom was becoming more and more anxious as they came closer to their goal. All roads eventually led to the capital, and the closer they got, the more folks they met. The number of folks on the road increased the chances of discovery. Each night when the night wolves would leave, Lom feared that one or both would either be discovered or not return. He worried that they would find hunting some farmer's livestock easier than hunting wild game, raising a hue and cry, causing folks to hunt the night wolves.

A small niggling worry at the back of his mind was whether he had been too quick to trust Theora. After all, did being accompanied by a night wolf really mean she was on the side of the Crown and was truly helping him get to the royal forest? Or was this just a ruse to get him to find the piece of the oppgave ringe and then take it away from him? He shook that thought off, for how would she have known what he was looking for? But she had come from the eastern mountains. Maybe she had somehow gotten the information from Ealdred or Master Opeline. *No, that could not have happened, could it?*

# CHAPTER FORTY-ONE

Lom needed to pull himself together, or he was going to go mad. It was bad enough he did not know if he could trust Theora. He was also so alert he was jittery almost all of the time, jumping at the slightest sound, peering at shadows, convinced that something moved within. He worried that every rider, walker, or wagon driver that came near them would know who he was and what he was trying to find. *And was that not a laugh*, he thought. *I, Lom, lowly laborer who pulls weeds for a living, am supposed to find a piece of the oppgave ringe, in the royal forest no less?*

Several other worries had crept in recently to add to the others. What if Aldys, the woman who had left the box at Ealdred's, had hidden the piece of the oppgave ring in a cloth or pouch made of golden pine spider silk? No matter how sensitive he was supposed to be, he would be hard-pressed to feel any kind of pull, if that were the case. Or what if Aldys had told someone where she had hidden the ring, and that folk had picked it up, so it was now long gone from the royal forest?

Since worrying never seemed to solve anything, Lom finally decided to do something else. They had camped in a beautiful wooded spot. The night wolves had left almost the minute the wagon had stopped, not even waiting until dark. So far, no one else had pulled into camp where they were. Lom busied himself with gathering wood. In addition, he had foraged in the woods and returned with mushrooms, early summer berries, and a variety of edible tubers to add to their evening meal. Theora, returning to the campsite after hauling water from a nearby stream, found Lom skinning a rabbit Taarig had dropped off before slipping back into the woods.

"Looks like we will eat well this night," Theora commented, as she began to scrub the dirt off the tubers. "We should talk about what happens next, for we are getting close to the royal forest. So far, the night wolves seem to be well able to take care of themselves and stay out of sight. I do worry about what will happen when we camp in the royal forest. There will be more folks there."

"I would understand if you and Tala want to just drop me off anywhere and head on to your family's place. The closer we get to the royal forest south of the capital, the greater the chances are that someone is going to catch a glimpse of the night wolves. It certainly will put you in danger."

"To be quite honest, I don't think either of us has that choice. Tala was quite insistent as to where I was to go. I believe there is a reason that she has brought me to you. I don't know what that is, but I feel we should trust it is important, so I think we will stick with you and Taarig."

While Lom was not convinced that Theora was to be completely trusted, he was still relieved that she wished to continue to the royal forest with him. She was a good companion and comfortable to travel with.

The day finally arrived when Theora pulled off to the side of a lane just on the edge of the royal forest. "It would appear that we have arrived. Now what?"

"It would be helpful if we had a map," Lom suggested.

"To get a map, we would need to find a forester and ask if they have one available. What good is a map going to do us? It's not like there is going to be an *X* marking the spot of what you are looking for."

"Don't I wish it would be that easy? No, I have no expectations of them having a map with a convenient *X* on it. I had hoped they might have a map showing where the quirrelit groves are located. This royal forest is huge. I had hoped to eliminate wandering around through grove after grove of trees trying to find the quirrelit groves."

"Good idea. We probably would have come across a forester if we had come into the royal forest on the royal road from the capital. Coming in the back way reduces the likelihood of a chance meeting. Sitting here is not going to get us any closer to finding what you came here for, so we had best just start looking for quirrelit groves and see what will happen."

With that said, Theora gently snapped the reins to start the horse moving. Lom quickly jumped down, saying he needed to stretch his legs. Mostly, he wanted to be alone with his thoughts. He was surprised when Taarig fell in beside him. He noticed that Tala had also left the wagon and was headed farther into the woods. From time to time, he would catch a glimpse of her as she kept pace parallel to the lane. Lom wondered about both of the night wolves being no longer content to ride in the wagon. He also wondered why, at this point in their travels, he was not feeling concerned that they were in the open.

The forest was quiet and peaceful. Sunlight sent rays through the leaves, lighting up pockets of ferns. Small animals went about their business in the underbrush and in the tree branches overhead. Birds flitted and flew, calling to one another. Lom found himself relaxing for the first time in weeks. He could almost pretend he was just out for a nice walk on his day off, accompanied by his dog. Only he was not on a day off, and Taarig would certainly never be mistaken for a dog. Shaking himself, Lom pulled his attention back out of his daydreams. It was then that he became aware that something was pulling at his senses.

*Could it be this easy?* Lom wondered, only to have his hopes dashed when he realized that it was the firestar gem in the ring on his finger that had captured his attention. It had grown warm. He glanced down at the ring and saw there was a slight glow within the firestar gem. He quickly looked all around, trying to spot anything or anyone that might be causing the ring to heat up and glow. Lom quickened his pace until he was next to the driver's seat of the wagon.

"Pull to a stop, please," he called to Theora. As she complied, Lom looked around, trying to spot Taarig, who had silently slipped away.

"Is something wrong?" Theora asked.

"I'm not sure. The firestar gem in the ring I wear has begun to warm and glow. Taarig has disappeared. I can no longer spot Tala, and ..."

"And?"

"... and the forest seems to be closing in."

"How can the forest close in? Are you doing that to the ...." Theora stopped mid-sentence when Lom had answered her with a "no" and was shaking his head. Tree branches had intertwined, bushes had spread out. The forest surrounding them had become so dense that, except where they were, the woods were deep in shadow. Oddly enough, they stood in bright sunlight surrounded by the dense forest.

"So, all right, this does not seem right," Lom suggested. He kept glancing around, trying to spot a break in the forest. He was very worried about Taarig.

"The night wolves gave no warning?" Theora asked.

"No, none. One minute Taarig was walking beside me, and then I lost track of him when I moved to catch your attention and ask you to stop the wagon. It was when you stopped that I noticed the forest closing in. I tried to concentrate and cause the plants, bushes, or tree branches to return to their original places. I couldn't even budge a leaf."

"I have to tell you I'm finding this quite alarming," said Theora.

Theora jumped down off the wagon and asked Lom to help her set the chocks on either side of the wagon wheels, to prevent the wagon from moving should the horse become spooked. Oddly enough, the horse paid no attention to what was happening, just dropped his head and began nibbling on the grass that grew between the ruts on the lane. Once the wagon was set, Theora climbed back up and grabbed her bow and quiver. She did not think what was happening in the forest was natural. She wanted to be prepared for whatever might come.

An hour passed, then two. The forest remained dense and ominous. It was very quiet within the small space left on the lane. The only sounds were the jingle of the horse's tack and quiet talking between Lom and Theora. The normal forest sounds were shut out. Lom and Theora had considered trying to slip past the foliage. Lom had even walked past the horse and a little way into the brush. He had returned quickly. He told Theora that once he had entered the area, everything around him became so tangled and dark he could not get very far. Even with several axes, they would not be able to chop their way through.

Theora had taken up a position in the driver's seat of the wagon, watching the front and both sides. Lom had settled himself, leaning against the back of the wagon, every once in a while moving out from the wagon to glance around and stretch his legs.

"Theora," Lom whispered, having moved to the side of the wagon facing the woods.

"Yes."

"There is a patch of forest that seems to be moving, just there," Lom said pointing. "Do you see it?"

"Yes," Theora answered, jumping down to stand beside Lom, alert, her bow at the ready.

The brush, plants, and tree branches continued to pull back, forming a corridor that stretched back into the forest. Within moments, Lom spotted movement within the corridor and quietly mentioned it to Theora. Soon they could make out what was approaching. Flanked on both sides by the night wolves was a young woman. She slowly approached them, one hand on the head of each night wolf walking beside her. She was dark-haired, very slight, with skin the color of tree bark, dressed in clothing that allowed her to blend into the forest. Her clothing was not quite that of a forester. Most noticeable was the firestar gem pendant hanging around her neck, emitting a soft glow.

Lom had a swift moment of panic. *Had this young woman taken over command of the night wolves? Had Taarig and Tala just been using Theora and him to transport them here?* The minute the idea entered his mind, he shoved it right out again. The idea that she was somehow controlling the night wolves did not leave him, however. His other concern was that this young woman approaching them could be the one who controlled the forest, and she was far better at it than he was. He felt a sense of great relief when she raised her hands, extending them palms forward in a gesture of peace. The two night wolves trotted forward and came to stand next to Lom and Theora.

"Please lower your bow, wolf friend. No harm comes from me. Which one of you called?"

Lom and Theora exchanged looks of puzzlement. It was at that moment that the ring on Lom's finger sent out an arc of light that was met by an arc of light from the firestar gem on the pendant.

When her eyes once again adjusted after the flashes of light, Theora remarked, "I would guess you were the one who called."

"Again, I ask that you lower your bow."

"Theora, please do as she asks," Lom requested. If I understand how these firestar gems work, that arcing of light suggests she is a friend, or at least not an enemy."

Theora slowly lowered her bow and un-nocked the arrow. Tala leaned in against Theora's leg as if reassuring her that doing so would be all right. When Theora looked up, she noticed the woman had moved closer, hands still outstretched in a gesture of peace.

"I am Taren, and you are?"

"Lom," said Lom, "and this is Theora."

"Taarig and Tala travel with you?" Taren asked.

*How had this woman known the wolves' names?* Lom wondered. He looked to Theora and saw the same questioning look on her face.

"You, you know their names?" Lom asked, the surprise in his voice evident.

"We are old friends. Please tell me which of you called."

While this exchange had been going on, the tree branches, brush, and undergrowth had begun to untangle and untwine. Streaks of sunlight once again filtered through the leaves.

Feeling a bit more relaxed and not quite so hemmed in, Lom tried to answer her question. "I think I might have. I just didn't know I was doing it at the time."

"Perhaps I need to ask another question. Why did you call?"

*That is an even more difficult question to answer,* thought Lom. He did not quite know what to make of this folk standing before him. *I do not think she is a forester. The night wolves obviously know her and seem to trust her. How do I answer her question? Maybe the best way to handle this is to ask her a question.*

"Who are you? Are you a forester?"

"No, I am not of the forester clans. I am the caretaker of the quirrelit groves here in the royal forest. I have been expecting you," stated Taren.

Now Lom was really confused. *This complete stranger suggested that Theora or I called her, and now she is saying she has been expecting us.*

"I can see by the looks on your faces that you are confused. We need to get off this lane and farther into the forest. Once we are in a less travelled place, I will explain. I know you might not know me or trust me. Know that the night wolves trust me. Trust your night wolves," Taren stated, as she began to move down the lane ahead of the horse.

# CHAPTER FORTY-TWO

Lady Farcroft was pacing back and forth across the dais that held the high-backed chair she normally sat in when presiding over her loyal followers at the ancient keep high on the hill overlooking the manor house.

"Hunting cats, griff falcons, even that strange little animal, what was it, ah yes, a halekrets, I can understand, but a night wolf?" scoffed Lady Farcroft.

Bode knew Lady Farcroft's moods well and was reluctant to speak up. Braving it, he said, "Begging your pardon, m'lady. It was reported that there were the tracks of two night wolves."

Flinging herself into her high-backed chair, Lady Farcroft suggested that Bode explain.

"Yes, m'lady. As you know, we have been alerted that a number of rovers have begun to gather in the royal forest south of the capital. A gathering of rovers in numbers of more than three or four wagons is not unusual, for families often gather once or twice a year. What brought this gathering to our attention is that it is not one of a clan or family group. This gathering is made up of a number of elder rovers across clan and family."

"What does this have to do with night wolves?" Lady Farcroft asked impatiently.

"We have had folks loyal to you patrolling the border of the royal forest. One of them, a good tracker, was following some wagon tracks that he thought might be that of a homewagon, when he ran across a place where someone got out to walk behind the wagon. When this folk got out, so did not one but two night wolves."

"How could this tracker even know the tracks belonged to night wolves? Maybe it was just tracks of two regular wolves, or two dogs for that matter."

"Said he learned tracking from his grandfather who had learned tracking from his father. Had a book that had been passed down for generations that held drawings of all types of tracks. Even had a drawing of the tracks of a halekrets and other animals that haven't been seen in Sommerhjem for longer than folks can remember."

"So either the original maker of this book of tracks made up the animals and their tracks, or animals such as halekrets and night wolves existed in Sommerhjem," mused Lady Farcroft. "Well, did he find the night wolves and those they travelled with?"

"Not exactly," Bode replied.

"Not exactly?"

"No, m'lady. He reports that he followed the tracks of the night wolves, the walker, and the wagon down the lane. They stopped again and were joined by another folk. They went farther down the lane for a short way and then disappeared."

"If this tracker was any good at all, he would be hard-pressed to lose three folks, two night wolves, a horse, and a wagon."

"He could not understand how they could disappear, so he went and gathered several more good trackers to help him. They, too, could not follow the trail. It is as if the forest swallowed them up."

Lady Farcroft sat for a long time, silently thinking over what Bode had reported. She knew she was right in her conclusion that pairings of folks with uncommon animals was the key to who found and brought the pieces of the oppgave ringe to the capital. Folks traveling with night wolves, if this tale was to be believed, suggested they might know where one or more of the pieces were located. They had to be stopped. At least one of the pieces of the oppgave ringe needed to be in her hands before the opening of the summer fair at the capital.

"Send a message to this tracker and to others near the royal forest. Increase the number of those looking for these folks. Tell them to find them," Lady Farcroft commanded. "Also, see if we can find out more as to why the rover elders are gathering."

Lom and Theora followed Taren just a short way down the lane before she stopped and walked back to them. "With your help, Lom, we will ask the forest to uncover the lane hidden here. If you will take the front, I will close up behind us. There have been watchers along the border of the royal forest for the last month. They are not, I think, friends to you or to the rovers who are gathering in the royal forest right now."

*This Taren knows way too much about me*, Lom thought. *Right now is not the time to question how.* Lom was feeling an urgency to be off the lane. He did not know where the feeling was coming from. He also sensed that Taarig was growing impatient. Though Lom was feeling less confident in his abilities to move even a leaf off the lane, much less the foliage he was facing, he told Taren he would try.

The plants, bushes, and tree branches responded readily to Lom's requests and drew back revealing a narrow lane, just wide enough for the wagon. Theora turned the wagon onto the lane, and Taren closed the lane up behind them. When she was done, not even a blade of grass was out of place.

After quite a long while, Taren moved to the front of the wagon and told Lom he could stop. He had been concentrating so hard, he had not noticed that the wagon had stopped behind him. Stumbling to a stop, Lom bent at the waist, put his hands on his knees, and took several deep breaths. He felt like he had been running for miles rather than walking.

"It is just a little way farther," Taren told the two. "There is a good camping spot ahead, and then you both can rest."

Once camped, Lom once again asked Taren to explain just who she was and how she knew the night wolves. He also asked why she had been expecting them.

"As I said, I am the caretaker of the ancient quirrelit groves here in the royal forest, as was my mother before me. As to the night wolves, they pass this way every so often, and have rested with us a while. I knew someone was coming because Taarig and Tala came and found me several nights ago, and urged me to be near the lane you entered the royal forest on. As I am sure you are aware, either one of them can be quite persuasive, and it is difficult to withstand the two of them," Taren said.

Lom could hear the laughter and fondness in Taren's voice when she talked about the night wolves.

"Now then, wolf friends, tell me why you have entered the royal forest by the back way. Tell me, how can I help?" Taren asked.

Lom looked at Theora, who gave a slight nod of her head. He knew that without help or a really good map, they could wander the royal forest for days and still not find all of the quirrelit groves. Many of the groves could not be reached by wagon. He knew that they could become hopelessly lost if they tried to wander on foot, and would be very vulnerable. Lom decided to trust Taren since she wore a firestar gem and was certainly trusted by both the night wolves. Taking a deep breath, he turned to Taren.

"I have reason to believe one of the pieces of the oppgave ringe was hidden in a quirrelit grove in this royal forest. Whether it is still here is unknown. Finding it will take more luck than skill. We need a guide or a map that will show us where the quirrelit groves are."

"And how will you find so small an object in a grove of quirrelit trees?" Taren asked.

"It seems that I'm sensitive to objects of power. I should feel a pull toward the ring if I get close. At least that is what others think."

"But you are not convinced," Taren said.

"No."

"And you, protector, what do you think?" Taren asked, directing her question to Theora.

"Months ago I would have told you that night wolves were the stuff of legend. I would not have believed that anyone could get trees, shrubs, bushes, grass, and other green leafy living things to move at their will. Now, I'm more open to possibilities I previously would have thought were impossible. I don't think it has been just chance that has brought all of us

291

together. So, to answer your question, I believe Lom can feel the pull of objects of power. For the sake of Sommerhjem, I hope he succeeds."

"Yes, there is that. It is not just the former regent's rule that has caused disturbances in the land. There is a great need to go back to the old ways. The land of Sommerhjem needs it. So tell me, when was this folk here who was supposed to have left a ring in a quirrelit grove?"

Lom did not answer right away, for he was thinking about what Taren had just said. *Just what did she mean when she said that the land needed to go back to the old ways?* Finally, Lom gave an estimate of when Aldys may have been in the royal forest.

"Unfortunately, that does not eliminate any of the groves. Do you know where she came from?"

"I'm afraid not. All Ealdred said was that she escaped the removal of her family from their farm, and others of her clan got her away safely. One of the stops along the way to a safe place was Ealdred's. She never made it back home. She did not tell in her note when she had hidden the ring, nor exactly where."

"I guess there is no help for it then. We will just have to start in the morning at the quirrelit grove not far from here and hope for the best. I will guide you as I am honor bound to help one of the Neebing blessed. Get a good night's sleep. Be ready early to go hunting," Taren said, as she slipped back into the long shadows cast by the surrounding trees. She quickly disappeared from sight.

Once Taren had left, Lom slowly sank to the ground, his shaking legs finally giving way. Ealdred had warned him that working with plants and asking them to follow his requests could drain one of one's energy. He had felt tired after his lessons. Never this exhausted.

"Lom, are you all right? Did she do something to you?" Theora asked anxiously.

Lom could hear the concern in Theora's voice, yet hardly had the energy to answer her. "No, just really tired and …" Lom gathered more strength. "… working with plants … takes a lot of …" Lom's voice drifted off. "… energy. I think I need some food."

Quicker than Lom thought was possible, Theora thrust a cup of hot broth into his hands. Shaking the cobwebs out of his head, Lom realized he must have fallen asleep. His look around confirmed it was toward the end of dusk and nearly full night. Lom was glad Theora had put the broth in a cup, for he found his hands were shaking. The heat of the broth warmed him, and he began to feel less groggy.

"Better?" Theora asked.

"Yes, thank you. Clearing the path took more out of me than I expected."

"Do you think Taren can be trusted?"

"I think so. The firestar gem in my ring is not supposed to react to anyone wearing a firestar gem who is not a good folk. I'm not quite sure just who she is. She seems so much older than she appears. She certainly is very skilled."

"I agree with you on the skilled part. When you were napping and I was through with chores, I had a chance to look at where we came into this campsite. While I'm not an expert tracker, I think anyone would be hard-pressed to know we had come here. There are no disturbances in the grasses and plants. You cannot tell that two wolves, three folks, a horse, and a wagon came through there. Now, let us hope Taren returns tomorrow and what you seek is in a quirrelit grove just a short way away from here."

Just when Theora finished speaking, both of the night wolves stood, facing away from the fire, alert.

# Chapter Forty-Three

Theora stepped away from the fire and swiftly walked to her wagon. She picked up her short bow and quiver, which she had leaned against a wheel. While she knew the rules for the royal forest stated no one should be harmed, that all were safe in the sanctuary of the royal forest, not everyone followed the rules. The royal forest and the royal roads fell under the same rules. However, the royal roads were well patrolled and traveled. The royal forest, while well looked after by the forester clans, was much harder for the royal guard to patrol.

Lom had come to stand beside Theora, and the two were flanked by the night wolves. "Listen," Lom whispered to Theora. "We must be closer to a road or lane than we realized. It's a good thing the fire is down to coals. It's awfully late for a wagon to be traveling. I'm going to try to catch a glimpse of it."

"Are you sure that's wise?" Theora asked.

"No, it's probably not wise. Something about the sound of that wagon has me very curious. I'll go with caution. Taarig, will you go with me?"

Taarig stepped off in the direction of the wagon sound and Lom followed. Working his way slowly through the underbrush, he followed Taarig onto a narrow animal path that wound its way around trees and bushes. Surprisingly, he found the lane not more than one hundred yards from where they were camped. When he saw the light of a lantern being held aloft by someone walking in front of an approaching wagon that had twin lanterns hung above either side of the driver's seat, he quickly ducked back behind a wide tree trunk. As the wagon drew closer, Lom became aware that it was a rover homewagon that was headed toward where he was hiding. The homewagon was close enough that he could hear the conversation between the walker and the driver.

"We need to stop soon, Grandfather."

"Of that I am more than aware, Gersemi. I am weary to my very bones, especially the ones in my bottom. How is it that the driver's seat cushion becomes harder and harder as the day goes on?"

The woman carrying the lantern just laughed at her grandfather's grumbling. "We should meet up with the other rovers on the morrow."

The homewagon was fifteen feet from the tree behind which Lom and Taarig were hiding when suddenly Taarig slipped out from behind the trunk and walked to the center of the lane.

"No, Taarig, come back," Lom whispered frantically.

The night wolf did not heed Lom's call. Lom stood frozen, afraid to come out from his hiding place, and afraid not to. Meanwhile, the woman walking in front of the homewagon stopped abruptly, as did the homewagon behind her. For long moments, nothing and no one moved. Finally, Lom stepped out from behind the tree trunk and walked to stand beside Taarig, who was sitting patiently in the middle of the lane.

Placing one hand on Taarig's shoulder and holding the other hand out palm up in a gesture of peace, Lom said, "No harm here."

"Gersemi, tell me my old tired eyes have not finally failed, for I think I am looking at a lad standing in the middle of the lane with his hand on the shoulder of a night wolf," Gersemi's grandfather, Zeroun, said.

"If your old tired eyes have failed, then so have mine," Gersemi said.

Before anyone could say anything more, Tala padded out onto the lane to sit next to Taarig.

"Oh my," Gersemi exclaimed. "Now I'm seeing double."

"And so it has come to pass," Zeroun stated cryptically. "So, young man, if you mean us no harm, perhaps you would let us pass, for we have travelled this day since before dawn and are beyond weary."

At that point, Theora stepped out from behind the tree where she had been hidden. "We would be honored if you and your granddaughter would share our campfire, Elder."

Lom gave Theora a questioning glance, and she smiled at him reassuringly. He had not had very much contact with rovers, so he decided to trust Theora concerning the two in front of him.

"It is going to be an interesting next few days, I think," Zeroun told his granddaughter. "Those few remaining rover elders who are doubting what is happening will no longer be able to deny that the Neebing blessed are abroad. Change is coming." Directing his comments to Lom and Theora, Zeroun graciously accepted Theora's invitation.

"Lom, would you please go on ahead and make sure the lane is clear?" Theora suggested.

*What lane?* Lom thought. *What lane is she talking about?*

Seeing the confused look on Lom's face, Theora said, "You know, the one about twenty feet down, just around the bend. The one we will be heading out on in the morning."

"Sorry, it's been a long day," Lom said over his shoulder as he started down the lane. He had been so exhausted from moving the foliage out of the way into where they were camped, he had not given a thought as to where they were to go in the morning. Taarig apparently knew the way, for he padded on ahead of Lom and stopped at a slight opening in the trees. Fortunately, the moon had risen, giving Lom enough light to see by. He stilled himself, hoping he had enough energy left to clear a path for the homewagon. Fortunately for him, the way into the campsite from the lane was neither very overgrown nor very wide. It would be just wide enough for the homewagon to move through.

Once everyone was settled into the campsite, introductions were made, and the fire was stirred up so the rovers could cook a hot meal, Theora asked Zeroun if he and his granddaughter were just traveling through.

"No, lass. There is going to be an ingathering of as many of the rover elders as can make it. It is time to put our collective heads together to try to separate tale and legend from fact. We feel the need to compare what we know is happening now to what has been handed down through the generations. As elders, we are the keepers of the oldest stories among the rovers. For example, I remember my grandfather telling me something about night wolves. Something about when two night wolves join with two folk. I know it is important. I just cannot grab a hold of that memory. I am weary. Maybe I will remember in the morning."

After everyone had gone to their wagons, Lom was more than willing to bank the fire once again and roll up in his blanket roll. It had been a long and exhausting day. He was still unsure why Taarig had chosen to show himself to the rovers. He hoped it had not been a mistake to invite them to share the campsite.

In the morning, just as they sat down to a shared breakfast, Taren entered the campsite, coming in from the lane. A surprised look of recognition passed across Zeroun's face. Turning slightly, so he could lean close to his granddaughter, he whispered, "Night wolves and now a guardian of the quirrelit groves. That a guardian would be helping these two folks. This is important. If only I could pull why out of my old mind. Something about two night wolves and a protector and a discoverer. Discoverer is not quite right. Let me think more on it. Also, if you can, take a close look at the ring the lad is wearing. A firestar gem for sure. I want a description from you as to the markings. I want to know if these old eyes of mine are playing tricks on me."

When Taren reached the gathered group, she looked directly at Zeroun. "Well met, Elder. Other rovers have gathered a quarter of a day's ride from here, near the oldest of the quirrelit groves. Glad I am that you are here. We will need your wisdom in the coming days." Turning to Lom and Theora, she held out a rolled piece of parchment. "I am sorry I cannot stay and help you as I had hoped. There has been an infestation of kvele vines in the quirrelit groves. The vines are growing unnaturally fast, the why of which I have no explanation for. If the foresters and I cannot stop their spread, the groves will suffer. It will then affect those who live in or depend on the quirrelit trees. Unfortunately, we think someone has planted these vines. We just do not know why. Again, my apologies for needing to run off and not being able to help you personally. This map should help you find the areas you want to search. I wish you good hunting."

Before any of the others could say anything, Taren turned and began swiftly walking into the forest. One minute she was visible within the trees, and the next minute she was gone.

Zeroun sat sipping his tea in quiet contemplation. He still could not bring the elusive memory concerning night wolves forward. He did suspect, however, that the two folk across from him were important to the future of Sommerhjem.

"We will be joining other rovers today. As I mentioned to Theora last night, this is to be an ingathering of the oldest of each of the clans. We hope we can put our collective memories together and see what we actually might know about the oppgave ringe and the Gylden Sirklene challenge, among other things. The time draws near to the anniversary date of when the challenge was called. Two of the rings are still out. In addition, no one is quite clear as to what will happen once all nine of the rings are in place in the vessteboks. One thing is very clear," Zeroun stated. "The former regent and his followers are getting desperate and will use any means possible to prevent the remaining rings from being brought to the capital."

"Grandfather and I talked it over last night and both of us have come to the conclusion that, even if Grandfather cannot quite recall why folks and night wolves pairing is important, he nevertheless wishes to extend the invitation that you continue to travel and camp with us," Gersemi stated. "There is always safety in numbers. It is obvious you have some task here. We will help if we can."

"I thank you for your kind offer," replied Lom. "We will keep it in mind as we travel the royal forest over the next few days. I'm not sure our path leads to where you are headed just yet. We will need to look at the map Taren left us. I know you are anxious to head out, so we do not want to delay you."

After the rovers left, Lom and Theora spread out the map Taren had given them on a flat rock. Lom was amazed as to how detailed the map was, and after studying it for a few minutes, was extremely grateful to Taren.

"There are quirrelit groves scattered all over the royal forest," Lom remarked. "Without this map or a guide, we would be wandering the royal forest for days and would still probably miss half the groves. I think we are camped here," Lom said, putting his finger on the spot on the map he thought was their campsite.

"And here is where the rover elders are gathering, I think," said Theora. "You were right in wishing to study the map and make a plan rather than wandering around the royal forest willy-nilly. It looks like the nearest quirrelit grove is fairly close. How do you want to proceed?"

Lom was a little surprised that Theora had deferred to him as to what to do next. She was a trained border guard, used to making decisions about more important things than he was. After all, over the last few years his most important decisions had concerned whether a plant was a weed or not, whether it should be pulled or not. *I'm used to taking directions, not figuring out directions*, he thought a little hysterically, laughing at his own pun. Lom had been feeling the weight of the task that had been set on his shoulders for some time now. Today, that weight almost doubled him over. *Folks are counting on me, looking to me to make the right decisions.* He felt overwhelmed.

At that moment, Taarig walked over and sat next to Lom, placing a front paw on Lom's knee. Lom felt the warmth of the night wolf beside him. Just having Taarig close gave Lom a sense of peace. Taking a deep breath, he turned to Theora and suggested they head toward the nearest quirrelit grove.

"I have noticed something," Theora said. "The quirrelit groves spiral outward from the grove where the rover elders are gathering. Unfortunately, the roads do not follow the groves. Perhaps we need to move my wagon to here," Theora said, pointing to a place on the map. "If we leave the wagon there, we can walk back here. Then we can follow the spiral of the groves inward and eventually end up at my wagon."

"That would work. The question is, do you want to leave your wagon unattended for as long as it takes for us to walk back here and follow the spiral inward to your wagon? That could take several days."

"Normally in the royal forest that should not be a problem and the wagon would be safe. On the other hand, we are still so close to the time that many folks were displaced and desperate, I'm not sure how safe the wagon would be. Leaving the wagon unattended is a risk."

"Then maybe we should follow Zeroun and his granddaughter to the most ancient quirrelit grove. I think your wagon would be safe with them."

"How would we explain why we wish to leave the wagon with them while we walk off for a number of days?"

"I don't know," said Lom. "The good thing is, if we choose to camp with the rovers, we have a quarter of a day's ride to figure it out."

Lom decided he did not want to make any snap decisions. He and Theora talked over what to do next, and decided to camp where they were one more night. Their camping spot felt very secluded and safe at the moment, especially after Lom once again had the foliage next to and overhanging the narrow lane in and out of the campsite move, obscuring their spot from passersby. There were a number of quirrelit groves they could check out during the day and still make it back to Theora's wagon before dark. Slinging a small daypack over his shoulders, Lom, Theora, and the two night wolves set off to locate the nearest quirrelit grove.

"Once we reach the quirrelit grove, do you know what you will do?" Theora asked.

"I haven't any idea," Lom replied. "All I know is Aldys said she left the ring in a quirrelit grove in the royal forest. Maybe her children would have known which grove or which quirrelit tree. At this point, there is no way of knowing, and no time to find them and ask. Ealdred thinks I will somehow be drawn toward the ring if I'm in the right grove. I'm not sure if his faith in me is mistaken. I think our chances are really, really slim."

"Oh, I don't know. Would you have ever expected to be walking about the royal forest accompanied by not one but two night wolves?"

"No."

"Me neither, and yet, here we are. I can't help but think luck may be on our side," Theora said optimistically. "That being said, do you think you will have to actually climb each quirrelit tree?"

"I certainly hope not. Our search would take months and months if that is what needs to happen. We don't have that much time. I'm hoping that as I wander within a quirrelit grove, I'll know whether there is anything important about that particular grove." *How am I going to know? That is the question*, Lom thought. *If I do not figure it out right away, I could miss the ring, and never know I have done so.*

# Chapter Forty-Four

An hour's walk brought them to the closest quirrelit grove. Lom had been in a quirrelit grove before, but never one of this age and size. Looking at the enormous tree trunks and the size of the grove, his heart sank. Taarig, who had been ranging ahead of him, came back, sat down next to him, and leaned against him. Taking deep breaths, Lom gathered himself together and stepped into the grove. The sunlight seemed brighter, the leaves greener, and even the air about them seemed to change. Everything felt fresh and crystal clear. What struck Lom the most was the fact that all of his fears just melted away. He felt strong, capable, and at peace with the task that had been set on his thin, narrow shoulders.

As Lom wandered from tree to tree, he got the distinct impression he did not need to climb any of the trees. He was not sure where the idea came from and wondered if it was just wishful thinking on his part. *Wishful thinking or not, I need to trust my instincts,* he concluded When he reached the middle of the grove, Lom stood silently, trying to feel if anything was pulling at him. Nothing was.

During the whole time Lom had wandered through the quirrelit grove, Theora had remained quiet and on guard, with Tala by her side. It seemed important to her that she let Lom take the lead, while making sure she was there to guard his back, not that she expected trouble. She then reflected that trouble often appeared exactly when you least expected it.

The morning passed by swiftly as the four moved from quirrelit grove to quirrelit grove. In each, Lom would stop at each tree. When he reached the center of each quirrelit grove, he would stand very still and concentrate with all his might. In none of the quirrelit groves did he feel any type of pull. Tired and discouraged, Lom pulled out the map Taren had given them and looked at it with Theora peering over his shoulder.

"I think we can look at one more quirrelit grove before we head back to the campsite. It will take us almost as much time to get back to the campsite as it took us to get here, minus the time we spent in the quirrelit groves," Theora said.

"Or maybe we should just head on back," Lom answered. It was difficult to keep the discouragement out of his voice. Reluctantly, he agreed to try one more quirrelit grove before heading back to the campsite.

Squaring his shoulders, Lom hesitated to step out of this quirrelit grove and on to the next. He had certainly begun once again to doubt that he even had the ability to feel the pull of something that held power. Maybe he had just been dazzled by all of the beautiful and unique objects in the cases in the royal palace. He had just made it all up in his mind that he could feel something from some of them. Even finding Aldys' box had not been his feeling a pull. Rather it was Taarig who had really found the box, not him. He should just quit now, head back to the capital, and hope he could get his old job back. Maybe no one would notice.

Lom almost went flat on his face when Taarig came up behind him, reared up, and planted both front paws squarely on his back, sending him sprawling. Fortunately, he managed to catch himself. Rolling over, he looked up into the face of the night wolf, who was snarling at him. Looking into the face of a snarling night wolf was frightening beyond belief. Before Lom could open his mouth to make a remark, Taarig sat down and began to lick the fur on his shoulder.

"What is wrong with you?" Lom asked, sitting up, and brushing dirt and leaves off his front.

Taarig gave him a look which tossed the same question back at Lom.

"Maybe he was trying to knock some sense into you," Theora remarked wryly. "I appreciate that the task set before you looks impossible. Today's results so far certainly have not held anything that might lift your spirits or keep your hopes up. It is just the first day, you know."

"I know, and I'm sorry. I just got overwhelmed."

"Who wouldn't?" Theora said, reaching down to give Lom a hand up. "Now let's check out that last grove before we head back."

It was midafternoon when they entered the final quirrelit grove of the day. No sooner had Lom stepped foot into the grove when he felt that familiar pull he had felt in the corridors of the royal palace. As he walked farther and farther into the grove, the pull became stronger and stronger. Finally, he arrived in the center of the grove at the foot of the mother tree.

Theora noticed that Lom had not searched this grove the way he had the others. Rather than circling the grove and working his way inward, he had walked almost straight to the very center of the grove. Following him, she stopped and watched him circle the trunk of the quirrelit tree and then stop.

"Lom?"

"Sorry, I felt a pull, and it led me here. Can you give me a boost up so I can catch that lower branch? Whatever is causing the pull is up in the tree."

Theora did as Lom asked, admonishing him to be careful. "It does us no good if you fall out of the tree and break something."

"Yes'm," Lom said, giving Theora a mock salute.

Lom felt he had to be quite close to whatever was pulling at him. He cautiously climbed up another level of branches, and then a third, before he spotted an object just resting on top of the broad branch of the tree, not more than an arm's length away from him. It was a short-handled billhook, the kind used to cut brush and vines. Typical billhooks had a wooden handle and a knifelike blade that was curved at the tip. Lom had used one for pruning vines in his work in the royal palace garden. One of the assistant royal palace gardeners had taught him to use it in an upward slicing motion, toward himself, rather than in a downward chopping motion away from himself.

Lom stood for long moments looking at the billhook. He could not imagine how it might have gotten where it now rested. It definitely was what had been pulling at him. Leaning forward to get a better look, he was surprised to see the blade was not rusted, as he might have expected, since it was lying on the branch exposed to the elements. Upon closer inspection, Lom saw the blade was not made of metal at all. It looked like

wood, but not quite. In fact, it looked like it was made of the same material
as the ring on his finger. In addition, the billhook's handle was carved in
a pattern similar to the patterns he had seen on both the box at Ealdred's
and on his ring.

Tentatively, Lom reached out his hand to pick up the billhook, and
then pulled back. After a quick, silent debate with himself as to whether
he had any right to pick up the billhook, he reached out again. The minute
his hand closed around the handle, he felt a rightness in his decision. He
did find the heat of the handle slightly unnerving, and the tingling feeling
that ran through his hand was a bit disconcerting.

Now that the billhook was in his hand, Lom took a closer look at it.
Though it was made out of a material he could not name, being neither
metal nor wood, the craftsmanship was beautiful. Even more surprising
was the fact that the blade was very, very sharp. For some reason, he felt
it was an object of great age. Now Lom's only problem was getting down
out of the quirrelit tree with the billhook, since he was going to need both
hands to climb down.

As he stood on the branch of the quirrelit tree, trying to work through
how he was to get down with the billhook and not cut himself, something
brushed the top of his head. Balancing himself on the broad branch, he
reached up with the hand not holding the billhook and brushed it across
his hair. Something brushed the top of his hand. Looking up, Lom had
thought he could not feel much more surprised after finding the billhook
in the quirrelit tree. He had been mistaken. Hanging from the branch
above him was a sheath. He was sure it had not been there when he was
climbing up the quirrelit tree. He slowly reached up, and the sheath came
away in his hand. He was not sure if it was because he had tugged it down,
or because the slim branch holding it had released it.

The sheath, upon closer inspection, was not new and was also not as
weathered as he might expect. Rather, it was in good condition and well
cared for. The sheath was decorated with the same design as the billhook.
Lom took the billhook and slipped it into the sheath. It slid in easily and
fit perfectly. It was obvious to Lom that the sheath had been made for the
billhook. Tucking the sheathed billhook in his belt, he climbed back down

the tree. Theora was waiting at the bottom of the trunk when Lom dropped down from the lowest branch.

"Did you find the ring?" Theora asked.

"No, but I did find something surprising," stated Lom, as he pulled the sheathed billhook out from behind his back. "It's a billhook for cutting vines."

Lom pulled the billhook out of the sheath so Theora could look at it. She did not reach for the billhook.

"This is what drew you?"

"So it would seem. It's one of those good news, bad news types of things," said Lom. "The bad news is I didn't find a piece of the oppgave ringe. The good news is it seems as if I really do feel a pull toward objects of power, for I think this billhook is more than it seems."

"I'll have to take your word for it."

After Theora suggested they needed to get moving so they might reach their campsite before darkness fell, Lom asked for a few minutes while he unbuckled his belt and slipped the billhook sheath onto it. Once the sheath and billhook were secure, he followed Theora, who had quickened her pace. On the walk back to their campsite, Lom turned over and over in his mind how the billhook had ended up resting on a branch of a quirrelit tree. He also was absolutely sure he would have seen the sheath when climbing up the quirrelit tree. He had been paying very close attention, since he had been looking for a very small object. Something as large as a sheath would have caught his eye, especially since the lower branches were bare where he was climbing.

The way back to the wagon seemed faster than the way out, but that was often the case. The long walk and needing to concentrate hard in each of the quirrelit groves had left him feeling tired and drained. He was glad when they finally arrived back at the campsite, which was undisturbed. The evening meal was a quiet one. Once the cleanup was done, Lom and Theora settled down, with their feet to the glowing coals of the cook fire.

"We need to decide what to do next," Theora suggested. "Whatever we decide, we are going to have to move from here on the morrow. While we have been lucky so far, I don't think we are going to go unnoticed for much longer. At some point, we are going to have to travel the more well-traveled roads."

"Aye, I think you have the right of it," Lom said. "The more I have thought about it, the more I think we should check out the quirrelit groves between here and where the rovers are gathered. There is safety in numbers. For some reason I can't explain, I trust Zeroun and his granddaughter. Your wagon would be safe with them. I also think the rover elders might not be too surprised by the night wolves."

"Your idea has good and bad points. Those who are looking for folks who travel with uncommon animals might get wind of us sooner rather than later if we camp with the rovers. On the other hand, I don't think the rovers would be easily bullied into giving us up. You also have the right of it that I am reluctant to leave my wagon unguarded for several days in a row. It certainly is not as grand as the rover homewagons, but it suits my needs. I built it myself over the long, cold winter months in the mountains and am really quite fond of it. So we are decided then? We should plan to camp with the rovers?"

"Yes."

Lom felt the decision to camp with the rovers was a good one. As he rolled up in his blanket roll that night, he felt calmer than he had in days. He was up with the breaking of dawn the next day, eager to be on his way. The quarter-day's ride it should have taken them to reach the rover campsite took much longer, since Lom made side trips into the quirrelit groves along the way. His search of each of the groves was disappointing, for none of them pulled at him the way he had been pulled by the billhook the day before.

It was midafternoon before they came close to the ancient quirrelit grove where the elder rovers were gathering. Theora pulled her wagon over and stopped. Turning to Lom, who was sitting on the driver's bench next to her, Theora asked, "Are we still sure about our decision?"

"The closer we have gotten, the more I think it's the right thing to do."

"How should we proceed?"

"Well, since it is going to be difficult to hide the two night wolves once they climb out of the wagon, I guess we should just drive in and ask

Zeroun and Gersemi if we are still welcome to camp with them. I suspect we will cause some talk," suggested Lom. "If not us, the night wolves certainly will."

"And turn a few heads."

Pulling into the campsite, they spotted Zeroun's homewagon right away. Lom was surprised at the number of other rover homewagons lined up neatly beyond Zeroun's. Zeroun himself was sitting in front of his homewagon in a gathering of other rovers. Glancing up, he smiled, stood, and walked over to Theora's wagon.

"Glad I am that you have come. We were hoping you would. You are welcome here. Are the night wolves with you? I am, I am ashamed to say, looking forward to the looks on the faces of a few of the other elders who have questioned both my honesty and my eyesight." When Lom answered in the affirmative, Zeroun chuckled, rubbed his hands together, and said, "Oh, this is going to be fun."

The night wolves' appearance when they jumped down out of Theora's wagon had Zeroun's expected effect on several of the rover elders who were gathered there. Once the surprise was over, Gersemi suggested strongly that all of their questions could wait while Theora and Lom took care of the horse and set up camp. Once the others had grudgingly grumbled their way back to their own homewagons, Zeroun drew Theora aside.

"I'll be right back. Taren left something for you with me earlier this day. She must have known you were headed here."

# CHAPTER FORTY-FIVE

Zeroun left for a short while, slowly climbing in and out of his homewagon, and returned carrying a leather-wrapped bundle. With quiet dignity, he handed the bundle to Theora. Lom and the two night wolves gathered close as she untied the lacing holding the bundle together and slowly unrolled the buttery soft leather.

"The covering is so beautiful and soft, I almost don't want to unwrap whatever is inside. I could just run my hands over the covering for a while," Theora said a little self-consciously.

"Take your time, lass," suggested Zeroun. "It is not every day that a guardian of the quirrelit groves leaves a gift."

Lom heard Zeroun follow with a mutter, "Most unusual, oh my indeed, most unusual." He did not think Theora had heard the rover. She was focused on slowly unwrapping the bundle. When the last layer of soft leather was folded back, the three found themselves staring down at a beautifully crafted bow of medium height and a tied-together bundle of arrows, equally beautifully crafted.

Handing the leather wrap to Lom, Theora asked him if he would be so kind as to set it inside her wagon on the bench. He did as he was asked. When he returned, stepping carefully over the arrows Theora had laid on the wagon's steps, he took a good look at the bow Theora was examining.

"If these old eyes are not mistaken," Zeroun said, "that bow is made of quirrelit wood. How very rare. And the carved design on the bow …."

"What about the design?" Lom asked.

"It is an old, old pattern, the use of which had almost faded from memory until very recently. A rover lass, name of Nissa, a woodcrafter by trade, has begun to carve the old patterns again. Designs like the one on the bow you hold used to be carved on door frames and window shutters, not only on rover homewagons, but on huts and cottages of folks who lived in or near the grand woods of Sommerhjem. Mind you, that was a very long time ago. As the forests grew smaller, as the land changed, the old ways were either forgotten or discarded. The keepers of the stories of the rover clans tell one suggesting that when the Neebing patterns come around again to grace the land, great change is on the wind, and one or more Neebing blessed will arise."

*There is that phrase again*, Lom thought. *What does Neebing blessed mean? For that matter, what or who are Neebings?* Before he had a chance to ask, Theora suggested he show Zeroun the billhook he had found. Lom did as she asked, pulling the billhook out and handing it handle first to Zeroun.

"Do you think the rover Nissa made these?" Theora asked.

"No, lass. Both the bow and this billhook have the look and feel of great age, nor do I think Nissa has ever worked in the material this billhook is made of. The pattern is similar to the one on the firestar gem ring you wear, is it not, Lom?"

Lom, who had been looking at Theora's bow, looked up sharply at Zeroun's words.

"Don't look so surprised, lad. After all, I am a gem cutter by trade. I notice things like firestar gems and rings."

"Yes, sir, the carvings are similar."

"Could I ask how you came by the billhook?"

Lom glanced at Theora hoping for some type of sign as to what he should tell Zeroun. None was forthcoming. Clearing his throat he said, "I wonder if we might set up camp first ...."

"Ah lad, forgive an old man's curiosity. Why don't you go ahead and settle in? Once you are set up, perhaps you could join Gersemi and me for the evening meal. Would that suit you?"

"Thank you, that is a kind offer. Theora?"

"We would be delighted to join you. I found some good tubers when we stopped to rest the horse. Also, some fine shelf mushrooms that I can add to whatever you are cooking. Just give me a moment to grab them."

Lom excused himself and got busy unhitching the horse. Once he had it hobbled and settled with a feed bag, he went back to Theora's wagon to see what else he could busy himself with, giving him time to think over what to tell Zeroun. He also needed time to talk to Theora. When he came back from hauling water, he found Theora sitting on the steps of her wagon, examining the arrows that had come with the bow. Both Taarig and Tala were lying at her feet. Settling himself on the bottom step, he began to talk quietly.

"So far we haven't needed to talk to any of the other rovers. I can't see that lasting for long. They and Zeroun are going to begin to ask questions. How do you think we should answer?"

"I grew up with rovers visiting my town. They always struck me as good, honest, hardworking folk. While they are fiercely independent, they also seem to be very loyal to the Crown," replied Theora.

"I heard some things when I was working in the royal palace gardens. The rovers don't have much love for the former regent, I can tell you that. He was hard on them, more than on most folks.

"The fact that there is a group of rover elders gathered here to try to put more information together about the oppgave ringe and the Gylden Sirklene challenge speaks well of them."

"Maybe I can just tell Zeroun that we have been charged with a task by the Crown. Maybe that will be good enough," Lom suggested. "In its own way, it is the truth."

"That's brilliant," Theora exclaimed. She watched the red creep up Lom's neck and his face turn red. "Ahem, ah, well, I had best put these arrows away before we head over to Zeroun's homewagon."

The evening meal with Zeroun and Gersemi was a comfortable one. Zeroun had asked the other rover elders to give the newcomers with the night wolves time to settle in before bombarding them with questions. He told Lom and Theora they should not be surprised if other rover elders began drifting in to settle around the cook fire toward dusk.

When the last plate was washed and the last pot scrubbed, the four settled in around the fire. The night wolves, who had left the campsite shortly after Lom and the others had sat down for dinner, returned and were now resting by the fire.

"Will you folks be staying with us for a few days, or are you off on the morrow?" Gersemi asked.

"Actually, we're off on the morrow. We would like to leave Theora's wagon here with you." Lom looked up and saw he was going to have to explain, based on the quizzical looks on Gersemi's face and a raised bushy white eyebrow on Zeroun's. "We, err, I have been charged with a task by the Crown. It involves looking for something in quirrelit groves that are not near lanes or roads where a wagon can go. We did not want to leave Theora's wagon unattended for days. If you are going to be here for a number of days, it seems safer to leave Theora's wagon here where you might watch over it, if you would." Lom had said all this in a rush and hoped he had done all right. He looked at Theora for support.

"We know the royal forest is supposed to be a place of sanctuary and safety. Nonetheless, I would feel better if I knew someone was watching over my wagon. If you are not staying, or if this would be asking too much, I would understand," stated Theora.

"We would be happy to keep watch on your wagon. Elders are still arriving. I anticipate we will be here for about a fortnight. Will that suit?" Zeroun asked.

"We would be most grateful for your help," said Theora.

"How do you intend to check out the quirrelit groves?" Gersemi asked.

"Let me get something," Lom said. "If you will excuse me, I'll be right back."

Lom got up and went to fetch the map Taren had given him. He spread it out on the small flip-up table attached to the side of Zeroun's homewagon. Zeroun and Gersemi stood and came over to look.

"Taren left us this map. You can see that we are here. You can also see that the quirrelit groves spread out from here in a spiral. We intend to walk out from here on the morrow and follow the spiral outward," Lom said.

"Your plan for searching the quirrelit groves is a sound one. Theora, is your horse also a good riding horse?" asked Zeroun.

"Yes."

"Do you have gear for riding?"

"Yes."

"I would suggest then that you, Lom, take one of our horses and riding gear. It would make your search easier and faster," suggested Zeroun.

Lom was astonished that Zeroun would offer one of his horses to him. Instantly seeing the wisdom in the offer, he gratefully accepted. He quickly rolled up the map, for Zeroun had been right in his prediction and the other elder rovers began to wander in.

The elder rovers began to ask Lom and Theora questions, once it had been determined that the two animals now lying at their feet were indeed night wolves.

"You've given us quite a bit to think about, showing up here with not one but two night wolves," a woman elder stated. "There are old tales about folks and night wolves pairing. Pair is the key word here. The tales I have heard never speak of just one folk and one night wolf. Always two folks and two night wolves. Never thought about that before."

"I have been trying to remember the tales," said Zeroun. "Wherever they are hidden in my head must be a place covered in cobwebs, for I just can't seem to recall them."

"Had something to do with a vine cutter and a protector," another elder said.

Lom and Theora exchanged glances, as did Zeroun and Gersemi.

"Theora?" Zeroun asked questioningly.

"Yes, I will get it," said Theora, knowing that Zeroun was asking her to get her gift from the guardian of the quirrelit groves. "Lom?"

Lom sat where he was for several moments thinking. He knew now that they were sitting with the rover elders, and those folks were aware of the night wolves, he and Theora had already put some trust in the rovers. If he showed them the billhook he had found in the quirrelit tree, he would be putting more trust in folks who were really just strangers to him. Taarig took the decision out of his hands when he stood up, walked to

Lom's side, and nudged his cloak away from his side, exposing the handle of the billhook.

Hoping the night wolf knew what he was doing, Lom took out the billhook, holding it out to the firelight so those gathered could see it. As he put his hand out, the firestar gem flashed in the firelight.

Zeroun motioned Lom closer, so he could examine the billhook again. After careful study, he told the gathered elders, "I know some of you have seen Nissa's work and the patterns painted on her homewagon. She did not make this handle or the ring Lom wears. Both are very old. Both look like they were carved out of quirrelit wood."

"I am curious as to how you have come by both. Were they passed down in your family?" the rover sitting to Zeroun's right asked.

*Here is certainly a way of explaining how I am in possession of both the ring and the billhook,* thought Lom. *I could just tell them that both items had been in my family for years and years, but that would be a lie. Somehow I do not think lying to these elders is a good idea. It is always best to stick to the truth.*

"No, sir, neither the ring nor the billhook have come to me from my family."

Before Lom had to speak further, Theora returned carrying the bow that had been a gift from Taren.

"A bundle to be given to Theora was left in my care by the guardian of the quirrelit groves," Zeroun explained to those gathered around the campfire. "Please note that the design on the bow matches the design on the billhook."

"Maybe the billhook belongs to Taren," Lom said reluctantly, explaining he had found it in a quirrelit grove.

"I do not think so," stated Zeroun firmly. "I think it is time you start at the beginning of your tale." Seeing the look of reluctance on Lom's face, Zeroun suggested in a gentler tone that what Lom said to them would only add to their knowledge.

Lom glanced at Theora, who nodded her head encouragingly. Taking a deep breath, Lom told of being kidnapped and why, being taken to the Raven's tower, and escaping with Aaron Beecroft. He did not elaborate on how he had escaped. He told them of being given the ring by Aaron Beecroft and being taken to Ealdred's by Journeyman Evan. Here he hesitated in his telling.

Sensing his hesitation, Zeroun said, "I sense you have been sent here to search for something using this ability of yours. It is enough to know you are here at the request of the Crown."

"But ...." one of the elders said, starting to object.

"Remember, putting together bits and pieces of the knowledge we carry with us is why we have assembled here. That, hopefully, will be helpful. However, knowing some things can be dangerous. What we do not know, we cannot tell," Zeroun stated.

"You speak the truth," the elder who had objected said.

The assembled group broke up a short while later, heading off to get some rest. After Lom and Theora had left the campfire, Gersemi urged her grandfather to move into the homewagon and get some sleep.

"In a moment. I want to sit here in the quiet and think on what we have heard this night. Lom having the billhook and Theora the bow is important. If I could only draw out that memory about night wolves."

# CHAPTER FORTY-SIX

Early the next morning, Lom took his time walking through the oldest quirrelit grove they were camped next to. He felt an overwhelming sense of calm, peace, and great age within the grove. He did not feel the pull he had now come to both understand and believe in. When Lom returned from his inspection, Theora had both of the horses saddled and ready to go.

"Anything?" Theora asked.

"Nothing, no. It would probably have been too much to ask that what we are looking for would be here. Thank you for getting the horses ready and tying my pack and blanket roll on," Lom said.

Theora and Lom had spent a little time before they left Theora's wagon going over the map Taren had given them. They wanted to double check their ideas of how to most efficiently get to the quirrelit groves in the royal forest. It was a big forest and there were more quirrelit groves than either had imagined. The two had concluded that working their way outward from the oldest grove was the right choice. Being able to travel by horseback would speed up the searching. Knowing her wagon was being watched over had eased some of Theora's concerns.

Lom tried to enjoy the morning ride. The sun was shining, the sky was a clear brilliant blue, and the trees were fresh with new leaves and growth. The ferns had unfurled, and late-spring flowers were in bloom. On such a day, which should have brought lightness to the heart, Lom felt weighed down by the seriousness of the task before him, the sheer challenge of trying to find a small ring in the huge forest.

As they halted their horses at the edge of another quirrelit grove, Theora suggested they take a break for their midday meal. Lom was in full agreement.

"You can see Taren or the foresters have been here before us fairly recently," Lom told Theora.

"How can you tell?"

"If you look closely at the base of that quirrelit tree over there," Lom said, pointing to his right, "you can see where someone has cut away greenery. I suspect they were cutting away kvele vines. You can still see some of the vine dangling from that branch there, about the third one up. The leaves on the vine are just beginning to wither and dry up. The vine was probably cut several days ago. It gives me the shakes thinking what kvele vines can do to a tree or a grove if allowed to grow. They are very fast growing. It almost looks as if this vine was planted here," Lom said.

"Why would anyone want to destroy the quirrelit groves?" Theora asked.

"I can't imagine." Taking one last bite of his noon meal, Lom stood, dusted crumbs off the front of his shirt, and wiped his hands on his pant legs. The night wolves, who had been lying in a sunny spot, rose with him. Once again, nothing pulled at him as he wandered through the quirrelit grove.

By the third day, Lom was feeling very discouraged. Doubts had been creeping in as the day drew to a close. They had covered over half the quirrelit groves and still nothing. Lom worried that Aldys had never had a piece of the oppgave ringe, or someone from her family had retrieved it long ago. His worst fear was if Aldys really had hidden a piece of the oppgave ringe in a quirrelit tree in the royal forest, she had hidden it wrapped in golden pine spider silk. If that were the case, even if it were hidden in a quirrelit tree here, he would never sense it.

"I think we should stop for the day," Lom suggested to Theora.

Theora, hearing the discouragement in Lom's voice, agreed. "Why don't you set up camp for the night? I saw a pool a ways back. If you'll be all right alone, I think I will take advantage of it for a bath."

"I'll be fine. You go ahead."

After Lom had taken care of the horses, he began to gather firewood. Tala had gone off with Theora, and Taarig was nowhere in sight. The quiet of the woods settled in around Lom as he picked up more branches. When he straightened and looked up, he saw he was no longer alone.

"Now, just what has we here?" a small, very thin man asked.

"It looks like we's got ourselves easy pickin's. Now son, if'n youse don't wants to be harmed, I'd thinks youse should stand very still while we's takes a look at what youse might be have'n to share wit' us," stated the other man who was holding a wicked-looking long knife. The jagged scar on the man's face suggested he had fought with knives in the past.

Lom quickly thought through what he should do. He knew he did not want to return to Zeroun minus his horse nor did he want to give up Theora's horse. On the other hand, he also knew he was no match for two men and one wicked-looking knife.

"Kind sirs, I would gladly share a meal with you, for I have not much else. Please do not take the horses, for they are not mine."

"A horse thief, are ya now," said the small thin man. "Hear that, Hamill?"

"Ya, I hears ya. So very kind of him to offer to share a meal," replied Hamill, grinning at his companion. "I's thinks we's should take him up on his offer, don'ts youse, Blain? Youse, lad, get that fire goin'. Well, what's youse waitin' for?" Hamill asked, motioning with his knife that Lom should carry his wood over to the fire pit.

*They do not seem to know I am not here alone. I need to do something before Theora comes back. I do not want her hurt,* Lom thought. He was so anxious that he dropped half of the wood he had gathered.

"Pick that wood up right fast and get those feet movin', lad," said Blain. "Hamill and I are a might bit hungry."

When Lom looked up, he saw, much to his relief, that Taarig was moving in behind the two men. When Taarig was about three feet behind the two, he let out a loud, low growl. Both men jumped, turned, and saw a huge black wolf, hackles raised, growling and ready to spring. Hamill yelped, dropped his knife in surprise, and ran, followed closely by Blain.

"Thank you, my friend," Lom said to Taarig who was sitting, his head turned, watching the retreating would-be-thieves. "I don't think the evening would have ended well for me if you had not returned when you did."

Theora walked in from the direction opposite the men's retreat and asked what was causing the thrashing and crashing coming from the woods, and whether she should be concerned.

"I don't think so, at least not any more. Just two folk who thought they should unburden me of our horses and possessions. Taarig gave them quite a scare." Lom thought for a moment before he spoke again. "Well, maybe we should be concerned. So far, we've managed to avoid being seen other than by the rover elders. That allowed us to get here. I don't think those two are going to be quiet about seeing Taarig."

"I don't think they are going to go bragging to all and sundry that they were interrupted robbing someone by being threatened by a night wolf," Theora stated practically.

"I think you are right about them not bragging about being fumbling, bumbling robbers …"

"I hear a 'but' here."

"… but I can't imagine them not talking about the night wolf. When others scoff at their tale, they will probably mention me, as in they saw a lad with a night wolf. That tale could get back to those who are looking for ones such as us. Those two men Taarig sent scurrying off might, once they get their wits about them again, even know folks traveling with uncommon animals are being sought after."

"You are right. I had not thought of that. Well, there is no way to prevent them from telling others. We had best just be prepared. I'll take first watch this night."

The next morning, both Lom and Theora were tired from not getting a full night's sleep. The morning's search of quirrelit groves provided only frustration. At midday, Lom had just reached the mother quirrelit tree in a small grove when he discovered kvele vines had grown up the trunk and were entwined around the lower three branches. No matter how urgent his task was to find a piece of the oppgave ringe, Lom knew he could not leave the grove until he had cut down the kvele vines.

"Theora, Taren or the foresters haven't gotten to this grove yet. I need to cut the kvele vines down before we move on. I'll cut them off at the ground, but then we have to pull them down."

"Let me get my bow first, and then I will help. I don't want to be caught unprepared."

Lom pulled out the billhook from its sheath. It was a tool he was very familiar with, having used its like working in the royal palace gardens. He hesitated a moment, wondering if he should be using a tool of such great age and made of a material he was unfamiliar with. He knew the billhook was sharp. He hoped it was as sturdy as it looked. The only other tool he had to cut down the very thick, tough vines was his knife, which he knew would not do the job as well as the billhook. His thoughts were interrupted by Theora returning with her bow and quiver.

"Ready when you are," said Theora.

Remembering the royal palace gardener's frequent statement about work always going better and being easier if one had the right tool, Lom made the first cut into the central kvele vine with the billhook. It sliced right through the tough vine in one cut. Lom stood staring at the billhook in surprise. He had expected to have to take at least two or maybe even three strokes to cut the vine in half. He quickly cut the other vines that had grown up from the base of the tree.

"If we pull together, we might be able to get the vines down," Lom told Theora.

His suggestion worked for all but the thickest vine. Theora gave Lom a boost up and he quickly cut the stubborn vine away from the branches. Theora was then able to pull it down. Before he began to climb down, Lom rested his shoulder against the tree trunk, balanced himself on the tree branch, and pulled out a kerchief to wipe his forehead. He thought for a moment something was on his shoulder, and had the sensation of something brushing his cheek, sending a warm and peaceful feeling through him. When he tried to get a look at what might be on his shoulder, the sensation was gone as swiftly as it had come. Having no reason to remain in the quirrelit tree, Lom climbed down.

"There's nothing more here for us. We should move on," Lom told Theora.

"Nothing pulling at you," Theora asked.

"Unfortunately, no."

The rest of the day followed the pattern that had been set in the quirrelit grove with the kvele vine. Lom would circle the grove, moving ever inward until he reached the center and the mother tree. Theora and the two night wolves would stand guard, alert. If the grove had kvele vines on any of the trees, Lom would cut the vines, and he and Theora would pull them down. Taking the time to cut and pull down vines was certainly slowing their search, and Lom continued to be torn between helping the quirrelit trees and looking for the piece of the oppgave ringe. Even though he did not know if he could explain to Theora how both actions felt equally urgent to him, he knew he needed to do both.

By midmorning of the next day, Lom and Theora were moving more swiftly from one quirrelit grove to the next. Someone had already been through this section of the royal forest and removed the kvele vines. By late afternoon, Lom, looking at the map, realized they had covered over two-thirds of the quirrelit groves. As they had moved out the spiral, the groves were farther and farther apart.

"The next grove is about an hour's ride from here," said Lom, pointing to the grove they were heading for on the map. "We should be able to get to it and search it before dusk."

"Lead the way."

Once Lom, Theora, and the night wolves came within sight of the quirrelit grove, Lom's heart sank, and he changed his opinion about being able to search the grove before dusk. Unlike the other groves they had searched, this quirrelit grove was covered with kvele vines from the outer edge inward, blocking out the sun. The ground cover beneath the trees had withered and much of it was brown and dead.

"This does not look good. It will take us hours to clear away these vines," stated Theora.

"You are right. We can't leave it this way. Instead of cutting and pulling, why don't I just begin by cutting the vines off at the ground? That will at least kill them."

"I can help. That big ol' knife that thief Hamill dropped looks sharp enough to cut vines. I may not be as fast as you, having to take two to three cuts to your one."

"It will certainly speed us along."

*There is something terribly wrong in this quirrelit grove,* Lom thought. *It is as if the life within the grove is being snuffed out. I only hope we are not too late.*

# CHAPTER FORTY-SEVEN

Neither Lom nor Theora had taken a break since they had arrived at the quirrelit grove. His body was drenched in sweat. His arms felt like they might fall off if he took another swipe with the billhook. The sun had almost set, so it was getting quite dark, and yet he did not want to stop. With each stroke of the billhook, Lom felt as if the grove was coming more alive. It took Theora calling three times before her voice penetrated the exhausted fog of Lom's mind.

"Lom, you need to stop. This task will still be here in the morning. You won't be helping the quirrelit grove if you cut off a limb instead of a vine. Come, let's get camp set up while we have a little light left. I don't know about you, but I could eat a whole deer by myself, if we had one roasting over a fire," stated Theora wearily.

"Just a couple more vines, and I will have this tree done," Lom replied.

"Lom ...."

"Please, I need to do this. I promise, I will come when I have all the vines cut off this tree," Lom pleaded.

"All right. I'll get things started in camp."

The evening meal was a quiet one and, soon after, Lom was curled up in his blanket roll and asleep. It seemed to him that Theora woke him only moments later to take watch. Just as dawn was breaking, Lom became aware of voices. He glanced around to see if the night wolves were on alert. Neither of them was in sight. He quickly walked over to where Theora was sleeping and woke her up. Theora was instantly awake, asking what was the matter.

"I heard folks talking close by. Neither of the night wolves is here."

Theora was already out of her blanket roll and nocking an arrow in her bow before Lom had finished speaking. "Which way did the voices sound like they were coming from?"

"It is always hard to tell in the woods. I think from the west," Lom said, turning in the direction he thought the sounds of voices had come from.

Moments later, Taarig and Tala entered the campsite followed by Taren and half a dozen foresters.

"Well met, Lom, Theora," said Taren in greeting. "Thank you, Theora, for lowering your bow. Glad I am to see you are putting it to good use, protector. I can see you have been busy in this grove already. We thank you. Ah, is that a kettle I see over the fire? All of us could use a good cup of hot tea, for we have been up since before dawn. Let me introduce you to my companions."

After everyone was settled around the cook fire with cups of hot tea, Lom felt compelled to ask Taren about the billhook he had found. When he had originally found it in the quirrelit tree, he had been torn. On one hand, he thought he should leave it there, thinking someone might have left it and would return looking for it. On the other hand, he thought he should pick it up, and not leave it out in the rain and sun, for it was too fine a tool to be left out.

"Taren, a word with you, please," Lom said. When Taren nodded her head, Lom went on. Taking the sheathed billhook off his belt, he held it out to her. "I found this in a quirrelit tree a number of days back. I felt it should not be left out. Do you know whom it might belong to?"

Taren took the billhook in its sheath from Lom. She spent some time looking at the sheath before she pulled the billhook out. Again, she took her time examining the billhook. Finally, she addressed Lom.

"It belongs to you, now. It is very old, and one like it has not been seen in a great long time. It was a gift from those who dwell in the quirrelit groves. You are indeed Neebing blessed. Come, let's put it to good use this day," Taren said abruptly, standing and handing the billhook and sheath back to Lom.

Before Lom could ask any more questions, the foresters all rose and began talking about how to most efficiently go about ridding the quirrelit grove of the kvele vines. It took all of the morning and half of the afternoon to clear out the rest of the vines, until finally they reached the mother tree. It took almost a half hour to cut the vines away from its base.

"Lom, would you mind going up the tree and cutting the vines away up there? This must have been one of the first groves where the kvele vines were planted, judging by the age and thickness of the vines. I think they were first planted next to this mother tree, and spread out from here. Normally, I would have found and destroyed the vines with the help of the foresters. The former regent pulling the foresters out of the royal forest left me greatly shorthanded. So much to be done and so little help for too many years. Well, that's water under the bridge now. Anyway, would you mind going up? That billhook of yours should do the job right quick. Get as high as you can first, before you start cutting."

Lom climbed higher than he had ever been off the ground. He thought he should feel afraid to be so high up, but he was not. He was surprised that the kvele vine did not reach as high up in the tree as he had expected. Strangely enough, when he got to the end tendrils of the vine, they looked like some of them had already been cut. Knowing that others were waiting below to try to pull the vines down, he began to cut them away from the tree branches. One by one, the massive vines were pulled down and cleared away.

Not wanting to climb down before the last of the vines were cleared away, Lom sat down on a limb to rest, leaning his back against the trunk. It felt good to take a break. He shifted this way and that, trying to get comfortable, but could not. Something was poking him right in the middle of his back. He stood up and bent down to see just what had been poking him. When he brushed his hand down the trunk, he knocked a chunk of bark off, revealing a hole in the trunk.

Squatting down, Lom looked inside. He could see nothing. Curiosity overcame caution, and Lom reached into the hole. He felt something soft and quickly removed his hand. At the same moment Lom removed his hand, he felt a slight weight on his shoulder. Turning to look, he could see nothing. Strangely enough, he felt compelled to reach back into the hole, which he did. He once again touched something soft. Gripping whatever it was between his thumb and forefinger, Lom slowly drew it upward. When he saw what he had drawn out of the hole, he abruptly sat down. Dangling from his fingers were ten golden pine spider silk pouches.

Taking a closer look, Lom noticed that each pouch was a different color. Gently feeling each pouch to see if there was something inside, he discovered that there was. He opened the pouch the color of quirrelit leaf buds and tipped the contents into his hand. What he saw made his heart race, for lying in his hand was a ring. Upon closer inspection, Lom realized it was made not of gold but of quirrelit wood, and carved in a design similar to that on the billhook. The pouch the color of spring quirrelit leaves also had a ring made of quirrelit wood, as did each successive pouch, until there was only one left.

Tucking the rest of the pouches in his pants pocket, Lom looked down at his hand. Lying there on his palm was a pouch made of golden pine spider silk the exact color of the quirrelit tree trunk he was sitting next to. Cautiously, Lom untied the cord of the pouch. He had barely opened the pouch before he could feel the pull of the contents. It was the strongest pull he had ever felt. He was so startled he almost dropped the pouch. He barely managed to grab it by the cord as it began to slip out of his hands.

Taking a very deep breath, Lom pulled the pouch open and very slowly tipped the contents into his hand. He could not believe what he was seeing and had an almost hysterical need to roar with laughter. Stifling the urge, Lom continued to stare at the misshapen golden ring lying in his hand. Looking at it closer, he could see what looked like scratch marks on the band. The ring felt very warm to the touch. From the descriptions he had been given, he was sure he was looking at a piece of the oppgave ringe. If he had not been sent up this tree to cut down the kvele vines, he could have wandered these woods checking out quirrelit groves from now until forever, and never have found the ring. Hysterical laughter bubbled up inside him again. *Being a sensitive did not lead me to the piece of the oppgave ringe. Sheer dumb luck led me here*, he thought. *Or did it?*

"Lom. Lom, are you all right up there?" Theora called. "All the kvele vines are down and cleared away. You can come down now."

"Be right down. Just enjoying the view," Lom answered, continuing to gaze down at the ring in his hand. Finally, he put the ring back in the pouch, put the cord over his head, and tucked the pouch of golden pine spider silk under his shirt. Slowly, he climbed back down the tree.

At the bottom of the trunk, Taren greeted him. "The foresters and I are grateful for your help. We have only a few more quirrelit groves to go. Theora tells me you have already taken care of about half of what we had left, so again, thank you. Have you had any luck in your task?"

Lom did not know what he should say, surrounded as he was by foresters he did not know. If it had just been Taren, he would have had no difficulty answering. Taarig took that moment to walk over from where he had been resting and lean against Lom. Reaching down, Lom brushed his hand over Taarig's ruff, stalling for time.

Taren, sensing Lom's hesitation, asked if he would show her his billhook again. She was interrupted by a forester asking what she wanted next. She thanked them for their hard work and asked them to proceed to the next quirrelit grove, and check for kvele vines growing there. If there were, they could get started cutting, and she would catch up. Once the foresters had left the grove, Taren once again asked if he had had any luck in his search.

"Yes," Lom said, and saw the surprised look on both Theora's and Taren's faces. "When I cut the last of the vines away, I sat down to wait until you folks had pulled them all down, or to see if you needed me to cut off any of the lower vines, if some of them proved to be stubborn. I sat down but could not get comfortable."

"Poor thing, having to sit down on the job while the rest of us toiled below," Theora teased, to lighten the tension she was feeling.

"Yes, well, ah, anyway, I got up to see what was poking me in the back. I brushed away what looked like a piece of bark, and it fell off, revealing a hole in the tree trunk. Inside were these," Lom said, pulling the nine golden pine spider silk pouches out of his pants pocket. Opening the pouch the color of deep summer leaves, Lom tipped the ring out onto his palm. "Each of these nine pouches holds a ring similar to this one. They are all made of the same material, I think, as the billhook. The rings I looked at had designs on them similar to the ones on the billhook, Theora's bow, and the ring I wear. Each ring is just a little bit different."

"These are very beautiful," Theora commented. "I'm a bit confused, for I thought you said to Taren that you had been lucky in your task. How do these nine rings help you find the piece of the oppgave ringe?"

"They don't. I actually don't know what they are for, or if they are even meaningful. It was the tenth pouch I found that is important." Grasping the cord attached to the golden pine spider silk pouch, Lom lifted it over his head, opened the pouch, and tipped the piece of the oppgave ringe into his hand.

"I, for one, think I need to sit down," commented Theora, when she looked at the ring resting in Lom's hand. She walked over to a downed tree trunk and sat down with a sigh. Tala went with her and put her head in Theora's lap.

"A very good suggestion," said Taren, joining her.

Lom and Taarig followed the three, and Lom joined Theora and Taren on the log, sitting between them.

"Could we see it again?" Theora asked.

Lom held his hand out, the ring resting on his palm. Neither Theora nor Taren reached out to take it from him.

"Keep the ring safe, you two," Taren stated solemnly. "I think your journeys are not at an end just because you have found this piece of the oppgave ringe. You will have more tasks before this is over. Travel with caution. I must leave now and catch up with the foresters. They will wonder what has kept me."

Before either Lom or Theora could say a word, Taren rose abruptly and walked swiftly into the quirrelit grove, disappearing from sight almost instantly.

"I want to know how she does that," Theora said, looking the direction Taren had headed. "One minute you can see her, and the next she is gone." She turned back to see Lom tucking the piece of the oppgave ringe back into the golden pine spider silk pouch. "Your biggest fear was we would wander the royal forest checking out each and every quirrelit grove and never find the piece of the oppgave ringe because Aldys would have hidden it in golden pine spider silk, and you would never sense it. Luck was surely with you this day."

"So it would seem," said Lom, with a very thoughtful look on his face.

"What is it, Lom?"

"Just a minute," Lom said, standing. He pulled the other pouches back out of his pocket and laid them out on the log, side by side. He placed the pouch containing the piece of the oppgave ringe next to the others. When he was done lining the pouches up, he turned to Theora. "Do you see it, too?"

# Chapter Forty-Eight

"I can see that each pouch is a different color," said Theora. "What is it that you are seeing?"

"I see two things. Look at these four pouches here," Lom said, pointing to the last four pouches. "They are the color of quirrelit tree bark from new growth to mature tree. The oppgave ringe was in the pouch the color of a middle growth tree, like the one I found the pouches in."

"What of the other five?" questioned Theora.

"They are the color of the quirrelit leaves from bud to late fall. The real question, or maybe the real two questions are, why are there ten pouches, and why do each of them hold a ring?"

"Not questions I have any answers for, that is for sure. What I do know is daylight is passing swiftly by, and we should get a move on. Let's look at the map, and see where we are, and how far we might be from a main road or lane."

"Do you think it's wise for us to travel down a main road?" ask Lom.

"I'm nervous about traveling anywhere with what you now carry, to be honest with you. I do think that if we are near the royal road, we should take it. It's better patrolled and will get us back to my wagon sooner. Once we are back with the rover elders I will feel better, since there is safety in numbers. At least, I hope that will be the case. Much as I feel the urgency to get to them as soon as possible, I don't think we should call attention to ourselves by galloping down the royal road, but rather we should go at a slower pace."

"I agree. There is one thing though."

"And that is?"

"I think you might have forgotten about Taarig and Tala," Lom stated. "Whether we walk our horses or ride swiftly down the road, we are going to attract attention, since we will have two night wolves running or walking by our sides."

"You're right. I think my mind is still in shock, preventing me from thinking clearly," Theora stated ruefully. "Let's take a look at the map."

Lom picked up the pouches, putting the one containing the piece of the oppgave ringe back around his neck and the others back in his pocket. He then smoothed the map out on the downed tree trunk the pouches had been spread out on. When he took a good look at the map, he was surprised to see how close they were to the royal road. Though they had crossed it several times in their searching, he had been concentrating on kvele vines and searching one quirrelit grove after another. Upon further examination of the map, Lom came to the conclusion that the shortest and easiest route back to where they had left Theora's wagon would indeed be by the royal road.

Pointing to the map, Theora said, "We are at the far southern end of the royal forest. It is a good two or two and a half days' ride from here to the capital. If we travel on the royal road through the rest of this day, camp, and then start again at the break of dawn, we should be able to reach my wagon by midday on the morrow. I think it's time to take a risk and travel more openly. Those two scoundrels who tried to rob you, I'm almost certain, will have talked to someone about seeing at least one night wolf. Nothing we can do about that now but be prepared."

With the decision made, both Lom and Theora mounted up and set off at a fast pace. Lom had wondered if the night wolves would fade away into the forest and meet up with them later, or if they would travel on the royal road with them. He had a troubling worry at the back of his mind that, now that he had found the piece of the oppgave ringe, Taarig would not stay with him. He was very relieved when they turned their horses onto the royal road and Taarig and Tala kept pace with them, sometimes staying at their sides, sometimes leading.

If it had not been so worrisome when they either approached other travelers or passed them by, Lom would have found great humor in the looks on folks' faces when they realized just what they were seeing.

It was close to full dusk when Theora called a halt. "Let's stop here. Are there enough plants, bushes, and trees here that you could hide us from folks traveling along the road?"

"I think so. We probably should not light a fire this night. No sense hiding in the shrubbery, only to have folks find us by following the smell of wood smoke."

Sleep did not come easily that night. Lom was surprised by the number of travelers he could hear passing by on the royal road late into the night. He felt they were concealed well enough to escape anything other than someone stumbling across their campsite by chance. He knew the next day was going to be the most dangerous, until they reached the elder rovers' camping place.

Rising at first light, Lom and Theora quickly saddled up. The road was clear for the first hour. After that, they frequently met folks or passed slower travelers. By midmorning, though he was loath to do so, Lom knew they needed to stop to rest the horses. As uncomfortable as he felt about the idea, nevertheless, he slowed his horse down. Theora pulled alongside.

"While I really would like to just keep going, my horse is tiring. I have to tell you though, I have had a very uneasy feeling this last stretch of road, like someone is behind us, just back behind the last bend. Have you felt it also?" Lom asked.

"Yes, I have. I too am loath to stop, and yet we cannot run either of our horses into the ground. That will do none of us any good. If I remember from the map, there is a wayside rest area with a spring not too far ahead. It is as good a stopping place as any."

Once they arrived at the wayside, both dismounted. Theora told Lom she would be right back and stepped into the woods. Lom walked the horses to cool them down before he let them drink. The two night wolves drank their fill at the spring and then faded into the forest.

Lom's uneasiness increased with each passing minute. He knew they could not keep riding the horses as hard as they had without rest, and yet, the urge to climb back into the saddle was almost overwhelming. Suddenly, he heard the sound of several horses racing his way. Lom moved to mount his horse and then had second thoughts. He felt a strong urge to flee, yet he could not abandon Theora. He was still frozen with indecision when four riders galloped into the wayside clearing, one of whom Lom, with a sinking heart, recognized.

"Well, well, well, looky here, if it isn't the escape artist, my old friend Lom. Never expected you to be one of the two folks traveling with night wolves. I'm going to enjoy getting you to tell me how you got out of the Raven's tower. That's for later, however. Right now you need to tell me where the other rider is, not to mention the two night wolves. I would suggest you answer carefully if you do not want to get hurt," suggested Dubhlainn.

Lom looked at what he was facing before he answered. He was already shaking in his boots at the sight of Dubhlainn. The three others who accompanied him were rough-looking men, who all had arrows nocked and ready.

"You must be mistaken, sir. There are no night wolves with me. My companion has just stepped into the woods to, ah …."

"It is really not wise to lie to me," Dubhlainn suggested menacingly. "We know it is you we have been following. The tracks are quite clear. Two horses, two night wolf tracks, leading us to this wayside. I don't see any of those tracks leading back out down the road. Now you need to cut this nonsense out and tell me what I want to know."

"You want an honest answer?" Lom asked.

"Yes, and I want it now."

"I honestly don't know where the other rider is. I also don't know where the night wolves have taken themselves off to. I don't know why you won't just leave me alone. I am of little use. I just sometimes feel the pull of certain objects, but what good will that do you?" Lom said, stalling for time, though he did not know just what that would do for him.

What Lom did know was he had to get away. It was one thing when he had been picked up before by Dubhlainn's men and taken to the Raven's tower. His being held captive then did not mean much one way or the other for the country of Sommerhjem. Not much would have changed if he had just disappeared. Now, however, with what he had in the golden pine spider silk pouch hanging around his neck, much could be lost if he were captured.

Just as Lom thought that he would need to do something, anything, and started to center himself as Ealdred had taught him, a number of things happened all at once. Tree limbs and brush branches began moving, swaying, and thrashing as if being moved by a heavy wind. An arrow zipped past Lom and struck the earth just in front of Dubhlainn's horse, causing it to rear and throw Dubhlainn to the ground. The two night wolves flowed out of the woods behind the other three horses and began nipping at their back legs, causing the horses to panic. The three horsemen dropped their bows and grabbed the reins, trying to no avail to control their horses. Lom jumped out of the way as one of the horses almost ran him down.

When the dust settled, Lom looked over to where Dubhlainn had fallen, worried the man could still cause him trouble. He was less surprised than he thought he should be when he saw that Dubhlainn was pinned to the ground by creeping vines. Hearing movement behind him, Lom whirled around.

"Well met," Taren greeted Lom. "It looks as if you were having a bit of trouble, wolf friend."

"Ah, well, yes, you could say that. The man you have so neatly wrapped up is certainly no friend of mine or the Crown. We have met before. That meeting did not go as planned for him either," Lom said.

Before Lom could say more, Theora stepped out from the edge of the woods. Her bow was lowered, but still at the ready.

"Very nice shooting, for which I thank you," Lom said.

"Glad to be of help. We are still not out of the woods, for this man's companions surely will return once they have their horses under control. We also have the problem of this man Taren has tangled up."

"As far as the other three men, my feeling is that, once the night wolves break off chasing them, they are going to be very lost. The royal forest can be quite dark and ominous even during the day, if you do not know where

333

you are. You should be all right until morning. As for this fellow I have trussed up, what would you like to have happen to him?" Taren asked.

"His name is Dubhlainn. He is the one who had me picked up and taken to the Raven's tower. He is the one who was holding Lord and Lady Hadrack's nephew Aaron Beecroft there," Lom stated.

"I imagine the Crown would be very interested in getting their hands on him," suggested Theora.

"It will be arranged," said Taren. "I would suggest you move out right now and put some distance between you and this place. I will take care of those who would follow."

"Thank you. We are in your debt," stated Theora.

"You are not in my debt. It is an honor to serve one of the Neebing blessed. Guard him well, protector." With that said, Taren once again slipped into the trees and was gone.

"I really wish I knew what she was talking about, don't you, Lom?"

"Yes," Lom replied as he mounted up. He had been worried that their horses might have run off or followed the horses of the men who were chased by the night wolves. With relief, he had found them just a short distance away, calmly grazing.

It was no more than an hour later that the two night wolves joined back up with Lom and Theora. Several hours after that, Theora reined her horse to a stop.

"I don't know about you, but I need to stop for a while. My horse is beginning to falter, and so am I. I'm having trouble keeping my eyes open. We could just pull a little way into the woods here. Or we could push on and make it back to my wagon, for I do not think we are all that far away now. What do you wish to do?" Theora asked.

"Stopping for a little while might be a good idea."

"Do you feel up to taking first watch?"

"I will take first watch. I still feel very wound up after meeting up with Dubhlainn this day. I had hoped never to see him or his like ever again. I have much to think about, so I probably would not sleep right away anyway."

Once Lom was settled, Taarig came and lay down beside him. A cloud cover had moved in. The air smelled of coming rain. Lom hoped the rain would hold off until morning. He was glad he had time during this first watch to think about what had happened over the last few days, or weeks for that matter.

Seeing Dubhlainn had brought him full circle back to when he had been walking home from a day's work in the royal palace garden. Though Lom had come to accept that he had some skill recognizing objects which held some type of power, he still questioned why he had been given that skill. More importantly, he wondered why he was the one sitting here now with a piece of the oppgave ringe tucked in under his shirt. Before he could ponder those questions further, Taarig stood up, alert.

# CHAPTER FORTY-NINE

Tala joined Taarig, who was now facing away from the lane and toward the south. While not quite dusk, the woods beyond where Lom was sitting were in deep shadow. Lom stared in the direction the night wolves were looking. He could see nothing moving. Feeling movement to his left, he quickly glanced that way and saw Theora had awakened, grabbed her bow and quiver, and moved to stand beside him.

"What is happening?" Theora asked in a whisper.

"I don't know. Ah, look, there, by that large pine. Something is moving."

Theora raised her bow in preparation, and then lowered it, as Taren appeared out of the shadows.

"You must leave quickly, wolf friends. Dubhlainn was much cleverer than I had expected. He not only had those men who the night wolves chased off, but also three who were about an hour behind as backup. I could not hold them all off. It will take them some time to cut Dubhlainn out of the vines, which will keep entangling them all, but eventually they will get him loose and follow your trail. Come, grab your horses' reins, and follow me. The way we will take is a shortcut to the place where the rover elders are camped, but best walked. Hopefully, we will arrive there before Dubhlainn and his men find you," said Taren, turning and blending back into the trees.

Lom could see that the path they followed was a very narrow animal path. If it were not for Taren moving the brush and tree branches away from the sides of the path, it would have been very difficult to travel down the path with the horses. Those following would find the going very challenging on horseback, or even leading their horses. Following on foot was another matter.

The shadows became longer and longer as they followed Taren, making it difficult at times to see her and the path. Finally, Taren signaled they should halt. Walking back to them, she said, "The lane we are approaching is a very short ride from where the rover elders are camped. I will cover your back trail. Theora, you and the night wolves need to protect Lom. Make sure he gets to the capital. Safe journey. Now go swiftly."

Lom mounted his horse and turned to thank Taren for her help. She was nowhere to be seen, having slipped back into the woods. Turning forward, he urged his horse to move toward the lane. Following Taren's directions and galloping full out, it was just minutes until the four arrived at the rover camp.

It was Gersemi who spotted them first. She ran to hold the reins of their horses while they dismounted. "Quick, unsaddle the horses and stow the tack. I will get someone to take care of them and settle them with the other horses. You might want to ask the night wolves to make themselves scarce, for there have been folks by looking for folks with night wolves. Theora, quick, change into your border guard uniform. Lom, come with me, for you are about to become a rover for a few days."

"It's a good idea for us to change our appearance. Unfortunately, my looking like a border guard and Lom pretending to be a rover will not do us much good, since at least one of those looking for us knows what we look like. We either take our chances by leaving in my wagon this night, or stay here, hoping safety in numbers will be enough," stated Theora grimly. "If we stay, it will put all of these good folks in danger."

"Oh, I do not think those looking for you will try anything here. Look around you."

Both Lom and Theora did as Gersemi suggested. The number of rover homewagons had more than doubled.

"I only suggested the change of appearance because it might confuse those who might be looking for you. This gathering is breaking up on the morrow. The rovers gathered here will be heading in several directions."

"I think the time has passed to continue to hide," Lom stated, speaking up for the first time, surprising himself with his bold statement. Drawing himself up and placing a steadying hand on Taarig's shoulder, Lom asked, "Might any of the rovers be heading to the capital? I found what I came looking for and need to go there."

"I think a great number of rovers would be honored to escort you there," stated Zeroun, who had stepped up behind his granddaughter while they had been speaking. "A grand procession of rover elders up the royal road accompanying you four would certainly cause a rather nice commotion. We would undoubtedly be noted by the many we passed on the royal road. Anyone trying to harm us would certainly not further their cause. I think they would need to think long and hard before they attempted to prevent you from making it to the capital. I will call a meeting right now to see who would go with us."

Lom fell asleep that night to the murmur of voices from the campfires nearby. He had been invited to join Zeroun, his granddaughter Gersemi, and others, but had declined. He was incredibly tired due to too little sleep and too much weighing on his thin shoulders. He had thought he might have trouble falling asleep this night, owing to the fact that he was carrying one of the pieces of the oppgave ringe. That certainly was not the case. Lom awoke the next morning, refreshed.

The rovers were up and bustling at the break of dawn. It took very little time for the rovers to break camp. Lom helped wherever he could, stacking firewood, hitching up horses, filling in fire pits, topping off water barrels, and filling water skins. Soon it was time to head out. What surprised Lom the most was the number of rover homewagons that were lined up on the lane leading to the royal road.

Gersemi waved Lom over. "Grandfather would like you to ride with him today, if you don't mind. I will ride with Theora. The night wolves are welcome to ride in our homewagon if they choose. We should reach the capital by early evening, if all goes well."

Lom settled into the driver's seat of Zeroun and Gersemi's homewagon. Zeroun had asked him to drive. Lom motioned to Taarig he was welcome to come into the homewagon, or ride up front on the driver's seat, for

Zeroun was content to ride inside. Taarig chose to walk in front of the wagon along with Tala, leading the way.

"Oh, this is going to be a grand parade. Most folks have never seen this many homewagons at one time. I will bet none of them have seen this many rover homewagons in a row, and being led by not one but two night wolves at that," Zeroun stated, chuckling.

"Ah, sir, riders approaching."

"Can you make out who they are?" Zeroun asked, concerned, moving to climb into the driver's seat next to Lom.

"Foresters. At least by their clothing, they appear to be foresters."

"And a large number of them."

One forester came ahead of the large group of foresters and cautiously approached Zeroun's homewagon. The night wolves came back to flank the homewagon as she approached.

"Well met, my old friend," the forester greeted Zeroun. "Taren sent us to make sure you folks make it to the capital safely."

"I thank you, Verna," Zeroun replied. "It is neither I nor the rovers who need to be kept safe, but this lad sitting beside me. This is Lom, and that is his night wolf, Taarig, sitting in front of you. We also need to keep safe the young border guard in the wagon behind me. She is the companion of the other night wolf, Tala.

"It will be done," Verna stated calmly, turning her horse and riding back to the other foresters.

"I think, lad, you can now loosen the white knuckle grip you have on the reins," said Zeroun, as he moved back into the homewagon. "We are in very good hands now. For myself, I think I will settle in and take a nap. It is going to be a long ride."

No one stopped the rovers escorted by the foresters. Word had spread ahead of them, and folks lined the royal road to get a glimpse of the night wolves. As they came closer and closer to the capital in the waning light of day, somehow the night wolves looked bigger, grander, darker, and more dangerous. A quiet stillness fell over those gathered as they passed by.

"The summer fairgrounds are just ahead," Zeroun pointed out. "Most of the others are going to draw in there and camp. You and I, Theora and

Gersemi, and the night wolves are going to head to the royal palace. They will know how to keep you safe. Those looking for folks traveling with uncommon animals might be more reticent to try to go after one or both of you if you are being looked after by the Crown. Ah, look, here comes the royal guard. Seems we will have double the escort at this time. Let's get a move on, lad. The sooner we get to the palace, the sooner I can stretch these old legs."

*How can Zeroun be so calm?* Lom questioned. *I just want to crawl into the homewagon and go unnoticed. All this attention is making me very nervous.* He had not driven very far when two folks approached. Lom identified them as both belonging to the Glassmakers Guild. After consulting with Verna and the captain of the royal guard, the two approached the homewagon.

"Hail, Zeroun. Seems you have made some new friends since we last met," stated Master Rollag. "May we approach?"

Zeroun nodded his assent. Turning to Lom, he asked if he knew the two who were approaching.

"I know of Master Rollag and Master Clarisse. I have seen both of them in the royal gardens, walking and talking with Lady Esmeralda."

The two guild masters drew up close to the wagon. "We had word before you arrived that a long line of rover wagons were heading up from the royal forest led by two night wolves. At first, we just thought it was another of the rumors that fly around the capital on a daily basis. Then Master Clarisse received a messenger bird confirming the foresters were escorting many homewagons and two night wolves. We have been on the lookout for you folks."

"It is the lad, Lom, here that you need to talk to. He is the companion of one of the wolves. The other wolf companion, Theora, is in the wagon behind us." Zeroun said. Turning to Lom, he told him that these two folks could be trusted.

"Lom, is it?" asked Master Clarisse.

Lom nodded his head in the affirmative.

"Would you care to stretch your legs and walk with me for a while? It is good that you have come here. There is certainly room for you to stay at the royal palace and hopefully it will offer you some measure of safety.

Messages have been sent out throughout the land that folks like yourself who travel with uncommon animals would be best served if they gathered here in the capital for protection."

Since both of the night wolves had come to stand next to Master Clarisse, allowing her to scratch both of them behind the ears, Lom had few qualms about stepping down from the wagon and joining her.

"You go on now, lad. I am going to continue to the campsite and camp with the others. These old tired bones need to rest. You are in good hands. I will see you on the morrow," said Zeroun.

"Thank you for all you have done, sir," Lom said. "I hope you can remember what you know about folks and night wolves soon."

"I'll keep thinking on that, lad."

While Lom was giving his thanks to Zeroun, Theora and Gersemi walked up from Theora's wagon and joined them. Gersemi climbed up to take the reins of their homewagon.

Turning to Theora, Master Clarisse introduced herself and asked if it would be all right for one of the royal guards to drive her wagon to the royal palace.

"As I suggested to Lom, with so many different factions on the lookout for folks traveling with uncommon animals, we think you might be safer at the royal palace. Let's walk a ways," suggested Master Clarisse. "I have been expecting you four for some time now."

Both Lom and Theora looked at her questioningly.

"How could you have been expecting us?" Lom asked.

"When we get to a more private place, I will try to explain. Right now, we need to get you all to the royal palace. Do I understand correctly that you have brought a piece of the oppgave ringe?" Master Clarisse asked Lom.

"Yes, and a few other items," Lom answered. "How did you know?"

"A little bird told me," said Master Clarisse.

Once they reached the palace, footmen came out to take care of Theora's horse and wagon. Master Clarisse led the four of them through the palace out to the back garden. "I thought you might be more comfortable here. Oh, before I forget, Lom, Journeyman Evan sends his greetings and will try to see you soon. He has been a loyal friend and very determined to keep you safe. He would tell no one where he had taken you. Now then, first things first. You do have the eighth piece of the oppgave ringe?"

"Yes. I also have nine other rings. They were hidden with the piece of the oppgave ringe."

"I had wondered if they would show up."

"You know something about them?" Theora asked.

"Only a little. It seems the Book of Rules only gives up its secrets a few at a time. It mentions the rings. There is a mention of the need for the gardener and the protector accompanied by night wolves. Like everything else in the Book of Rules, nothing is specific. I suspect that for each of you, your journeys are not at an end with your arrival here with a piece of the oppgave ringe."

"Begging your pardon. I think you might be mistaken as to me being the gardener. I was just a day laborer here in the royal palace garden. I certainly would never call myself a gardener here," Lom said.

"The head royal palace gardener would beg to differ," said Lady Esmeralda, who had joined the five in the garden. "He told me he had been about to make you an assistant royal palace gardener when you disappeared. I am sure the offer is still open, and certainly something to think about over the next few days. Now then, Master Clarisse, have you talked to these two about what is likely to happen in the coming days?"

"No, not yet. Lom, tomorrow you will be escorted to the Well of Speaking to place the ring in the vessteboks. After that, there will be receptions and other gatherings. Many folks will want to see and talk with you, both you and Theora." Seeing the look of terror on Lom's face, Master Clarisse tried to assure him that it would all be over in a few days. "You, like the other ring bearers before you, would probably like to skip this part. Would that I could let you. Folks are becoming more and more convinced that the Gylden Sirklene challenge is real. They need the continued ceremony."

"Now then, enough of this serious talk. You both must be tired and hungry," Lady Esmeralda said. "Come into the palace, and we will get you settled."

Seeing reluctance in the faces of both Lom and Theora, Master Clarisse explained that it was the safest place for them at the moment. With Lom in possession of the eighth ring, folks who did not want the challenge to happen might try to prevent Lom from getting to the Well of Speaking. Anyone would be hard-pressed to get to him in the royal palace. At least that was the thinking of the head of the royal guard.

# CHAPTER FIFTY

Lom was awakened early the next morning and escorted to the bathhouse. He was surprised when Taarig followed him there. The look on the rather stuffy attendant's face when the night wolf joined him in the bathing pool provided some much needed mirth, though Lom tried not to laugh out loud. He could only hope when he was emerging from the bathing pool that Taarig would not go over to the poor man and shake water all over him. Fortunately for the attendant, Taarig had better manners.

All too soon breakfast was over, and it was time to head to the Well of Speaking. Lom ran his hands down the jacket he was wearing, marveling at the softness of the cloth and leather. He had never worn such finery. He had added the billhook in its sheath to the clothing that had been provided. Lom did not know why that was important, but it felt right when he slipped it on his belt.

Theora was dressed in her border guard uniform, which had been cleaned and pressed. Lady Esmeralda had asked Theora if she would stay on at the palace until after the great summer fair in the capital. Theora had agreed.

When it was time to go, the night wolves flanked Lom and Theora. Their black coats glistened in the sunlight, the silver tips of their back fur shining. Lom knew that neither of the night wolves had grown overnight, and yet they looked even bigger and fiercer than they had the day before.

When Lom reached the top entrance of the Well of Speaking, he wanted to turn around and head back to the palace. There were folks crammed into every available space in the amphitheater.

Lom glanced at Theora and saw her take a very deep breath, square her shoulders, and adjust the bow and quiver she had insisted on bringing with her. Turning to Lom, she reached over and placed her hands on his shoulders, giving them a squeeze.

"I'm sure that, like me, you would rather be in the rover camp settled into a camp chair having a nice cuppa' something warm. For whatever reason, our travels have brought us here, so we might as well go do what we came here to do, don't you think?"

Lom nodded assent. Whether he felt he had been chosen to bring the piece of the oppgave ringe to the capital or had merely chanced across it by luck, he needed to go down the steps and place it in the vessteboks.

Before he could take that first step through the entrance, a voice called out, asking him to wait. Surprised, he turned around to see Ealdred striding toward him, accompanied by Journeyman Evan. Theora swiftly placed herself between Lom and the strangest man she had ever seen, reaching for the long knife at her side.

"It's all right, Theora," Lom said. "Those two are my friends."

Theora stepped back. She sheathed her knife but kept her hand on the hilt.

"So, lad, you found Aldys' ring, did you?" Ealdred asked.

"Yes, sir."

"Proud of you. You, however, are not dressed proper, and we can't have that now, can we?" Ealdred exclaimed.

Lom looked down at what he was wearing. He thought he had properly put on the clothes that had been laid out for him that morning. Now he was not sure.

"Oh, the clothes are fine, lad. Just a little something is missing." Ealdred reached into his pocket, pulled out a ball of moss, and carefully broke it apart. Inside the moss was a small thin vine that had been gently wrapped in a circle. Ealdred pulled the vine out of the moss, untwined it, and handed it and a bit of the moss to Lom. "Can't have you showing up in front of all those folks without you being dressed proper, now can we?"

Lom was profoundly touched that Ealdred would even be in the capital, much less seek him out. That he brought him some vine was more important to him than he would ever be able to explain to anyone. Very carefully, Lom placed the moss in the top pocket of his jacket and tucked the vine in the moss. Centering himself, he invited the vine to move upward until it was twined in his beard.

"There now, now you can go," Ealdred stated. "Journeyman Evan and I will see you in a little while."

Just having that little bit of green growing vine calmed Lom down more than any words, reassurances, or gestures ever could. Squaring his shoulders, he thanked Ealdred, nodded to Theora he was ready, and stepped through the gate.

Once he, Theora, and the night wolves started down the stairs, a hush came over the crowd gathered in the Well of Speaking. The silence was not broken the entire time Lom, Taarig, Theora, and Tala descended the steps. Lom was thankful that Master Clarisse had told them what to expect when they reached the bottom of the steps. She was waiting for them next to the sea wall.

"Are you ready?" Master Clarisse asked.

Lom nodded. Looking at Theora, he asked her to walk to the vessteboks with him.

"Tala and I will stand guard here. That is our task. Yours is to place the piece of the oppgave ringe in the vessteboks."

Accepting what Theora had said, Lom placed his hand on Taarig's shoulder and walked to the sea wall. The small golden box set into the sea wall opened easily. Inside were nine posts carved of quirrelit wood. Seven of the posts held gold misshapen rings that looked very much like the one Lom had found in the quirrelit tree. Drawing out the pouch containing the ring, he lifted the cord over his head. Tipping the ring onto his hand, Lom reached out and placed the ring in the vessteboks.

The stillness in the Well of Speaking was profound. Nothing and no one moved. It was as if all those folks sitting or standing in the amphitheater had stopped breathing, waiting. Slowly, ever so slowly, a thin rope of dark green light rose out of the vessteboks and climbed higher and higher. To Lom's amazement, the green light sprouted branches and leaves, moving ever upward until it bent inland and branched out north, south, and east.

As far as the eye could see, the sky over the capital and beyond was filled with the vine-shaped light. It lingered there, dark green against the clear blue sky, for long moments, and then the colors of the leaves began to change to reds, oranges, and yellows. Once all of the leaves on the vine of light were in fall colors, the vine slowly began to fade, until finally it was gone.

Theora and Tala came to stand next to Lom and Taarig when the vine of light began to fade. There was still no sound or movement coming from the folks gathered there. Suddenly, there was a collective gasp from the crowd. Lom, who had turned to look at the crowd, turned back around and saw another light was rising from the vessteboks. This one was much paler, the color of new spring growth. Again, the light was in the shape of a vine, a new young vine. This vine of light did not reach up to the sky. Instead it bent toward Lom, Theora, Taarig, and Tala, twining itself around them. Then, it too faded.

When the second vine of light faded, murmurs began, and folks began turning to one another and talking. Finally, the gathering began to break up.

"Let us wait until the crowd disperses before we head up," Master Clarisse suggested. "Are you two all right?"

"Yes, I am. You?" Lom asked Theora.

"Yes, I'm fine. More surprised than anything."

"It looks like most of the crowd is gone now. I suggest we had best get on with the day's activities," said Master Clarisse.

By the end of the second day, Lom was more than tired. He was not used to being the center of attention, or spending that much time with crowds of folks.

The morning of the third day after he had placed the ring in the vessteboks found him near the bottom of the formal part of the royal palace garden, sitting on a bench watching the water fall gently from a fountain. Theora, understanding that Lom just needed to sit quietly for a while, stood several yards away. The night wolves lay between them.

Lom's time of quiet did not last long, for Ealdred, accompanied by Master Clarisse and Lady Esmeralda, walked up to the four.

"I am sorry to interrupt, but I would like to have a word with you both," Lady Esmeralda said.

Lom rose, quickly snatching his hat off his head. In all his time as a laborer, he had never had the occasion to talk to the former heir to the throne. He did not know if he should attempt a bow, or what he should do.

"Do you mind if we join you?" Lady Esmeralda asked, as she gracefully sat on the edge of the fountain. "We would speak with you of important things." When both Lom and Theora nodded assent, Lady Esmeralda went on. "In far too few weeks it will be time for the great summer fair here in the capital. As you know, in order for the Gylden Sirklene challenge to happen, all nine pieces of the oppgave ringe need to be in the capital by the third day of the fair. Thank you for bringing in the eighth piece. We are coming ever closer to being able for the challenge to happen and a true ruler of Sommerhjem to be chosen. We would like to ask another boon of the four of you."

"The rover elder Zeroun contacted me yesterday," said Master Clarisse. "He still has not been able to put his finger on just what legend or folktale he has heard concerning the pairings of night wolves and folks. He is convinced that it is important, and your journeys have not ended here."

"In light of what Zeroun has suggested, the interim ruling council would ask that you both remain in the capital. Quarters will be provided. Zeroun strongly feels you both, with your night wolves, need to be here for the summer fair. Theora, Zeroun suggests that you need to continue to be Lom's guard. In the past, there has been a special branch of the royal guards who looked after folks of importance to Sommerhjem. That group has recently been reformed. Would you be willing to become a member?" Lady Esmeralda asked.

Theora did not hesitate to answer that she would be honored.

"Lom, Ealdred and Journeyman Evan have suggested that you are less than comfortable with groups of folks. No, lad, that is quite all right," Master Clarisse said, when she saw Lom's face begin to color red. "Ealdred has a suggestion."

"I know the head royal palace gardener has offered you a chance to be an assistant royal palace gardener. Know that you are welcome to make that choice. I have another offer for you. I would like you to continue to be my student. We can stay here through the summer fair for there is still much work to be done here in the royal palace garden that we could help with. After whatever it is you are needed for here, should circumstances allow, you could come back to live and study with me."

"You would stay here for the time being and continue to teach me?" Lom asked Ealdred.

"Yes, lad."

"Would you all excuse us? I would like to talk alone with Theora."

"Take your time," Lady Esmeralda said.

Lom, Theora, and the two night wolves walked away from the three seated at the fountain.

"Theora, how do you feel about staying here? You have used up a great deal of your leave looking after me already. You have not had a chance to get home to visit your family."

"I am honored to be asked to join this special unit of the royal guards. Besides, I kind of like looking out for you and the night wolves," Theora said.

Both of the night wolves swiveled their heads toward Theora.

"Let me rephrase that. I like being able to guard you with the night wolves."

Lom was sure he saw both of the night wolves just barely nod their heads before they lay down.

"What do you want to do, Lom? Do you want to become an assistant royal palace gardener, or do you want to take up Ealdred on his offer? Do you want Tala and me to continue to guard your back? Should we stay here as we have been asked?"

"I want to accept Ealdred's offer rather than the offer from the head royal palace gardener. I can't explain it, but for some reason, I think we need to stay. I feel as if there is something that is unfinished."

"Then we had best return and give our answers to those who are waiting."

Printed in the United States
By Bookmasters